AS THE
ECHO
RISES

JESSICA LYNN MEDINA

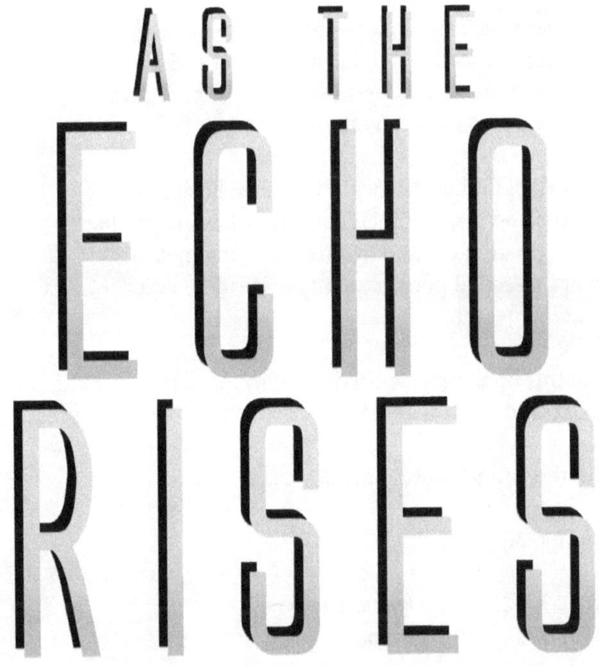

THE ECHO SERIES BOOK THREE

Printed in the United States of America

First Printing, 2025

ISBN 978-1-7336145-3-5 (*paperback*)
ISBN 978-1-7336145-5-9 (*ebook*)

Library of Congress Control Number 2025906651
Rising Moon Creatives
Seattle, WA

www.RisingMoonCreatives.com
www.JessicaLynnMedina.com

Editing by Marinda Valenti
Cover Illustration by Allie Preswick

For my grandmothers.

My claims to gumption began, first and foremost, with them.

PROLOGUE

Kiyo Alloura crept around the perimeter of the fence, the bands of orange lasers hissing ominously in the quiet. The air was stifling against his skin without even a hint of a breeze to offer relief. His shadow grew long in the late twilight, but the heavy heat persisted as sweat beaded down his back, making him itch.

Kiyo never thought he'd visit the central wastelands himself. The detention camps he'd seen in briefings were usually housed in advanced facilities controlled by the Federation. It was strange to find one so far away from civilization, much less in the barren landscape left over from the Final World War.

But that was the entire reason Minister Klein had placed it there: no one would come looking.

Ground missions weren't exactly Kiyo's area of expertise. He definitely wasn't trained for them, and Mayven had never asked him to do one. The honor of camp liberation was usually a task delegated to Avery Vey and her team. The powerful So'Reange could accomplish more with her powers than with any trained squad the Citizens Liberation Front could compile—and Avery even made it look easy.

Kiyo had never been prouder of his Reange lineage than on the day Avery accepted the CLF's invitation to join them. Mayven Thula, the group's leader, had waited weeks for Avery to make her next steps after the Gate's fall. In those initial days, Earth had descended into chaos. They had needed Avery then more than ever. But she had needed time.

Now Kiyo stuck to the shadows, moving slowly enough that his thighs burned. Compared to the other camps, this one was barely fortified. He supposed the environment itself was a natural deterrent. If anyone did escape, the radioactive wastelands would take care of them soon enough. At least the subpar security meant he had a better shot at succeeding.

The CLF had caught wind of rumors about this place weeks ago, a camp where humans were held alongside Reanges. Where Klein sent her own to rot with the Reanges, who would camouflage their unlawful incarceration. Where Klein experimented on them.

Mayven hadn't disclosed the intel to Avery. Kiyo wasn't surprised—Mayven played her hand close to her chest. She always had. She wanted equality between the species more than life itself, and that required a certain element of confidentiality, especially with information that had the potential to send their most powerful weapon back into emotional turmoil.

Kiyo reached his target at last. It was only a small building made of metal plating, no more distinct than a shoddy warehouse. He edged along curved structure, scanning the periphery. There were only two guards, who stayed close to their post at the front. Their heads were armored with UV helmets, but the blasters they held drooping at their sides hinted at boredom. That would serve Kiyo well.

He made his way to the rear of the building and pulled a laser blade from his belt. His earpiece beeped.

"Go quickly. Get in, find him, and get out," Mayven directed. She watched his progress from their ship, hidden just beyond the blast crater hills, out of reach from Federation scanners.

He gave her a thumbs-up, knowing she'd see the gesture from his wristport cam.

The mere existence of this place hadn't been the only piece of intel the CLF had managed to gather. There had also been whispers of who had been sent here and why. And that information was important enough to warrant an undisclosed rescue attempt. Mayven had formed this plan with Kiyo alone—only one other person knew they were there.

Kiyo suppressed a smile as he activated the laser, pushing the deep gold blade into the side of the metal. The fact that Mayven trusted him so completely, above everyone else on their team, had to mean something. He hoped it did, at least.

And once Kiyo found their target, it would change everything. Maybe the CLF would finally have a chance, a real chance, to alter the course of history. If their intel was right, it would push Avery toward—

Something slammed into the back of his head. It knocked Kiyo off his feet and straight into the hard-packed ground.

"Looks like we found a stray." The soldier's voice was robotic, digitized by the mouthpiece on their cobalt helmet. "How did you get out of your pen?"

Again Kiyo's earpiece beeped. He fought against his throbbing head, trying to focus.

"Kiyo!" Mayven panicked. "Get up, Kiyo—get up!"

Woozily, he started to push himself up to stand. A booted kick connected with his jaw, slinging him violently into the metal-sheet wall behind him.

"Get up!" Mayven said again, her command wavering and desperate.

But Kiyo couldn't. The hot breeze picked up, blowing dust into his eyes, making them water. Or maybe his blurred vision was from the blow to his head. He'd failed Mayven, the only woman he'd ever cared about impressing. And now she would watch him die.

The soldier stepped over him, kneeling to pick up the knife Kiyo had dropped. They looked out to the horizon. The visor on their helmet flashed, scanning the distance in the wastes.

No! Kiyo had to give Mayven time. She was the face of the CLF. If the Federation caught her trying to infiltrate a sanctioned camp, it would ruin everything they'd worked for since the Front's inception.

Why had she come with him? It had been stupid of him to agree to this. Neither of them were prepared, especially Kiyo. But he refused to let his failure bring Mayven down with him.

Kiyo gathered what strength he had left and threw himself at the soldier. He wrapped his arms around their waist, twisting violently, trying bring them down.

The soldier snarled, struggling against Kiyo. They brought their blaster down, driving it into the side of his face again. Kiyo fell back, an arc of blood sailing through the air on his way to the ground. He lay there with his face in the dirt, tears mingling with dust until his cheeks were caked in grime.

And as he drifted in and out of consciousness, Kiyo could still hear Mayven in his ear. Her words scared him more than what awaited him in the camp that was meant to break any Reange held within its barrier.

"Don't worry, Kiyo. I'm on my way."

CHAPTER ONE

Avery watched the city of Alexandria pass around her as she soared upward. The capsule elevator rose up to the top level at an alarming speed. Hulking buildings of the city were a blur of reflective metal and mirrored glass that extended into the lower levels, signs of the city's wealth. Even citizens who lived closer to the ground could afford massive windows that looked out over their capitol.

If only the same could be said for the Reanges who had found refuge there. Avery knew for a fact that her people feared the earth's capital city more than any other on the planet. Reanges had always been hunted there, seen as a scourge that thumbed its nose at World Council regulations. And after the Gate fell, things had only gotten worse.

Interspecies relations on Earth had reached a breaking point in the fifteen months after the Gate disaster. Riots broke out weekly across the globe. Disagreements quickly escalated into outright violence. Humans and Reanges on both sides fought throughout the levels. They injured one another, even killed one another, for no other reason than fear.

Avery's jaw tensed.

Klein had been reinstated as Minister after the global vote last year. She blamed the Gate destruction entirely on the Reange refugees and the Citizens Liberation Front by default for supporting their integration. Klein had renewed her entire platform on the promise of eliminating the threat from within. Following her widespread support, the World Council narrowly approved the Reange Containment Law. All nonhumans were to be arrested on sight. Later months were filled with raids and arrests on every level in every city.

Avery had joined Mayven Thula to help the Citizens Liberation Front soon after. As the most recognizable Reange on Earth, Avery couldn't serve as a public figure for the CLF. She could never hope to give speeches or rouse crowds. But she was determined to help in any way she could. Especially after the first detention camps were established.

It didn't take long for the government to realize they had no secure place to hold such an enormous influx of arrested individuals. So they created containment camps to house the thousands of Reanges taken in daily by Federation soldiers. Each major city on Earth now featured at least two or three of them. It was deplorable.

For the first time in her life, Avery was ashamed to have ever considered herself human. And that realization alone had been enough to drag her out of the stupor of grief she'd inhabited for weeks after the Gate's collapse.

But Mayven had known what would tempt Avery back into action. She'd offered a unique position, one suited to Avery's skills and training, in a new division within the CLF committed to completely liberating the camps. And Avery had wholly thrown herself at the opportunity. The mission gave her life meaning when she thought she had lost it completely. It had pulled her out of the endless oblivion that had been her life after the Gate's destruction cut her off from everything and everyone she'd ever—

Avery took in a sharp breath. She gripped the railing of the elevator pod, her knuckles turning white on the cool metal. She didn't need the agony of her memories. Not now, not when she needed to focus. Cora Najisuki rarely called her in for a meeting. Whatever the owner of the galaxy's most influential tech corporation had to say, it was important. And Avery refused to seem incompetent in front of her.

The pod continued to climb, up and over Alexandria's shining jewel: the Biodome. The enormous glass dome top spanned four blocks, protecting the extensive cultivation of plant life within the otherwise-artificial park. An entire river wound its way through the center, walkways and paths crisscrossing over and through the forests and gardens. Humans came from all over the planet to marvel at its beauty, to experience a green space somewhat like what Earth had once been.

Avery had been inside the Biodome a single time before. A few months earlier, she had been invited there by Cora herself for a fund-raising event. Grigg and Nova had complained the entire night. Grigg had been especially unhappy to have to confine himself to the styles of the upper-level echelon of Earthen society.

It was the largest park of its kind on Earth, a testament to Cora's influence and wealth. Najisuki Nano Tech was a key donor in the creation of the Biodome. And Avery had been invited to view it by the woman herself.

Before any of this, Avery had only ever been in one tree park in New San Fran. The visit had been part of a government-sanctioned class trip. Gran could never have afforded the membership fees required for regular entry. Most lower-level dwellers couldn't.

"I can't believe you have to pay to look at plants here." Grigg now leaned against the pod glass, nonplussed by the staggering height of the structure. He looked out at the Biodome, following Avery's line of sight. "Why is everything on Earth at the expense of credits?"

Beside him, Nova rolled her eyes. "The Biodome is free now. Even Reanges are welcome. You'd remember that if you'd paid attention at all to Cora's speech at the gala."

"I was distracted by those little fruit tarts."

Avery let out a puff of laughter.

Grigg shrugged. "Besides, free entry won't make a difference. No Reange would be caught dead aboveground in this city."

Avery sighed as her heart sank. It was true enough. Cora had hoped to make a statement with her gesture. Granting everyone free access to the Biodome was a noble idea. Not to mention, openly offering Reanges sanctuary was in direct opposition to World Council law. But practically, the act did little. Tree parks were meant for those who had little to worry about in their lives. Lower-level citizens and

Reange refugees had plenty else to occupy their time.

"Cora has never invited us to her personal apartments," Nova said. "And if this couldn't wait for our weekly meeting with Alex, then it must be something big." Her gaze flickered away from Avery's fingers clenched on the railing, always in tune with Avery's moods.

"Why did she need to drag us across the continent?" Grigg crossed his arms over his broad chest. "A holocom would have worked just as well. And we could have avoided stepping foot into this blazing city."

"I don't like it either." Nova shook her head as the pod slowed to a halt. "There's too much risk for us here. Too much risk for Avery."

"I assure you, Nova, my facilities are the most secure in the galaxy."

Avery whirled around.

The pod doors had already opened behind them and Cora stood at the threshold, watching them with calculating eyes that missed nothing. She had come to greet them in person. Avery had expected some kind of attendant, not the woman herself.

"Cora!" Avery exclaimed, her cheeks flaming. "We didn't think—"

"Welcome, Avery." Cora smiled thinly. She nodded to the other two. "Grigg. Nova. Follow me, please." And she turned on her platformed heel, stalking away almost as swiftly as she had greeted them. She could often be as cold as the pale blue marble covering every inch of the entry hall.

Avery jumped to do as Cora had bid. Even though Avery was a So'Reange and a symbol for the Rebellion on Earth—powerful in her own right—this was still Cora Najisuki. She had built a tech empire at the age of seventeen with nothing more than the skills of her own mind. She had done more in her thirty-seven years than most people could dream of accomplishing in an entire lifetime.

As Cora strode ahead, she looked every bit as valuable as her brain in a cream mock-neck sweater with matching trousers that billowed out around her legs. The outfit—a Cora Najisuki staple—made her bronze skin glow. The dewy surface of her face was flawless, a product of the best gene coding money could buy.

Seeing her in person was always surreal, no matter how many

times they had met. Avery tried not to stare.

Cora descended a curved staircase into a courtyard—*a court-yard*—before passing a few more rooms of marvels. Priceless pieces of wood furniture. Ancient oil paintings. A complete skeleton of some ocean creature with a horn on its skull.

And I thought Qav's shit was weird, Grigg mused through the group's bond. Nova's answering laughter curled up and around them. The comment was just like something Finn would say. Only, he wouldn't have kept it to himself—even in front of someone like Cora.

At that thought, Avery blocked the others off from the grief that pierced her chest. She let the vision of Finn's laughing face filter through her mind. His smiling blue-gray eyes, his deep dimple. The pain blossomed, spearing Avery from inside, just beneath her ribs. She would never see Finn again. He was gone. But somehow the physical agony of his memory made her feel close to him. It was its own kind of sacred torture.

"Make yourselves comfortable." Cora's voice snapped her back to the present.

They'd made it all the way to Cora's office. She pointed to an enormous blue couch that took up a quarter of the room before perching on one of the matching floral chairs that sat its opposite.

You okay? Nova silently asked Avery.

Avery ignored the question, taking a seat. Grigg and Nova followed suit, settling on either side of her.

"We're here," Avery said, clearing her head to focus on the woman before them. This was why she had thrown herself into the CLF: to atone for the guilt that came with her grief. "What was so urgent that you needed us to come all the way from New San Fran?"

Cora dipped her chin. "Apologies if it was inconvenient. I'm used to having people jump to my whims. Perhaps I should have taken that into consideration." Her dark eyes drifted to Nova. "But as I said earlier, my home here is one of the most secure locations in the galaxy. I cannot say as much for Qav's Sanctum."

Avery tensed. She didn't want to discuss Qav.

"We wouldn't need the *most advanced security in the galaxy* if you hadn't Avery to step foot into the capitol," Nova replied ominously.

"As I assured you in the spring, Nova, I can guarantee her safety. I swear it to you," Cora replied.

Something stirred in Nova, sidling up to Avery's notice, a private memory that she was doing her best to keep below the surface. Avery pulled away from her entirely. If something had happened between Nova and Cora, it was none of Avery's business. Besides, they deserved whatever happiness they could find for however long they could claim it. Avery had learned that lesson the hard way.

"Why are we here, Cora?" Avery asked, redirecting the conversation. She was eager to dispel the anxiety that had curled in her gut since they'd left the Sanctum.

"A woman after my own heart. You always get straight to the point." Cora smiled tightly. "But I'm afraid you're not going to like this. I did tell her going in alone was a mistake."

"Who?" Avery pressed.

Cora sighed, tapping the illuminated skin on her wristport. A holovid materialized over the low marble table between them. Another tap, and it began to play.

It was a wristport vid, shaky and blurry from the constant movement of the user. Avery saw the dark uniforms of Federation soldiers, their heavy boots at eye level. A group of people huddled against a far wall, their eyes wide and frightened.

Avery's gut twisted. She knew that look. She had seen it on the faces of hundreds of Reanges. Grigg sat forward. Nova stiffened. They realized it too. The footage was from a Reange camp.

"No!" the user yelled, his voice scratchy and weak. "Don't hurt her!" He grunted when a soldier slammed a boot into his chest.

"You can't do this!" a woman screamed. Her voice was familiar somehow. "I'm a human! A citizen of the——"

She gasped in pain, whimpering as she fell to her knees in the dirt. Right into frame of the wristport vid.

Mayven Thula, leader of the Citizens Liberation Front, looked up at the soldier who had butted their gun across her face. Curling brown hair fell into her eyes, wide and defiant and angry. She spat blood at their feet. "You'll pay for this. I don't care who you work for. I have people who will—"

Cora cut off the feed.

"What is Mayven doing in a camp?" Grigg had leaned forward, his arms braced on his knees, his body tense. His outrage vibrated against Avery's skin. "She's supposed to be at a citizens' rights meeting on Mars."

Avery let out a low, steadying breath. Mayven had lied to them about her absence. Grigg's response was of little surprise. He'd grown closest with Mayven during their year working with the CLF. The subterfuge would hurt him most.

"I suppose this explains the urgency," Nova said dryly.

Avery turned to Cora. "Where is Alex?"

As one of Earth's most beloved politicians, Alex Peña was the antithesis of everything Minister Klein stood for. She was the linchpin in the trio of powerful women—Alex, Mayven, and Cora: the politician, the activist, and the tech genius. Together, they were some of the only humans with power to stand up against Klein and her policies, a true force to be reckoned with. Even Qav didn't interfere with them.

If anyone would be able to help get them out of this mess—to extract Mayven from a government facility without hurting her reputation as a public leader—it would be Alex.

"Not here," Cora replied succinctly. "And she will not be. It was Mayven's explicit request. If things went south, we were not to involve her. Klein would take any opportunity to drag Alex down from her seat on the World Council."

Grigg stood and paced over to the window. He stared out at the city below, staring blankly at the Biodome winking back in the sunlight.

"The last time I checked, Mayven recruited me to lead the camp liberation efforts," Avery pointed out.

"She doesn't even have any combat training," Grigg reasoned, shaking his head.

"Whose vid was that?" Nova asked.

"Mayven's admin—Kiyo Alloura," Cora answered. "I offered one of my own security personnel, but Mayven refused. She only wanted him. Part of whatever plan she concocted."

"Why am I not surprised?" Grigg muttered.

Avery echoed his sentiment. They'd come to know Kiyo almost as well as they had Mayven. Those two had been making eyes at each other for weeks. No matter how professional Mayven tried to keep things, Kiyo couldn't conceal his feelings. Especially from Avery.

"You're asking the wrong questions," Cora said sharply, clearly growing restless. She crossed one sleek leg over the other, and her heel bounced energetically.

Mayven wasn't an idiot. In fact, she was incredibly capable for her young age. She never would have been able to start such an impactful group like the CLF without a considerable amount of capability and charisma. Her warmth brought people together the way Cora's intellect awed others into acquiescence.

If she had tried to infiltrate a camp with only Kiyo as her accomplice, Mayven was doing so to keep her actions fully under the radar. She needed a Reange to slip easily into the camp—that much was clear. But she hadn't informed Avery. Mayven hadn't even asked Avery for help even when she knew it would be the easiest way to gain access.

"What doesn't she want me to know?" Avery tried.

"Better." Cora smiled, her eyes sparking. "But Mayven also requested I let her explain to you."

Nova laughed derisively. "You expect us to go along with that?"

"We don't hide things from one another," Avery said. "I think you know that by now."

"You'll understand once Mayven—"

"Explains," Nova finished. "We get the picture."

Cora's dark brows rose. Her sharp jaw ticked.

Easy, Avery chastised. Cora's patience only went so far. Avery had seen her hit her threshold before. And it hadn't been pretty for the person who had pissed her off.

Avery sighed, rubbing a palm over her forehead. If Cora was bound by Mayven's request, they would have to honor it. Whatever they were hiding didn't matter. She wouldn't leave Mayven in the hands of the Federation. Not when her discovery could bring Alex down with her.

"How long, then?" Avery asked.

"Six hours," Cora answered. She tapped her wrist and pulled up a map on the holo in front of them. It showed Alexandria on the eastern coast before zooming out and across the continent to the middle wastelands. "I'm sending her location to your vessel. You'll need to move quickly—if Klein discovers who they caught, this won't end well for the CLF. Nor for you, by extension."

Grigg snorted. "Then why did you waste time by having us come here?"

"I couldn't risk the possibility of a hack," Cora replied simply. "The only way to truly guarantee privacy is via in-person interaction."

"Aren't you supposed to be a genius? Seems like you could have figured something out."

She studied Grigg as though seeing him in a new light. "What a peculiar combination of compliment and insult."

"This camp isn't on any of our logs." Nova pinched the blue holo-map, rotating the figure with a flick of her wrist.

"It's in the wastelands," Avery noted. "Nobody has been stupid enough to build anything there in at least a century. I thought the air wasn't even breathable."

"A slight exaggeration. Nothing an irradiation patch can't fix," Cora clarified. "The biohazard regulations allow the government to maintain its hold on the land. If anybody were to casually look, they'd see a generic sanctioned Reange detention facility."

"And if they looked closely?" Avery asked.

"Even the Federation has people who step out of line. If they can't be trusted within the system, Klein still finds a purpose for them."

Avery caught her meaning immediately. "Humans?"

Cora nodded.

The camp wasn't just for Reanges. The Federation had placed humans in the middle of one of the most inhospitable places on Earth for a reason. Klein was trying to hide something.

Avery's gut clenched. They'd never found any Reange testing labs within the city camps, but she couldn't help herself from wondering. The public at large seemed to have forgotten about the unsanctioned testing, the same experiments that had stripped Avery from her parents. Or maybe people just didn't care anymore.

Avery had hoped that maybe Klein had given it up, that they no longer needed to tamper with the Reanges. Her scientists had finally been able to alter a human's genome to grant him So'-like powers. In fact, Nick Lunitia was even strong enough to take on Avery by himself. That in itself was worrying, even though he couldn't mimic her telepathic abilities.

But if the Federation figured out the key to duplicate the merge . . . If Klein could control the minds of humans along with their government, there would be no way to stop her.

Avery would throw herself into a black hole before she sat by and let the world descend into that kind of hell. If there were still innocent people she could help—Reange or human—then she would do everything in her power to support them. She had already made too many mistakes in the past. Too many had been opportunities lost because she hadn't acted fast enough. Because she hadn't trusted herself. Because she hadn't trusted those around her.

It wouldn't happen again. She wouldn't let it.

And Mayven trusted her. Not enough to reveal this plan ahead of time, but Avery could deal with that revelation. Mayven had her reasons. She would disclose them when it was necessary.

Avery stood, and Nova quickly after her. Grigg turned to them.

"We'll do what we can." Avery nodded.

Cora rose to take Avery's hand, her lithe fingers cold. "Be ready, Avery. This one is different."

CHAPTER TWO

A very sprinted across barren dirt, hard and immovable beneath her boots. Grigg and Nova trailed close behind. With Avery's power amplifying their speed, they moved like shadows beneath the hazy night sky overhead.

Avery could feel the Reanges held at the camp ahead of them. The group was cramped together in a small metal building with nothing but the bare ground underfoot. The oppressive darkness of the enclosed space was made worse by the stifling heat. Avery couldn't imagine what the temperatures climbed to during the day. None of them had eaten in days. Even the three children among them.

Rage surged through Avery, boiling her power out of her veins and into the ground in great rivulets that rattled the dirt as they ran. The sound could easily be mistaken for dry thunder careening out across the wastelands.

Avery sent her awareness out in the distance, reaching the Reanges easily and filtering through their perspectives. Their fear—their desperation—was palpable. It rushed through Avery with such intensity that it set her own heart racing. But she had been prepared for this. She steeled herself against the sensation. She had felt this same terror from hundreds before them.

So few? Nova asked through the merge, her confusion sliding up the bond.

Cora had been right. This camp *was* different. They had been used to hundreds of Reanges at the camps they'd infiltrated, not a measly fifty.

Avery didn't slow as they reached the laser fence, vaulting up and over the ten feet of glowing orange barrier with ease. Grigg and Nova followed, trusting in Avery's gifts to carry them alongside her. They hit the ground one after the other, rolling to their feet to keep running.

Two guards at the front of the building offered no challenge. They never even saw them coming. Avery slowed and let her friends make quick work of the obstacles.

Grigg took the taller soldier, slamming his blaster into their neck hard enough to dislodge their helmet. He drove his fists into the young guard's face, two hits knocking them flat on their back. Nova latched onto the other's shoulders with her legs, throwing them up and over her body until they hit the ground. Neither opponent stirred.

Avery forced open the door, leaving Grigg and Nova to contain and hide the soldiers. The guards' absence wouldn't go unnoticed, but it would give them time.

Dozens of faces looked up at her in the shadows. Through their perspectives, Avery saw herself standing in the doorway, her golden eyes piercing in the blackness that had become their entire world. Someone gasped. A man let out a relieved sob. One of the children started crying in earnest.

Avery blew calming breath between her lips, fully relaxing into her power, letting it loose. And on the next inhale, every Reange in the room was in her grasp.

Avery's eyes widened with her new awareness of the merge. Her power connected them to one another, allowing them to share in that awareness, to combine knowledge and perception and emotion. Avery filtered their minds together, diffusing their fear and replacing it with the assurance and skill of her team. Someone let out yelp of elation, their joy coursing through them all as one.

Now—get up. Avery sent the command down the merge and into her people, urging them to rise to their feet. They complied immediately, gathering themselves to stand.

Avery needed to move fast. Even with her speed, their presence would have been noticed by now. Except . . . There was a distinct lack of security at this facility. Avery studied the details of the Federation patrol patterns through the Reange memories. The soldiers barely kept watch over this building.

I've seen poorly executed security protocols before, but this is a new level, Grigg mused, making his way to the group inside. He helped an older woman who was struggling to stand.

It's like they don't even care about containing the Reanges, Nova thought. She stood by the door, a blaster in her hand. Her blue eyes scanned the other buildings across the wide dirt path that bisected the facility.

The Reange containment area had been left wholly in the dark. But the other structures were well used, illuminated by soft blue spotlights at each entrance. Even so, the buildings were no more than concrete boxes with small windows.

"That's because it's not about us," someone croaked, shuffling to the front of the group.

"Kiyo!" Avery breathed. She was at his side in a moment, grabbing his arm to help him stay on his feet. His charming smile was gone, replaced by a stale grimace. One of his eyes was swollen shut. He looked like shit.

I didn't know if you'd come. Kiyo's relief was nothing short of euphoric. *She knew you would, but I wasn't so sure. Not when you—*

Where is Mayven? Grigg asked.

Kiyo dropped his head, a tear escaping his one good eye. Memories flashed through his mind and flowed to the others effortlessly. The soldiers had beaten her when she'd arrived. Mayven had tried to lie her way into the facility, a disastrous attempt that failed completely. And when they'd scanned her DNA and realized she was human, they'd taken her to one of the other buildings.

The humans go in there, but they never come out. The thought emerged from a young girl. No more than ten years old, her father held her in his arms. She stared at Avery, fascinated by the So'Reange, mesmerized by her eyes.

Avery turned back to Kiyo. His feelings for Mayven were so vibrant within the merge—so clear. She placed a hand on his shoulder.

"I'll find her, Kiyo. I'll get her out of here."

His shoulders straightened against the pain of his injuries. "I'm not leaving without her."

Grigg shook his head. *You can't come with us. I don't care how much you care about her; you'll only slow us down.*

I won't, Kiyo argued. *With the merge, I'm just as valuable as either of you.*

"You're beat to shit," Grigg replied aloud. "It's your body that can't keep up, not your mind."

He's right. You're going with the others, Avery agreed. She turned away from him, already heading for the door and slipping out into the night. Kiyo's anguish speared through her, the only indication that he struggled against her order. Avery had felt a similar kind of torment before. With Finn. She stopped the memory short, as well as Kiyo's emotion.

A bead of sweat slid down her temple as she paused beside Nova. *Get them to the ship—you'll need the head start without me. Grigg and I will get Mayven. We'll be right behind you.*

Nova nodded, gathering everyone into groups to move more efficiently. Avery felt Kiyo's guilt. But he voiced nothing.

Avery and Grigg kept to the dark, scaling one of the single-story structures and moving silently across the compound from roof to roof. The occasional guard passed on the walkways beneath them, but none ever looked up. The compound was quiet in the late hours of the night.

Avery's heart sunk as their navigation through the facility revealed her worst fear: the buildings were mainly labs. Though they were unassuming and plain on the outside, the rooms within were pristine and state of the art, not unlike the ones she'd seen on the Port Station when the Klein's general had first captured her. The Federation program had been intent on studying Avery, eager to discover the secrets of her powers.

But whatever they were doing, the Reanges had been largely untouched, beyond the occasional beating and general maltreatment. None of them had endured any experimentation. It didn't make sense.

They found Mayven quickly. The largest building was little more than a rectangular one-story prison, with twenty cells running along either side, each with its own window. They filtered through the occupants.

In fact, things were going more smoothly than Avery had anticipated. In nearly every mission they'd attempted before, they had to fight their way out of high-security holdings. They had to rely on the merge to allow the Reanges to fight alongside Avery and the others. Security wasn't just lax in this facility—it was virtually nonexistent. Someone had gone out of their way to make the compound appear as unassuming as possible.

An alarm sounded, the high-pitched wail pulsing in the air around them, stinging Avery's ears. The soldiers must have found their holding pen empty at last.

Looks like we're out of luck. Grigg pulled out a sonic-pulse emitter, latching the small disc onto the roof under their feet. He tapped on its back. The disc pulsed green, then red before the concrete dissolved into sand and collapsed into to the cell below. It left an open circle, three feet in diameter. Avery lay on her belly, then dropped her upper half into the cell as the dust settled.

Someone was coughing, waving at the cloud of disintegrated concrete billowing around her. It cleared, revealing a wide-eyed Mayven staring up at the two of them in shock.

They grinned down at her. "We heard you needed a ride."

CHAPTER THREE

"We can't leave without him."

"Who?" Avery pulled Mayven up onto the roof beside them. Her tight curls were coated in dust, their usual mahogany now a powdery gray.

"Kiyo is with Nova," Grigg assured her.

"Not Kiyo—*the engineer*," Mayven said desperately. She was clinging to Avery's arms, her fingers digging into her jacket sleeves. Her wide eyes were panicked. "He's the whole reason we came here. He's the whole reason I didn't want to ask you to—"

"Slow down, Mayv," Grigg said gently. He brushed off her shoulders, sending dust flying. "Where is this guy?"

We don't have time for detours, Avery reminded him. The group was making good time across the desert, but she was worried the Federation might pursue them. Though they had extra weapons, Avery didn't relish forcing innocent Reanges to fight if they didn't have to. Sometimes killing was unavoidable.

If the Feds are worried about you and me, they'll be distracted from the others, Grigg reasoned.

"He's three cells down from me, on the left," Mayven replied. "He worked for the Federation, Avery. He—"

"I don't need details right now, Mayven. Let's just get out of this first." Avery leaped down into the cell, grabbing the displaced sonic and shoving it into the pack on her hip. There was no point in stealth anymore. In fact, Grigg's point argued against it. She looked back up at him through the perfect hole in the ceiling. *Get her out of here. I'll meet you by the northeast corner.*

Avery wrapped her hands around the black bars that had locked Mayven inside and wrenched the sliding mechanism open. A guard was on her as soon as she stepped out, drawn by the cement cloud that had mushroomed out into the central corridor.

Avery dropped to the ground, sweeping a leg out from under him. He began to topple backward and she was already up, slamming a fist into his chest as he fell. His head hit the floor. He didn't get back up.

The door at the end of the corridor slid up with a whoosh. Another guard emerged with his blaster raised. Avery turned to him and he froze. His eyes widened with fear.

Avery charged at him. The guard fired wildly, missing every shot as Avery jumped up the cell wall, running along the bars and overhead to land behind him. His weapon clacked to the ground before she could strike. He fell to his knees and cowered before her.

Grigg's amusement slithered through the merge. *I guess he recognized you.*

Avery snorted. She brought a swift hand down on the man's neck, subduing him immediately in a move Syla had taught her. He'd wake up in a few hours with a nasty headache.

Avery stalked the cells, trying her best to ignore the faces that watched as she passed. Some were gaunt, others fearful. Her heart wrenched in her chest. They couldn't afford to save all of them. She couldn't bring humans together the way she could Reanges. She wouldn't be able to mobilize them effectively enough to combat the Federation soldiers outside. It was an agonizing brush with reality. But for the mission at hand, Avery had to walk past them.

Finally, she reached the cell Mayven had indicated. An older man stood near the back wall, eyeing her warily. He wore a suit—like he'd just left work. But its condition suggested otherwise: dirty and wrinkled beyond repair. The sleeves were torn. His pants had a hole in one knee. He'd been there for a long time.

"Are you the engineer?"

He nodded.

Avery grabbed his cell's door, forcing it open with a single, decisive jerk, the metal crunching. She stepped inside. A fine sheen of sweat coated the engineer's richly tanned forehead. His long fingers shook at his sides. Perhaps he recognized her, too.

"Do you have a name?"

He nodded again but said nothing.

Avery moved past him, pulling the sonic destabilizer out of her pack and attaching it to the wall. She tapped its back, and the small disc flashed green, then red, before dissolving the surface beneath it. A hole opened before them clear through to the outside. The shrill wailing of the warning sirens were still piercing the air.

Shaking, the engineer's dark eyes flickered between Avery and the outside.

"You don't have to speak . . ." Avery said softly. She took his arm and led him to the opening. It was no small relief when he climbed through without protest, though his progress was slow, impeded by exhaustion. Avery crawled out after him into the warm night air. "But you do have to hold on." And she slung him over her shoulders. He grunted, but he clung to her jacket, following her command feebly.

Avery skirted the buildings, avoiding the patrols that ran toward the Reange area. She kept to the edges of the camp. The soldiers were distracted, but they'd discover their missing human hostages soon enough, and Avery would like to be well into airspace by then.

They made it to the outer fence, and Avery crouched low by the hissing laser wire. She shifted the engineer on her back and paused to catch her breath. Someone would be monitoring the vid feeds by now—she couldn't risk leaping over.

A hover bike whizzed behind them, and Avery pulled farther back into the shadows. The fence shimmered, blacking out completely as it briefly disengaged to let the bike pass. Three more followed behind, speeding out into the wastelands beyond.

In an instant, Avery bolted after them, making it through just as the lasers sizzled back on. She broke into a sprint, ramping up her pace to an unnatural speed. Those bikes would soon be after Nova and the group ahead. They wouldn't have the time to finish their ten-mile trek to the ship before the soldiers reached them.

Avery shifted the merge back into focus. She was with Grigg and Mayven, who were no more than a mile out. Another two miles farther, Nova and the others were making good time. But it wouldn't be enough.

Three hover bikes on your tail. Stay alert, Avery warned, only letting Grigg and Nova hear her direct thoughts. For the other Reanges, she tried to assuage their anxiety, to bolster their courage. *You won't make it to the ship in time. We won't be slipping out of here quietly like we planned.*

Grigg bristled, almost offended. *We can handle a few Feds on bikes.*

Nova sent a command to their ship to meet them en route. If they had to give up their stealth, it would make their escape easier.

Within minutes, Avery caught up to Grigg and Mayven. She extended her power to Grigg, pushing him and Mayven faster. They could hear the hover bikes searching in the dark, their electric whines zigzagging around them in the shadowed haze of the wastes. It wouldn't be long before they found the others nearby, even hunting blindly.

Ahead, Nova halted her group as the ship descended from the mottled night sky, one of Qav's personal vessels. The large black hull was a curving shadow, perfectly camouflaged by the starless night for whatever underhanded needs it had been commissioned. Avery had commandeered it from the Sanctum for her own use. She didn't bother with asking for his permission. Not anymore.

Grigg and Avery reached them just as they were loading the ramp into the underbelly of the ship. The purple lighting along the walkway was a faint beacon fighting against the murky, polluted air.

Mayven jumped off Grigg's back before he could slow to a stop and threw herself into Kiyo's arms. The pleasure that coursed through Kiyo as he held Mayven was enough to make the mission worth it. Avery hadn't realized their attachment had been so deep—at least for Kiyo's part.

As Avery set him down, the engineer collapsed and vomited onto the dirt. Mayven pulled away from Kiyo to kneel beside the man. She delicately rubbed his back.

Behind them, the high-pitched whines grew louder. Hover bikes were heading straight for them. And from the sound of it, they'd multiplied.

"That's more than three," Nova noted ominously. She pulled the blaster from her back. It beeped as she disengaged the safety.

"Good." Grigg wiped his forehead and stepped over to Avery. "I was worried they thought *three* would actually be a challenge."

Avery turned to Mayven, her eyes traveling over the Reanges, who moved too slowly into the ship. "Keep loading them. This shouldn't take long."

CHAPTER FOUR

Avery bolted into the night with Grigg and Nova by her side. Blue smears of light in the haze were the only warning before the bikes were on them. Avery threw her hands up, erecting a shield of pure power that stopped the four in the lead. The riders slammed against the invisible barrier, their bikes crumbling, bodies tumbling across the desert floor.

Five more bikes sped at them from behind the leaders, pivoting at the last moment to avoid Avery's shimmering wall. They doubled back into the shadows, the whining pitch of their machines confirming they hadn't gone far.

Grigg and Nova were already on the fallen Feds. Two struggled to their feet, trying to fight. The others didn't move. But Grigg and Nova made quick work of them anyway, subduing them before they could threaten more trouble.

Avery stalked forward, exposing herself in the open, a temptation the soldiers wouldn't be able to resist. In her experience, many of the Federation soldiers liked to play with their prey. Especially at the camps.

She smiled when two of the bikes returned. They circled Avery, surrounding her in a blurring blue ring of light that danced in her vision. They hoped to intimidate her. To frighten her. If only they knew that kind of fear had been driven out of her months ago. It was the only benefit of losing everything—she had nothing left to lose.

Avery stood still, watching. Waiting.

The leader peeled out, whirling around and driving right at her. Avery dropped to one knee and slammed her fist into the dirt. The wave of her power shot into the bike, sending both machine and rider careening into the sky. The wave kept going, hitting the rest only half a second later. Their bodies sailed off their bikes, disappearing alongside their cycles into the black. None of them returned.

Your flare really makes these fights worth it, Grigg admired. His smile was wide as Avery jogged back to the others.

"Jealous?" Avery taunted, grinning back.

"Always."

"Should we cart them inside? They saw your face." Nova towed one of the four Feds they'd knocked out and tied up. Grigg had removed their helmets. They were barely adults.

The CLF had prioritized keeping Avery's identity a secret during the camp raids. It had been a concession Avery agreed to when Alex had protested against her involvement in any capacity. Mayven had to fight with Alex to even be able to offer Avery a position.

Many humans who disagreed with the Federation's policies on Reanges saw Avery as a symbol for that resistance. She had become a beloved public figure on Earth, and with that came a certain level of immunity where Klein was concerned. If the liberation of legal Reange camps were ever pinned on Avery, things would get more complicated. Alex argued it would irrevocably hurt the progress of the whole movement.

Avery stared at the humans by her feet. Freeing incarcerated Reanges was one thing, but absconding with Federation soldiers would bring Klein's support base down on their heads. Either way, Alex would not approve. Worse than that, she'd be disappointed.

"Leave them," Avery said. The guard in the facility had seen her either way. Maybe she should take Syla's advice and start wearing glasses.

Mayven and Kiyo still waited by the ship. Avery had come for only these two and were leaving with a vessel full of innocent Reanges. That had to be worth something.

A soft whirring was the only warning Avery had before she pivoted on instinct. A laser knife sailed through the air, missing her back by inches.

Avery pushed Nova and Grigg behind her, and turned to face the dark as pain sliced through Avery's abdomen. She looked down, grabbing her stomach and finding no wound.

"Avery!" Mayven screamed as Kiyo collapsed in her arms.

The knife intended for Avery had found a different target. Mayven slid to ground beside him as Avery threw up a haphazard shield behind her. There would be no more surprises.

"Get to the bridge," Avery commanded Nova, who was already on her way up the ramp. They had lingered too long.

Grigg had his blaster out and trained on the shadows beyond. "Someone's out there."

Avery didn't have time to worry about who. She dropped to the ground, then ripped the knife from Kiyo's side. He gasped and cried out. Left inside, the laser would have continued to melt his flesh. Blood oozed from his wound, surging with each beat of his heart. It was a life-threatening blow. Avery pressed her fingers into the gash, trying to stanch the bleeding. Kiyo panted, fixating on Mayven.

Avery pulled his pain away from him, drawing it into herself. Her breathing shallowed as Kiyo's leveled. His face relaxed, draining of color. Avery gently ushered him into unconsciousness.

"What are you doing?" Mayven asked sharply, her dark hands moving frantically down Kiyo's arm before clutching desperately at his sleeve. Her fingers were stained with his blood.

"Helping," Avery bit out between pained breaths.

"That gash is too deep." Grigg backed up to stand over them. His blaster never left his shoulder while he kept his focus on the shadows. "He needs a healer."

Mayven shook her head emphatically, perfect brown curls bouncing at the sides of her face. "There's no way we'll get him to one in time. We never should have come here alone. This is all my fault. This is all *my fault!*"

Mayven struggled against her lurching breathing, devolving into a full panic that Avery was helpless to dispel. As much as she may have wanted to, as much as it may have helped, she couldn't influence humans.

But Mayven found her own control. She leaned back on her heels, straightening her shoulders. And when she looked up at Avery, her wide brown eyes carried the weight of the two worlds within them. "Please, Avery. *Please.*"

Avery knew the torment behind that look. Had felt it. Had been destroyed by it.

"What do you want me to do, Mayven? I can't exactly—"

"Heal him."

Avery flinched. Kiyo stirred in her hands before she seized her control again.

"I know you've done it," Mayven continued, tears spilling down dirty cheeks. She placed a hand on top of Avery's, skin slick with Kiyo's blood. "Please—*please.* You can at least try."

The last time Avery had healed someone, she had been asked in nearly the exact same way. Pleading. Desperate. It had been a stretch for her to attempt it even then.

Ready when you are, Avery. Nova had made it to the bridge. The ship was prepared to leave.

We don't have time for this, Grigg argued, anxiety making him flinch at the slightest shifting of shadows. The person out in the dark still hadn't shown themselves.

Mayven held her gaze. Her fingers had warmed and steadied on Avery's.

"I don't make any promises," Avery said tightly. She shifted, dragging Kiyo up onto the ramp until they were bathed in soft purple light. Mayven followed, crawling on her knees. Avery swallowed hard. "Back away from him. Give me some room."

Mayven scrambled back, farther up the ramp. She tucked her knees under her chin, those wide eyes making her look younger than she was.

To focus wholly on Kiyo, Avery let the other Reanges go from her connection, and once again she was alone in her mind. She kept her hold on Kiyo. His life force struggled, flickering in and out of vibrancy with each gush of blood that pooled through Avery's fingers. He was fading rapidly.

It wouldn't help to waste more time thinking it over.

Avery ripped open his shirt where the blade had melted through the beige fabric. Fresh blood flowed from his side, accumulating on the ramp beneath. Mayven whimpered.

His skin was hot under Avery's hands. She closed her eyes, blocking out everything but the feel of her power deep within, of the warmth that called out to Kiyo. The warmth built, seeping from the core of her chest, surging up and through her veins and straight into her palms. She could *feel* Kiyo—feel his life leaking out through his wound. And if she could feel his life, then she could grab hold of it.

Mayven gasped.

Avery opened her eyes. Where her hands hovered above Kiyo's skin, her fingers glowed bright with a warm light that diffused as it reached up under her sleeves. Kiyo's blood seemed to stop flowing entirely before retreating back into his body.

The sheer influx of raw power made Avery lightheaded. Warmth surged up and through her, filling her and pouring into Kiyo's wound to do her bidding. Some part of her remembered this. She relished in the sheer rightness of it, the utter and complete belonging.

And Avery was struck with a sudden clarity: she knew what she was doing.

CHAPTER FIVE

"How could you be so stupid?" Alex Peña paced the room, pausing every few seconds to level a serious glare at Mayven.

Avery sat on the couch beside Mayven, avoiding Alex's eyes. But she kept her shoulders as square as she could. Avery would be damned if she would appear weak in front of a woman whose opinion she valued so highly.

"How could you let this happen?" Alex threw a wild hand at the holovid playing on the wall of the expensive hotel room.

In the vid, which was currently making the rounds on every major newscast, Avery and Mayven knelt together on a ship ramp with Kiyo between them. Avery faced the cam, her braid draped over one shoulder. She leaned over Kiyo as her bloodstained hands began to glow. Light poured from her fingers into his abdomen.

The vid cut to more footage of Avery attacking the Federation soldiers who had pursued her on bike. And then again to the jail where she took down two guards.

Alex fumed, turning to read the headline aloud. "Avery Vey, Known Native Elite, Viscously Attacks Federation Facility.'"

Avery grimaced. Her shoulders faltered. Censure from Alex was worse than any lecture Gran had ever delivered.

"Easy, Alex," Cora purred. She stared down at her wristport, typing in something with fingers that moved faster than light. "They didn't have time to prepare for this one. There were bound to be hiccups."

"*Hiccups?* Is that what you call this? This one stunt is going to cost us an entire *year's* worth of progress with our voter base!"

Avery's cheeks heated. "We didn't have a choice. If Klein had found Mayven there—"

"Is that what Cora told you?" Alex laughed humorlessly. "Mayven losing her standing would have been regrettable, yes. It would have set the CLF back. But it's nothing compared to *your* public appearance, Avery. Don't minimize your importance to our goals here. Don't minimize the power of your image. We agreed you should limit the use of your powers for a reason, and you just gave Klein an enormous avenue to fearmonger her rabble."

Avery held Alex's gaze, refusing to look anywhere else. There was some truth to Alex's words. Maybe she was right. People carried Avery's image on banners during protests; they painted her profile on the sides of cruisers. Others mimicked Avery's style or gen-modded their eyes to be as light as they dared. Avery's visage had become a political statement that existed outside of herself. It was an unforeseen responsibility—one she didn't relish. It was a distraction from her real purpose, her real work. The missions she filled her days with were the only things that kept her guilt at bay.

Mayven cleared her throat delicately. "This is why I didn't want to tell you, Alex. I knew you wouldn't understand."

"Wouldn't understand?" Alex ran a frustrated hand over her dark cropped hair. She dropped her lanky frame into one of the large chairs that faced them. "You mean I wouldn't let you set off—without Avery—on some kind of idiotic assignment that was little better than suicide?"

"That's exactly why." Cora sounded amused. "It's her life to risk as she sees fit."

"Don't even get me started on you." Alex glared again. "It was your intel that got Mayven started on this absurd scheme in the first place."

Mayven leaned forward in her seat. "And it was my idea to keep it secret. From both you and Avery. I'll be the first to admit that was a mistake."

"Why keep it from us at all?" Avery asked. "Alex is right—you should have come to me with this. What you did was reckless, Mayven. It could just as easily have been you instead of Kiyo with a knife in your gut last night. And if it had been, I couldn't have done anything to stop it."

Mayven's eyes narrowed, her round face tilted downward. "I've heard otherwise."

Avery frowned.

"You've healed a human before," Mayven clarified. "Finn Lunitia."

Avery's breath caught in her throat. A thousand memories came flooding back to her at once, threatening to knock her off her feet. She hadn't heard his name aloud in weeks. To have it hit her here, when she was so unprepared . . . Her head spun. The darkness that had haunted her for months following the Gate's collapse wound its heavy fingers around her heart, threatening to drag her back down into its depths.

"Mayven." Alex said her name like a command and shook her head. This was clearly a conversation they'd had before, and Mayven was going off book. Even Cora stilled.

"*This* is why," Mayven said quietly. She softly placed a hand on Avery's knee. "This is why I kept it from you. I was worried about the impact. You've worked so hard to move on, to put the past behind you. I know how it was for you after the Gate fell."

A chill ran down Avery's spine. What did rescuing some Federation engineer have to do with the past? With Finn?

Is everything okay? Nova's question curled around Avery's mind.

Avery had nearly forgotten she kept a loose merge with Nova and Grigg. When they were outside of the Sanctum, Nova insisted upon it.

I'm fine. Avery reeled herself back in.

Nova and Grigg had been frustrated enough to be barred from this meeting. It would serve no purpose to worry them further.

Cora studied Avery closely. "What I wouldn't give to know how that works."

Avery's spine stiffened. "You're not the only one. That sounds dangerously close to Federation sentiment."

"Settle down. I didn't mean anything by it. But Klein was able to replicate your abilities in at least one test subject. It would be interesting to see the research."

"Is that what that facility was for?" Avery snapped. "Is that what all this is about? Nick Lunitia?" She hadn't seen or heard from Finn's brother since he'd attacked them in the Sanctum last year.

Cora pulled something out of her briefcase. It clanged heavily as she placed it on the low table in front of Avery. The hilt of the laser knife from the wastes. The one intended for Avery. Avery picked it up, running her fingers over the cold metal. Carved into the base were two letters: *N. L.*

No human could have thrown that knife from such a distance. At least, not one without powers. And someone had filmed that footage of Avery healing Kiyo. Had Nick been there, watching them from the shadows?

"That facility was more than just a Reange camp," Avery said, piecing things together aloud. "There were labs in those buildings. But they weren't testing on Reanges. The human prisoners were the priority."

"Which suggests . . . ?" Cora prompted, a brow quirking with excitement.

"They were testing on humans."

"It's *who* they test on that is more interesting," Mayven leaned in toward her. "Klein sends humans there whom she's deemed dangerous. Whom she wants to hide. Like the engineer we were trying to find."

"Why not just have them killed?"

Mayven shrugged a bandaged shoulder. "Mercy?"

"I'd hardly call becoming a test subject mercy," Alex muttered.

Avery shook her head, trying to follow. "Why would you care about some Federation engineer? What could be important enough to risk your life for him?"

"Because he's not just 'some Federation engineer,'" Cora explained. "He's spent his career monitoring signals from the outer planets. Sifting through meta data. Categorizing anomalies."

"So, what, he spilled his coffee on Klein's white pantsuit or something?"

"He flagged the wrong code—he delved too deeply into its origins. He asked too many questions."

"Avery." Mayven took Avery's hand in hers and squeezed gently. "He was convinced there's been regular data entering our galaxy from Echo's star system."

Avery blanched.

"That's impossible," Alex breathed. For once, the politician was shocked into abject silence.

Cora nodded. "It should be impossible if the wormhole we used to connect the Gates had been truly severed. Any comms launched without some kind of fold jump would take decades to reach us. I spent the whole morning with him going over his work once I got him to talk. His figures are sound—the data is authentic."

"What about a delay?" Alex asked. "How long between origin point and reception?"

Mayven smiled. "This is where it gets really interesting. Delivery delay of under an hour."

"Which means," Cora continued, "that whatever is receiving that data from their system is somewhere in our galaxy."

Avery's breath caught, her heart clenching in her chest. Her entire world was shifting in the space of a few minutes. The table began to rattle as her control faltered. "But . . . that would mean . . ."

Cora smiled. "There's another Gate."

CHAPTER SIX

Avery couldn't believe what Cora was saying, could barely hear anything beyond the ringing in her ears.

Moons above. Grigg's voice trickled down the merge to jerk Avery out of her stupor. She'd lost control of herself again. Grigg and Nova had heard everything. Had felt everything.

The two of them sat together on the ship docked on the parking level, their hands tangled together with hope. Avery couldn't fault them for listening in on her. She wished she had insisted on bringing them with her.

"I've been poring over satellite scans all morning and haven't found anything yet. I set up an algorithm to run constant searches." Cora kept talking, growing more animated by the second. "Even though it's within our star system, that's still a lot of empty space to cover. But if it's out there, we'll find it."

"How could Klein hide a worm gate?" Avery asked. "I thought they were massive."

"It may not be a full Gate," warned Cora, "so prepare yourself for that possibility. It could be anything allowing the data to get through to us—even some kind of anomaly."

"The fact that Klein had this man thrown into a human test lab suggests otherwise," Alex said darkly.

"The facts support that theory," Cora agreed. "Klein doesn't want this information getting out."

"Then we need to move. We need to act." Avery stood, her sudden anxiety making her restless. At least she had managed to settle the table's rattling.

"We all agree," Mayven said. "It's why we went to pull him out in the first place: we need more information. Working around Klein will take time."

"We don't *have* time." Avery tried her best to not sound as desperate as she felt. "I left Echo in turmoil. Even if we can only send comms through . . . If there's even a chance, then we can't afford to linger. That Gate is gone because of us—because we didn't—"

"Whatever happened to the Gate wasn't our fault," Cora argued, her hazel eyes narrowing. "We stopped Klein's attempt to destroy it."

"But you still refused to release that vid," Avery accused, casting a glance over all three of them. Bitterness boiled in her gut. "If you had, Klein never would have been reelected in the first place. She never would have regained power."

Alex let out a sigh as she closed her eyes and pinched the bridge of her nose. "We've been over this, Avery. That vid wouldn't just bring Klein down—it would cause mass panic. If citizens discover the earth has a limited number of years left before it's uninhabitable, they'll dissolve into chaos. Just look at what happened after the Gate's collapse. The destruction from those gravitational waves was just the beginning. Think about the riots you dispel or the camps you liberate. You believe Klein would be able to manipulate the public so easily if they weren't scared? If they weren't desperate? That vid would make things exponentially worse."

Avery bit her tongue and stared at her feet.

"And that was before your little adventure with Mayven and Kiyo last night," Alex continued, her voice ratcheting up. "We'll be lucky if any of this even matters once Klein makes her next public address. Mark my words, she will not waste this opportunity. We will all suffer for it."

"Alex," Mayven censured firmly, a glassy look on her face. "It was my fault. I'm the one who begged Avery to use her powers. I'm the one who went in alone. And I'd do it again."

They fell into silence.

At least Kiyo had survived. He was recovering in Cora's personal cruiser under the careful watch of the best healer credits could buy. The same one who had treated the engineer so that he could help Cora with calculations that morning.

We should ask him *for help*, Grigg suggested.

Avery flinched. "Absolutely not."

Cora tilted her head. "Why did we explicitly exclude your friends from this meeting if you were going to include them either way?"

Avery shrugged. "Where I go, they go."

Alex crossed one long leg over the other. "Well? Are you going to share their thoughts with us? It seems like one of them had a decent idea."

Grigg has a point, Avery. Nova's soothing energy reached Avery. *Time is an issue here and we can't afford to wait for more information. Not when we all know who can get it for us.*

Avery sighed, gritting her teeth. "Qav."

Mayven sat up, her eyes lighting. "That's not a bad suggestion, actually. If information is what we need, well, Qav has always been a steady source of it."

"He brought us information from Klein before," Alex conceded. "And I was skeptical it could be done even then."

"Yeah," Avery confirmed. "With a great deal of *my* help and by nearly killing everyone involved in the process."

Mayven's brows drew together. "Didn't you just say we don't have time to waste? We have no idea what Klein's next move is or how it will affect our maneuverability. She'll know we took her engineer. She'll know what we're after."

Cora crossed her arms over her chest. "What are those powers of yours for if not this?"

We're with you either way, Nova assured achingly. Her hope was tender, a raw and beaten thing that mirrored Avery's own.

Avery let out a long breath. Nova was right. If there was even a chance at finding the truth they needed sooner—if there was even a chance at knowing if Finn and the others were still alive—then Avery would make a deal with the devil himself.

And Qav wasn't exactly that—but he was close.

CHAPTER SEVEN

A very swiftly took the stairs up to Qav's mansion as the artifical daylight dimmed toward evening in the dome overhead. Grigg and Nova flanked her. The stone beneath her boots was pristine, a pure ivory speckled with gray that had yet to be sullied by much use.

Rebuilding his island sanctuary had been the first item on Qav's agenda after things had settled. Although he had spared no expense to rebuild the city first. He was many things she hated, but Qav did care for the Reanges who called his underground sanctuary their home. He took his responsibility as caretaker seriously.

Still, what he had done to Avery . . . What he had cost her . . .

Avery quickened her pace, surging ahead of her companions and through the barren courtyard. If she was sorry for anything, it was the gardens she had destroyed when she leveled Qav's home. The flowering trees that had once lined the walkway had taken Avery's breath away. It would take years to regrow them.

Before she could reach the massive metal double doors at the entryway, they opened.

"Avery?" Syla couldn't hide her surprise at the approaching trio, her pink eyebrows rising as she strode forward to greet them. Her outfit was casual but finer than what Avery was used to seeing her in. The deep maroon jumpsuit offset her vibrant pink hair and made her dark skin almost glisten in the twilight. "I thought you canceled our training session today. Was I supposed to meet you at your place?"

"Change of plans," Avery said cryptically. It was difficult enough bringing herself to come here. She'd rather get it over with as soon as possible so she could leave.

"Just as well, Sy." Grigg finally reached them, jogging to keep up with Avery's pace. "I would have bested you today. I could feel it."

The tall warrior grinned, throwing a punch into his shoulder that nearly made him stumble. "In your dreams, Big Grigg."

Grigg glowered, rubbing his shoulder. "You know I hate that blazing nickname."

"Aw." Nova laughed loudly as she came up behind him. "But we all love it so much."

Avery couldn't bring herself to enjoy their banter, much less participate in it, but she was glad they had become friends. Syla had taken on the role of their trainer the past year. Her skills in classic Reange fighting techniques had advanced their trio to a new level of combat.

"Avery. What a surprise." Rem appeared in the doorway looking as regal as ever, his long nose turned up beneath yellow-lensed glasses as he ran his gaze over her outfit. His disapproval floated around Avery like a haze that rendered the grimace he tried to hide pointless. "You're not dressed for dinner."

"Why would I be?"

Rem paused, eyes flickering to Syla and back. "Then you haven't finally accepted one of his invitations?"

"Is he in?" Avery ignored Rem's question, pushing her way past the lanky secretary and into the foyer. It looked exactly the same as it had the first time she set foot in this place.

Rem nodded, dazed. "In the dining room. With Ennis."

"Avery, wait." Syla grabbed her arm, strong fingers circling around her bicep. "What's this about?"

Avery dropped her eyes to Syla's fingers and back up again. Syla immediately let go.

"Just . . ." Syla tucked a loose strand of hair behind her ear. She hadn't cut it since the collapse. "Go easy on him."

Avery sighed, trying hard to ignore the fear emanating from Syla. Fear *for Qav*. For what Avery might do to him. "If he makes this easy, then I'll go easy. That's all I can promise you."

Syla nodded once and Avery turned, the rest of them following as she marched to the dining room at the end of the hall. The veined granite doors were already open, and Avery didn't falter as she strode over the threshold.

Ennis jumped up from her seat near the head of a massive dining table, a smile spreading over her heart-shaped face and pulling at the scar that slashed across one eye. "Avery! You're here . . ." She trailed off as she saw Avery's expression, her reflexive joy deflating.

Qav leaned back in his tall chair at the head of the table, one elbow resting on its ornately carved arm, those silver eyes trained on Avery. His long pale hair fell in stark relief over the shoulders of his deep mauve jacket, fully loose and straight.

"You came just in time. We were about to sit down to dinner," Ennis said lamely as silence stretched. She looked at Qav, widening her eyes meaningfully. "Right, Qav?"

A corner of his mouth tipped up. Syla snorted, then maneuvered around Avery to take a seat at his other side.

Rem sniffed. "But she's not dressed for—" He cut himself off, dipping his sharp chin until it sunk into his floral buttoned collar. He shuffled past Avery to join the others.

Qav was speaking to them silently, leaving her out.

She could have easily walked into his mind and forced the connection between them. There was no wall Qav could build that Avery could not break down. He had lost the upper hand a long time ago, and they both knew it. But Avery wanted to stay out of his head, if possible. She had set boundaries that she wanted to maintain, and she had a better chance of him respecting those if she did the same.

Months ago, the last time they had spoken, things had not gone well in any stretch of the imagination. But Avery was ready for a fight with Qav. A part of her yearned for it—the only way to dispel the rage that simmered just beneath the surface of her skin.

"I thought you never wanted to step foot on this island again," Qav finally said, his familiar voice dancing over the enormous quartz dining table and across the room.

Ennis shifted and something thumped beneath the table, dislodging Qav from his repose, his elbow slipping off the chair. He snapped his head to glare at his companion, dark brows drawing together.

Avery cleared her throat to cover the laugh that nearly surfaced. It was such a quintessentially Ennis move. But although Syla and Ennis had become her friends, Qav had not. Avery needed to remember that.

"I love what you've done with the place," Avery said flippantly. She sauntered into the room, looking from the twisting glass chandelier above their heads—identical to the one she smashed last year—to the arched windows framing the city.

"Yeah," Grigg added behind her. "It's so . . . different."

"I put a lot of thought into first iteration of my home," Qav said simply. "Why would I change anything? It's not like I asked for it to be pulverized."

Avery ran a finger over the shards of amethyst inlaid along the white quartz of the table. It sparkled beneath the soft lighting overhead.

Qav noted sourly, "Unfortunately, I couldn't find a replacement for the wooden banquet table. The last one took me five years to obtain."

Avery looked up, leveling Qav with a golden stare. "Whoops."

Grigg snorted on a laugh while amusement poured from Nova thickly enough that even Qav would feel it.

Qav's mouth twisted, but he said nothing. He took his glass of pale wine, downing it in one swig. "Why are you here, Avery? As much as I'd like to believe you took me up on an invitation, I doubt you've found it in your heart to forgive me quite yet, so I—"

"You're right, I haven't." Avery stopped him before he could continue. Before he could force her to think about what she had endured. Before the memories could touch her. "I'm here for a favor. I think you owe me at least that."

His eyes brightened. "Anything." He said it so quickly and with such intensity that Avery found her assuredness plummeting.

"What?" she croaked. It sounded idiotic even to her own ears. She had expected a fight from him. Annoyance and inconvenience, at the very least.

Qav stood. He placed his hands on the table before him, leaning forward. "Anything," he repeated. "I want your trust again, Avery. And I will do whatever it takes to regain it. Just name your price."

Of course he would phrase it that way.

"Trust cannot be bought."

"Are you certain? I have fairly deep pockets."

"Not deep enough."

Avery almost felt sorry for him, but that was what had gotten her here in the first place. It's what had cost her everything and everyone dear to her.

He studied her, as though determining how much to test her limits. In the end, he straightened, spreading his hands out wide and sweeping them over his companions and the extravagant room.

"Well, then. I'm at your disposal either way. What do you need from me, my So'?"

No, this had not gone as Avery expected. At all.

CHAPTER EIGHT

Qav took a deep swallow of the expensive liquor in his glass, surveying the lights of the Sanctum coming to life as the domed sky brought them into an artificial night. The city had rebuilt fast. Qav had made sure of it. But his people had adapted to the damage the Federation had wrought during its attack better than he'd anticipated. The Sanctum was finding its footing again.

While the battle itself had brought great destruction, it was paltry compared to the loss of the Gate. That had wrought an invisible, irreparable blow to every Reange in Qav's city.

Thankfully, they had built this place with enough foresight and planning that the Sanctum had been spared the worst impacts of the gravitational waves. Compared to the human cities on ground level, they had been left relatively unscathed. But the destruction of the Gate itself . . .

As much as Qav hated to admit it, that portal had *meant* something to the Reanges here. Even if Qav didn't care about the connection to Echo—even if he never wanted to see that planet for himself—many people under his protection did. Plenty of residents within the Sanctum had been born on Echo and brought to Earth only in an attempt to avoid the bloodshed of the war. And although they had left their home world, they held on to the hope that they'd see it again one day.

Especially after Avery showed up in the world above and fueled that dream to reach new heights. Even Qav's friends had abandoned him to try to save that promise alongside Avery, despite everything he had given to them. Despite everything he had built from the ground up *for them*. Despite the safety he provided.

But the Gate's decimation had stolen any hope of returning to their home.

Qav's fingers tightened on his glass. He could easily manipulate them, as he had done for years. Turning the tides of public sentiment toward his schemes had been his strategy for nearly a decade. A way to keep the peace and endear himself to every Reange in the Sanctum. He had always seen it as his right. He was different. A So'Reange.

But after what Qav had done to Avery . . . After the way she had reacted to it—to him . . . For some reason, things had changed. And he wasn't entirely sure why.

"Do you really think it's possible? Could there be another Gate?" Ennis's light voice drew Qav from his thoughts and back to the room behind him. She sat on the large couch beside Syla, both nursing their glasses of amber alcohol. Rem stood by the holofire, staring quietly at the leaping artificial flames, his long fingers clasped behind a straight back.

"Avery's instincts are usually spot on," Syla replied thoughtfully, but her excitement curled through the air, mingling with the others—even Rem, no matter how much he tried to conceal it. "At the very least, we'll have more answers to the questions that have been plaguing us since the Fed attack."

"That may be, but the risks are amplified. Maybe it's not Avery's instincts so much as a desire to get Finn back," Rem suggested.

"Remmington," Ennis chastised curtly.

Syla frowned, focusing on the ornate navy rug that spanned the entirety of the room.

"I'm just enunciating what we're all thinking. We all saw how she handled losing him. Are we willing to take on a mission this hazardous for her love life?"

"Don't be ridiculous," Ennis snapped. "We all lost something when that Gate was destroyed. Every one of us. And it wasn't just Finn, Rem. Except for Grigg and Nova, Avery's entire family was on the other side."

It was something Qav had considered. This urgent need to find answers, to dive straight into Klein's reach, could be propelled by her grief. Her pure desperation to have Finn back in her life. If there had been a way for Qav to see Veena again . . .

"Even so," Rem continued, an undercurrent of fear rippling around him, "with the open hunt on Reanges, it will be more difficult than ever for us to traverse aboveground. I don't like the idea of rotting in a Federation prison for life."

"You say that like you'll be rotting with us. When have you ever come on jobs before?" Syla pointed out dryly, picking at a piece of meat stuck in her teeth. "Nobody expects you to start now."

"Can you not do that? It's disgusting." Rem scrunched his nose. "And you need a hacker. Avery said so herself."

Qav sighed, reaching out to Rem to soothe his anxiety. Qav may not control anyone anymore, but a little nudging toward calm never hurt anyone. Especially Rem.

"She also said we'll have Cora Najisuki on comms the whole time," Qav pointed out as he took a seat in the winged-back chair to face the others. He casually threw one leg over the other. The more relaxed he looked, the better off they'd be. "Moons above, Rem. I thought I paid you good money to pay attention."

"I'll have you know I took extensive notes," Rem sputtered, pushing his glasses up on his nose. "But what if you run into another blackout scenario, like the desert operation last year? If you lose comms, you'll be completely blind in there. You need a Reange."

Syla laughed. "Since when are you on the same level as Cora blazing Najisuki?"

Rem bristled, turning back to the holofire. If only Syla knew this was Rem's way of worrying about them. Maybe Qav *would* suggest Rem come along. On the ship, he'd be away from explicit danger but close enough to feel useful. It was never a bad idea to have a backup pilot.

Avery and the others had left shortly after dinner. Qav was surprised that they'd stayed to eat after all. After Avery's revelatory news,

Syla dropped into silence while Ennis had immediately launched into a full inquiry. Not that asking more questions helped. Avery didn't have many answers. It was the entire reason she had come to them. It was why she needed Qav.

Avery looked good. Healthier, anyway. Her cheeks had more color than the last time he saw her, and her eyes glowed brighter, a sure sign of the use of power in the in the wastelands. He'd seen the vids circulating the news feeds. While their gifts could drain them in the immediate aftermath, an influx of energy always followed. But dark circles lingered under her eyes, there since she had lost half her family to the other side of the universe.

"At least we have two days," Syla offered.

"At least?" Ennis eyed her. "We'd need two *months* to run through all the possibilities."

"Seems like Cora has already done that for us. If we have to trust anyone's calculations, she's not a bad option."

Ennis made a sound of agreement and tucked her bare feet up under her. Her gray eyes found Qav's, looking larger in her face than ever, her shorn hair accentuating their intensity. She had always been able to read him from the moment he'd first met her as a child. *Are you okay with this?* Her thought drifted to him.

He couldn't very well answer that no, he wasn't okay. He couldn't admit that the prospect of working so closely with Avery again frightened him. He couldn't admit that what he had done to Avery had been a mistake. That he was terrified she would force him to acknowledge it. Like she had tried to do a few months earlier.

So instead he tipped up his mouth in a convincing grin. *Why wouldn't I be?* He drained the rest of his drink and stood. "I need some air. You all should get some sleep. I want us on top of our game tomorrow for the meeting with the others. Let's show them how a real team works."

Ennis glanced at Syla so quickly that if Qav didn't know them, if he couldn't feel their emotions, he would have missed it. Since he didn't particularly want to hang around and get bombarded by their silent analysis of him, as they been doing for months, he left.

Stalking through the halls of his newly completed home didn't make him feel much better. Although he'd had the place reconstructed in an exact replica of his original plans hoping it would bring him peace, all it seemed to do was anger him. Familiarity didn't do anything to ease the oily sensation in the depths of his chest. It was always there, waiting for a quiet moment to suffocate him from the inside.

He made his way to the back veranda that curved around the natural formation of the island rocks, overlooking a rectangular swimming pool that glowed purple. It cast a soft stain against the white stone of the archways, the potted trees sending dappled shadows that danced in the warm wind of the night. Qav breathed in the sweet air, letting it fill his lungs.

Well, that took long enough. He realized the thought wasn't his own just as a shadow emerged from behind the closest arch.

Qav nearly jumped out of his skin. His hand shot out in front of him along with a substantial pulse of energy.

"Really?" Avery almost laughed on the word, the slight rise of her chin the only indication that she had exerted any effort to deflect his attack. "I guess you really are going soft if you didn't sense me out here. Syla would be livid I got the jump on you."

Qav glowered at her, his heart racing. She had crept back onto the grounds after leaving with the others. They were alone together for the first time in months.

"And why should I have?" Qav asked. "You've been shielding yourself from me for weeks."

"We both know you could feel my presence if you wanted."

Perhaps. But he *hadn't* wanted to. Not that he'd admit that, especially to her.

"Where are your guard dogs?" Qav moved leisurely over to the water's edge, peering down into the depths. "Dropped them off at their kennel?"

Avery only shrugged. Qav suddenly realized she had changed her clothes. Instead of the casual garb at dinner, now she wore an all-black ensemble with twin blasters strapped to each thigh. So it wasn't a social call. He supposed he should have guessed as much.

"I didn't hear a boat," Qav said, still reeling from the fact that she'd been able to sneak up on him. Avery was right—even without his powers, he should have been more alert.

"Do I need one? It's not so far from the shore."

Qav crossed his arms over his chest, meeting her golden stare. "You're telling me you jumped it?"

Her only answer was a smug smile and a tilt of her head.

He let out a laugh in disbelief. "You're joking."

"It's not that hard. You just need to work on the physical aspects of your gifts. You rely too much on the merge and mind control."

As soon as the words left her mouth, the air shifted, turning awkward and stiff. Avery's brows drew together as she looked away, staring instead at the swaying trees. The soft whooshing of their leaves was unnaturally loud in the silence between them.

Qav's chest twisted as he floundered for something to say. He hated the quiet. Especially like this. Especially with her. But he had to do something.

"Is that an offer?" He laced his voice with what he hoped was innuendo. If he couldn't delve into her mind, maybe he could distract her enough to give himself some breathing room.

Her golden eyes sliced back to him, glowing in the darkness and cutting straight through him. Qav forced himself to hold his ground. He'd faced harsher things in his life than this girl's censure. He could survive her.

But he wanted Avery's trust again. He needed it. And he was afraid to ask himself why.

So Qav simply grinned, running a nervous finger over his bottom lip. "Sorry. Old habits."

Avery paused for a moment, considering him. "I want us to go alone." At last, she had revealed her intentions.

Qav blinked. "What?"

"We're going alone. You and me. To get this intel from Klein." She broke it down into short sentences, like he was an idiot.

And maybe he was. Qav scrambled for some kind of adequate response. "Are Grigg and Nova on board with that? I didn't think they let you out of their sight these days."

"I'm here, aren't I?" She gestured to herself. At his disbelieving look, she added, "They don't know. And if I have my way, they won't know until it's done and we're back."

Qav studied her. "Why?"

"We have no idea what we're walking into." Her voice strained as she pulled her braid over her shoulder, running her hand down its length. "I know Cora has her plan for us, but I don't like putting them at risk like this. I won't."

"Then we don't have to go at all. We can take things slower. Cora's scans will find something eventually and—"

Avery stopped him with a look. "You know that's not an option. I won't wait around for Klein to block us entirely. The only advantage we have is speed. She won't see us coming."

Qav sighed. She had made up her mind. He would not be able to change it. Avery was immovable where he was concerned.

"Syla and Ennis . . . They'll be furious with me." It was the only excuse Qav could think of that would truly hold him back. He had been working hard to rebuild what he had broken between them. And they were just becoming a unit again.

"So will Grigg and Nova."

Qav eyed her. "They can handle it, you know. They've been through worse."

"And whose fault was that? We nearly died on that last mission with you, and without my ability to heal, Syla *would* have. I'm not going to put them in the line of fire again when you and I can do this alone."

"Isn't this what got you into trouble the last time? Doing things alone?" He wasn't sure why he said it.

Avery held his gaze, gold clashing against silver. "I won't be alone."

Qav was the one to turn away. He moved over to the pool's edge, focusing on the water moving in soft laps against the custom tiled walls that had taken him weeks to source. Avery was in his home, asking for his help. She was giving him another chance to prove . . . He didn't know what.

Her boots clicked on the stone as Avery walked up beside him. Together, they stared into the water, purple light dancing over their skin. She knew he was going to say yes. Despite keeping their walls up, she could still see through him.

"Fine," Qav said shortly. "So, what, you just want to sneak out in the dead of night while they're all sleeping?"

Avery tilted her head up, grinning at him for the first time in what felt like a millennium.

Qav flattened his lips. "You're joking."

"Looks like you're going to jump that lake sooner than you thought," she said brightly, already taking off around him and disappearing into the shadows of the night.

And Qav followed her.

CHAPTER NINE

❚❚ust so we're clear on this, I'm not certain you'll find anything in there." Cora had been reiterating the fact for the past two days.

"It's our best shot," Avery replied. She doubled-checked the laces on her boots, one foot braced on the copilot's seat of Cora's ship. "The longer we wait, the more time Klein has to regroup and move against us."

"You said she was certain," Qav muttered, his hands busy gathering his long hair into a bun at the nape of his neck. A few shorter pieces escaped and fell forward against his sharp cheekbones. He'd changed into an outfit similar to Avery's, a fully black ensemble that hugged his form for easy movement, with practical black boots laced up to his mid-calves.

"I said 'pretty' certain," Avery clarified.

"Well, that explains it," he said dryly. "I stand corrected."

Cora eyed their plain clothes. "Is that all you're wearing? No protective gear?"

Avery shook her head. "Mobility is more important."

"It's not too late to change your mind, Avery. Going in with just the two of you—" Avery gave her a look, and Cora threw up her hands in defense. "Look, I didn't tell Alex or Mayven, as requested. I don't think you should have to answer to anyone, but they're not going to be happy."

"They'll have to get in line," Qav said. "She's going to be busy answering to a lot of people after this one." He avoided Avery's eyes, making a show of checking the laser blades secured to his calves. He wasn't doing much to help convince Cora this was a good idea.

Really, both of them should be grateful Avery had at least asked for *Qav* to come with her. She'd given serious thought to going in alone. Surely anything would be better than putting her life in his hands again. The thought of trusting him blindly was . . . unpleasant. In fact, she was planning on avoiding the merge with him entirely. He didn't need her skills to hold his own in hand-to-hand combat.

But Qav was right about one thing: Avery had learned her lesson about going solo once before. She wasn't likely to repeat it anytime soon. If she had listened to Finn when he—

"I can answer for my own choices," Avery said resolutely, bringing herself back to the present.

Qav raised his eyebrows. "You say that now, but—"

"Enough," Avery snapped, frustration crawling through her veins, her power running rampant. The holoconsole in front of Cora flickered briefly as the components rattled ominously.

"Easy, Avery." Cora's eyes cut across her tech, assessing any damage. "I know you like to throw around those fancy powers, but the cloaking tech on this ship alone is worth more than that whole city you have beneath the surface. Not to mention, it's company property."

"You're the majority owner and it's privately held." Qav crossed his arms over his chest, taking offense to the valuation of the Sanctum. "And don't act like you don't have five more of these."

"That's what I've always liked about you, Qavarion. You've got more brains up there than you let on. Besides"—Cora smiled with a nonchalant shrug in her crisp white jacket—"who's counting?"

Avery moved closer to the front of the ship, watching the lights of Alexandria fast approaching. Her palms turned clammy, her heart rate climbing as something wild came alive inside her. It paced within her rib cage, eager to be unleashed.

Qav stepped up beside her and they watched the city together in silence, sharing in a moment of breathless anticipation before their fight. He felt it, too, this strange excitement. Like their power knew it would be set free in the hours ahead.

Avery cleared throat. "When we get down there, you follow my orders. Got it?"

A grin tugged his lips, but the only thing that came out of his mouth was an acquiescent, "Of course."

The response annoyed Avery. She spun to face him. "Do you have something else to say?" She stared at his profile until he turned those silver eyes on her. They moved over her face, like he was looking for something, like he was restraining himself from finding the answer.

Do it, she taunted, daring him to cross the boundary she had laid between them. Daring him to try to read her.

The only sign he'd heard her was a slight dilation of his pupils. It infuriated her—she should've stepped straight into his mind and showed him what true power looked like. She would welcome the fight, the opportunity to stretch herself in a way she'd been unable to for almost a full year. She would revel in it, as well as the opportunity to put him in his place again.

But now wasn't the time. She turned back to the windows.

"Coward," he whispered, quietly enough that she barely heard him. In fact, she wasn't certain he hadn't said it to her in mind.

She spun around, grabbed a fistful of his shirt and pulled him up from the ground—

"We're here," Cora said. She concentrated on the map in front of her as she brought the ship off autopilot. "You two better move to the hatch. Drop point in two minutes."

"Let's go," Avery sneered at Qav. She dropped him to his feet, and he landed gracefully. "You better not pull this shit when we're down there." She strode away, grabbing her earpiece from the console on her way out.

"Turn that on as soon as you land," Cora called to them. "I'll track your progress from here."

Avery didn't wait for Qav, but he trailed behind her in silence. They moved through the ship's sleek white interior in seconds, arriving at the hatch door that was now open from Cora's command on the deck. Air whipped up violently around them, the noise drowning out any attempt at conversation. And Avery was glad for it.

She had nearly let Qav goad her into a reaction. This was what she had expected from him at dinner—where had his conciliatory mood gone? She needed his cooperation, not his constant probing.

Beneath them, the buildings flew by, slowing only when they dropped into civilian airspace. Thanks to Cora's cloaking, no scanners would be able to detect them, nor would the naked eye. The large vessel was rendered completely invisible. They could get as close to their destination as they needed without any alarms sounding.

They descended sharply, and Avery held on to the edge of the hatch. It was almost laughable that Avery had once been afraid of heights. But those days were long behind her. The lights of the ship flickered red. Cora's signal.

Avery tumbled forward, letting herself free-fall toward the building below. Her stomach dropped out from beneath her, wind whipping hair against her face as she spun through the air. Qav's lithe form followed in a similar tuck behind her, strands of silvery white flying out around his head like some kind of bird in the night.

They were ready for this. They had to be.

Avery unfolded herself, arms plastered to her sides. She narrowed her focus, using her power to direct her velocity straight at the roof of Klein's apartments.

CHAPTER TEN

They rolled together hard across the surface of the roof, picking up into a run toward the only blind spot. Avery crouched down behind the row of solar panels, breathing heavily. She scanned the shadows, hunting for any threat.

"You landed right in position. I'm swapping the cams with the AI feed. Hold." Cora's voice came through the earpiece Avery had activated on the way down. Since neither Avery nor Qav used wristports, Cora would be able to navigate them and monitor any movement via the building's security system.

Qav took a knee beside Avery, fiddling with his own earpiece. "Not quite the merge, but I guess it will do."

Avery ignored him, running through the layout of the rooms below in her head. She had studied them relentlessly for the past twenty-four hours. No matter how advanced Cora's tech was, there was always a possibility of it failing.

At least once they were inside, there wouldn't be many humans to maneuver around. While Klein had a full official squad of Federation security at the main entrance on ground level, there were only two posted on the roof. They weren't expecting threats from above, at least none that they'd be unable to detect.

The Minister's apartments spanned the entire top level of the building, in direct view of the capitol seat itself. Avery peeked over the edge of the roof. Through a curtain of zooming cruisers, the open platform of the capitol building was only a few levels down from them. The wide expanse of its courtyard was eerily quiet, the great mirror pool that ran its length reflecting the glimmering neon lights of the city rising up around it. Great spotlights lit up the columns of the building itself, casting oppressive shadows along the grand doors that spanned two levels high. During the day, the area bustled with politicians and activists, a rush of breathless activity. But now, in the small hours of the night, it slept in shadows, resting heavily with the weighted silence of potential change.

"Speaking of . . ." Qav drew her attention back to him with a whisper. "When are we going to . . ." He trailed off, waving a finger between them.

Avery turned away, craning her neck around the edge of the angled solar panel. So far, Qav had followed her lead on avoiding the topic of the merge. She had hoped to continue the trend.

"Avery," he snapped, an emotion something like fear winding its way out from him to brush against her, cold like ice. Cold like him.

She suppressed a shudder. "We're not using the merge."

"What?" The question came out louder than he intended. Fabric rustled as he looked over his shoulder. "We can't go in there without it. That's beyond stupid."

Avery turned back around, regretting not having had this conversation on the ship. They'd had at least an hour of travel from New San Fran, most of which she'd spent dodging him when they weren't briefing for their plan. It was an amateur move. And now she was paying for that poor judgment. "We both have powers on our own. It's not like we're going in helpless," she reasoned.

Qav frowned, wind blowing his hair across his face. "It's like tying one hand behind our back for a fight." *Why do it if we don't have to?* The question brushed over her boundaries, sending a true chill down her spine. He hadn't used his gifts to step into her space in a long time.

"Stay out of my head," she spat, pushing his presence away. Having his thoughts in her mind was more than she could stand. "I already told you, we're doing this my way."

"That was before I knew you were going to be stubborn to the point of lunacy." When she turned away again, his hand shot out to grab her arm and whip her back around. *"Avery."*

She heard the near command in his use of her name, and it ignited anger in her blood. "I'm not going to do it. Drop it and focus."

"And you think I want to?" His whispered question was fierce, his fingers digging hard into her jacket. "The last time you were in my head, you hollowed me out completely. You left *nothing* unseen—nothing untouched. I'm not exactly jumping at the chance for a repeat performance."

"Like you left me a choice," Avery hissed. Her throat tightened as she remembered the desperation of that day. The agony that had consumed her, finally breaking her free from Qav's manipulation that had led to the loss of everything. She wrenched her arm away from him. "We can do this without the merge."

His silver eyes darkened. When he spoke, it was like a warning. "I'm only here because you asked me to be."

"What's that supposed to mean?"

Their earpieces beeped, Cora's voice interrupting them. "Clear to move forward—the guards ahead just changed position to the north corner patrol."

Heat climbed up Avery's neck. Cora had heard their conversation.

Avery knew she wasn't making much sense, but she didn't want to examine it further. The idea of opening herself up to Qav again . . . It brought an unnecessary and unfamiliar panic. She was more powerful than him. Hadn't she proven that? He wouldn't control her anymore. He couldn't.

"Let's move." Avery wound stealthily around the row of solar panels, crouched in a run. Her feet barely made sound as she approached the raised structure on the south edge of the building that housed the stairwell. The control pad by the entrance was flashing red, heralding its locked door even before Avery tried to open it. But they had prepared for this. She already had Cora's hacking device in her hand, pressing the small black rectangle up to the metal security panel.

The light changed to yellow. Avery shared a worried look with Qav, her heart lurching. He turned to scan behind them, silver eyes moving rapidly in the shadows, looking for a threat.

The latch clicked and turned green. Avery let out a breath, pulling the door open and slipping inside with Qav close on her heels. The door snicked shut and they were alone in a dimly lit stairwell, all concrete and functionality. A short staircase lead them to another door.

"One more guard in the hallway ahead. The remaining two are stationed at the elevator around the corner. I'll signal you." Then Cora went silent. They had agreed on communication only when necessary.

Avery pressed her back against the wall, ready to move on Cora's mark. Qav took the position opposite.

"It means," he whispered, his forehead wrinkled in frustration, refusing to let their conversation go, "that if you didn't want my blazing help, why did you ask for it?"

"If you'd shut up for one second, we'd already be done," she bit out. "Remember, on Cora's signal, I'll move in first while you—"

Qav grabbed the door handle, yanking it open and surging through in a flash of black and silver. Avery reached for him too late, catching only air. Her stomach dropped, fear lodging in her throat as she kept herself from calling his name.

"What are you doing? I said wait!" Cora's admonishment was ignored.

Avery peeked out from the doorframe. Qav sprinted down the hall in complete silence, like some kind of ghost.

The guard walking toward him was outfitted in the full dress uniform of deep blue that suggested she was more for show than anything else. Thank the moons her vision was trained on her wristport. Something amusing made her chuckle. By the time she saw Qav, or the shadow he became, it was too late for her to do anything but widen her eyes on a gasp.

Qav threw his feet up in a leap, spiraling his body as he wrapped his legs around the guard's neck. The momentum from his spin brought her body around, slamming into the ground hard enough to knock her out. He rolled to one knee, and looked over his shoulder at Avery.

You coming or not? he asked, in her mind and out of it before she could force him away.

The two other guards rounded the corner, drawn by the commotion—something Cora had intended for them to bypass. Their blasters were raised and ready to shoot.

If Qav had only kept to the blazing plan.

They fired, and Avery was in the hallway on her next breath, throwing her hands up. The blasts dissipated into the air, inches from Qav's back. He hadn't even turned. He only stared at her.

The guards jerked their weapons at Avery. Their eyes widened as they recognized her. That wasn't good. Damn everything—this was not working out the way Cora had advised.

The soldiers hesitated only a moment before letting loose on their weapons, firing one blast after another. Avery kept her hands raised, catching each shot as it came at her, knocking the energy away and into the burgundy-papered walls.

Qav made use of the distraction, already on his feet. He lifted his chin, throwing one guard into the wall hard enough that the man slumped onto the carpet, a mass of dark blue against the swirls of gold. Swinging to the final guard, Qav knocked the blaster from his hand. He drove his free fist upward in a swift cut, the energy Qav added to the blow carrying the man's body into the air. Qav spun. He raised a leg to slam his heel down on his opponent's chest as he fell. Neither guard stirred.

Qav looked up at her. *Was that good enough, my So?*

Avery raced to his side, kicking the blasters strewn about the ground away from the guards. "You are an absolute—" One look at his smug smile and Avery clamped her mouth shut. She wouldn't give him the blazing satisfaction. "Just help me move them."

They picked up the unconscious guards, securing them with ties and gags in stairwell. If they woke, they wouldn't be any trouble for a while.

"Cora?" Avery asked. "Any movement downstairs? Did they call this in?"

A few seconds passed before she replied, "No. You're in the clear."

"Sorry." Qav shrugged, looking over the guards he'd taken down. "I guess I got a little antsy."

Avery glared.

She turned back to the hallway, heading to massive double doors of their target. It was late, the lighting dim and soft, muted against the burgundy walls. Avery glanced up and down the long corridor. She'd feel better once they were inside.

Avery pulled the hacker out of her thigh holster, tapping it on the security pad. This one took longer, but the latch clicked in a few moments. They slipped inside.

It was quiet and dark, the only light spilling in from the wide windows that overlooked the capitol. Klein was attending some conference on the eastern continents, leaving her place blissfully empty. The open living space was cast in neon shadows, staining the furniture with mottled splotches of blues and reds.

"Remember, no cams in here." Cora's voice almost made Avery jump. "I'll monitor the hall. Let me know once you've placed the hacker on her drive."

"Lower floor," Avery whispered to Qav, crouching over to the staircase that spun down to a second level. Alex was the one who had revealed Klein held unofficial meetings in her home office. If she had ever been to one, she hadn't said. But if they were going to find anything Klein was hiding in analog or on-prem, that would be the place to start.

Klein's office was enormous and hard to miss, encased in electronic reinforced glass doors, also locked. Avery pulled the hacker back out, holding it up to the bio reader embedded into the clear surface. Avery's blood went cold. Cora hadn't mentioned bio security when briefing them on the device. She prayed it could bypass that kind of tech, too.

Qav watched the shadows. Despite his posturing in the hallway above, he was nervous. Avery could feel it.

"Why wasn't there any alarm system?" Qav whispered.

Avery shushed him, focusing on the bio pad and the hacker that she held against it. It was taking too long. Longer than either door before. Avery's heart rate sped until she could barely hear past the rushing in her ears. Cora had sworn this blazing thing would work.

The door beeped at last, sliding open in a soft whoosh. Avery nearly let out a giddy laugh. They were in.

Avery. Qav's silent voice was a torrent of ice, tearing swiftly through the defenses she held against him.

She whirled on him, his panic scaring her enough to knock every bit of anger straight out of her system.

But Qav wasn't looking at her. His eyes were trained on the darkness behind them, his head angled, his body tense.

That's when Avery saw *him*. Alive and well and walking straight at them. His tall frame emerged from the shadows and into the pool of blue light that stretched across the empty hallway.

Nick Lunitia.

"Avery," he said, that smooth voice melding with his smile in a show of practiced artifice. "It's been a while."

CHAPTER ELEVEN

Nick paused a few feet away from Avery and Qav. He tucked his hands into the pockets of his gray pants, the expensive fabric falling in graceful folds from his hips, the image of relaxation. Dread hung heavy in the pit of Avery's stomach.

"And you brought a friend," Nick said, tilting his head at Qav. A lock of dark hair fell over his forehead, the movement so much like Finn that Avery's heart skipped.

Finn had said more than once that Nick was the consummate politician. Every action he made was in service to his ultimate goal, his every move intentional. Controlled. Nick's nonchalance was nothing but an act. It had to be.

Avery kept her voice low. "I should have known you'd be here. Hiding like a rat in her shadow."

"Not a rat, surely. He's far too well groomed." Qav meandered forward, regaining his own prowess as he placed himself closer to their enemy. His silver eyes ran the length of Nick's body, assessing. Avery had been the subject of that tactic once before. "More like a faithful pet waiting patiently for its owner. A pity she didn't leave the lights on for you."

Nick's smile faltered as his attention shifted to Qav. "Qavarion Tsetski. You've been a thorn in the Federation's side for quite a while. It's almost an honor to meet you at last."

"We aim to please, Ambassador—" Qav let out a small gasp, lifting a finger in question. "Do we still call you that? I don't think there's an official title for your current position . . . Minister's Houseboy, perhaps?"

Nick's jaw ticked. Qav was good at this.

"You two came alone. Together," Nick observed. "I have to admit, Avery, I'm a bit disappointed. I had expected a bit more loyalty from you. Who knew you'd move on from my brother so quickly?"

A feral sound emerged from her throat as Avery took a step forward.

"How quaint." Qav shifted his body to stop her before she did something stupid. "It must have stung when Finn chose Avery over you. Especially after you dropped that bombshell about your father." A smile spread across his face, evolving into outright laughter. "What was it Finn said to you? 'She is my home'—"

"Now I see the appeal." Nick took his hands out of his pockets. "You talk almost as much as he does."

"Walk away, Nick," Avery said gravely. "You still have a chance to turn this around. To help us. If you ever loved Finn, he would want—"

"You have no idea what he would want. And neither does he. He never did." Nick fumed, the anger spilling over and distorting his features. The glass doors of the office rattled ominously. One wall split with a loud crack, fissuring down the middle. Nick still had powers; that much was obvious. But he had little control over them. "Rest assured, I will make Finn see reason even if—"

"See reason?" Avery stepped around Qav to face Nick. "He's gone. Your precious Minister made sure of that."

Nick's eyes flared, his cheeks flushing. His blunder was obvious. He had no recourse to correct himself. The loss of control had worked in their favor.

Avery's heart raced. "So it's true, then? There *is* another way—another Gate?"

Nick lifted his chin as his eyes narrowed at Avery. He stepped closer. "What if there is, Avery? I wonder . . . What price would you pay to access it? To get back to him?"

Their earpieces beeped. Cora. "He's stalling—guards are on their way up. I barred the roof and disabled the elevators, but they'll counter soon. You've got five minutes. Get out of there."

"She's not going to pay you anything," Qav drawled. "Given how loudly you're barking for your absent owner, I'm willing to bet all the information we need is right here. And rest assured—we will be walking out of here with it."

"I'm afraid I can't let you do that," Nick warned grimly, bracing his feet. The air was charged, thick and metallic.

Qav clucked his tongue disapprovingly. He stepped forward again, and it took the curling of his finger behind his back for Avery realize it was only a ruse. Qav was distracting him.

Avery welcomed his silent words into her mind: *Get the blazing files. I can handle one power-tripped human.*

Qav shook his head at Nick as though he were a misbehaving child. "I'm not sure what powers Klein has had her humans cook up in the lab for you, but you're not exactly—"

In a second, Nick had moved from the hall and was on Qav before Avery could even clock him. One punch to the chest sent Qav sailing, slamming him hard into the wall behind them, narrowly missing the glass.

Qav caught himself on one knee. The concrete wall was a mess of cracked indentations that crumbled around him. He looked up sharply, his eyes blazing through a curtain of white hair that had escaped its bun. "Okay, then." He spit out a mouthful of blood. "We can do it this way, too."

Go! Qav yelled into Avery's head.

And for once, she did as he said.

She scrambled to the huge white desk in the office, scanning for some sign of a hard drive or physical computer among the stacks of tablets and digital glass sheets. She ducked beneath a curved edge, running her fingers underneath, looking for a compartment or a drawer. Beyond the office, the two men fought, the sounds of each blow resonating throughout apartment.

Nick wouldn't be guarding the place for nothing. He had been in the wastelands—she knew it had been him. He had come here with the explicit goal to intercept them. *Something* had to be there.

Avery lifted the enormous desk and slammed it down, desperate to dislodge something. But still, it revealed nothing.

A loud crash reverberated through the hall. She glanced up to see Qav straddling Nick in the rubble of the adjacent sitting room, his fingers wrapped around Nick's neck. Nick flailed, clawing and sputtering to try to free himself. Qav wouldn't release him. He would enact ultimate vengeance on the man who had nearly destroyed the Sanctum. But Qav was too focused on his win, too sure of the victory—a mistake Syla would have chastised him for.

He didn't see Nick swipe his leg around until it was too late.

Qav went down hard. They struggled against each other in a blur of fists until Qav was on his feet again. One eye was already swelling. His face was smeared with blood. His chin dipped, determined. Qav could handle it alone—he'd said so himself. If nothing else, Avery would trust his estimation of his own skill.

But Qav had never fought Nick. Avery knew too well the weight of those manufactured powers.

They charged at each other, and Avery spun back to the shelving lining the wall. She pulled out trinkets—holoframes and marble obelisks and a sizable collection of miniature crystal fruit—throwing them to the ground in her haste. They shattered into rubble at her feet.

In the room beyond, Nick roared, the sound mingling with a cacophony of breaking glass.

Avery leaned across the desk, throwing the tablets to the ground until the white surface was bare except for a blue orbed lamp balancing on its geometric onyx platform. Pointless. This whole thing had been totally *pointless*. She growled, and the orbed fixture flew across the room in the wake of her frustration, shattering loudly against the window that looked out onto the lights of the city. The view of the capitol building was clearer here; they were only five levels above its expansive courtyard, close enough to see the wind blowing ripples in the mirror pool.

Avery's pulse rang in her ears as her mind spun. Cora was never wrong. The drive had to be there. Klein wasn't some mastermind . . . She would have hidden it somewhere functional. Somewhere within reach. Somewhere—

Avery's eyes snapped to the shards of the blue glass she'd just shattered. She leaped over the desk, sliding to her knees. The black stone pedestal had broken in two. And from one side, winking up at Avery in the shadows was . . . an analog drive.

There was no sense in hacking it anymore, not when it was small enough to shove into her pocket. Klein would know they had been there regardless.

The building rocked, the walls shaking from a loud explosion above. Cora's voice came through. "Auxiliary guards are breaching the stairwell doors. You need to leave now! Backup plan—emergency route through Klein's private service entrance."

Avery tucked the drive into her pocket as she got to her feet. She'd have to help Qav after all. But her limbs locked in place as she turned, shock paralyzing her.

Nick lifted Qav by his neck with one hand, squeezing until a pained yowl choked its way out of his flattened throat. Qav's eyes rolled, his body going slack.

Avery threw out both hands, ripping the two men apart from where she stood in the office. They each went flying in opposite directions. Qav lay still on the floor, and Avery panicked, sending her mind out to him immediately, her boundaries thrown to the wind. He was still alive.

Nick pulled himself to his feet, brushing glass from of his hands. They glistened red in the shadowed room, stained with blood. His own wounds or Qav's, Avery couldn't tell.

"I'm getting sick of your attitude, Avery." All traces of civility were gone as Nick stalked toward her. Another boom sounded above them. "You think you're special? Because you have powers? Because you're an *Elite*? Let me tell you something—you are nothing but a *little girl.*"

Avery lunged forward, driving a fist into Nick's gut. He stumbled back, wheezing. Avery frowned, studying him. The force in that hit alone should have sent him into the air. She spun on her toe, lifting her body to bring her leg down in a wide arc into his neck.

A blast caught her off guard, piercing her side in a searing slice of pain. It knocked her out of the attack and onto the floor. She wheezed, the air gone from her lungs. Her vision spotted, threatening to go black.

The soldiers had arrived. One had taken her shot from the top the stairs. The rest were descending on them too rapidly. Qav was still down.

Nick didn't hesitate. He was on Avery in a flash, his boot slamming into her ribs. The hit connected with her fresh wound, and her vision eclipsed in a kaleidoscope of stars. The impact sent Avery careening across the floor and back into Klein's office. She slid through the mess of glass she had left, her head slamming violently into the windows. Avery glanced down at the blast wound in her side. Blood seeped through her fingers, pooling onto the cold floor.

Nick walked through the glass doors, stopping to pull a shard of glass from his forehead. Blood dripped from his eyebrow, running in a rivulet down his cheek. In the shadows, his profile was so similar to Finn's.

He motioned over his shoulder, and the guards halted on the stairs. Clearly, he wanted to finish her himself.

Avery would have laughed if she had the capability to breathe.

Qav had been right. She should have brought the others with her. She should have just trusted Qav—should have merged with him. Maybe then he would have stood a chance against Nick. If only she had known how strong Nick had become. If only she had known how Qav's fighting skills had lapsed.

Nick's shoes crunched on the glass as he approached. He squatted beside her, frowning as he pulled a piece of blue glass from her braid.

"You're a little girl," he repeated, his expression almost pitying, "struggling to survive in a war she barely comprehends. You have no idea what's coming for you. What she has planned. And now that you've played right into our hands, it will be easier than ever."

Blasters fired behind them, and Nick shot up, spinning around at the guards' screams. A flash of white and silver was the only warning before Qav hammered into Nick.

With one arm locked around Nick's waist, Qav fired off a few blasts at the window as he kept dragging them both straight for it. And he drove them through the weakened glass, out in to the open air.

Qav couldn't use his powers to land safely. She wasn't even sure if she could do that herself from such a great height. He had taken Nick to his death and gone right along with him.

She clawed her way to standing, her palms digging into the edges of the shattered glass. There was no time to think. Even if she'd been able the consider her next move, it would have been the same.

Avery vaulted over the edge, throwing herself out after him.

CHAPTER TWELVE

Avery fell through the air, wind making her eyes tear. Below her, Nick and Qav were a tangle of limbs dropping through the sparkling lights of the city. Avery jerked her chin, using what power she had left to pull their bodies apart. Nick went careening out of sight into the veil of cruisers beyond.

Qav angled himself toward the capitol lawn. He twisted as he fell, and his eyes locked with Avery's across the distance. He was too far away. She would never catch him before they landed. But this plummet was farther than anything she'd ever attempted to buffer herself against before. It was more than just absorbing impact; she needed to pull off something more akin to flying. But with her wound, there was no way she could bring Qav with her. As it was, her vision blurred in and out of focus.

Qav had barely been able to leap across the lake in the Sanctum. Avery had to use her powers to bolster his attempt. She doubted he'd be able to direct himself to the safety of the platform without her.

There was only one way to save him. One way he would be able to stop from crashing into the concrete a thousand feet below. And Avery didn't have time to talk herself out of it.

She opened her mind, reaching out to Qav across the night air. The ice that greeted her was familiar—almost soothing—as she expanded the merge between them. Her pupils dilated as the world expanded to dual perspectives. Qav looked up, and she saw herself falling toward him from above. Her golden eyes shimmered as she speared through the air, her long braid whipping up behind her.

About time, he said through the bond. Satisfaction prickled along his words, making her giddy.

Just shut up and focus. Avery trained what energy she had left on stopping her descent, shifting to maneuver toward the capitol block. She would have actually taken flight if she'd had her full strength. The realization was enough to make her breathless.

Through the merge, Avery's experiences were as easy to understand as Qav's. He mirrored her movements, manipulating the air, forcing his body to arch toward his destination. Qav's attempt harnessed less raw power, but the concept remained the same. His speed slowed, his body plunging gracelessly beneath her in lurches.

When Avery reached his side, she grabbed his hand to pull him close. She aimed for the large mirror pool. They hit the water hard before sinking underneath. Avery kicked off the bottom to rise back up. Breaking the surface, she gasped for air as Qav sputtered beside her, pushing wet hair out of his face that had finally come out of its bun.

He grinned, an adrenaline-laced thrill racing through them and their bond. *We're alive!* he whooped before letting out an audible yelp of exhalation.

Avery threw her head back and laughed. She spread out to float on her back, but pain stabbed her side and she doubled over, choking on water as she began to sink.

Qav threw her over his shoulder in an instant. He dragged her onto the grass, kneeling beside her as he ripped open her jacket and tore her black shirt to expose her wound. Brisk fear clouded her thoughts—his.

How do I heal you? His eyes darted from her face to the mottled mess of flesh that used to be her stomach.

That looks disgusting. Avery squeezed her eyes shut.

"Obviously," he said aloud. His brows drew together. His face was pale. "I need to know how to heal you. You have to show me."

Avery looked over his shoulder to the gaping hole in the building five levels above them. Fed guards peered down into the sky traffic. Qav's stinging fear ebbed, fading from her. The bond was disintegrating.

The edges of her vision dimmed, leaving only a blue halo around Qav's head. His hair was more silver than she'd ever seen it, unruly strands streaking across his cheeks and plastered along the side of his face.

"Your hair is nicer wet. Like moon dust," Avery whispered. The blood loss must have made her loopy.

"How do I heal you, Avery?" He was yelling now, shaking her by the shoulders. "Damn it, don't close your eyes!"

"Sorry," she slurred. Her eyelids were too heavy. The dark was too tempting.

A new chill reached her that had nothing to do with Qav's powers, and this time she surrendered to it. But somewhere far away, he was still calling her name.

Broken glass crunched beneath Rebecca's heels as she made her way from the winding marble staircase through the debris that was left of her home. The sitting room had been reduced to a pile of rubble. And her office hadn't fared much better. Her shoulders stiffened beneath her perfectly tailored blue suit as she passed over its threshold, sidestepping shattered remnants of figurines that had taken her whole life to collect. They had been priceless.

"Minster Klein!" a cleaner exclaimed, rising quickly from their crouched position. A heavy bucket full of glass shards slipped from their hands to the floor. "We didn't expect you back so soon. If you'll just wait upstairs—"

"Out," Rebecca commanded shortly. The cleaner blushed furiously and scurried around her and up the stairs.

She walked to the gaping hole in the outer window and peered down to the capitol building. It was a view she had taken in hundreds of times before from that exact spot. Wind snapped up through the jagged opening, threatening to pull her blond hair from its intricately styled updo. She stared at the bustling masses of people traversing the capitol landing, her long fingernails biting into her palms. They had no idea the lengths she had gone through, that she was still going through, to give them peace.

"You're back."

She turned as Nick limped into the room. His left arm was in a sling that rested heavily against his white shirt. His left eye was swollen shut and blackening. A freshly sealed cut ran red and angry over his eyebrow.

"I thought you were handling it," she said simply. Nick had been progressing beautifully in his trials. They had been confident he would hold his own against Avery in a second battle.

Nick cracked a pained smile. "She brought Tsetski with her."

Rebecca turned back to the window. Yes, that would have presented a problem. One Elite, Nick could handle. But two? The odds had been decidedly against him.

Just because the Lares Project hadn't found any new Elites in decades, that didn't mean they weren't out there. Rebecca had spies littered throughout Echo searching for more. And of course, she kept a close eye on the Reanges on Earth. There were always rumors of children who showed evidence of the gift. But finding them had been difficult. Even Leviathan—the crazed Elite who now ruled over Echo—hadn't found any in the year since the Gate's fall.

Klein congratulated herself on maintaining her connections on Echo. They had provided her with invaluable information on the current state of affairs there. Leviathan ruled without anyone to challenge her, establishing an Elder Council in name only. It was a matter of time before she rounded up what Elites they had left there, which would serve Klein's purposes well enough. Once she returned to Echo, she would have the perfect opportunity to eradicate the genetic anomaly once and for all.

But she'd need more power to accomplish that. Nick wasn't enough anymore. At least Avery wouldn't have found anything on their research. She should have finished the job at the facility, not come to Klein's home. Avery's grief was making her sloppy.

"She took something," Nick said quietly. "Picked it up from the broken pieces of your orb lamp."

Rebecca sucked in a breath. Her personal files. The one circumstance she hadn't foreseen. Keeping such important documents in an archaic storage system was the very reason Rebecca thought it would be secure. The pedestal that housed the drive should have been impenetrable to scanners. How had Avery found it? She hadn't told anyone about it—not even Nick.

So Avery hadn't been after information on the wasteland facility. Rebecca had been so sure it had been the reason for her rash attack. They should have had that engineer killed instead of sending him to the wastelands. But wasting his skills had seemed juvenile. That had been a mistake. She'd been too soft-hearted.

"If she has that drive, then she knows everything," Rebecca said tersely.

Nick was silent for moment before asking, "And *our* work? Does she have that, too?"

"No, thank God. That is Federation-sanctioned—she'd have to go back to the wastes for it, and we both know that will be impossible for her now." Rebecca smoothed down her hair. "She either ignored the tests or still doesn't know how close we are. But it means—"

"We need to move faster," Nick finished. "If only I had caught her, then this would be over."

"Yes. But you didn't. You let them goad you into a fight."

"I tried to take her down. She's more powerful than before."

"Evidently." Rebecca turned away. "Even in the wastelands, you let her leave without so much as a fight."

"I got you that footage of her healing the boy. The blow to the CLF's reputation is worth more than—"

"There is nothing worth more than her!" Rebecca snapped. "Not when we *know* she is the key to making this work a success. Her genome is unique. We need more samples."

"Then why haven't we raided the Sanctum? If you would just let me—"

Rebecca let out a breathy laugh. "Because that went so well for you last time? No. They're too powerful en masse."

Nick said nothing. The sounds of the city filtered in through the window, carried by the wind.

Rebecca needed the tests to finally work. The weight of their species' survival was on her shoulders. She had access to Echo, but it would be useless without the force to take it back from the Reanges. Nick needed more control, and they needed more soldiers like him. Unfortunately, additional tests to replicate his transformation had been unsuccessful.

Avery's blood had been the ultimate solution for Nick's transformation. But they'd used up what had remained in the labs from Avery's time imprisoned on the Port Station. Without the unique energy emission of her cells against the human genome, any attempts at genetic modifications were unsuccessful.

And now that Avery knew about the second Gate, gaining access to her would be nearly impossible. There was some hope, though. Even with her influential friends, they'd find the second portal more difficult to access than anticipated. That, at least, would give Rebecca time. She would need to act quickly.

"Comm the wastelands and—" She lost her balance, her right heel slipping on something wet. Rebecca grabbed the window, glass digging into her palm. She hissed, looking down. Her once white heel was stained red at the edges. Blood.

Nick was at her side, reaching for her hand and gingerly inspecting the wound. "This will need a healer."

"Is this yours?" Rebecca asked sharply, looking into his striking eyes. Hope churned in her veins, temping her with its promise.

Nick frowned, shaking his head as he replied, "No. It's . . . Avery's." His eyes widened as he followed her train of thought. His uninjured hand moved to the side of her head, pulling her in for a hard kiss. "You are a genius."

"We need someone here immediately to collect this." Dark liquid pooled under her feet. There was so much. Nick had clearly wounded Avery more than he realized, perhaps even enough to kill her this time.

Even contaminated—even half-dried—they'd have more than

what they needed. The relief made Rebecca almost dizzy. After all these months of scrambling for solutions, things were finally looking up.

She stopped Nick as he turned to do her bidding, pulling him back into her for a longer kiss and running her fingers through his hair. She bit at his lip as she broke away, thrilled by the growl it elicited from him. His gray eyes worshiped her. She smiled at the delicious sensation.

"Let her find the blazing Gate," Rebecca whispered. The promise of control surged through her system, making her feel more alive than she had in years. "That girl just gave us everything we need."

CHAPTER THIRTEEN

A very awoke to the sound of distance raised voices, her eyes fluttering open in a dimly lit room she didn't recognize. The low ceiling above her was rimmed with soft green lighting, and in its center was a giant scripted *N* that glowed from within. Her head throbbed.

Someone shouted. It was enough to wake her fully. Avery dragged herself to sit, ignoring the way her brain screamed. The viewing bubble caught her eye first, or what was beyond it. The large extension of glass looked out onto the vast expanse of a star speckled universe.

She wasn't on Earth anymore.

Avery finally registered what had woken her. The door to her chamber remained open.

". . . can't just leave the Sanctum behind entirely." Qav's voice, sharp with anger.

"We're not," Ennis countered calmly. "You have a well-established system to handle this kind of situation. We've done it before."

"She's right." Syla's low confirmation. "Remember that month in the Andalusian pleasure houses?"

"A whole month?" Grigg's familiar laugh floated on the end of the question. "You all are more fun than I thought."

"You have no idea," Syla purred.

"Can you both give that a rest?" Ennis sounded disgusted. "It's starting to make me uncomfortable."

Qav spoke again with no trace of humor. "The point is, we don't know the risks here. The Sanctum is an entire city of vulnerable refugees. I can't just leave them without protection."

"Alex Peña has guaranteed its safety."

"*Alex Peña* has less power than she lets people believe. If Klein decides to move on our home while we're gone, the people wouldn't stand a chance. We'd be leaving them to be massacred."

"And what do you think you forced Avery to do when you kept her on Earth?" Nova's voice was nearly unrecognizable. Her question vibrated with hostility.

Qav didn't reply.

Nova continued, "Even now, we could be too late. If Leviathan has killed every human on Echo—if Finn is gone, if Petra and the others failed . . . what do you think *that* will do to Avery?"

"I don't need to be lectured on what I did to her." The silence in the wake of Qav's declaration was cold and impenetrable, a wall of pure ice.

Guilt slashed through Avery, robbing her of breath. If that reality awaited them, it wouldn't just destroy Avery. Nova and Grigg would be devastated too. Even after the months they'd spent fighting together—becoming closer—those two still put Avery above themselves. It felt wrong. It *was* wrong.

But who was to blame for that except Avery? What she had done last year . . . . How she had behaved as she settled into her role as a So'Reange . . . . She had been naive. She had thought her experiences so far removed from the others that she'd isolated herself completely. It was the exact reason Qav had been able to burrow his way into her mind.

Avery swung her legs from beneath the silk sheets of the bed. The heated floor was delightful beneath her bare feet. Spots flooded her vision as she clutched at the sharp sting in her torso.

Right. She'd been shot. Silly of her to forget that detail.

Memories came flooding back to her. The drop through the city. The graceless plunge into the mirror pool. Qav leaning over her in the shadows, his face contorted by something like panic.

A soothing chill replaced the sharp pain so swiftly that if left her breathless. Avery pressed a hand to her clammy forehead.

"You're awake."

Avery's eyes snapped open.

Qav stood in the doorway, looking as composed as ever in a long coat of deep gray that fell to his knees. He was shielding Avery from her pain. Before Avery could decide if that in itself was an invasion of privacy, Nova pushed around him, carving her way into the room. Her blond hair was down for once, curling in luscious waves down her back. She seemed rested.

"You shouldn't be out of bed yet," Nova chastised, but she grasped Avery by her elbow anyway to help her stand.

"I'm guessing I've been out for a while." Avery walked unsteadily beside Nova.

"Three days," Nova said tensely as they passed the threshold into a circular lounge room. The others relaxed on a curved couch set into the floor. Grigg was standing, relief etched onto his face.

Another viewing alcove dominated the far wall of the room, offering a spectacular view of an enormous cobalt planet. Neptune. They were at the ends of the solar system, billions of miles from Earth.

"It's good to see you up at last," Ennis said easily. She and Syla kept their seats beside each other.

"This one was close, Avery." Nova's hands tightened on her. "Too close."

"They're all close these days," Avery said with a grin, shrugging a shoulder.

Nova didn't laugh. "You sound like Finn."

Avery's heart lurched, pleasure seeping painfully into its cracks. Images of him flashed through her mind. His easy smile giving way to a deep dimple. Dark hair falling over his forehead. The honeyed sound of his voice.

Grigg took her arm from Nova, leading Avery down to the couch. "Ignore her. We've just been waiting for you to pull another resurrection on us," he said and winked. "Even a shot to the gut can't hold our So' back."

Syla nodded in agreement. "The scar you'll bear is a testament to your strength."

"Don't encourage her." Nova settled beside Avery. "This was as stupid as Mayven's plan. Avery only survived because of luck."

"And Qav," Syla added.

"Syla," Qav snapped, frowning.

"No—she should know," Nova said, an edge in her voice. She turned to Avery. "You lost too much blood. And as a So', not just anyone can give you a transfusion. And we only knew *that* thanks to Ennis's research. Do you know how close you came to dying this time?"

Avery's hands curled into fists in her lap as heat flushed her cheeks. Qav had given her his blood? He looked no worse for wear. He must have recovered quickly. And back at Klein's apartments, he had thrown himself through a window to save her from Nick without any idea that he'd survive. She'd nearly lost both their lives.

In the end, the decision to leave the others *had* been idiotic. Avery's plans had a habit of turning sideways lately. No matter how good her intentions were.

"I told you, going alone was my idea," Qav said before Avery could sputter some kind of apology. She glanced up at him, stunned. He leaned against the curved doorframe with his arms crossed over his chest. "The rest of you would have just gotten in the way. We didn't know we'd have to deal with that overgrown lab rat."

Nova's blue eyes assessed Qav. She wasn't buying his story, no matter how many times he'd told her.

Nick had been stronger than Avery had ever seen him. His powers were advancing, even if they were artificially derived. Still, if the Fed guards hadn't shown up, she would have been able to handle him. They could have gotten out with the drive and never—

Avery tensed. "The drive! Where is—"

"Relax, Avery." Syla cocked an eyebrow at the theatrics.

"Qav found it on you when you were in the hospital," Ennis explained, smoothing a hand over her scalp. "Cora made short work of it. Klein barely had more than a password protecting the data."

"And? What was on it? Did we find the receiver?"

Ennis grinned, unfolding her petite legs from the couch and leaning forward to showcase the projection from her wristport. A miniature holocast of Neptune appeared, floating in the air above her arm.

"You're gonna love this," Grigg said under his breath with a grin.

"That's . . . a planet," Avery said flatly. Clearly, she was missing something.

Grigg snorted.

Ennis ignored them both. "If you wanted to hide one of the galaxy's largest pieces of machinery, where's one of the only places you could pull that off?"

Avery looked up, realization dawning. "It's . . . inside? The Gate is inside Neptune? How is that even possible?" No wonder Cora hadn't been able to find it on any cursory scans. She hadn't exactly been looking *through* any celestial bodies.

"We're not sure, exactly. Neptune's atmosphere is the equivalent of a subzero hurricane on steroids, so by all rights it should have been impossible. Only a few exploratory vessels have ever even descended past its upper atmosphere."

"This solar system is bizarre," Grigg said in wonder. "Why are there planets made of gas? All fifteen of ours are terrestrial."

"Fourteen," Nova corrected wryly.

"What?"

"There are fourteen planets in—"

Avery held up a hand. "I'm going to stop you there before you two get to the arm wrestling section of this argument. So how are we supposed to make it into the center of a volatile planetary atmosphere?"

"We don't have to make it to the center," Ennis replied. "The Gate is just beneath the cloud cover, but the real trick is getting the blazing thing out. We can't exactly activate it in the middle of a frozen ice storm."

"Not to mention the Fed patrols," Syla added, pushing her pink hair behind her ear. "We've been floating around out here for days just trying to avoid them. They're going to notice if we pull out a piece of equipment the size of a small moon."

"At least we have a ship that can handle the haul. Good thing you make friends in high places." Grigg winked at Avery and nodded to the ceiling. There was another *N* embossed on its white surface, back-lit by the same green glow. *Najisuki Nano Tech.*

"Cora?" Avery said in surprise. "This is her ship?"

Memories surfaced, nothing more than flashes. Cora's ship materializing from on the steps of the capitol, shimmering into existence like some kind of magic . . . Her worried face beside Qav's, yelling something unintelligible as they shifted in and out of focus.

"She gave us one from the new Najisuki exploration fleet," Qav said, shaking his head as though he didn't fully understand it either. "Well, *give* is a strong word. I think her exact phrasing was 'loan on pain of death if you damage it.' That woman—and I don't say this often about anyone—is frightening."

"No wonder I like her," Syla muttered. She blushed, clearing her throat and clarifying, "For a human."

"It's built to withstand deep space meteor fields and close proximity solar bursts," Nova added. "If anything can get us in and pull the Gate out, it's this ship."

Avery leaned back. They were going to owe Cora a large debt by the end of everything. She wondered what kind of favor the powerful woman would ask for in return. But that was a concern for the future. Assuming they had one.

Ennis twisted her wrist, a new projection loading on her arm. It was the Gate, nearly identical to the original that had once floated above Earth. "Rem is still running simulations based on the schematics we recovered of the Gate's build. It's much smaller than the original, so the jump will be bumpy. But once we get it clear of Neptune we should be able to remotely access the controls. They didn't exactly build it to the same security standards as the government required."

"We don't even know if it's functional. Nobody's ever traveled through it," Qav stated harshly. As far as Avery knew, he'd barely been farther from Earth than the moon. Qav had been born on Earth—like Ennis. It was the only home they'd ever truly known.

Grigg slapped his thighs and tilted his head. "Well, isn't that why we have this luxury battle ship? I say we punch it. I'm ready to be out of this dump heap of a galaxy." He glanced at Syla. "No offense."

The tall woman only crossed her arms. "Qav's the one dragging his feet."

Avery looked at him at last, meeting silver eyes that were already watching her. "Are you?"

"Am I what?"

No more games, remember?

He smiled, the pull of his lips lacking their usually irony. *Did you finally decide I'm worth trusting?*

Avery narrowed her eyes. *You threw yourself out a window to save my life.*

"Maybe I knew you'd throw yourself out after me. You never can resist a good hero moment."

Avery held his gaze, refusing to give in to his challenge. He was playing down what he had done. But Qav couldn't have been certain she would follow him, let alone have the strength to save him. It had been . . . selfless.

The others shifted, the silence intensifying in the room until they could all feel it. Grigg widened his eyes at Nova in a silent question. A soft shake of her head was the only indication that she thought they should stay out of it.

Avery sighed, saving them. "Look, you don't have to come with us, Qav. You're right—leaving the Sanctum unprotected is a risk. A big one. I could use your help on the other side . . . But I'm not going to force you." *Even though I could.* She let the silent point travel to Qav alone. His eyes tightened. "And if Syla and Ennis choose to accompany us, then I'll protect them just as—"

"We'll see who does the protecting," Syla quipped, brown eyes turning molten.

Even Ennis looked offended as she shut off her wristport and stood. "I'm going to check on Rem." She disappeared out the door. Syla was quick to follow.

Qav pushed off the doorframe. "I thought you wanted to avoid unnecessary danger. So eager to see Lunitia that you're willing to throw us into an unstable wormhole?"

Grigg stiffened beside her as Nova shot to her feet, snarling, "I told you to watch your—"

"Nova." Avery touched her arm and rose, unsteady on her feet. "I want to go home, Qav. *Home.* There are people who need me there, as much as the people in the Sanctum need you. I want to see my Gran. And Megan and Petra. And yes—I want to see Finn, if he's still—" She stumbled over the words, choking on an embarrassing sob, her eyes burning. "If he's still alive. If any of them are."

Qav was still. His eyes closed briefly before he said quietly, "He is."

Avery tilted her head. "How would you know that?"

"I *don't* know—you do," he said cryptically. His continued on reluctantly, "In the merge, when I was trying to find a way to heal you . . . I ran through your mind, digging through anything I could think of, any memory that would show me some way to save you. I tripped right over your tether."

"My what?" Avery whispered.

Qav frowned. "You didn't know? Has no one ever taught you—?"

"Clearly not," Avery snapped. The reminder that he'd been able to rifle around unchecked in her mind was not exactly a warming thought. He might have proven something to her by saving her life, but that was a far cry from full trust.

"That connection you have to him—you felt it first after you healed his wound on the Port Station. We call it a life tether. It only happens when we bond deeply with another Reange. I've studied it closely enough that I can harness the general idea with any Reange. That's how I feel the Sanctum even when I'm halfway across the solar system. And you still feel it." He paused. "You're still connected to him."

"How is that possible?" Nova asked. "Finn is human."

"I'm not exactly certain," Qav said slowly. "So much has been lost about the truth behind our powers, and I only know what Ennis has been able to gather from her years of research. Well . . . that and the folklore I was able to squeeze out of Bedria. But I do know what it feels like to bond with someone's life force. What you have with Finn is no different. I've felt it before."

Avery's breath caught, the pain of Qav's memories piercing her from across the room.

Veena. Ennis's older sister. The girl with lavender eyes whom Qav couldn't save. The one Qav had loved.

Ennis thought of her sister often but never in Qav's presence—she was careful with that. And they certainly never spoke of her. Even after Avery had torn the memories out of Qav last year, he still refused to speak of it. Of what happened. Of the girl he had loved and lost. Qav thought he kept it locked away safely, but Avery knew the truth. The grief was festering inside of him, like a wound that refused to heal. She had seen it.

Avery reached out to him, taking a chance. *If you talked about her, it might help. Ennis would be—*

"She's dead, Avery. There's nothing more to talk about." He turned on his heel and left without a backward glance.

Grigg let out a low whistle, dropping back onto the couch in a heap. "Now, there's a guy who knows how to make an exit."

"And he knows it," Nova hissed. "If he wants to stay on Earth, then let him. We can't afford to wait any longer. Klein knows we're out here. She'd be a fool not to."

Avery nodded. "You're right. We can't hide forever."

"What's the alternative?" Grigg asked. "We can't go anywhere until Rem finds a way to get the Gate out of that giant ball of gas."

Avery bit the inside of her cheek, looking out the window at Neptune in the distance, a perfect sphere of glowing cerulean in the inky velvet folds of deep space. Pale clouds swirled over its surface, turning the entire planet into a smeared watercolor of blues and teals. Syla was right: there was no way they could get something so enormous out of those depths without Klein noticing.

But they could try something different . . . something Klein would never expect.

"If we can't bring the Gate to us . . ." Avery turned back to her friends. "Then we'll go to the Gate."

CHAPTER FOURTEEN

"Impossible." Rem shook his head vigorously, his glasses slipping to the tip of his nose. "It can't be done."

Ennis looked at Avery like she had grown three heads. "You can't honestly mean to get the portal operational while it's still *inside* the planet."

Qav chuckled in the corner, rolling his eyes to the ceiling.

"Why not?" Avery countered. "You said yourself this vessel was intended for deep space exploration."

"For deflecting the occasional meteor rock. Not for crossing into a subpar wormhole device in the unstable atmosphere of an ice giant." Rem stood at the ship controls clutching a small tablet. "I don't think you fully understand. The storms on Neptune are incomparable to any other planet in our system. The winds alone surpass the speed of sound which results in swirling masses of supersonic methane clouds churning at different rates along its axis. That's not even considering the magnetized lightning storms or the torrential downpour of pressurized liquid frozen at temperatures barely warmer than the vacuum of space itself."

Avery raised a brow. "So you're saying it'll be hard."

Rem looked to Nova. "Is she being serious? I honestly cannot tell."

"You forgot about the diamonds," Syla mumbled.

Rem whirled on her. "Enough with the diamonds, Syla. It's not like anybody can mine them—which is my whole point. Nobody with a brain in their head goes *inside* Neptune."

Avery crossed her arms. "I didn't ask if anybody goes in. I asked if it could be done."

Rem frowned, frustration billowing out around him. He glanced at Qav and back. More silent conversation. "Theoretically we could survive a few minutes in this ship, but—"

"Great." Avery smiled. Anticipation made her bounce on her toes, turning to Nova and Grigg. They were finally going home. All of them.

"*But* this vessel wasn't crafted for those conditions," Rem finished. "It would take me days to run through the scenarios to ensure we don't hit critical failure once we descend into the storm itself."

"We don't have days."

"I'm aware. Which is why I suggest we continue with our original plan."

"Have you figured out how to pull out the Gate without the Feds descending on us?"

Rem's mouth pursed. He glanced at Qav.

"We can afford a few days, Avery." Qav sighed, finally standing from his relaxed seat. "What's the rush? If Rem says he can—"

"You're assuming I want your opinion? After everything you've done?" Avery snapped. She couldn't believe Qav would try to convince her to wait. This entire mess was his fault to begin with. The familiar rage that had been a constant in Qav's presence for the past year suddenly surged once more to life. It clawed up her ribs, digging painfully into her throat. "You want me to wait a few days? We can't even afford a few *hours*. You think Klein won't come after us? She'll have figured out what we took from her apartments. She wants Echo for herself—she won't hesitate to bring the entire Federation down on us to keep me from getting back there. We need to move *now* while we still have an advantage."

Qav nodded once, holding up his hands and backing away.

Rem swallowed awkwardly and stared at the floor.

Avery sighed, shifting her weight. For some reason, Qav's immediate compliance made her uncomfortable. She had lost control of her anger and he seemed unfazed. He'd even yielded.

"Look, I know it's dangerous." Avery gestured to Grigg and Nova. "But for the three of us, everyone we've ever cared about is on the other side of that Gate . If all we have is this one chance to get back to them, then we need to take it."

Nova's hand slipped into Avery's and squeezed. Grigg brushed his shoulder against hers in a soft bump. Warmth emanated from them, pouring into Avery like bright sunlight, chasing away the cold rage that had flooded her system.

"Let's say we go through," Qav said carefully. "What happens when Klein follows us to Echo? You'll be right back where you started."

"She couldn't mobilize a response that quickly," Ennis reasoned. "She'd need approval from the World Council to bring in Federation support."

"And according to Alex, Klein is unlikely to get that approval either way," Nova added.

"Which is why I need you," Avery pleaded to Qav. "By the time Klein makes her move, we'll be well established on Echo. There are weapons left from the war—there are ships. We can keep her from implementing whatever plan she has to reclaim it."

Qav tilted his head. "And what about the Elder So' who drove you out of Echo in the first place? Given the state you came to me in, she may prove more of a challenge than even Klein."

Avery's jaw set. "Leviathan won't catch me off guard again. I know what I'm going up against. I'm stronger than I've ever been. And we have a weapon she'll never see coming."

Qav lifted a curious brow.

"You."

He let out the barest hint of a laugh and looked away. Avery had used his preferred method of manipulation against him: flattery. Strangely, it seemed to work. And more bizarre still, it was the truth.

Syla leaned forward. "So the ship needs to withstand harsher conditions. Why don't we just reinforce the hull?"

Rem eyed her skeptically. "And how would you suggest we go

about that? We're millions of miles away from the nearest station."

"Avery and Qav." Syla nodded to them both. "They did it before. When the main Gate was destroyed, they buffered the ship from being torn apart in the aftermath."

Avery's shoulders straightened. Syla was right. They *had* been able to protect the ship then. It had been nothing more than instinct, a desperate attempt to keep them alive, but it had worked. If they had done it once, they could do it again.

"Are you insane?" Qav scolded. "Both of us nearly died."

"I'm hearing a theme," Nova muttered.

"You're a genius, Syla." Avery placed a hand on her shoulder.

Syla raised a brow at Qav, daring him to say something about her support of Avery's scheme. But Syla didn't want to give up on the second Gate, either. As much as she held a place by Qav's side, she had been born on Echo. And she wanted to return one day. Or at least make it possible for her parents to do so.

But for Syla's idea to work, Avery would need Qav on board. Regardless of anything else, they were stronger together.

"We can do this, Qav," Avery pleaded. "You're the one who told me our powers aren't stagnant. They expand the harder we push them."

"You *do* have a death wish," Qav said darkly.

"Lucky for you, it hasn't been granted yet."

"I'm not sure *lucky* is the word I'd use."

Avery looked to Rem. "Would it work?"

He nodded hesitantly. "Perhaps."

"Avery, you're still healing. You're not even at full strength," Qav protested softly, like he was talking to a child.

"I'm fine—I can handle it."

"Just listen to reason. We can at least wait until—"

"I know my own blazing limits. I said I can handle—"

Pain seared through her abdomen and Avery folded into herself. She clutched her side with a gasp as her wound throbbed to life with agony, robbing her of breath.

"Avery!" Nova supported her arm, helping her stand.

Avery looked at Qav through the curtain of loose hair that had fallen into her face.

His brows drew together. His shoulders were stiff. "You can't even stand."

She had forgotten Qav was shielding her pain. A foolish mistake, and one she wouldn't make again. She took a breath and steadied herself, rising to her full height. The sensation wasn't unbearable; it had merely startled her for a moment. Qav hadn't had permission to alter her reality, no matter how well meaning the gesture had been.

Qav's mouth turned up, his familiar self-righteousness slithering against her mind more viciously than a slap to the face.

Avery flew across the room, slamming her hands into Qav's chest and sending him soaring into the paneled wall. He barely caught himself, leaving handprints indented on the metal.

"I said I'm fine," Avery bit out. She ignored the lancing in her gut that the show of power had caused. "This whole thing is *your fault*, Qav. And by the moons, you're going to help me fix it."

Qav's eyes narrowed as he sent her a silent counter. *Not my fault entirely, gnima.*

The sinking guilt was immediate and disarming, but Avery stood her ground. She wouldn't give him the satisfaction. Qav was right. And that hurt the most. Avery's choices—her conviction to keep herself separate from her friends—had led to the disaster that had nearly ruined both worlds.

"Avery." Syla stepped in front of Qav. In her dark eyes was a fierce understanding. Syla knew better than most the cost of Qav's manipulations.

Still, she was asking Avery to back down. To slow down.

Avery let out a heavy sigh, placing a hand over her healing wound. Compromising would be the best avenue forward.

She had told Qav she could go through this alone, but it would be helpful to have him with her. If he was so determined to gain her trust, this would be the way to go about it. But trust went both ways.

"Twelve hours," Avery conceded. "Rem can run projections, we all get a good night's rest, and in the morning, we do it my way."

✳

Another nine hours of sleep actually did help restore Avery's strength. After eating something, she returned to her rooms and stumbled into the gargantuan bed. She was asleep before her head hit the silk pillows. By the time she woke, her wound was barely a twinge in her side.

The speed of her healing surprised Avery. She ran her fingers over the mottled pink flesh on her abdomen as she showered, marveling at the change even during her sleep. Perhaps her ability to heal had expanded to include her own body.

Avery changed into more sensible clothes that had been packed for her. While rifling in the small room that served as a closet, she came across a smooth white box on the round table in its center. There was a pale cream card on top with a single line of handwritten text.

Avery, let's not repeat the performance.
- C. N.

Avery touched the surface of the box and it unlocked with a soft snick. She lifted the lid to reveal a dark swath of thick fabric folded neatly inside. Avery pulled out the first piece and held it up to the light. The shimmering fabric was soft to the touch but retained its structure. It was a chest piece, curved and shaped perfectly for Avery's measurements.

Avery laughed in disbelief. Cora had created some kind of gear for her. And there were more additions in the box: arm plates and pants and a holster to accompany them. Avery brushed her fingers over them reverently. She had never seen anything like the fabric—she was scared to even wonder about its cost.

But they wouldn't need it yet. She closed the box and grabbed her boots to leave. Thankfully she could bend over to lace them as easily as if she'd never been shot in the first place.

Grigg was waiting for her as she bounced over the threshold into the living space.

"You look better." He was grinning, his optimism echoing her own bubbling excitement. "That's a relief. For a moment I was worried I'd actually have to take Qav's side on something."

"So little faith in me?" Avery pouted. "And here I thought I was your favorite."

"You had a hole in your gut seventy-two hours ago," Grigg said, sobering. "But I underestimated your will to prove Qav wrong. Don't worry—it won't happen again."

"It better not." Avery laughed. She grabbed the jacket she'd laid out by the door and shrugged into it. "Did Nova send you to babysit me?"

Grigg chuckled and slung a heavily muscled arm over her shoulders. "She'll settle down eventually. You just scared her—you scared *us.*"

Avery bit the inside of her cheek as they passed through the central corridor. "Getting shot wasn't exactly part of my grand plan."

"You know, it never is, yet it happens to us more often than you'd think."

Avery laughed, falling into step easily beside him. He was always a source of comforting warmth. It was easy to see why he and Finn had been such fast friends, close as brothers.

Which was why Avery slowed as she felt hesitation bubble up between them. Grigg was uneasy, worrying over how to say what was on his mind. He rubbed the back of his neck, dropping to Avery's pace, staring at the floor.

Had he and Nova discussed the danger of Avery's plan? Maybe they had changed their minds about going through with it. If there was even a bit of reticence on their part, Avery owed it to them to listen. She had barely asked their opinions before running to the others with her idea. Avery wouldn't budge for Qav, but Grigg and Nova were another story.

"Whatever it is, just say it," Avery encouraged with a grin. "If you think we should wait—"

"No, Avery. We're with you all the way." He laughed awkwardly, kicking his boot against the floor. "It just—about Nova. She only hovers over you because she made a promise to Finn. When you told him to get lost." His panicked eyes flickered up to her, his cheeks flushing as he struggled to comfort her. "Not that you meant it—I mean, you weren't *you*. Moons above, I'm bad at this. What I mean to say is, she made a promise to Finn before he left. That she'd take care of you, since he couldn't. I think it's just her way of trying not to disappoint him."

Avery's throat constricted, her eyes stinging. No matter how Grigg tried to spin Avery's actions, she knew the truth. Avery *had* told Finn to get lost. The memory of that moment cracked open her heart every time she shut her eyes. The tears on Finn's cheeks. Petra's disgusted betrayal. Megan's mouth falling open in shock just before Avery had used her power against her. It ached more than the wound in her side ever could.

How was she even going to face them? It wasn't something she had let herself think of yet. And now that the question was in front of her . . . She was utterly terrified.

Avery had made so many mistakes. She had wanted to be the perfect leader. She had *needed* to be perfect. She had wanted it so badly that she'd hidden herself away from those who mattered most. And for what? To appear infallible? If the past year had taught her anything, it was that infallibility was a trap. That road only led to isolation and suffering.

Grigg stretched his arms over his head, cracking his neck. "Don't worry about it so much. We all know Qav was an asshole. He still is half the time. But Nova and I don't blame you for that. And Finn won't, either."

Avery leaned her shoulder into him, her eyes watering. Maybe Nova wasn't the only one who noticed things. "Thanks, Grigg. But he's not the only one I have to answer to."

He let out a dramatic breath through pursed lips. "Yeah, well, Petra is a different story. I've got zero advice for how to handle that live wire. I try to stay away from the scary ones."

"Now, Grigg, what did we say about giving people advice?" Nova jogged up behind them, completing their trio. "I told you to wait for me."

"I got restless," Avery offered.

"I know the feeling," Nova said excitedly. Avery hadn't heard her so animated in ages. "It's not every day you get to go home after thinking it was gone forever."

Grigg laughed. "I can't *wait* to see the looks on their faces when we waltz in there."

Nova linked her arm with Avery's. "Do you think Qav is right about your tether with Finn?"

Avery shook her head. "I don't know. The pain when he . . . when he left this galaxy . . . It was excruciating. I think that's what pulled me out of the haze Qav had placed over my mind. I thought it was the grief of losing everyone, but now . . ."

"You're thinking maybe it's more," Nova finished quietly.

Avery nodded. "For once, I hope Qav is right about something."

"Only one way to find out," Grigg said with a smirk. "Who's ready to narrowly escape death in an insane attempt to beat the odds?"

"Insane?" Avery laughed, feigning offense. "What happened to 'we're with you all the way'?"

"Let's be honest, your track record isn't the best." Avery swiped at him, and he sidestepped her, dancing away.

Avery jerked her chin up, casting a leash of power to pull Grigg's feet out from under him. He came down hard on the white floor, wide-eyed and wheezing. Nova cackled as they stepped over him.

They were still laughing when they entered the bridge. Grigg had caught up and, despite Avery, was grinning ear to ear. Syla stared at the three of them like they had lost their minds. Rem was muttering over figures on the holocontrols with a concerned Ennis peering over his shoulder. Qav stood with his back to them, watching Neptune through the large windows at the nose of the ship.

"You seem fairly upbeat for a group of soon to be frozen corpses," Rem muttered under his breath. His eyes never left the lines of data floating in the air in front of him.

"Lighten up, Rem," Syla said.

"We ran the numbers," Ennis added. "If Qav and Avery can generate the same buffer they did during the gravitational waves that hit Earth, then this is going to work."

Rem's mouth twisted. "That's assuming nothing will go wrong. And something *always* goes wrong."

"Of course it will with that blazing attitude," Grigg growled.

Avery approached the holocontrols, looking over the map outlining their descent into Neptune's atmosphere, straight for the northern section of its axis, where the Gate would be waiting.

"Is everything ready?"

"As ready as we can be." Ennis moved to Avery's side. "Federation patrol is making its rounds on the far side of Pluto now, so we have a half-hour opening."

Avery turned to Qav, waiting for him to say something. He just stood there in silence, his hands clasped behind his back. He watched the large blue planet that filled their view.

Qav. Avery opened the path between them. His shoulders stiffened. *Are you ready to do this?*

His took in a long breath and released it, his shoulders lifting and falling as his fingers tightened together. But he didn't turn toward her. The air in the room grew heavy.

Avery walked to his side. She glanced up at his profile, the stern lines motionless. Avery reached out to him with her power, needing to know at least some semblance of what he felt. She could do so without him noticing—he had been the one to teach her how—though she had been too ashamed to use the skill until now.

She flinched at the cold onslaught of pure fear. Avery couldn't prevent the quick intake of breath that followed. Qav was afraid.

He turned his head to her slowly, meeting her eyes. His brows drew together, thoughts rioting through his head that Avery refused to touch. Maybe he had felt her invade the privacy of his emotions. He certainly couldn't blame her for it, even if he had.

For a moment, Avery thought he might tell refuse to join her. After everything, Qav still had an opportunity to control her future. Despite the power Avery had gained, Qav could keep her here—trapped on Earth. At least, for a time.

Avery could force him. Her power had grown to such a level that she knew she could do it, and Qav would have no one to blame but himself. Avery swore to never stoop to his level, but if it meant getting back to the others? To Gran . . . To Finn? She wasn't sure she had the strength to resist.

Avery placed a hand on his arm. The gray fabric of his coat was cold beneath her fingers. "I'll get you back home. I promise you that much."

The corners of his lips turned upward. "Careful, *gnima*. I'm not sure that's a promise you can make."

"With your help, I sure as hell can."

He studied her briefly before turning to share a long look with Syla whose expression gave away nothing. Ennis stepped up beside her, dipping her pert chin in a nod.

Avery realized then: Qav wasn't doing this for her. Certainly he had come with Avery to Klein's apartments in a bid to gain her trust, but this choice was different. Going to Echo was for *them*.

For Syla and Ennis. His family.

"Let's do this, then," Qav said, marching over to them. "Before I change my mind."

"A part of me was still hoping you would," Rem groaned. "Everybody strap in. This is going to be a bumpy ride."

Qav took one of the three viewing seats lining the front, pulling his long white hair into tie at the base of his neck. Avery settled in next to him with Rem on her other side. She pressed the touch pad by her leg and a restraint system unfolded over her shoulders and down her chest, locking her in. Grigg and Syla dropped into the row behind, anticipation snapping off them like electricity.

"Once Nova pulls us out from behind this moon, we're going to make a dive straight for the coordinates," Rem explained. "The Fed patrols are out of reach for our window, but if we ping on their scanners, they'll be on us in minutes."

"*Will* they scan us?" Nova asked. Without Petra, she was by far the best pilot in the group. Ennis took the command center to Nova's left, ready to control the Gate via the ship's system once they reached close enough proximity.

"Not if you don't waste time getting down there."

"Haul ass—got it," Nova replied dryly. She leaned forward and the blue holocontrols materialized in front of her, swaths of light wrapping around her hands. Her eyes met Avery's, a smile tugging at her lips. "On your command."

Avery faced forward, straightening her back. Her eyes slid closed. The cool air of the bridge filtered in through her nostrils, slowing her heart rate. She reached out to Qav, opening entirely to him. If they were going to do this, she'd do it right this time. His icy energy expanded, surging out around her, like he'd been holding himself back.

On your command, he parroted, irony slithering along Avery's spine with the thought.

Still, she couldn't prevent the smile that pulled at her lips. Together, they let their awareness expand throughout the ship, flying outward and down the passageways, through the rooms and cargo hold until they completely encompassed the vessel. It was encased fully in a protective shield of their energy.

Avery's opened her eyes and zeroed in on Neptune ahead of them. Somewhere beneath its spinning blue clouds, the second Gate waited for them.

"We've got one shot at this." Avery gripped the arms of her seat. "Let's make it count."

And they took off like a falling star into the swirling cerulean depths that promised them a way back home through the infinite folds of the universe.

CHAPTER FIFTEEN

Their world turned white as they hit the outer atmosphere, engulfed in the barrier of swirling clouds that blanketed Neptune. The ship jerked, struggling to maintain its trajectory as it plummeted through layers of supersonic winds. Avery's muscles tensed as she reinforced her shield, doing her best to buffer the intensity of the onslaught. Qav was already struggling. He rose his hands to concentrate his power, his fingers shaking.

"How long are we doing this?" Qav bit out through clenched teeth. A bead of sweat dripped down the side of his face.

"Five minutes." Ennis's reply was immediate. "Counter winds should reside as soon as we drop out of the upper atmo."

"Should?"

The ship lurched to the side and Avery homed in on her control, countering the tilt. Her breath quickened, a fine sheen of sweat breaking out on her own forehead.

I don't know how much more I have, Avery. Fear ran like an icy rivulet behind Qav's thought, digging its claws into Avery. Qav's strength was fading quickly—faster than Avery had anticipated.

We have to hold on! She would get nowhere by blocking his emotions. Instead, she welcomed the terror, displacing it along with her own. They had to let the pass through them, the same way they were passing through the tumultuous atmosphere around them.

A memory flashed, sudden and vibrant. It was Qav's, seeping through the bond and straight into her mind. Syla and Ennis, younger than Avery had ever seen them, laughing hysterically as they curled into each other to stay on their feet. It was a vision of pure warmth, soothing and clear. Treasured. Avery clung to that feeling, pulling it out of Qav and spreading it through both of them until the chill of his fear seemed to wane.

The ship burst out of the clouds. They dropped into the lower atmosphere, the vast world opening up in front of them in a wide swath of deep blue. Nova leveled out the ship and gravity pressed down on them, harsher than any Avery had ever felt. She sunk into her seat until it seemed her skin would stretch out against her bones.

"The gravity sensors are failing!" Nova called out. "The ship can't keep up—"

They dropped, hitting an air pocket that sent the vessel rapidly spiraling, leaving their guts floating miles above them. Anxiety gripped Avery's spine. She fought against the strange sensations as visions of the serene blue planet blurred past them. Qav wasn't the only one afraid anymore. Still, he faltered beside Avery. His breath came in sharp pants as he fought to hold on.

Avery grabbed his hand, his fingers even colder than hers. *Stay with me, Qav.*

She squeezed her eyes shut, fixating on her shield and pulling the ship in a counter motion to balance out its death spiral. They could do this—*they had to do this.*

The ship slowed enough for Nova to regain control. They dove into an air stream and surged forward with the movement of the clouds around them. When Avery opened her eyes at last, Neptune itself careened around them wildly. They weren't done yet.

Avery gulped in air. Sweat gathered at the small of her back and along her temple. Qav gripped her fingers as harshly as she did his. Their power bolstered together to fight against the rippling winds that still threatened to take the ship off course.

"There!" Ennis pointed ahead. In the distance, a speck of black floated in an eerie pocket of calm, the surging clouds billowing around it. Like it was encased in a bubble of protection against the violent landscape.

It disappeared as they flew into an enormous cloud, their view replaced by nothing but endless white. A bright flash, and the world cracked in two on the boom that followed as lightning struck the ship. Pain lanced through Avery, filtering its way through her system via every spare inch of her veins. She screamed, squeezing Qav's hand, unable to release him. But he remained silent, his face going deathly pale. Qav's head dipped, his eyes closing. Blood began to drip out of his nose, coursing down to stain his lips.

Hold on! Avery screamed at him, shaking their hands together, willing him to stay awake. "Hold on!"

They burst out of the clouds and the Gate was closer than ever before. Avery's eyes traveled up its looming arch, taking in the mass that extended beyond their ship's field of vision.

Alarms began to wail, filling the bridge and assaulting their ears with a painful warning.

"Shit!" Nova twisted her arms sharply, bringing the vessel into a swift roll.

They spun and the seat restraints cut into Avery's shoulders as her weight shifted against the rigid gravity. Something slammed into Avery's shield and she tensed, enhancing the barrier. Avery knew that feeling, she had stopped it before—blastfire. They were under attack.

"The Gate has a blazing security system," Ennis bit out as her fingers frantically tapped across her touch screen.

Syla gripped her restraints. "We went over every inch of those schematics—there were no guns."

"Well, there are now!" Ennis replied. Panic surged out from her as she frowned at the screen. "I can't get into the blazing system."

Nova jerked the ship around, taking them up and away from the artillery that protruded from the edges of the gargantuan metal ring.

Rem slammed on the control pad to release his restraints. He bounded over to Ennis and she grabbed his belt, holding him steady as he looked over the screen. His eyes moved rapidly, inputting commands with the yellow coding classes that tracked his movements.

"Hang on to him!" Nova yelled. They crested over the top of the Gate and down.

Ennis wrapped an arm around Rem's waist and Avery pulled her attention away from the ship to brace him.

"I'm in!" Rem whooped.

But it was too late—a final blast caught the ship, penetrating Avery's and Qav's defenses. The ship spun out in a wild pirouette. Rem went flying, slamming into the ceiling. The alarms were still blaring. Avery pushed all her power to Rem, leaving a deteriorated Qav to protect the ship. Rem floated aloft in the cabin as the vessel lost control.

"You can do this, Nova!" Grigg bellowed.

Nova's face contorted as she counteracted the violent pull of centrifugal force. They began to slow as Nova regained control at last. And when she pulled them up to aim for the Gate, they passed through its shield easily. The chaos of Neptune's storms evaporated as they piloted into calm.

Avery brought Rem gently to the ground. His eyes were closed, long lashes resting against pale cheeks. He didn't get up.

"Ennis?" Avery asked desperately.

"Ten seconds!"

If there had been defensive measures on the Gate, then Klein knew they were there. The Gate's design already differed from the schematics they recovered . . . What else had been modified?

Ennis fell silent as she focused on her work. She tapped purposefully on her screen, coding her way through the activation protocol. At last, she looked up, her eyes bright and hopeful.

A low hum began to resonate around them. The Gate was powering on.

"Is it working?" Grigg leaned forward.

The giant ring began to glow a soft, unblemished white. The open space in its center oscillated, turning a familiar texture of rippling translucence as it came alive. The protective bubble enshrouding them shuddered in a cacophony of booms as lightning cracked across its protective sphere.

"The open wormhole is distorting the magnetic fields," Ennis said nervously. "I need to run a quick diagnostic to make sure—"

"We don't have time for that!" Avery shouted.

"Ten seconds! I just need ten sec—"

"You said that already," Syla snapped. "If we wait any longer, the Gate could collapse entirely."

Qav's hand went limp in Avery's. He slipped away from their connection, as his mind went dark. He slumped in his seat, blood coating his chin. If the bubble collapsed, Avery wouldn't be able to get them out of Neptune alone. Not without him helping her. Forward through the Gate was the only way out of this.

"Now!" Avery yelled. She swung her head to Nova. "Go now, Nova—we can't wait any longer."

"Wait!" Ennis pleaded, her eyes wide with panic. "Let me just—"

Nova didn't hesitate.

Their ship speared through the shimmering surface of the portal and into the shadowed unknowns of the other side. There was nothing Avery could do but hope that the risk had been worth taking.

CHAPTER SIXTEEN

Fifteen months earlier

Finn grimaced against the brightness that dragged him into consciousness. His head throbbed. But his face . . . his face was on fire, a steady pulse of searing pain that ran the length of his jaw, jolting him into awareness. He groaned and lifted his hand to explore the bandage that covered most of his right cheek.

His mind filtered through memory, unable to conjure more beyond the basics. Their battle with Origin forces. Their frenzied escape from his mangled ship. The wave that surged out from the Gate, throwing their pod off course and sending them crashing into the mountains.

He was separated from Avery forever. He'd never see his brother again, or his home world. And Grigg was . . . Grigg was dead.

Finn tried to sit up against the pillows behind him, squinting against the early-morning light. He grunted when more pain lanced down his arm. It was in a sling, limp at his side. Fabulous—another injury. Their descent to Echo must have been more crash and less landing.

He finally noticed the bed beside his own. A girl with blond hair lay still as death tucked beneath a wool blanket, her pale face dirty with soot. Megan. And in the corner, slumped in a simple chair cast in soft shadows, Petra slept. Her chin was tucked into her chest. Her blue-black hair fell gracelessly over sharp cheekbones. Of course she was frowning, even in her sleep.

Finn's mouth turned to sand when he caught sight of the water set out on the side table. He rolled to grab it with his good hand, but the pain made him clumsy. It fell to the stone floor, shattering.

Petra was on her feet, blaster out of its holster, aimed straight at him. Her green eyes were wild.

"Easy," Finn croaked, falling backward into his pillow. His face pulsed with each heartbeat.

"Why didn't you wake me?" Petra snapped. Her eyes flicked to Megan. Like she had hoped the noise might stir her.

"Just felt like testing your reaction skills." Finn closed his eyes and let out a long, pained breath. "You passed."

Petra jabbed the blaster back into its holster on her thigh. "At least you're conscious."

"Not sure I'm grateful for that at the moment. What happened?"

"Your pod went down in the far north mountains. Thank the moons our scanner was still operational—we were able to find you pretty quickly."

"The others?"

"They're—"

The door flew open as Markes barreled inside, eyes bleary with sleep. Linderly shoved past him, halting when she realized Megan was still unconscious.

"You're up!" Markes exclaimed. A bruise spread out across his forehead, the chartreuse skin nearly matching the yellow of his hair that stuck out in every direction. "I told you he'd pull through it," he crowed at Petra.

"That was just wishful thinking." Linderly sat on the edge of Finn's bed. She placed a tattooed hand to his forehead, her fingers blissfully cool. "The fever broke."

"Looks like wishful thinking worked." Markes leaned against the doorframe.

"Remind me to thank you once the room stops spinning," Finn replied, resting his head on the pillow. He'd been in better shape.

"I'll grab you more water," Linderly said after she noticed the mess of glass at her feet. Then she disappeared through the door.

"Where are we?" Finn asked.

"A village in the Northern Mountains. Nos Mulda," Petra replied.

Nos Mulda. Finn knew it. The small town was rudimentary at best but a decent location for staying off the radar. It wasn't far from Nova's hometown. She and Grigg had dragged him back there to visit her family at least a dozen times. The wouldn't know—Nova's family wouldn't know yet. That she was separated from them forever. That Grigg was . . . gone.

Finn grimaced against the stinging in his eyes. He couldn't think of that now. He couldn't afford to. Not yet.

"You've been out of it for days," Markes explained. "Fever. That sick gash on your face got infected."

"I gathered," Finn bit out, resisting the urge to touch the burning flesh running up his cheek. "Do I want to know how bad it is? We're talking scarred for life, right?"

"Don't be vain, Lunitia." Petra was quick to chastise him. But her eyes shifted to Markes and back.

Finn laughed softly. "That bad, huh."

"You're alive," Petra stated. "Be grateful for that."

"Ever the empath," Finn muttered.

Linderly bounced back into the room, saving him from further discussion of the topic. Finn took the fresh water, in a metal cup this time, and downed it greedily.

"He's awake." Tai had materialized with Linderly to linger in the doorway beside Markes. Dark shadows ran beneath his eyes as he looked to Petra. "We should relocate, then. Lingering here only increases our chance of discovery."

"I guess that means we lost?" Desolation dropped down from Finn's heart, sinking into the marrow of his bones. They had failed. "Leviathan killed the humans, then."

"No!" Linderly exclaimed, making Finn jump. "Leviathan pardoned the humans. Just after the Gate malfunction."

"Malfunction?" Finn laughed bitterly. "Is that what she's calling it?"

"The official story is that Earth destroyed their own Gate. Leviathan claims they did it to themselves."

"Out of fear," Markes added.

"Wait, she *pardoned* the humans?" Finn sat up, keeping his head steady. "Why? Earth is cut off from us. She has all the power she could ever want."

"Indentured servitude," Petra answered, plopping into her chair. "All humans on Echo are pardoned under the condition they work of their life debt. Reanges can now register for a license to purchase them for their households."

"*Purchase?*" Finn choked out. He grabbed the blanket that fell to his hips. Someone had changed him into a nightshirt.

Maybe it had been Leviathan's plan all along. The Origin fighter ships had been waiting for them as soon as they crossed back into Echo's star system. Leviathan had clearly expected some kind of fight from Avery once they returned. Finn had barely been able to evade the advanced Federation warships.

It was Linderly who'd discovered that the Origin had hacked the wormhole's system from Echo's side. Leviathan had been the one to destroy Earth's Gate. She clearly hadn't foreseen the repercussions of such an explosion—that the gravitational waves would surge through both sides of the wormhole.

The destruction would have been worse on Earth's side. And Avery had been up there, trying to stop it from happening. She had come back to Finn. In the end, she had freed herself from Qav. Finn's heart ached, rivaling the pain from the wound on his face.

Finn swallowed hard. He looked to Petra. "And Avery?"

Her eyes hardened. She shook her head, a slight, swift movement.

"We haven't heard anything from the other side," Linderly said gently. "The Origin Council claims the earth's Gate was obliterated. No chance at recovery."

"Judging from the way we got projectiled into the mountains, I'd say that's an accurate assessment," Markes drawled.

Avery was gone, then. Lost to him forever.

Finn let the truth settle into him, as foreign and unwelcome as a steel rod lodging beneath his ribs. Nova was with her. Grigg was dead. Everything they'd tried to accomplish had been for nothing. He'd lost everything that had ever mattered to him in one staggering error in judgment. They never should have gone to Earth in the first place.

Finn's eyes watered and he looked out the window, clearing his throat. He stared at the bright light of the rising sun until his skull hurt.

"So what do you have planned?" Finn asked roughly. He needed to act. He needed a path forward—even if it wasn't toward *her*.

"What do you mean?" Petra frowned.

"I mean, how are we going to take Leviathan down?"

"Take her down?" Tai crossed lanky arms over his chest. "Maybe the impact really did scramble your brains."

Finn struggled to rise. "We can't just let her have Echo. She's controlling people against their will. *You* know that better than anyone."

Tai flushed, his green eyes dropping to the floor. Only weeks ago, Leviathan had turned him into a glorified assassin bent on destroying every human he came into contact with. Surely he wanted retribution.

"But we don't have Avery," Linderly said softly. She tucked a lock of jet-black hair behind her heavily pierced ear.

"It's *because* of her that we have to fight back." Finn leaned forward. "This isn't the future any of us wanted for Echo—Leviathan isn't the future. We fought for so long to gain independence from the Federation. I won't stand by and let Echo fall from one corrupt government to another. Avery wouldn't have wanted us to give up."

"We don't have any weapons," Markes said dryly. "No resources. No intel. How do you propose we go about dismantling an Elder Council with an all-powerful So' at its helm?"

"She's hardly all-powerful." Petra leaned forward to sweep back a lock of hair from Megan's cheek. "Even So' have weaknesses."

"Especially ones as ancient as that fossil," Finn murmured. He looked to each of them, at what was left of their crew after they had been torn apart. They weren't entirely without hope. They could still do this. "We can't help Avery now, but we *can* help Echo. We can give the people a chance for a better future. If we don't try, then no one else will."

His words floated around them in the silence. Finn knew they thought he was insane. And maybe he was. But he had trained his whole life to free Echo. He had joined the Reange Rebellion and fought alongside them for years to bring about that reality. To let the people of Echo choose their future for themselves. Finn wouldn't sit by and let it fall into the hands of another extremist obsessed with nothing more than power and control. He'd sooner die.

"Megan needs a doctor," Petra said softly, looking up. "If we're going to start somewhere, let's start there."

Megan's face was still. Her pale hair spread out over her pillow like a halo. She still hadn't woken from the blow Avery had dealt. Megan would be trapped there with them on Echo, separated forever from her family and her world. A human adrift. Like Finn.

"Then I guess first we'll need a human healer. At least that one will be easy. With any luck, Dr. Vey is still in the city."

Petra's eyes widened, and her long fingers pressed into the mattress. "Avery's grandmother," she breathed in wonder. "Why didn't I think of that?"

"Let's hope she and Dr. Brinstal are still hiding with the humans they rescued before we left." Finn's mind was already swirling, despite the headache. It didn't fix the gaping hole where his heart used to be, but it helped.

He couldn't stand by Avery's side anymore. She was on her own somewhere across the stars.

No—not alone. Nova had promised to keep her safe. At least Finn could trust that his friend would never abandon the woman he loved. Even if Grigg had been . . .

Finn pulled his legs over the side of the bed. The floor was freezing beneath his bare feet, distracting him from the sudden pain of the gash in his calf. His vision turned spotty and he leaned into the sensation, glad that it wiped out any other feeling.

"First things first," Finn said resolutely, his good hand settling on his bare knee. "Where are my pants?"

CHAPTER SEVENTEEN

Present day

Petra was well ahead of the others by the time she entered the snow-covered village. The straps of her heavy pack dug into her shoulders and she adjusted it, grateful that its weight made the journey that much more difficult. She paused at the top of one of the final ridges and looked back down the hill she had climbed.

The humans they had rescued were doing an admirable job of keeping up with her pace. Even if Petra had slowed herself down for their benefit. Finn had harped at her more than once about forgetting that not everyone could keep up with her. Petra wasn't exactly jumping at the chance to repeat the lecture. From him especially.

Tai lead the group of eleven, his face drawn into hard lines of determination as he walked. He looked older than she'd ever seen him, even if his cheeks were pink in the cold. The past two years had put him through so much. Petra had tried to keep him safe, to shield him from the things that would change him. But Tai was no longer a child. It was difficult to watch her little brother turn into a man in one startling revelation after another.

He laughed suddenly, turning once more to the boy he had been as Linderly bounced up beside him. Petra was glad that he had found someone who made him feel less alone. As partners went, Linderly was a decent choice. She was brilliant and good in a fight. And judging by the ink that adorned her limbs, she could handle her fair share of pain. Tai could do worse.

When they finally reached her, Petra forced herself to stand still as the humans caught their breath. A few were coughing, unused to the high altitude and freezing temperatures. She ran a tally of heads for the millionth time. At least there were no children on this retrieval. That always made things more difficult.

"Are we there?" An older woman gasped as she clutched at her side. She looked like she was regretting the decision to leave Milderion, even if she had been enslaved for months there.

"Almost!" Linderly reassured them. "The town is just over the next ridge. You all are doing great." Her flawless skin was flushed pink in the cold, her large eyes bright from the exertion beneath black bangs that just covered her eyebrows. She must have actually listened to Finn when he'd discussed keeping up morale.

Things had been difficult when they first started bringing rescues to their Nos Lenti base. There were precious few supplies, and even fewer connections in the capitol. Many of the humans they brought to the small mountain village were despondent at best. Ungrateful at worst.

Those were the hardest for Petra. It should have been enough that they'd been saved from a life of perpetual servitude. Occasionally the rescues had the audacity to complain about their new lifestyle. Especially when they were told to deactivate their wristports. It was asinine. They were *free*—why did a blazing wristport matter?

But even liberation from forced labor paled in comparison to whatever wealthy version of reality they had lived in on Earth. The only humans who could afford to visit Echo in the first place were those with enough credits to dissolve. A part of Petra resented them for it. She had become a savior to those whom she once sought to destroy. That in itself was a certain kind of lunacy.

Many of the people Petra had come to love most in this life were humans. Avery had believed the two species could live side by side in peace. She had dedicated herself to achieving that goal. But that path had cost Avery her mind. Petra had to believe the fight to keep that dream alive was worth the same price.

"Let's go." Petra kept her words short. She hated leading these raids. The way the humans looked to her with hope in their eyes—with trust—was difficult. Noticing Tai's raised brows, she added over her shoulder, "There will be hot meals waiting for you."

That was as much coddling as they'd get from her, Finn's lectures be damned.

They finished the hike in silence, nothing but the sounds of heavy breathing and the soft crunch of snow beneath their boots to break it. They crested the final hill and passed beneath the stone archway that marked the village boundary. A few of the humans gasped with something between surprise and relief.

Nos Lenti was similar to many villages in the Northern Mountains, but it held its own kind of charm. The simple buildings pressed up against the base of towering craggy cliffs, their peaked gables hefting thick layers of snow while wide windows beckoned with warm glows of yellow light. A stone-layered throughway curved around the gully, disappearing beyond the bend along with the rows of houses that lined its path.

During the war, remote towns like this had been cleared out as residents feared what Federation forces might attempt so far from the prying eyes of the media. Many had simply joined the Rebellion forces at Nos Valuta. But some had stayed, trying to keep the traditions of the mountains alive. Like Nova's parents. They had welcomed Finn and his irrational scheme to liberate Echo with open arms. Even when he had brought news that their daughter was lost to them forever.

Thanks to their efforts, Nos Lenti had been reborn in the following months. It bustled with life as people walked through its streets, bundled up against the cold. Both humans and Reanges had gathered there. They had created a unique kind of refuge that attracted anyone looking for peace outside of Leviathan's rule.

A few faces below turned up to their approach, stopping to point from the village center. A man yelled and a gong soon followed, ringing out from the tower in the square and heralding their arrival. Someone would already be preparing to receive the new arrivals at the intake center. At least the drivel about hot meals wouldn't be a lie.

By the time they made it to the middle of town, people were already rushing forward to welcome the rescues, bundling them in blankets and offering platitudes, executing a dance that was already familiar to the veterans there.

Markes appeared from nowhere, launching himself at Linderly and wrapping her in a lanky hug that sent her tiny body stumbling. This mission had been the first time the twins had been separated since their time on Earth. Markes hadn't been happy about it. Linderly hadn't minded as much when she realized Tai would be with her.

"You're back!" Markes exclaimed, holding Linderly's face in his hands. His eyes were wet.

"Right on schedule, brother." Linderly smiled indulgently. "Told you it would be fine."

Tai watched them, smiling with something like envy. Petra had never been overly warm with him, not in the way of these two. She wondered if that had been a mistake. There had always been more important things to worry about—like keeping him alive.

But he didn't need her for that anymore.

"Here," Petra said, handing the small card with the manifest of names over to Tai. He took it with wide eyes, clearly shocked that she'd trust him with the responsibility. She was glad to be rid of it. "Make sure everyone is accounted for with registration. And clear the old logs before you—"

"Input the new values," he finished for her, grinning.

She frowned at him before adding, "And don't forget to—"

"Run a full debrief on the rescues and add the new intel to our database. I've got it, Petra."

A smile tugged at her lips. "Trust but verify."

He rolled his eyes. "I hate when you say that." But he was still smiling as he turned away to head for the tech quarters. "You guys coming?"

"Always," Linderly chirped. She hooked her arm together with Markes, pulling him along. "See ya, Petra!" she called over her shoulder.

"Don't linger—Finn will want a debrief from you two!" Petra

called across the snow, but they didn't acknowledge her, too busy laughing at something Markes said. Petra's mouth twisted. At least she liked the sister.

Petra sighed, shifting the weight of her pack again and heading for the lodge they'd commandeered as their headquarters. The sooner she updated Finn, the sooner she could sink into the steaming waters of the hot baths and melt the ache out of her muscles.

A flash of blond hair from across the road caught her eye and Petra froze. Megan appeared from behind one of the buildings, her hands wrapped around a woven basket overflowing with spare tech parts. She was dressed in the traditional garb of the mountain Reanges: fitted brown pants with sensible boots and a long overcoat of blue wool with embroidered trim. There were no skin-tight dresses or platformed heels for her here. A pelt draped over her shoulders, the golden fur a near match for Megan's platinum curls that fell against it.

She'd never been more beautiful.

As though she felt Petra's stare, Megan's eyes lifted, fair lashes fluttering over sky blue. Petra's fingers gripped the straps at her shoulders, her knuckles turning white. The air thickened in her lungs, making it harder to breathe than when she had climbed a mountain earlier that morning.

Megan turned away swiftly and the moment was gone before it had begun. She scurried toward the tech building where she spent most of her days. Petra didn't know why she had expected anything different from her, even for an instant. Whatever had been between them once was gone now. Ruined. Megan had been clear on that score.

Petra's eyes lifted to the clear sky above, watching her own breath curl into puffs against the azure sky. As she had done a thousand times before, she traced the daytime outlines of the three moons. They were almost full. Su'elben would be coming soon, when they'd celebrate their alignment at peak brightness. Even in this freezing town hidden in the mountains, in the snowy landscape that was the opposite of her beloved warm coastal home, the moons watched over them.

And despite everything, that had to be enough.

Finn held still as Dr. Vey positioned his face into the light from the window, her deft fingers cool along his jaw. He wondered what she saw as she looked over the freshly healed scar. Beyond a cursory acknowledgment in the mirror each morning, Finn didn't let himself linger on the mottled flesh that ran from the corner of his right eye down to his chin. It wasn't worth the consideration.

Once they'd found Dr. Vey and Dr. Brinstal in Milderion, it had been relatively easy to bring them back to Nos Lenti. That had been their first successful save after they'd set up operations in the mountains. The two doctors had taken over the medical residence in the village, but it didn't exactly offer state-of-the-art facilities. Any healers had abandoned this place years ago when the Federation began running raids. But the doctors did what they could with what they had, and that was more than most would be able to.

"You should let me use regenerative enzymes on this," Dr. Vey said gently, her eyes crinkling at the corners. Her fingers were gentle as they prodded the tender skin. "Linderly was able to find them in the city on your last run. We could reseal this wound and there would be no scar at all."

"I'm kind of used to it now." Finn shrugged. "Besides, I was getting tired of being all looks and no intrigue."

Her knowing smile made him uncomfortable. She grabbed a jar of salve from the metal cart beside her exam table and spread it over the raised flesh in a light layer.

The weekly check-ins were unnecessary. Finn had healed fully, even the busted ribs that had plagued him for months after their crash. But Finn knew Dr. Vey enjoyed having an excuse to see him.

If he was being honest, Finn enjoyed seeing her too. They weren't related by blood, but this woman was so similar to the Avery. The way she moved, her speech patterns . . . They were comforting. At least he had kept some part of the girl he loved this way.

Avery had made him feel like he wasn't alone in the universe. Like no matter what, he had someone who would always be on his side.

Until she wasn't. Until Qav betrayed her.

And now Finn was more alone than he had ever been.

Finn cleared his throat, stopping his brain before it ran away with him. "Besides, we should save the medicine. The trips into Milderion are getting more dangerous. Someone could actually need it."

"Hmm," she replied thoughtfully, sounding just like a disapproving grandmother. Or what Finn assumed one sounded like. He didn't have any family left, least of all grandparents. Not in this galaxy, at any rate.

Dr. Vey leaned back against the windowsill, studying Finn as he hopped off the table. She waved at the scars on his face. "What is this really about?"

"Not sure I follow." Finn kept his limbs moving, shrugging on his brown jacket. Adjusting his shirt. Running a hand through his hair.

"Don't be smart with me, Finn Lunitia. All that bravado may work with people your age, but with me it's just hot air." She waited for him to settle until he had no other option but to meet her gaze. "Keeping that scar . . . Are you punishing yourself?"

Finn inhaled, looking away. *Damn.* His gut constricted. No matter how much he did, no matter how much he tried to fill his days with momentum, it seemed he would he never fill the cavernous pit that had become the core of his being. One small misstep and it felt as though he would fall straight into it, losing himself in an endless plunge of terror.

Dr. Vey didn't speak, seemingly comfortable lying in wait amid the tense silence between them. Watching him. It was blazing unnerving.

"It's a reminder," he admitted. A reminder of what he'd lost. Of the mistakes he'd made. Of the things he should have done differently. Finn wouldn't repeat the past. But he sure as hell didn't want to talk about it, either.

"I don't blame you for what happened to Avery, Finn. And if I don't, then you shouldn't either."

Finn crossed his arms over his chest, studying the floor. He would take another scar on the other side of his face if it meant getting out of this conversation. But he couldn't exactly tell her that.

"She made her own choices," Dr. Vey continued gently. "And you did what was you felt was best at the time. The people here would have suffered a far worse fate without you." She let out a deep sigh, choosing her words carefully. "When you've lived as long as I have, you'll learn that we all have things we regret. Everyone has lessons they want to remember. Even if they don't carry the physical scars to prove it."

If anyone knew the pain of regret, it was this woman. She had only been able to save Avery from torture, experimentation, and death because she had been a part of that system in the first place. As one of the leading geneticists on Earth, Dr. Vey had been scouted for the Lares Project early on in her career. She had been a part of unspeakable atrocities.

And if what Finn learned from Nick was true, so had their father.

He hadn't allowed himself to think about the last things Nick had said to him in the Sanctum, about the claims he had made. That their father had been a leader of the Lares Project right along with Klein. Finn didn't want to believe it, even now. His father had been a good man. An honorable one, devoting his life to establishing peace between the two worlds. He had been the kind of man Finn always wanted to be.

And if his father *had* been a part of Lares, what did that say about his memory? Maybe it was all a lie. Maybe Nick was right after all.

Dr. Vey had never spoken about the secretive Federation program with Finn. She had been a part of it, too. But she had left, taking Avery with her to start a new life. She worked tirelessly beside Finn and the others to undo the damage she had wrought.

Avery had never blamed her grandmother. Finn even admired Dr. Vey. She had refused to leave Echo even when it meant death as a human under Leviathan's rule. Surely that was proof that people could redeem themselves.

Maybe his father had done so, before the end.

Finn's fingers dug into the thick fabric of his jacket, willing his thoughts to stop. He needed to leave.

A gong echoed through the village, the long peel weaving its way through the main street and into the small room. They both looked out the window.

"The others are back," Finn said shortly, some pressure alleviating in his chest. Thank the moons, he had an excuse to get out of there. He was already backing up toward the door.

"We're not done here," Dr. Vey said with a frown.

"Vitals fine. Scar treated." Finn held up a finger after each point, edging into the living area that served as the medic waiting room. "Sounds like we're done to me. Petra will be looking to debrief."

"Finn." Dr. Vey followed, leveling him with a harsh stare.

Lissande looked up from where she sat on the couch with her nose in a book, clearly trying to decide whether she wanted to interfere or extricate herself. The two women had done an elegant job making their shared home feel welcoming. They'd been able to find their place there.

Finn was already to the front door. "And you both probably need to make arrangements for intake evals. I'll check in later."

"Finn—"

He burst out into the bracing cold air that flooded his lungs, leaving the inviting warmth of the building and Dr. Vey's worried censure behind him.

CHAPTER EIGHTEEN

"Petra!" Finn ran carefully over the stones that lined the main street of the village. They might be charming, but the rocks tended to freeze over in new snowfall.

She paused and waited for him to catch up. Undoubtedly, she'd been heading to the lodge to find him.

"You look good. All parts accounted for," he said as he approached, his eyes running over her for any sign of injury. Her team had been out of reach for days. Even if signals could get past the stone foundations of the mountains—and that was a big *if*—they didn't maintain comms during missions. The risk of discovery was too great. "Where are the others?"

"Dealing with registration." She shifted her pack and kept walking.

"Good," Finn said. A group of children laughed from farther down the street, chasing one another in the snow. "They'll need to be able to handle everything alone soon enough. You and I can't keep holding their hands forever."

Still, Finn was surprised Petra was trusting the younger ones with the responsibility. She was borderline obsessive over the missions she led. Not that it was surprising. Petra was Petra, and she liked control.

They reached the lodge and she pushed open one of the heavy doors that arched high over its entrance. A wall of heat greeted them as they entered, their footfalls swallowed by the high ceilings. Thankfully, the cold couldn't penetrate the thick windows that lined either side of the gathering space. The arching glass offered a stunning view of the white-capped mountains that shrouded Nos Lenti. Petra dropped her pack heavily to the floor.

"How did it go?" Finn followed her to the long table that dominated the hall.

"No surprises." Petra shrugged out of her heavy coat and tossed it on the back of a chair. "You didn't greet the new arrivals."

He shrugged. Explaining that Dr. Vey had tried to pull an emotional reckoning from him would serve exactly zero purpose. Finn didn't need one more person analyzing his choices. Petra least of all.

She let it go, moving to the spread of nitchus laid out at the far end of the table where small plates had been prepared for a midday meal. Finn didn't have an appetite after Dr. Vey's inquisition. He took a seat instead.

"The humans will be disappointed," Petra said, setting her plate piled high with food at the seat across from him. She settled, taking a few bites before adding, "They wanted to meet the Shadow."

That did tease a grin out of him, the red scar across his cheek stretching tautly. "Well, they already did. You're the Shadow as much as me. We all are."

"Not according to Leviathan," Petra countered. "Your face is plastered on every vid screen in the city."

So Leviathan's propaganda was getting worse. The notoriety was one of the reasons Finn was effectively caged in Nos Lenti while the others continued their runs to the capitol. The Origin Council had found a perfect scapegoat in Finn, the face of the resistance—against them and against Leviathan. But it had been the people themselves who called him the Shadow. Leviathan couldn't have been happy about the sensationalism.

Finn had hoped the fervor surrounding his image might have lessened since their last mission. He wanted to *move* again—to do something other than sit around the village and wait. That was exactly what had trapped him once, when Nick had controlled his entire life. It was the whole reason Finn had gone to Earth and found Avery in the first place. He was no use to anyone unless he was in action.

"At least this finally has a purpose," Finn drawled, gesturing to the mottled skin running down his face. He didn't exactly resemble the image the Origin was using of him. "Besides, the notoriety is good. The more humans that know about us, the more we can help. And there are more Reanges sympathetic to our cause than we thought. Leviathan's reach can extend only so far."

"That we know of. Which still isn't much."

Finn couldn't deny that. Leviathan was virtually untouchable to them. She kept to the Council quarters and never exposed herself publicly. Even if she did, they'd have little hope of reaching her. Leviathan had complete control of those around her, and influence over most of the city.

They all preferred those early days of complete invisibility. The Origin Council had assumed their entire crew had died in the aftermath of the Gate destruction. Things had been smoother before Leviathan started noticing their movements. Less dangerous, at least.

"You should still keep a low profile," Petra advised. "Patrols were out in force on the streets. They're scanning for wristport documentation at every block after curfew."

Finn frowned, crossing his arms. "Curfew?"

"She's getting desperate."

"To find us?"

Petra nodded.

They had expected this, but Finn assumed they'd have more time. He *needed* more time. More freedom. The alternative was unacceptable enough that he shoved it into the dim recesses of his mind.

But he couldn't deny the truth—it would only get worse from here.

Finn let out a slow breath and focused on the beauty of the snowy peaks framed by frosted glass. The midday sun cast shadows between each crest, carving out jagged slashes of blue against the rock. At least he'd been building a backup plan. He wouldn't stay cooped up in this village forever, useless and wallowing in the hell that had become his mind.

"There's more," Petra said dismally. "The Council is dividing up assets in the city."

"Is that surprising? They weren't going to let those buildings sit empty."

"They're delegating properties according to So' lineage. We saw an advertisement to register for heritage rights verification."

Finn squinted. "Pretend you're talking to someone who has no idea what that means."

"They're establishing a hierarchy for social resources," Petra replied flatly. "Anyone with a So' in their family line will be granted premium properties."

"What?!"

Both Petra and Finn turned toward the shrieked exclamation from the other side of the room.

"But that's sacrilegious!" Bedria popped up from behind a high-backed chair that sat near the fireplace, looking disgruntled.

"How long have you been there?" Petra grumbled.

"A better question is how long has she been awake?" Finn chuckled. The older woman often snoozed in the great hall beside the cozy holofire.

After leaving the Sanctum with them, Bedria had settled her sister Brehna in their hometown on the coast. But the holy woman had chosen to join their cause in the mountains. She was helpful sometimes. Intrusive always.

"The power of the So' is not a directive for status." Bedria's spiraling dark hair bounced as she shook her head in disapproval, the mass barely tamed by a swath of deep emerald fabric.

A quick squeak preceded her pet's appearance on her shoulder. The squirrel sported a green vest that matched Bedria's wrap. Raki chirped agitatedly, clearly pissed to have been woken from his own nap.

"We're aware of your feelings about the So'Reanges, Bedria." Finn ran a hand through his hair. "If Leviathan is setting up this precedence, then we have to assume she's done waiting."

"We knew this would happen," Petra pointed out. "That she would search for more So'Reanges eventually."

Finn nodded. "But I'm surprised she's trying so soon. She can't control other So' the way she can everyone else."

"Even *that* shouldn't be possible," Bedria said with a tsk. "That woman is old, even older than me. Her powers should become more limited as she ages, not expanding. To influence that many Reanges on such a mass scale? Even Qav himself couldn't pull that off for such a sustained amount of time. It's unnatural."

Finn stiffened at *his* name, turning away. His teeth clenched as he gripped his hands behind his back. He focused on the way the snow sparkled in the sunlight. Anything to distract him.

But Bedria continued, "As much as that boy plagued me, Qav was the most gifted So' I've ever seen. At least when it came to mind infiltration. Of course, nothing could compare to Avery's gifts. But it was remarkable, considering his upbringing and how he—"

"Enough, woman. Stop your babbling," Petra interjected.

Finn could have kissed her. Or something less revolting. Something less likely to get him knocked out.

The door burst open on a wave of cold air and laughter, dispelling the tense energy that had settled over them. Markes and Tai were wrestling as Linderly begged them to stop, giggling uncontrollably all the while. Megan was the last to enter, smiling softly behind them.

Finn glanced at Petra. He wondered if they'd spoken since Petra's arrival.

Not that Megan went out of her way to make time for Petra. Pretty much the exact opposite. Ever since Megan had woken from her coma, she had changed. As Finn had worried, dragging Megan away from her home world, away from everything she had ever known, had been difficult for her. Petra had insisted on bringing Megan, true. But Finn hadn't stopped her.

Petra's eyes tracked Megan's every move, following her to the table along with the others. They laughed, grabbing plates and food and taking seats. Megan avoided the spread, walking around to Finn's side. He wished she wouldn't. Petra's jealousy speared through him like blastfire.

"I finished the systems layout on the capitol building. Cut through their security like butter," Megan said brightly. If there was one thing that lit her up, it was talking tech. And she had more opportunity to do that in this new life than she ever had back on Earth. "I don't think they expect much interference—their safeguards were laughable."

"Ah, the blessing of lazy security engineering," Finn crooned. He took the tablet Megan held up for him, looking over the schematics as they returned to table. He sat and threw Megan's work up onto a holoprojection. The map of the capitol building hovered between the plates of food, its passages and entries glowing a translucent blue.

"You got in!" Markes said happily around a mouthful of food. "We should make a Su'elben drop, no problem."

"Drop? On what?" Petra asked slowly.

"The capitol," Markes replied earnestly, oblivious to Petra's sudden rigidity.

Finn nearly slapped the kid on the back of his thick skull. He had intended to approach the topic with Petra on equal footing. So much for that plan.

"Why would we *drop in* on the capitol?" Petra aimed the question at Finn.

But Markes answered. "We've been planning a raid—Finn's tired of waiting for more information on Leviathan. So we're going in to get it directly."

Petra held Finn's gaze. "Su'elben is next week."

"Exactly." Finn couldn't back down. There was no way but forward with her. And there was no way he'd change a perfectly good plan that would get him back into the field. "There won't be a sober Reange left in the city on the holiday. It's perfect."

"We agreed to keep pulling out humans for at least another year. Stay under the radar. I literally just explained to you why that's more important than ever."

"Liberating the humans is working, but it's not fast enough," Finn countered. "You also just explained to me that things are escalating in the city. We have to get Leviathan out of there before she runs Echo down a path that it can't come back from."

"Why was this even a discussion without me here? You think because I was on a mission for a few days that you get to make all the decisions now?" Petra shoved her chair back to stand. She braced her hands on the table, leaning into him. "'The Shadow is all of us.' I guess that was just a load of shit."

"No. *All of us* agreed to bring her down." Finn tapped a single finger on the table in front of him. "This is how we do that."

Megan leaned forward, closer to Finn. "It wasn't a last minute decision, Petra."

Moons above, nobody was helping him with this one. Megan's move was more likely to get Finn shot than Petra to agree with him.

"We've been working on this for a solid week and a half, and Finn has gone through the scenarios for twice that amount of time," Megan added.

"Too bad Finn isn't in charge here. This isn't a dictatorship." Petra's fingers turned white as she leaned into the table. "And Avery is gone."

Finn flinched, the words striking him as painfully as any blow. She got her hit in, after all.

"And whose fault is that?" Megan hissed, standing. "You just left her there. *You*, who claimed to love her more than any of us—you just abandoned her."

"Megan," Finn said weakly. He grabbed her arm. The accusation wasn't fair. If anybody should be blamed, it was Finn.

He had left Avery. *He had left her.*

And it had broken him.

Megan shook Finn off, narrowing in on Petra. "At least Finn is following through with Avery's wishes. At least he believes in a world where we can live side by side."

Petra balked. "And what exactly do you think I'm doing here?"

"I don't know! Nobody here knows! You hate humans, Petra, you always have, and the bizarre thing is that I'm *one of them*. I don't even know why you bothered to drag me along with you to this stupid planet."

"You wanted me to leave you there?" Petra laughed maniacally. "She would have killed you, Megan! Avery would have killed you."

"You're wrong," Megan bit out, tears filling her eyes.

Anguish clawed up Finn's stomach, making him nauseous. He put a lot of effort into not thinking about this. Keeping the guilt at bay took all the effort he could scrounge together.

"We all saw it. We all saw her at the end!" Petra gestured wildly to the rest of the table.

Finn closed his eyes at the image that surged from his memory unbidden. Avery's bloodied face, her cheeks wet with tears, her beautiful golden eyes filled with confusion. The way she'd tried to listen to him. The way she'd tried to fight Qav's control.

It hadn't been enough. In the end, Finn hadn't been enough.

And when Petra spoke again, Finn hardly recognized her voice. "Avery would have finished you off, and I would have had to pick up the fucking pieces."

Finn wasn't the only one broken from that day. They all bore scars, as painful as the one burned across his face.

Megan lifted her chin, a tear escaping. Her next words were low. Lethal. "You're wrong, Petra. And if you think she would have, then you didn't know Avery at all."

A scream pierced through the thick windows, jarring them all. Adrenaline spiked through Finn, blissful and acute, removing any trace of the grief that had surfaced. The gong echoed loudly, one long peal after another, three in succession.

It only meant one thing: intruders through the archway.

Finn vaulted over the table, sparing a glance out the window. People scrambled across the village center, running for the shelter of their homes. They had a protocol, and they were sticking to the drills. He pulled the blaster from the holster at his thigh. He clenched the cold metal, its familiarity almost soothing.

Petra was on his heels as he pressed out into the snow. Maybe Finn wouldn't have to go looking for action—it had come looking for him.

And as he ran toward the fight, Finn was ashamed of his own truth. That despite the danger, despite the imminent threat to everything they had built, he felt more alive in that moment than he had in weeks.

CHAPTER NINETEEN

Petra slid behind the barricade beside Finn at the edge of the village. Markes tore open the container of long-range weapons, throwing scopes and guns to Tai and Linderly.

When he held one out to Megan, Petra grabbed her arm. "Get back to the lodge. This is no place for you."

"Not on your life." Megan jerked away. She took the sniper and knelt expertly in the snow, adjusting the viewfinder. When had she learned how to handle a weapon?

"Petra," Finn called her name tightly, handing her his zoom lens.

There wasn't time to deal with Megan's preconceived ideas of her usefulness in battle.

Petra moved to the front with Finn, holding up the clear tablet and zooming in. A group of six stood immobile just beyond the arching stone boundary at the top of the hill. They wore light layers, not suited for the harsh conditions. One stepped forward out of the pack, walking into range.

"I can take him." Megan's voice was hard. Bravado more than anything else. She'd certainly never killed anyone before. But Megan had always been a warrior whether or not she'd ever seen battle.

"Hold," Petra ordered. She zoomed the image in closer.

Their leader was a large man in his forties. His skin was dark, his hair cropped close to his scalp. Petra knew his face.

He nodded once, like he knew Petra was watching him. His hand lifted. A shredded scrap of white fabric fluttered in the cold mountain wind.

"Is that Krez?" Finn's question rocked Petra.

It *was* him. Petra's fingers enclosed around the lens, her muscles tensing.

Krez. Once part of their inner circle but now a pawn trapped in Leviathan's web. He had attacked Avery in Milderion when he should have protected her. It didn't matter to Petra that he'd been controlled. He should have tried harder to resist that old woman's grasp. Petra would have.

Leviathan had used them all. Petra. Krez. Even Markes and Linderly. The old So' had groomed Petra herself during her time in the Origin. She had bent Petra to her ideals. The extremist group had offered sanctuary under the price of unquestioning loyalty. Only Avery had been able to break Petra free of it. Only Avery could.

But Krez had been the first to force Avery down the path that had brought them to this reality. Separated. Alone. Broken.

He must have tracked Petra's group this morning. Her hand went to her blaster, guilt sinking into her gut. She hadn't been careful enough. Her stupidity had led Leviathan's dog straight to them.

But how could Krez show his face to them after all this time? The cold metal of her weapon bit into her skin. After what he had done . . .

Petra vaulted over the barrier, taking aim even though she knew it would never find its target across the four hundred meters of frozen ground.

"Petra, no!" Finn yelled.

She fired anyway. Three shots, one after the other. The charged energy burned holes into the snow near his feet.

Petra almost smiled. Her aim was better than she thought. The surge of rage dissipated enough that she lowered her blaster. Krez was holding a white flag of surrender. She wouldn't kill someone asking for peace, no matter how much she blamed him.

"I can't see Leviathan sending him up here with a crew of five and a plea for truce." Finn jumped over the boundary to join her.

"You think she doesn't know?"

"One way to find out," Finn said with a shrug. He cupped a hand to his mouth to shout, "Are you coming down here, or do you want to wait for Petra to shoot at you again?"

Krez turned to speak to his group, handing them the gun he carried on his belt before marching alone down the stone pathway.

"I wasn't sure you'd even let me get that far, if I'm honest," Krez said as he approached, his low voice raspy with disuse. Deep circles pooled under his eyes. Wrinkles dominated his brow. He'd aged years since they'd left him, as though he carried every one of his four decades on his shoulders.

"You trailed me from the city," Petra accused, angrier with herself for the negligence.

His brown eyes met hers. They were clear. Familiar. "I taught you how to cover your tracks, Petra. You still falter in the same ways now that you did at fourteen."

A flush crawled up her cheeks, embarrassment flooding her like it had as a child. The same unchecked anger followed.

Finn stepped in front of her. "What are you doing here, Krez? Kissing Leviathan's ass not doing the same thing for you anymore?"

"I was sent on assignment away from Milderion." He looked back and forth between them. "Away from Leviathan."

Finn frowned. "Is that supposed to mean something?"

"I thought you knew by now." Krez paused, shaking his head. "The farther we are from her, the more her control fades."

"Awfully convenient."

"Convenient or not, it's the truth."

Petra curled her lip. "And we're supposed to believe you just had a change of heart? That you turned your back on the Origin when you were one of its founding members?"

Krez didn't shy away from Petra's direct stare. "You were part of the Origin, the same as me. And those two." He nodded to Markes and Linderly behind the rocks. "We all were there for our own reasons. Mine was Fiora. And after she . . . I made a choice, the same as all of you. I followed Avery."

"Yeah? Well, she's not here."

"I'm aware." Krez let silence stretch as he held Petra's gaze. It was strange to see him again, a blend of relief and longing. Like wishing for something that could no longer exist. "Then why are you all still fighting?"

Finn said nothing. He would let Petra make the call. A part of her wanted to believe Krez. He had meant something to her once. In many ways, they were similar. They always had been.

"Who are they?" Petra nodded up at the group waiting at the arch.

"Defectors. Like me. They want a future for Echo different from the one Leviathan is molding. It just took some distance from her control to figure that out."

"Reanges?"

"Four of them. One human."

Petra looked to Finn again. He quirked his mouth, as good a sign as any. They would have to figure out what to do with the group one way or another.

"Fine." Petra holstered her gun on her thigh. "But you'll be under guard detail until we can figure out what to do with you. I won't insult you by asking if your wristports are still active, but someone will be by to scramble them anyway."

"Markes. Tai," Finn called over his shoulder.

The two were at his side in an instant. Linderly and Megan kept their weapons trained on their targets.

"Escort Krez and the rest of his group to the empty two story by the cliffside. Stand detail until you're relieved."

Krez's shoulders relaxed and he raised a hand toward his companions. The three that had been carrying weapons laid them to the ground. The rest made their way down.

Finn and Petra watched as they passed. Smiles and thank-yous were thrown their way with small bows and nods. Their behavior supported Krez's story. But why would Leviathan have sent Krez away? If she knew her hold on him would lesson, what would be the point?

"He seems in earnest." Linderly was the first to speak, slinging the large gun over her petite shoulder.

"Petra would know better than the rest of us," Finn pointed out, looking to Petra. "Did he sound like himself?"

"It's hard to tell. He never was big on talking," Petra conceded.

Finn snorted. "No wonder he liked you, then."

Petra grinned, the gesture fading as she noticed Megan was watching her. Shivers broke out on Petra's exposed arms. She had left her jacket in the lodge.

"We'll need to make a decision quickly," Megan said. "If we decide they can't stay, they're a liability."

Petra watched Krez walk away, escorted on front and back by Markes and Tai. Some of the residents had grown curious enough to peek out of their doors.

"Someone will need to address the town. This is going to put everyone on edge."

"I'll talk with Perthos. He and Dr. Vey should be the ones to speak," Finn said.

Perthos was Nova's father, the de facto leader of Nos Lenti for the past decade. He'd taken on the role when so many had abandoned the village in the war. And Dr. Vey was a natural source of comfort for the humans she treated. It was a sound suggestion.

"Once we calm everyone down, let's convene to discuss." Finn stared pointedly at Petra. "We make the choice together."

Petra nodded, flexing her muscles in an attempt to warm them. The Origin forces had been unable to find them in at least of a year of searching. Krez had most likely in charge of those efforts.

As far as they knew, Krez had been appointed to Leviathan's inner guard. She knew his connection to Petra. She would also know of his loyalty to Avery. It seemed unlikely Leviathan would risk losing such an important pawn.

If Krez was telling the truth, he would be an invaluable asset. It would be stupid not to at least consider speaking with him further. And Petra would be the one expected to do the talking.

Golden fur hit her in the face and Petra flinched, her cold fingers digging into the silken pelt before she clutched it to her chest. Megan was already walking away, her shoulders only covered by the deep blue of her coat. Petra stared, wide-eyed, throat dry.

"Nice, blueberry," Finn whispered. "Real nice."

Petra spun on her toes, giving him a hard shove. "Shut up, Lunitia."

She was glad to hear him use the annoying nickname, even if she hated it. Glad to see his smile infused with something other than artifice.

If Krez really was here to join them, if he really had been able to free himself from Leviathan's grasp, then maybe there was more hope than they thought. It was difficult to open herself to the possibility. But not impossible.

Petra shrugged the still-warm fur over her shoulders, ignoring the curl of pleasure in her belly. Finn was still smiling at her. She desperately needed to change the subject.

She cleared her throat. "I wasn't going to shoot him. I was just letting off steam."

"With you, Petra, I never know. I'm just glad you're on our side." Finn shook his head, laughing again in that way that didn't quite reach his eyes. The genuine humor from moments before had been fleeting.

Petra knew what everyone thought about her. That she was a stuck-up bitch who hated every human she came across. But they were wrong—Megan was wrong.

Petra couldn't explain when or how the shift had happened, but she had changed irrevocably in the past year. The truth was that two of the people she cared most about in this world were humans, and Petra would fight beside them.

Megan had accused Petra of giving up on Avery. Of leaving her when she needed them most. Maybe they had. But that decision couldn't be undone no matter how much they wished it could.

Petra had learned her lesson and she would never repeat it. She wouldn't give up on anyone she loved. Not ever again.

CHAPTER TWENTY

Perthos and his wife, Naileve, had been waiting for Finn when he walked through the door of their home. Perthos was ready to speak the town, eager to offer his support.

Nova's parents had been a great help to them since they arrived. They hadn't hesitated to offer sanctuary, even after Finn had told them about Nova. And Grigg . . . He had been like an adopted son to them. And Finn's brother had killed him. Telling Nova's parents of his death . . . It was a shame that Finn would carry forever.

Finn tucked his chin into his jacket as the wind picked up. The gathering of residents was already dissipating as the excitement began to wear down. Finn hoped that the choice to let Krez stay wouldn't be a mistake.

"That went well, all things considering."

Megan had crept up on him while he was lost in thought. Dr. Vey was with her, their arms tucked against each other in the cold. At least Megan had been able to keep some small part of home.

"One word from Perthos and all the feathers settle," Finn said. "He knows how to work a crowd."

"So do you," Megan said as she leaned further into Dr. Vey's warmth. "Or did you forget that you were once the heartthrob of two worlds?"

Finn laughed awkwardly. "I do my best to forget that entirely."

"You do have charisma, Finn," Dr. Vey said, gray brows drawn low over steel eyes. She had a constant intensity that never seemed to abate. "The people here trust you—you would make an excellent leader."

Finn kept his thoughts to himself. He disagreed. He'd never been good at the diplomacy. That had been Nick's domain, and their father's before him.

Drawing attention, sure, Finn was skilled at that trick. But it wasn't what they needed now. In fact, it was the very thing holding him back.

Finn cleared his throat, shifting to start the walk to the lodge where the others would be waiting.

Dr. Vey took pity on him and changed the subject. "I finished the physicals on Krez and his group. A few minimal cases of frostbite, but nothing serious. I'm surprised they took off into the Northern Mountains without proper gear. Irresponsible."

"Well, there's one element that corroborates Krez's story," Finn observed. "If they were on the run, they wouldn't have the time or resources to supply themselves."

"And their wristports were deactivated, so that alleviates another worry," Megan added. "Nobody would have tracked them."

"At least we know he's not stupid," Finn said. "Did you get any other information? Maybe I should talk with him before—"

"I think he's telling the truth," Dr. Vey said suddenly, growing pensive. "I barely know him, and yet . . . he apologized to me. He got on his knees and asked forgiveness."

"Apologized? For what?" Finn paused to open the lodge door, holding it for them. He could hear the others inside, laughter floating out along with the inviting heat.

Dr. Vey gave Megan a soft pat on the hand. "Megan, would you give us a few minutes?"

"Oh—of course," Megan replied clumsily. Her eyes met Finn's before flickering away, not enough time for him to implore her to stay as he let the door close. She backed away toward the square. "I need to check in with Lind to get these records archived before we meet with the others anyway."

Finn resisted the urge to kick the snow at his feet, forcing himself instead to meet Dr. Vey's stare. She was stern, yes, but there was warmth there, too. Like steel that had just begun to melt. She was strong in a way that Finn was unused to. Avery had much of that same immovability.

"Why do I feel like I'm in trouble?" Finn asked with a soft chuckle.

Her eyes shifted, like she could see straight through him. "Why do *you* think Krez apologized?"

Finn's hands clenched into fists.

Dr. Vey continued, "He seems to think what happened to Avery was his fault."

"Get in line." Finn tried to laugh. It came out as an embarrassing croak.

"We didn't finish our conversation earlier," she said gently. A couple passed by and she smiled at them, nodding. She pulled the black collar of her coat closer. "You ran out of there before I had a chance to say this to you."

Finn ran a nervous hand through his hair and shook his head. He'd *wanted* to leave that conversation unfinished. "You really don't have to—"

"You are so much like her." Dr. Vey's eyes turned glassy and she looked up at the late-afternoon sky above them that was turning orange in the light. "Not willing to listen to a single thing I have to say, even when it's important."

Finn went silent at that, his jaw locking. It was the last thing he'd have expected her to say. It was the one thing that could have knocked the breath from him.

Dr. Vey braced her shoulders, letting out a short breath, all trace of sentimentality gone. "You have questions that you haven't asked me. And after all this time, I owe you answers."

"You owed Avery answers, not me." Finn was surprised he didn't stumble over her name.

But Dr. Vey was right—Finn did have questions. They had been burning a hole in his chest ever since they got her and Lissande out of the city.

"I can't offer them to her now. She would want me to give them to you."

If Finn opened that door, he wasn't sure he'd be able to close it. After what Nick had revealed to him, after everything he'd gone through . . . Finn wasn't sure there was any part of his soul left. Would learning the truth about his father really change anything?

It wouldn't bring Avery back.

But hiding from the truth wouldn't help him, either. If he faced the reality of what his father had done—of who he had been—then it could prevent Finn from making the same mistakes.

He shoved his hands into his jacket, clearing his throat. "Did you know my father?"

"Yes," she answered without missing a beat. The smile that followed was soft, a ghost at the corner of her mouth. "And you look every bit like he did when we were young."

"So it's true, then?" Finn asked on the end of a breath. Something loosened inside of him, his shoulders slackening. "My father *was* a part of Lares."

Dr. Vey nodded, watching him closely. "When the project was started, they only had good intentions. We only wanted to understand the Reange powers, not exploit them. I wouldn't have signed on if I thought it would cause lasting harm. And I don't think your father would have, either. By the time I realized what they were doing to the Reange subjects . . . How they were acquiring them . . . disposing of them . . ." She lifted her chin to the sky again, staring out at the crests of the mountains beyond the angled rooftops. She was quiet for some time. "I was in too deep. And your father . . . He was already drowning."

Finn stared at the ground. It was packed down with weeks of snowfall, stained brown by dirt and grime. He hardened himself against her revelation.

"I'm not making excuses for what we did," she added. "But for me . . . I couldn't get out until I had to. Until they shoved a baby in my arms and told me to experiment on her. And I couldn't. She was worth the risk, so I ran."

Finn knew the rest.

Dr. Vey had escaped with the child, concealing Avery's identity with gen mods to mask her as human since infancy. Such modifications should have been impossible, but Dr. Vey was known for beating the odds of science. It was the entire reason she'd been recruited in the first place.

"I imagine it was the same for your father," she continued. "If I remember correctly, he became ambassador not long after your brother was born. When faced with that kind of innocence, that kind of responsibility over another life. Your priorities evolve."

Finn focused on the biting cold that numbed his fingers, hoping the sensation would stave off the pressure building beneath his ribs.

His father had been perfect in Finn's eyes. To acknowledge his dimensions was to see him as something other than a paragon of justice. Maybe Finn's mother had known, too. Had his parents lied to him his entire life? And what about Nick—when had he discovered the truth?

Finn may have idolized their father, but Nick had been the one to *become* him. He had walked in his footsteps. It would have broken him to realize everything he had become was based on a lie. To face that reality alone.

No wonder Nick had treated Finn like a child for so long. For all intents and purposes, he had *been* a child.

Finn could almost understand why Nick had betrayed them. Almost.

But none of it mattered now. Finn's parents were gone. Nick was gone, still somewhere on the other side of the universe. With Avery.

If Nick chose to go after her again, Finn wouldn't be able to stop him this time. And Nick had become . . . He didn't know what. A glorified attack bot for Klein. An experiment.

His brother was gone.

"Thank you for telling me," Finn said. "I know it's not easy for you."

She gave him a warm smile, her gloved hand coming to rest on his arm, squeezing him gently. "Does that mean you'll consider the enzymes?"

Finn let out a surprised laugh. "All this to get me to heal the scar? Doc, if you missed my pretty face, all you had to do was say so."

The door opened before she could reply. Petra's face was hard as she gripped the door. "Get in here. You need to see this."

Finn heard Leviathan's voice before he saw the holocast on the long table. The others watched silently. Markes looked up briefly as Finn approached.

It was a broadcast. A red band ran along its base indicating that the feed was live. Leviathan was sending out a mass communication to Echo in real time.

The old So' stood at a podium beneath the archways of the capitol building in Milderion, her cane gripped by her thin fingers. Despite the deepening wrinkles that pulled at her face, Leviathan looked stronger than Finn had ever seen her. Even though she held her cane, she didn't lean on it. Her back was straight, her head held high as she spoke.

"*. . . must bring an end to this injustice. The outrageous behavior of a single human cannot stand against the power and connections of the Reange people. We have defeated the humans once before, driving them off our planet back from where they came, and we cannot allow a single seed of their insurrection to be sewn on our fertile grounds again. This man.*" A picture appeared on the feed by her face.

It was Finn. Dressed in a suit and smiling confidently at the cam. They had used his official picture as ambassador, taken years ago. Presumably the same one they'd been spreading throughout the city.

"*Finnegan Lunitia, once known as a friend to Echo. He called himself an ambassador, but chose to stand against us. He took one of our own, a beloved and sacred So'Reange, and stranded her on another planet in an attempt to cripple us. In an attempt to subdue our power.*"

Finn's throat dried. He could feel Dr. Vey's eyes on him as the air grew hot.

"*He has now taken up arms to steal human servants who are working off their life debt to good honest Reange households, convening them to who knows what end. If he is amassing a human force to stand against us, you can rest easy knowing that the Elder Council and I are doing every-*

thing in our power to prevent these clandestine activities."

The door burst open and Megan entered on a wave of freezing air, Linderly close on her heels. She was breathing heavily, her pale face flushed. They'd ran there from the tech quarters.

"You've seen it," Megan said, panting, her shoulders heaving as she watched with wide eyes. Linderly closed the door behind them and moved to Megan's side.

Leviathan continued, "*Which is why I've suggested a special order to bring this miscreant to justice that has been approved by the Council via unanimous vote. Next week, during our celebration of Su'elben, Finn Lunitia will turn himself in for punishment as dictated by the Council.*"

Megan snorted as she walked up to the table. Petra looked at her sternly, not sharing in the humor. The others were stoic. Even Dr. Vey didn't say a word beside him.

"*If he refuses to relinquish himself to the proper authorities, it is my great regret to inform you that we will choose, by random lottery, eleven humans to be executed in his place. For each subsequent day that passes without his surrender, another human will be selected for execution.*"

A surge of nausea gurgled up Finn's throat.

"She can't mean it," Megan said, her voice barely above a whisper. Linderly grabbed her hand.

"Leviathan always means what she threatens," Petra stated.

Finn's eyes were focused on the broadcast, unable to even blink.

"*The life humans now enjoy on Echo has been gifted by the Elder Council. Their pardoning was a mercy that they would do well not to forget. Su'elben is a time to honor sacrifices, and we will do so. This is a reminder: what is given can also be taken away.*"

Leviathan paused to look directly into the cam. Finn knew that whatever she was going to say next was meant for him. She wanted him to see her, to hear her.

"*He will answer for his crimes, or they will answer for him.*"

CHAPTER
TWENTY-ONE

"Absolutely not. You're not doing this."

Finn leaned back as Megan slammed her hand on the table. "I don't really see how I have much of a choice."

Petra shoved her chair back and grabbed her coat. She said nothing as she jogged for the door and left.

"Where are you going?" Megan yelled after her, but Petra was already gone.

"Petra does what she does, and we're all just in her way," Finn said dramatically. "Don't take it to heart."

"I wouldn't dream of it," Megan replied stiffly. Whatever emotion crossed her face was gone in a moment, expertly hidden beneath the surface. "Leviathan is bluffing. Killing all those people would be a PR nightmare when the Council has made such a fuss over the pacifist ideals of their new society."

Markes nodded in agreement. "That *is* why Leviathan pardoned the humans in the first place."

"Even if she is bluffing," Linderly said quietly, "are we willing to risk playing that kind of game?"

"No," Finn answered firmly. "I'm not going to sit out here and hide while more innocents die. I'd rather take my chances in custody."

Markes leaned forward. "You won't be in custody. You'll be dead."

"That's not very helpful, Markes," Dr. Vey scolded from her place between Megan and Lissande. Her hands were threaded together beneath her chin. She was always careful to speak, more prone to observation, never pushing them in one way or the other.

"Why isn't it helpful? It's the truth," Megan refuted. "If Finn wants to surrender to Leviathan, then he needs to know what's going to happen."

Finn laughed. "I know what's going to happen. I'm just not that concerned about the eventuality."

"What?" Megan jerked at the question, like Finn had slapped her. Her blue eyes were fixed on him, glistening in the soft light. "What did you just say?"

Finn had made his decision already. Nothing Megan could do or say would sway him. But she would be the hardest to convince. After she'd recovered from her injuries, Megan had found a new purpose alongside their team. She had blended in seamlessly, and her vast tech expertise had made her a true asset alongside Linderly.

But beyond her utility, Megan was an exceptional friend. She was loyal and honest. Laughter came easily to her, even after everything she had endured and lost. It was not hard to see why Avery loved her.

Megan would never just let Finn waltz into the capitol to die. To be fair, the others wouldn't, either. Even Petra.

He closed his eyes, preparing for the battle. "I said I'm not concern—"

"It was a rhetorical question. I'm starting to understand why Petra finds you so irritating," Megan hissed. Her eyes slid to Tai. "Why the blazar did she leave? What could be more important than this conversation?"

"I've never claimed to understand my sister's choices." Tai gave her an apologetic shrug.

"Are any of us surprised? I'm not exactly her favorite person," Finn drawled. "She's probably plotting how to get more from a trade with Leviathan."

"Don't insult her," Tai warned, his hands fisting on the table.

Linderly sat up, looking quickly between them. "He didn't mean it, Tai."

"Easy, kid. It's just a joke," Finn waved a hand. "Ever heard of cutting the tension with humor? It's kind of my thing."

"You mean it's kind of your coping mechanism," Megan muttered.

"If it ain't broke." Finn cocked his head with a shrug. The propensity for analyzing his choices seemed to be spreading. First Dr. Vey and now Megan. He'd have to work on improving his deflection.

Megan rolled her eyes. "Can we just focus, please? This came from nowhere—something must have triggered Leviathan. We've been liberating humans for months."

"And we've barely made a dent in the number of those still indentured," Linderly added.

"Exactly. We're a nominal threat at best," Megan agreed. "Which begs the question: Why now?"

Finn tilted his head back as they debated. There were cobwebs in the corners of the arching rafters, like it hadn't been cleaned in decades.

"At least this proves Krez wasn't lying," Markes reasoned. "Leviathan wouldn't need to threaten Finn if she had a mole in our camp."

Tai shifted in his seat. "What I don't understand is how Krez freed himself so quickly. When she controlled my mind, not even dragging me to Earth helped."

Megan looked to Lissande who sat quietly beside Dr. Vey. "What's your opinion, Lissande?" As the only Reange doctor with experience treating So', she was the best resource they had on how their powers functioned.

"I would imagine that whatever Leviathan has been doing is costing her," Lissande said quietly. "Even if we didn't have laws against such things, the powers of the So' are limited, and for good reason. They are not meant to be used on such a mass scale, and certainly not for an extended period like this. And at her age . . ."

"You think her power is waning?" Linderly asked hopefully.

"There's no way to know for certain," Lissande clarified. "Not without more information on how she amplified her power in the first place."

"It's reprehensible," Bedria tutted from the end of the table. Finn had forgotten she was still in the room. She had a way of lingering. "This isn't the way So' are meant to wield their power, and Leviathan well knows it. To think of desecrating a sacred rite in this way—even the suggestion of it makes me ill."

"Ultimately, we don't have enough information to make an educated guess on how her power functions," Lissande concluded.

"So we're back to square one. I'm turning myself in." Finn held up a hand to stop Megan before she protested. "At least we can make this an opportunity to continue with our original plan. There's nothing more distracting than an exhibitionist execution of yours truly."

Megan glowered. "I swear to God, Finn, if you bring up turning yourself in one more—"

The front door swung open and Petra strode in, snow clinging to her dark blue hair. Krez followed her.

His eyes moved swiftly around the room, marking those present and any points of entry. Krez had always been the most vigilant of anyone in Avery's crew. At least time with Leviathan hadn't stripped him of his training. He would be a valuable addition to the team when Finn was gone.

"Nice of you to join us," Megan snapped.

"And you brought a friend." Finn waited for Petra's eyes to meet his before raising a brow.

"We need answers," Petra said simply. She reclaimed her seat at the enormous table beside her brother and looked up at Krez. "Sit."

He complied, taking the place next to her.

"And you said we'd never use a table this long," Finn quipped. At least Markes snickered.

Petra tilted her head. "I thought I'd avoided the entertainment hour of this discussion."

"There's a time limit?"

Her green eyes narrowed and she moved on. "Leviathan feels cornered. We need to know why."

"And since you brought a yet-to-be-cleared prisoner to our meeting, I'm assuming you think Krez knows the reason?"

"I think Krez *is* the reason." Petra smiled tightly, looking to the large man beside her. His face was stoic, betraying nothing. "And he's going to tell us if I'm right."

Krez dipped his strong chin, his voice rumbling as he replied, "You're not far off, at any rate. If she's made this move, it's safe to say that she's frightened."

"Of you?" Petra asked.

"Of what I know. Of what it would mean for her if you found a way to interfere. She must have worked out my intentions once she learned of my disappearance."

"You think Leviathan knew you would look for us?" Finn asked.

"She was inside my head for a long time," Krez explained. "There were moments when I had clarity, when I knew I was being used before she reined me back in . . . She had to have known I wanted to rejoin Avery."

"If she knew her influence would wear off, then why let you go at all?" Petra asked.

"She didn't. Mylan ordered me on the assignment."

"Mylan?" Finn sat up. Any mention of Leviathan's second in command was enough to grab his attention. Without Mylan, Leviathan would never have gotten far, with or without powers.

"He thought I'd have better luck finding Petra alone, so he sent me to the coast in case she tried going home."

"And yet you conveniently found me as soon as your mind was free?" Petra asked skeptically.

"As to that, it was nothing but luck," Krez stated. "You still use the old routes from our days in the Origin to sneak past patrols. Right place, right time. We followed you out."

"Why not approach her in the city?" Megan challenged.

Petra snorted. "I wouldn't have let him get one word out before blasting a hole through his gut."

Krez raised eyebrows on a nod, confirmation enough.

"You nearly did that here, anyway," Markes muttered.

"As riveting as a conversation on Petra's anger management issues makes, I'd like to know what this man knows." Bedria's squirrel chirped as she placed her elbows on the table. "If you have information on how Leviathan is amplifying her powers, then out with it."

Krez drew a slow breath, letting it out in a sigh. "That is not so easy to answer."

"Humor us." Finn had lost his patience.

"There are rooms beneath the capitol carved from the sacred stone," Krez began. "It is able to block the powers of a So' in the same way that our mountains can block comms."

"Leviathan held Avery captive in those rooms last year," Dr. Vey said solemnly. "That stone prevented her from using her powers to free herself."

"*Umethri*," Bedria confirmed quietly, nodding. "Much of it was stolen by human scavengers after the first war. I didn't know there was any left."

Krez continued, "What is less known is that this stone has a companion, even rarer than *umethri*. It has no name, except that which is passed down in memory via the So' themselves. Where the first constrains the So' power, the second amplifies it, extending its reach and the life of the user to unnatural magnitudes."

"Ha," Bedria scoffed, waving a hand. "I have never heard of such a thing."

Petra scowled. "And that means it can't exist?"

"It's unlikely." Bedria lifted her chin. "My parents were both So' trained in the holy order of the old ways. If there were such a thing, I would have come across it by now. What you are suggesting is an ability only achievable by direct contact with the Essence."

A hush settled in the room as her claim echoed up around them, disappearing into the rafters overhead.

"Am I supposed to know what that is?" Megan asked.

Linderly leaned close with a reverent whisper. "The Essence is what gifted the powers to the So'Reanges in the first place, at the beginning of all things."

"And it would be impossible to harness," Bedria insisted. "The location of the true Essence has been lost with time. It was forgotten even before humans arrived."

"Not necessarily," Lissande countered. "Even if its physical place was forgotten, the energy remains. It runs through the veins of every So' and tendrils of it through every Reange. There are waves of power that we cannot see. They pass through the air . . . beneath the ground. It is how So' harness power in the first place: they commune with the energy inside us all."

Finn's mind conjured the image of Avery leaning over him, her hands on his wound as he lay dying in her arms. She'd reached inside of him with that power, pulling pieces of him back together. No So' had ever been able to use their power on a human. Until her. Avery was different—special. She always had been.

It didn't matter either way. He'd never see her again. Avery was gone. And soon, Finn would be, too.

Bedria shook her head. "You're claiming this stone is part of the Essence."

"It's a theory," Lissande acknowledged. "Maybe not the Essence itself, but it could hold remnants. Echoes."

"Your theory is impossible," Bedria repeated. "The Essence cannot *be* harnessed. It is infinite."

Krez straightened his back, meeting the woman's eyes. "I speak the truth. Whether you choose to believe me or not."

Bedria cursed, angling away from them.

"Leviathan only has a small piece. She keeps it in the form of a pendant," Krez continued. "It hangs from her neck at all times. She is never without it, even in her sleep."

"He has no reason to lie," Petra defended.

"Unless it's a machination to entrap us," Megan countered.

Petra's eyes darkened. "If Leviathan wanted to trap us, she would have demanded all our heads. Not just Finn's."

It wouldn't make a difference either way. Finn had made his choice. There was a certain peace in his decision.

So he plastered what he hoped was a convincing grin on his face. "So she's got a magical rock that makes her brainwashing unstoppable. It doesn't change anything."

"Of course it changes things." Megan's pitched up. "You're not going to give yourself over to her. It's out of the question."

"What is she talking about?" Petra's focus was wholly on Finn.

"Look, even if we wanted to get rid of that necklace, we can't be sure how long her control will take to wear off," Finn reasoned. "Krez was free in a few days, but we don't know if that will be the same for everyone. We can't exactly just stroll in and rip it off her neck. There are too many variables and not enough time."

Petra's jaw clenched. She looked to Krez. "Mylan sent you away from her. He does nothing without reason. Nothing without a plan."

A deep frown appeared between his brows. "You're right," he agreed simply.

"Are you sure you weren't followed?"

"You may still make mistakes, Petra, but I do not," Krez said slowly. "If he had intentions for me, I do not know them."

"Then maybe we start with him," Linderly suggested.

"What is Mylan going to do for us?" Finn asked. "Last I checked, he was still a Reange. He's still under Leviathan's control."

"You don't know?" Markes asked curiously.

"They went to great lengths to keep it secret," Linderly explained. "Mylan is like Bedria, Finn. Immune to the So's influence."

"That is rare indeed," Bedria said quietly. The realization seemed to be the only thing able to silence her.

"Even so, Leviathan trusts Mylan implicitly," Krez added. "He is never far from her, but he abhors a personal guard. He will be unprotected. This is a good plan."

"What plan?" Finn snapped, panic rising. Things were spiraling out of his control.

Petra raised an eyebrow. "The one where we kidnap Mylan and interrogate him before we force him to take the necklace from her. Try to keep up, Lunitia."

"No," Finn said rigidly. "What if this is exactly what Mylan wanted in the first place? It's too dangerous."

"If this was Mylan's plan, then Leviathan wouldn't have resorted to theatrics to bring you in."

"It's the only option we have," Megan implored. "She's forced our hand, Finn."

"There are innocent lives at stake." Finn frowned. "I am not going to gamble with that. Not when I can prevent it so easily."

"Easily?" Petra barked. She had gone stiff, her eyes wary. "Don't be an idiot."

"I'm not. You, of all people, should understand my reasons."

She was quiet for a moment, watching him. "Finding the stone takes priority."

"Over the lives of the humans?" Finn shook his head. "They're only at her mercy because we didn't act quickly enough before. Because we ran to Earth when we should have stayed and fought. I won't make that mistake again. I won't run again."

"Finn," Petra said his name loudly, a flat accusation. "We need you here."

He laughed, running a hand over his face. "Twenty-four hours ago you were yelling at me about how I wasn't in charge."

"That was before I knew you were going to kill yourself," she snapped.

"I don't think Leviathan will actually let me do that part."

"Finn." Dr. Vey spoke his name calmly, a pained warning. The grief in her gaze mirrored his. She wouldn't stop him, that much he knew. But she would suffer for it.

"Enough," she said softly. A quiet chastisement.

Finn studied the table beneath his fingertips, willing the flush of shame to recede. He wouldn't change course. Not even for Dr. Vey and whatever his presence meant to her.

"And what about when they torture you for information?" Petra asked. "What about when you give away our location in a pain induced stupor? Will your death be worth it then?"

Finn stiffened. "I won't let it come to that."

He had fought alongside Reanges during his time with the Rebellion forces, trained to take his life rather than reveal the secrets of Nos Valuta. Before he left for Milderion, he would raid the medical supplies. There had to be something available that would ensure his silence.

But Finn hoped it wouldn't come to that. He'd rather die by firing squad than suffer the ravages of an unknown poison.

Finn leaned forward, resting his elbows on the table. "Look, I'll think about it, all right? We have three days before Su'elben. That's plenty of time."

Megan rose swiftly. She grabbed her long coat on her way out the door, slamming it heavily behind her. Linderly jumped up to follow but not before giving Finn a small smile. As usual, Tai went with her.

Petra watched them leave, her jaw tense. But she let them go, silent and still in her seat.

The others were quiet.

It's not like Finn expected anyone to agree with him. But his life wasn't worth much at this point. Petra was right—Finn wasn't the leader . . . They hardly even needed him. And since the Origin had begun actively hunting for him, Finn had been constrained to the borders of the village. He was trapped, stuck without any outlet to expel the anxiety that grew more unbearable with each day that passed. And he was tired.

But if there was value in his life this way, Finn would offer it gladly. Giving himself up was the one thing he could be sure of. The one thing he could carry out perfectly without fail.

Finn pushed his chair back. "We're not going to agree on anything tonight. Let's follow their lead and get some rest. We can sort this out in the morning."

But for Finn, everything made sense already. He wouldn't wait for them try to change his mind. He had already decided: the moment Leviathan had spoken to him through that broadcast. Despite Megan's wishful thinking, the So' wasn't bluffing. The others knew it, too.

If they took the riskier option and went after the stone, innocent people could die. In all likelihood, they would die if Leviathan even got wind of them trying to subvert her ultimatum. Finn was sure of that.

Leviathan had given Finn the illusion of a choice when here had never been one to begin with.

Choose them. It always has to be them.

The memory of Avery throwing his own words in his face struck through Finn with enough force to knock the breath from him. The confusion on her face. The anger. She had mocked him in those last moments together, under Qav's toxic influence. She had taunted Finn's encouragement to choose her people over everything.

Those words were fated to mock him all the way to his last breath.

He waited for the cover of darkness, for the hour he knew the volunteers posted at the archway would be distracted as they changed shifts. Finn didn't want anyone reporting to Petra before it would be too late for her to stop him.

And in the wee hours of the morning, when the moons were nothing more than pale circles hanging low in a star-filled sky, Finn slipped away from Nos Lenti, guided by nothing more than shadows and the will to die for something that meant more than what was left of his life.

CHAPTER
TWENTY-TWO

After a wasted hour of counting the divots in the ceiling, Petra gave up on the pretense of sleep. The lodge floors squeaked beneath her bare feet as she left her room, one of ten others.

The building had once been an inn, before Federation violence scared visitors from venturing out of the larger cities. There was a certain camaraderie to be found in living under one roof. At least she had her own room, and that was enough privacy.

She descended the creaking stairs, heading for the kitchen. A mug of hot tea and a short walk in the cold would clear her head. She passed the hallway to the lower rooms where a soft line of light spilled out from beneath Finn's door. Petra stopped in her tracks.

A peculiar feeling rioted in her chest, itching for freedom. Petra wasn't great at heart to hearts. But if anyone needed someone to talk to, it was Finn. She owed it to him to at least try.

Petra understood Finn's reasoning. She knew why he was willing to give up.

Avery was gone. Finn's brother had betrayed him. His entire world had been stripped away. As much of a family as they had created there, it still wasn't the same.

Finn wasn't the same.

But they did need him. Petra had been totally honest with Finn on that score. They could certainly get the job done without him, there was no arguing that fact. But Finn had a certain way about him that brought people together, held them together, when they would have otherwise fallen apart. He had never needed Avery for that.

Was Finn the most annoying man Petra had ever met? Yes. But his presence held value. Without him, they would crumble. She knew it as well as she knew herself. The mere thought giving pep talks sent shivers of revulsion down her spine.

And then there was Megan.

Losing Finn would break her. Petra would jump into the vacuum of space before watching Megan endure any more pain.

So Petra let out a tight breath, pivoting for his door. Better now than later. From the look in his eyes during their meeting, Finn was halfway ready to bolt.

Petra reached for the handle and the door flung open. She froze. Megan stood in its threshold, illuminated by a halo of light that poured out around her into the hall.

Petra flushed. Words lodged in her throat.

Megan. Megan was there. In *Finn's* room.

"What are you doing here?" Megan fumed.

It jerked Petra out of her stupor. She pushed past into the room. So Petra would be the one to kill Finn after all. If he had laid one hand on Megan, she would rip that idiotic tongue right out of his smug mouth.

The room was empty. His bed was made neatly, the blue blanket turned down over gray sheets. It hadn't been slept in.

"He's gone," Megan said curtly. She was angry, all right. But for once, it wasn't with Petra.

"Where?"

"I don't know, Petra. It's not like he left a note." Megan disappeared into the shadows, and Petra followed, trailing her into the common room, where they'd all convened hours earlier.

"It's not hard to guess," Petra said. In fact, it was obvious.

She tried not to notice the fluid way Megan's hair swayed against her back, pale and striking against her dark sweater. Megan didn't slow down, striding swiftly to the door, intending to follow Finn straight into the fresh snow and freezing temperatures of night.

Petra stepped in front of her.

"Move," Megan demanded. Her face was flushed, her white cheeks stained a soft pink.

"What are you planning on doing? Chasing after him in your pajamas?"

"Somebody has to. And we all know you don't give two shits about him, so it has to be me." She tried to get around her, but Petra blocked her again. Megan reared back, the pink cheeks deepening to a mottled red. "Get out of my way."

"You're not going alone." Anger bubbled beneath the stinging rejection.

"I'd rather go alone than with you," Megan claimed. Her eyes glistened in what light from the moons trickled in from the wide windows.

"You can't avoid me forever, Megan." Petra dared to step closer. "Talk to me."

"*Talk to you?* I can barely stand to look at you." Megan's eyes welled. She shifted her gaze, focusing on some spot behind Petra's head while her hand clutched at her chest. "Every time I look at you, it hurts. Right here. And I don't know how to make it stop."

Petra gut twisted. Megan hated her enough that Petra's very presence pained her. It was a cut that sliced straight through Petra.

She scrambled for a reply, for something to say—anything.

When Megan looked at her again, a tear escaped down her cheek that she quickly wiped away. The desperation in her eyes turned quickly to fury as she continued, "You pulled me through that Gate with you. Without ever thinking about how I would feel when I woke up. Without even—"

"Of course I did," Petra snarled, indignation rising. "You were dying. I couldn't just leave you there with the huma—" Petra cut herself off, her mouth thinning to a line as she bit her tongue to keep from going on. She had nearly said it aloud.

"Go on. Say it, Petra." Megan laughed derisively. "*With the hu-*

mans."

Petra let the silence hang too long before saying, "I didn't mean that."

"You always mean it," Megan countered. "You've always hated humans, and there's no point in trying to deny it now. And here's a revelation for you: I happen to *be* human. And so is Finn. So forgive me if I don't believe you have his best interests at heart. Even if your speciesism wasn't an issue—"

"Speciesism?" Petra stopped her. "What do you think I've been doing out here with you and Finn and the others? I've spent the better part of a year rescuing your stupid species. I don't think you understand what that means."

"No, *you* don't understand!" Megan yelled, taking two steps back. She glanced behind her, worried she had woken the others. When she spoke again, her voice shook. "Every time I think about being with you, I see Avery."

Petra recoiled, her chin tucking against the shock of Megan's confession.

"I see the way her face crumpled when she realized we'd been hiding this—this *thing* between us. The way we left her there. With Qav—in his grip. Controlled by him. And she's alone. She has no one. *No one.*"

Petra's pulse was loud in her ears. She thought of that moment often, too. But it wasn't pity she felt for Avery—it was anger. And perhaps that frightened her most of all.

"She wasn't herself, Megan," Petra said gently. She would do anything to ease the anguish Megan had revealed. How long had she been suffering in this way? Had she told anyone? Had she told Finn? Petra swallowed down the jealously. "There was nothing any of us could do to help her."

Megan's eyes narrowed. "Nothing *you* could do, maybe."

"She was going to kill you, damn it," Petra bit out. "Why can't you get it through that gorgeous brain of yours? Yes. You *are* human. And in that moment, controlled by Qav, Avery was going to kill you for it."

"You're wrong," Megan whispered, shaking her head. Petra wasn't sure who she was trying to convince. "You're wrong," she repeated, the plea even softer than before.

Petra took a small step toward her again, resisting the urge to touch her. To reach for her.

"You think I *wanted* to leave her there? With *him*?" Petra's voice was uneven. She didn't let herself dwell on these thoughts often. It usually ended with her driving her fist into something hard. "We had to, Megan. There was no other choice."

"You should have left me too," Megan whispered. Her shoulders sagged, giving into the weight of her grief. "My parents are there. My brothers . . . My entire family. They probably think I'm dead by now. And I'll never see them again."

Petra had no response. This was the one argument that silenced her completely. The one she hadn't slowed down enough to consider in those moments before they'd left Earth. And the burden of that mistake was Petra's alone to bear.

If Petra had been separated from Tai forever, the only family she had left, that loss would have consumed her.

And yet, if she hadn't brought Megan with them, Petra never would have seen her again. Somehow that thought was more terrifying than living with the guilt.

"I . . ." Petra cleared her throat, trying again. "I *am* sorry for that. But I—couldn't leave you there."

Megan studied her. "Why?" The question was soft.

"I think you know." It was Petra's turn to flush, warmth creeping up her neck. She prayed Megan wouldn't press further.

But Megan took a tentative step forward, until they were separated only by inches. Until Petra could see the flecks of darker blue sprinkled throughout the lighter colors of her irises.

"I want to hear you say it," Megan whispered.

Petra's blood sang. She felt more alive than she had in months. Megan was there, standing in front of her, close enough to feel.

"Megan," Petra breathed. Her fingers grazed Megan's cheek, tracing the path of the tear she'd wiped away. "I just want—"

"Finn's gone!"

They jerked away as Markes's yell filled the room. Petra growled in frustration as Megan turned to meet him. She made a mental note to push him harder in their next training session. The kid deserved to hurt.

"We're dealing with it," Megan said tightly.

Tai appeared behind Markes alongside a groggy Linderly. "So he decided to leave after all."

"But he can't go . . . He said he would wait," Linderly said quietly, shrinking at Tai's side.

"He's not going anywhere," Petra stated. And to her surprise, she meant it.

Petra grabbed her pack that still lay beside the door and pulled out the gear they'd need, tossing clothes at Megan. The only sign she'd been crying was in the mottled red of her flushed cheeks. Petra shrugged into a thick coat, shoving her feet into her boots.

Finn didn't get to make this choice alone. Petra wouldn't let him. She may understand his reasons, but she didn't agree with them.

They would fight together or not at all.

CHAPTER TWENTY-THREE

The mountains were more beautiful in the snow. Finn could barely feel his toes after the ten-mile hike, but at least he could appreciate the early-morning light glistening off the fresh powder. Their small ship was encased in a fine layer of white, its lines blending in seamlessly with the gargantuan boulders surrounding it. It was peaceful. Untouched.

Avery would have loved seeing the mountains, especially this time of year. The cities on Earth didn't have snowfall, a luxury that planet had left behind long ago in the wake of environmental decimation. Finn imagined her beside him, running ahead on the trail through the crisp frost of the morning, fresh snowflakes settling on freckled cheeks.

Finn had planned to bring her to Nos Lenti with Nova and Grigg. Before everything had fallen apart. Avery would never see it, now. Nova would never see her home again. And Grigg was dead.

Finn gritted his teeth against the fresh rush of misery that stole his breath. He hadn't said goodbye to Nova's parents. He hadn't said goodbye to anyone. He hoped they would come to understand why.

Something moved in his peripheral and Finn whirled around, bracing himself, his blaster in his hand. The wind died down to nothing until he could only hear the rush of his heartbeat in his ears alongside the puffs of breath from his lips.

And watching from its perch atop a slap of rock jutting out from the cliffside, a large white fox stared back at him, just as still. Its sharp ears were alert over its head, cold black eyes assessing. Waiting.

Finn laughed in disbelief. A tsek.

He'd never actually seen one before. The arctic animal was so elusive that it was little more than myth to most. Nova had spent much of her childhood hoping to come across one. Many people spent entire lifetimes searching for it among the high mountains of Echo. Some said that once caught, it would grant a wish for its release. The same animal for which Qav had garnered his nickname.

Avery's eyes filled Finn's memory, their beautiful golden depths flashing silver. *Qav* had done that to her. He polluted her mind, stealing away her free will. That disgusting excuse for a So' had snuck up on Avery before they even had a chance to fight him.

"Get out of here!" Finn's voice bounced off the mountains in an unsettling reverberation.

The tsek tilted its head, those vast eyes wide and cautious. Its voluminous ivory tail twitched, waving through the air like a taunt.

Finn's throat constricted. He clenched the cold metal in his hands. He hadn't even been able to detect this stupid animal when it had been right beside him. His lip curled.

He lifted his weapon and fired.

Finn pulled up at the last moment and the shot hit bare rock, sending ice flying. The fox bolted, its swooping tail disappearing into the white snow beyond the ship.

Good riddance. Finn didn't believe in superstitions, but tsek or not, the fox was still sacred. Killing it would serve no other purpose than to soothe the rage that burned like acid through Finn's veins. He hadn't stooped that far. Not yet.

But he was tired of resisting the chaos that stormed inside of him. To control it meant controlling everything around him. The anxiety that came with such a task was tearing him apart from the inside out. Ending it would be a relief.

After chipping off the ice around the access panel, Finn headed straight for the bridge to turn on the engines. The sooner he got the vessel warmed up, the better. As beautiful as he found the cold, Finn didn't exactly relish freezing his ass off. He took a hot shower in the single washroom and changed into the fresh set of clothes he'd shoved into his pack.

There hadn't been time to replenish the food stores from the last run, but he found coffee in the small galley. It paired nicely with the slice of pletch cake he'd grabbed from the kitchen at the inn. He sipped on the scalding hot cup in silence, staring out at the frozen landscape beyond the wide windows of the bridge. Long trails of water ran down the glass, turning the mountain ridges into a blur. The sun was just cresting over the farthest peak, sending streaks of warm light across blue-shadowed snow.

The others wake soon, rising with the dawn. None of them slept late anymore. With Petra in charge of training, their sessions would be more intense than ever. Finn would pay good credits to see Petra's face when Megan showed up to the sparring mat.

He shouldn't linger. Impending execution waited for no man.

Finn typed in coordinates on the analog keyboard, initiating flight. The holoscreen flashed blue and glitched back to the internal system controls.

Finn frowned, trying his credentials again. And again. The program refused to load.

He ran a hand through his hair, trying to remember someone else's login. There was no way he'd be able to pull that out of his ass. The alternative was to climb down the mountains on foot. Even with the right equipment—which he didn't have—that journey would take him days. He barely had three to work with.

Shit. He couldn't even do this part right.

Shame dug its sharp fingers into his gut, turning the coffee he drank acrid. Finn growled as he grabbed the empty cup and sent it flying into the window. The metal mug clanked loudly to the floor, nothing but a few trails of brown liquid left its wake.

"So things are going well for you, then?"

Finn spun, aiming his blaster straight for the voice behind him before he could register it.

Petra raised a brow. "Are you going to shoot me?"

"Damn it, Petra, you scared the shit out of me." Finn dropped his hand.

"Even if you didn't see me board, you should have heard me coming down the hall." Petra approached him, cocking her head. "You're slipping, Lunitia."

"Yeah, well." Finn should have known he wouldn't get away with sneaking out in the night. "I have other things on my mind."

"Undoubtedly."

"Are you sweating?" Finn asked. Strings of hair were stuck to the side of her face.

"I ran." She sniffed and wiped her nose with the back of her hand.

"You ran." Finn repeated with a doubtful laugh. "It's a full ten miles over rocky terrain."

Petra scowled, crossing her arms. "Somebody had to save you from your own idiocy. The others are behind me."

Right. Of course they'd be coming after him. If one had discovered his absence, they all would know. He regretted wasting time on a blazing shower.

Finn sighed heavily, turning away. "I'm trying to do the right thing, here. It would be great if you would let me."

"This isn't the *right thing*, Finn," Petra said to his back. "You need to get your head out of your ass and stop being so blazing selfish for once."

"Selfish?" Finn turned, eyes wild. "What part of trading my life for others is selfish?"

Petra retreated, her mouth setting in a hard line. "We should wait for the others."

"If you have something to say to me, then say it. It's not like I have a lot of time left anyway."

"Always a joke at the ready." She paused, and he thought she would ignore his bait. Her impulses won out in the end as the said sharply, "Don't act like you're doing this for the humans' sake."

"Who the hell else am I doing it for?" Finn raised his voice, disbelieving, and let out a beleaguered laugh. When Petra said nothing, he sobered immediately. "Then, please, do enlighten me."

"You think we haven't noticed you pulling away?"

The flush deepened on Finn's cheeks until a fine sheen of sweat broke out on his brow. His stomach curdled. He didn't want to have this conversation. Not with Petra, at any rate. Not with *anyone*. But he was the fool who had asked her to explain herself. So he stayed silent, swallowing around his dry tongue, refusing to break eye contact.

"We've all noticed, Finn. Every single one of us," she continued somberly. "You keep everyone at arm's length, receding into yourself. You overanalyze every choice we make because you're terrified we'll make the wrong one again. You may be a lot of things, but scared has never been one of them."

Finn smirked. "Maybe you *don't* know me."

"I know enough."

Finn's gaze dropped to the floor. She was right. For the first time in his life, he was petrified of making the wrong choices. Of losing friends. Of failing innocent people. He lived in a constant state of anxiety, worried that one wrong move would cost lives. Would cost entire worlds.

"You've lost yourself in fear," Petra said. "We all want to save those people, but not like this. Not if the cost is your life."

"That's a price I'm willing to pay." Finn's hands balled into fists at his sides. "What I do with my life is *my* decision. Not yours. Not Megan's. Not anyone else's!"

"You cannot offer yourself up to Leviathan without a fight. There is no honor in that."

"Honor? There is no honor for me now!" Finn beat a hand against his chest. "The humans are only in this mess because of me—Leviathan only has power because of *me*. I'm worth more to everyone if I just . . ."

Petra shrunk back at the part he left unsaid. The minutes of silence grew between them.

"It's because of *all of us*, Finn. Not just you," she said at last. "We're in this blazing thing together. We're saving the humans *togeth-*

er. You're the only one who seems to have forgotten that fact. You're not the only one who lost her, Finn."

"Don't," Finn warned, his body curling inward. Something visceral rebelled inside him, contorting his shoulders until his muscles cramped.

"We all made mistakes back on Earth—even Avery. And you're not the only one who failed her."

"I don't want to hear this, Petra." Finn turned back to the controls, jabbing in his command codes. Again, it denied him access. His chest burned, sending bile up his throat. A ringing filled his ears.

"Avery made her own choices."

"Why do people keep saying that to me?" Finn snarled.

"Probably because you're too stupid to actually listen. You've been moping around here like your life is over. Well news flash, we all have our own shit to carry. And I'm telling you that what happened to the Gate, what happened to Nova—and Grigg . . . That was on *Avery.*"

Finn gripped the console, his fingers taut on the freezing metal.

"Even if Qav was manipulating her, what Avery did is her burden to carry. *Hers.* Not yours."

"Petra." Her name was a low warning. If she continued, he didn't know what he would do. He didn't want to find out.

"You think this is all your fault? That's proof enough—you're only thinking about yourself." Petra had moved behind him, her accusations quiet and deadly in his ear. "The same Finn as always. Selfish."

"I said shut up!" Finn swung an arm around, throwing a punch straight for her face.

She ducked, driving a fist into his gut.

Finn doubled over as the breath whooshed from his lungs. The dull pain that followed was familiar, even welcome. It ignited his instincts, driving away all thought beyond the response of his training. He needed to dispel the rage, to hone it on the closest available target. And Petra had just given him one.

Finn drove his shoulder into her chest and they stumbled into the doorframe. Her chin caught on the metal and she shoved him away, spitting out blood. She paused to stare at him, her eyes filled with a fury that equaled his.

She launched herself at him and Finn braced his feet to prepare for her aerial attack. But she dropped, sliding on her knees to twist behind him. Finn's feet flew out from under him before he could track her movements. He fell hard, his skull slamming into the deck.

Black spots teased across his vision, tempting him with a promise. He yearned for the bliss of unconsciousness, for even a single moment where he didn't have to live beneath the crushing weight of his guilt. He was ready for it, in whatever form it came. Even from Leviathan.

Was he choosing this path for the wrong reasons? Finn wasn't sure he could trust his own judgment anymore. And that was the entire problem. If he didn't have his instincts, then what was left of him?

Petra loomed over him, hands on her hips. "Are you done?"

"Give me a second," Finn said, closing his eyes.

Petra was wrong about Avery. If Finn had trusted her more—if he had listened to her—then Qav never would have been able to manipulate her. Maybe she would still be with them. Nova would be with her parents, and Grigg would still be alive.

Avery would blame herself. Finn knew without a shadow of a doubt that she was suffering on Earth. That she was in pain. It was almost like he could still feel her.

Petra showed little understanding for the woman she had once claimed to love. But her loyalties had shifted—to Megan. And what Avery had done to Megan had wounded Petra more deeply than she would ever admit.

Still, Petra's attitude toward Avery pissed Finn off.

He grabbed her ankle, yanking her feet out from under her.

She hit the floor beside him, her eyes wide with surprise as she wheezed. She curled onto her side as she sucked in breath and cast a hateful look in his direction.

He knew that look—this version of Petra he could handle. This version of Petra, he even liked.

"Now I'm done." Finn grinned up at the ceiling as he realized the humor woven through his chest was genuine.

In that moment, lying beside Petra on the floor of a ship in the frozen mountains, he felt an infinitesimal glimmer of the man he'd once been. And more shocking still, it had been brought on by the fierce accusations of one chronically irritable Reange who sometimes called him friend.

"I hate you," she muttered between wheezes. Then she kicked his thigh hard enough to leave a bruise.

And for the first time since they crash-landed on this side of the universe, Finn's laugh was loud enough to bounce down the halls of the empty ship.

Finn barely caught himself when Megan shoved him with enough force to send him stumbling into the wall.

"You have some real nerve," she spat, advancing on him.

Linderly grabbed her arm. "Megan, come on. We talked about this."

"I don't care." Megan looked borderline murderous. "If he's so intent on killing himself, then *we* should be the ones to do it."

"Moons above, can we lay off the violence?" Finn nodded his chin toward Petra. "I'm pretty sure Petra already bruised my ribs."

Petra's mouth tilted up when Megan frowned at her. "If you wanted a piece of him, maybe you should have gotten here faster."

"Not all of us have the stamina of a long-distance mountain goat."

"What happened to all that combat training?"

Megan fumed, her face reddening.

"None of us can keep up with her, Megan," Tai pointed out. "Don't take it personally. Petra is nothing if not an overachiever."

Finn laughed. "I think that might be an understatement, kid."

Petra lifted her chin. "Am I supposed to apologize for being good at things?"

Megan snorted. Finn laughed harder.

"I never said she was humble," Tai muttered, rubbing his neck.

"Well, I agree with Megan." Markes was uncharacteristically serious. His arms were crossed over his chest, yellow eyebrows drawn low in disapproval. "You can't pull shit like that on us, Finn. We are in this together. To the end."

"Message received." Finn held up his hands in defeat. "Trust me, Petra's fist got the point across a while ago."

"You're welcome." Petra settled into the command chair, acclimating to the controls. She glanced at Linderly. "Want to take the nav seat? We need to reset the system."

"At least Lind's hack worked—she cut you off at the pass," Markes said, grinning. He slapped a hand on Finn's back. "You'll have to work harder to outsmart the lot of us."

Finn narrowed his eyes, putting pieces together. Linderly had blocked his login access, preventing him from being able to pilot at all. Finn hadn't even thought of that as a possibility. If he had, maybe he'd already be halfway to the city.

It was strange—his friends valued Finn's life more than he did. Ironically enough, there was guilt in that, too.

Finn moved cautiously past Megan. "Look, I'm willing to try this your way. But we're going to do things by the book."

"You're the one who said you had a raid fully planned out," Petra said. "If it was good enough for next week, it'll be good enough now."

"That was for an intel run, not the kidnapping of a Council Elder. And since when are you the one to dive headfirst into danger?"

"Since you decided we had to risk everything to save a few humans," Petra said. She glanced at Megan. "But you're right. We can't just let them die. It would make everything else we're trying to do here meaningless."

Linderly typed in commands, undoing her work. "We'll have to change our approach. After that broadcast, they'll be expecting us to try something."

"They don't know we have intel from Krez," Tai theorized. "I'm willing to bet Leviathan thinks she'll force our hand before he finds us."

"After your little show last night, Linderly and I sat down with Krez to corroborate some details on their security protocols," Megan explained. "I figured we'd need something to bail you out of your own imbecility at some point."

"I don't know whether to be insulted or impressed," Finn said wryly.

"You should be thanking her," Petra chastised. "That intel is the only thing that's going to give us a chance at all here."

"That's assuming this wasn't Mylan's plan all along. Leviathan could already be expecting us," Markes added dismally.

Petra shook her head. "I'm not so certain. Mylan followed Leviathan, yes. But he always had his own agenda."

"There's only one way to find out," Tai replied.

Finn was inclined to agree. Mylan had served as a liaison for the Origin when they'd needed information for the Rebellion forces in Nos Valuta. Finn had dealt with him personally on several occasions. He'd always seemed like someone who facilitated extremism out of necessity, as a means to an end.

"Speaking of the dashing warrior, I don't see Krez in your little rescue party," Finn observed. "Didn't he feel like trying to save me from myself?"

"You don't have to be an ass about it," Megan retorted.

"He's staying in Nos Lenti," Petra explained. "Once we get closer to Leviathan, he could be more of a risk than an asset."

"By that logic, you all are," Finn said. "She could turn any one of you."

"Unless she has direct contact with us, I think her manipulation is marginal," Petra theorized. "She has to establish some kind of immediate vicinity to establish full control. Like she did with both Krez and Tai."

"That's a big unknown to be messing with."

Markes shrugged lightly. "No problem—we'll just keep our distance."

"There are at least two people here she has no power over," Megan said.

Petra frowned. "Out of the question. You don't even know how to fight."

"I've been working on it," Megan countered. She nudged Linderly. "Tell her I've been improving."

Linderly smiled hesitantly. "You're definitely better."

"Better isn't going to cut it," Petra snapped. She looked at Finn. "She isn't going with you. We ought to send her straight back to the village. It's too dangerous in the city, especially for humans."

"Don't tell me what I can and cannot do. I've proven that I can handle it before."

"This isn't hacking into a computer with your daddy's fancy credentials," Petra said forcefully. "This is hand-to-hand combat with trained soldiers. With killers."

Megan's eyes flashed. "I said I can handle it."

Finn sighed, loathe to step into whatever was going on between them. "Megan, as much as it pains me to admit, I'm with Petra on this one."

"Will wonders never cease," Petra muttered under her breath.

"You're improving," Finn conceded. "But not enough."

Megan seethed, looking out the window, away from them. She was getting better, and her aim with a gun was above average, but there was no way Finn was prepared to let her see real action. She'd get herself killed. And Finn owed it to Avery to make sure Megan was safe.

But it wasn't easy for Megan to accept her limits. *No* wasn't a word she enjoyed hearing. She and Petra were annoyingly similar in the worst ways.

So he added gently, "But I don't agree that we should send you back to Nos Lenti."

Petra balked. "She can't just put herself in—"

"I agree with Finn," Linderly interrupted, boldly facing Petra's scowl. "It will make my job a lot easier if I have someone on the ship who knows what they're doing around coding."

Megan gave a clipped nod, but her shoulders were stiff beneath her blue coat.

"The element of surprise will be essential." Finn moved on. "Even if we do find Mylan and get him to talk, there's no way to guarantee we'll get access to that necklace. Using him as a hostage is a long shot."

"Besides that, the Elder Council might move forward regardless of Leviathan's influence," Petra added.

"Aren't Reanges supposed to be pacifists?" Megan asked angrily. "Surely they wouldn't condone the execution of innocent people."

The bridge fell silent. None of them wanted voice what they were all thinking: there was no way to know for certain what the outcome would be.

"We'll know soon enough." Petra's reply at last was quiet, almost a whisper.

If it came to that, Finn would still make the choice they'd try to deny him. There was no way he was letting those people die when there was a way for him to prevent it.

"I guess we'd better get comfortable then." Finn took a seat beside Linderly. He stretched his legs out, crossing them at the ankles. "Pull up the schematics of the capitol building, I want to see the information Krez gave you on Mylan. We'll also need to get up to speed on Leviathan's guard detail. We have a lot of scenarios to work through and not a lot of time to work through them."

Markes perked up. "I have a new projectile blaster I've been working on that would be—"

"Absolutely not," Finn stopped him. "The last time you tried out one of your weapon designs, you nearly brought down the entire lodge. We're not throwing that into the mix, kid."

"That was one time."

"It's not happening."

"Fine." Markes settled in beside him, sighing. "I guess if the only thing we have going for us is surprise, then we better make it good."

"That's putting it mildly," Tai scoffed. "Just the fate of Echo's future on the line."

"And Finn's life," Megan added.

"Never liked my life much anyway." Finn winked at her.

None of them laughed. Not even Markes. Finn rubbed the back of his neck awkwardly.

He probably deserved the blank stares. There wasn't much sympathy to be had for suicidal self-deprecation.

Grigg would have laughed.

Avery would have thrown him across the room.

It would be safer for everyone if they let Finn go, using his execution as a distraction. The advantage Krez provided was small. Best case scenario would see Leviathan ousted from her position and the country free to make its own decisions according to the law. Worst case, they'd all be killed.

Finn wouldn't let that happen. If things started going sideways, he would turn himself over to Leviathan willingly. Even if it meant the others would never forgive him. He'd be dead either way, but at least they would live.

And if Finn was honest with himself, that might be how he'd prefer it.

CHAPTER TWENTY-FOUR

Finn gripped the ladder rung beneath one arm, shifting his weight as he glanced down. Mistake. His limbs seized up as he looked past Petra beneath him. In the darkness of night, he couldn't even make out the ground below, only the occasional bright blur as cruisers sped along the adjacent airway.

A current of wind billowed through the small cavity of the access ladder and someone yelped beneath him—Linderly. Markes let out a loud curse from somewhere near the rear.

"Hold on tighter before I push you off myself," Petra threatened. She must have seen whatever blunder Markes committed.

"Everything good?" Finn raised his voice above the howling wind.

"If Markes doesn't end up smeared on the ground, it will be a miracle."

"I'm not big on heights!" Markes called, his declaration breaking on the next gust of air.

"Probably not the best time to be pointing that out!" Finn called.

"I can't hear you! But I'll assume you said something supportive!"

Finn shook his head, looking back up to the fifty feet left in their climb. The capitol residencies consisted of two towers, only separated by a narrow wind tunnel between. The access ladder ran up the length of one side from the central ground level to the upper levels. It was their only access to Leviathan's personal quarters. No cam feed monitored the ladder, nor did sentries. Krez had suggested that climbing the thirteen stories was tantamount to suicide.

They'd been climbing for almost an hour, long enough that Finn's fingers had gone numb. The wind made progress painfully slow. In order to pass undetected through the ground level, they'd been unable to bring much gear. A single tether ran between them, clipped to their belts and tying them to Finn at the lead. Their safety was dependent fully on Finn's ability to secure the line to each rung.

Still, it could be worse. The weather in Milderion wasn't all that bad. After months in the snow and freezing temperatures of the mountains, the coastline was borderline balmy.

Another half hour and they made it to the access door, no more than a lip on the edge of the tower, six inches deep.

Finn looked down at Petra and nodded.

She turned to Linderly. "We're ready for Megan."

Linderly held the only communicator—a rudimentary device that would hopefully avoid detection. From the ship, Megan monitored the building's security system, offering them instruction. Tai had stayed behind with her, unable to argue with Petra's edict for him to do so.

"Ten seconds!" Linderly yelled.

Finn counted down under his breath. His eyes shifted nervously to the empty air, like he could anticipate the next gust. If wind hit them when he removed their tether, Markes wouldn't be the only one splattered on the concrete below.

Finn lifted himself as high as the tether would allow, pressing his ear to the door, listening for the locking mechanism. The door shifted without warning, sliding to the side. Finn unclipped from the ladder, crawling over the ledge as quickly as his exhausted muscles would allow. He leaned back over to grab Petra by the belt, hoisting her up beside him. Linderly was next. Her body was halfway over the ledge when the wind shifted.

The gust surged, jerking Markes from the ladder entirely. He cried out when his line to Linderly went taught. Her body yanked violently as she clung to Finn's middle.

"Shit!" Finn held on to Linderly, supporting the weight of them both. Markes slammed into the side of the building, flailing to grab his line.

"Markes!" Linderly twisted, trying to see her brother.

"Don't look back, you idiot!" Petra said harshly, wrapping her arms around Linderly's waist, anchoring her. She nodded to Finn. "I've got her."

The ledge dug into Finn's stomach as he leaned out to grip the thin rope, his forearms going taught. The wind surged again, pulling the line through Finn's fingers, ripping flesh. He hissed. Markes swung away again, the vibrant yellow of his hair a teasing blur in the shadows.

Markes grabbed for the rung, his hands catching air as he swung backward on a pendulum. He looked up at Finn. His eyes were wide. Frightened. If he fell at this height . . .

Finn leaned out farther, his bruised ribs protesting. He wrapped the line around his forearm and hoisted Markes with a growl. Petra pulled Linderly to safety with the slack in the line. A final pull and Finn locked his arm with Markes's, dragging him haphazardly inside. They fell to the floor, chests heaving against a dizzying combination of exertion and adrenaline.

"We're clear," Linderly said quietly, pressing her finger to the earpiece that connected her to Megan. The access door slid shut with a soft whoosh.

Finn rested his head against the cold floor beneath them. "I've never been so glad that someone was a runt with no muscles in my entire life."

Markes snorted between gasps, running a shaking hand over his face.

"Get up," Petra ordered, her eyes scanning the dim hallway that stretched out in both directions on either side of them. "We don't have time for you to get your shit together."

Finn rose unsteadily to his feet beside Markes while Linderly rolled up the tether. He flexed his stinging hands, acclimating to the pain where the line had ripped his skin.

Petra paused just outside of the final door that would lead them into the main hall. She stared up at the cam bubble embedded into the frame above it. They had to trust that Megan would glitch out the feed. And that Krez's information would still hold true.

Finn had no way to control the outcome. His heart rate sped, a fine sweat trickling down the back of his neck. He had almost forgotten what it felt like to be in the line of danger: the heady combination of uncertainty and anticipation that set his blood on fire. It used to drive Finn, propelling him forward, fueling his purpose. But now . . . the terror was all-consuming.

As a soldier, that was the most dangerous reaction of all.

"Time?" Finn asked, trying to hide his shaking hands.

"Ninety seconds," Linderly replied.

It passed in silence as they crouched against the wall. The door clicked, and Finn pushed forward slowly as his eyes adjusted to the bright lights. Mylan's quarters were three floors down. The elevator was out of the question—they'd have to make their way down the stairs.

If they did this right, they'd be back in the ship with one disgruntled Elder and a stone necklace before anyone figured out they'd even been there.

They'd spent a few hours in the mountains running over options and had to wait for cover of nightfall to head into the city. That meant two nights since Leviathan had issued her ultimatum. One more before Su'elben. And there was still no guarantee. Once they found Mylan, there was every possibility he'd refuse to talk. Finn wasn't sure he had the stomach for torture.

Linderly took the lead as they moved down the rear stairwell. Krez had been honest about Mylan's distaste for security. The hall outside of his apartments was empty. In his position, the lack of respect safety measures was astounding.

Far be it from Finn to shrug off the opportunity Mylan's negligence presented.

It was well past midnight by the time they slipped silently into

Mylan's quarters, roughly two hours after they'd begun their ascent. The entryway was dim, illuminated only by the soft glow of the city lights. They found his bedroom easily enough, following the sounds of shallow snoring. Linderly lingered at the threshold as Finn and Petra approached the bed. Markes had stayed behind at the entrance.

Mylan was a back sleeper, his mouth slightly open as one hand rested on his chest atop the white bedcover. His wrinkles were deeper than the last time Finn had seen him, even smoothed by the ease of sleep. His gray hair stuck out in disarray. It was hard to imagine him as the hard-ass Origin leader Finn knew. In the stillness of his bedroom, sleeping so soundly that his snores carried out into the hall, Mylan looked . . . vulnerable.

Finn peered across the bed at Petra standing on the other side. He dipped his chin in signal. Together, they brought their blasters to either side of Mylan's head.

"Wake up, Mylan."

Mylan's eyes opened groggily, registering Petra in degrees. The metal of her gun was heavy in her hand as she pressed it into his skull. He pulled away on a harsh intake of breath, only to run into Finn's weapon on his other side.

"What is this?" Mylan rasped, his voice dry from sleep. And no wonder, given the amount he had been snoring.

"We were in the neighborhood. Thought we'd stop by for a chat." Finn waved his blaster around. Mylan watched its movement warily.

"Are you insane?" Mylan shifted himself up to lean against his pillows. His eyes caught Linderly in the doorway, widening. "You brought the young ones? She will kill all of you. Even them."

Linderly raised her chin, her eyes bright.

Petra shoved her weapon harder against his skull. "We were old enough to risk our lives for the Origin. This is no different."

His gray eyes lifted to her. "We had no choice then, Petra. You should know that better than anyone."

Petra's throat tightened. She remembered when the Origin had found her and Tai huddled in a cave, hiding from Federation forces. Mylan had been with them. Petra had been thirteen, younger than Linderly was now.

The Origin should have let them go, not recruited them. Offering such a promise as vengeance to a child . . . It was wrong. Petra hadn't been old enough to understand what vengeance even meant, much less if it was an avenue to peace. A part of her still didn't.

But she knew the Origin didn't care about peace. Only control.

Petra's lip curled in disgust. "You had a choice when you recruited us. When you talked *children* into joining your campaign to sow more violence."

"As I recall, you didn't require much convincing. We offered you safety. Security. It's rather hypocritical to be questioning the avenues we took to ensure that when you would be dead without them."

"Security?" Petra almost laughed. She slept with one eye open. She trusted no one. "You and Leviathan *poisoned* me. You used my grief as a weapon, honing me until I knew no other reality than yours. And look at what it cost me."

"Ah." He nodded slowly. "We're discussing Avery now. I find it hard to believe that you broke in here just to chastise me when it was you who left her behind."

Petra saw red. She shifted, shoving the tip of her weapon into his forehead.

"Petra," Finn cautioned.

Her blaster didn't move. "The necklace. We're here to take it from her."

Someone who hadn't spent her childhood training for covert operations might have missed the way Mylan's breath caught. His eyes betrayed nothing.

"You sent Krez away." Petra pressed her gun harder. "Why?"

"Maybe don't shove the gun through his forehead," Finn said.

Mylan said nothing.

"You're going to talk, Mylan," Petra warned. "One way or another, we're walking out of here with that stone. You can either be dead or alive when we do."

Mylan held her gaze. "What stone?"

Petra pulled her blaster back to bring it down in a heavy strike against Mylan's chin. He fell sideways onto the pillows with a cry.

"Damn it, Petra," Finn cursed, kneeling on the bed. He placed a hand on Mylan's shoulder as the older man dabbed at the blood that tricked from his mouth. "We need him conscious."

"He's lying," Petra countered.

"No shit he's lying. That's not an excuse to beat him."

"Should I shoot him, then?" Petra asked, making a show of aiming toward the outline of Mylan's leg.

"No!" Mylan cried, his legs jerking to the side beneath the cover. He looked up at Finn, frowning. "Moons above, is she always like this?"

"Yes, I'm *always like this*," Petra said carefully. "I'm like this because you *made* me like this. Now you're going to tell us how to get our hands on that rock or I'm going to blast a hole straight through your kneecap."

Mylan studied her warily. A part of Petra wished he would test her.

Mylan pushed back the covers, setting his bare feet on the floor. He leaned his elbows onto his knees with a resigned sigh. "I thought Krez would find you, just not this quickly. How did he do it? When we've spent months hunting for you."

"Quit stalling."

He smiled. "You always were quick, Petra. I'd forgotten how valuable you were. We should have done more to keep you."

"My loyalty is to Avery."

"Yes, well, as admirable as your conviction is, I don't see Avery here." He spread his hands out, looking around him. "Is she hiding in the shadows?"

"Careful, Mylan." Finn's warning was deep and menacing.

Whatever Mylan saw in Finn's eyes made him shift in his seat. He cleared his throat. "There isn't a way to take it from her."

"Another lie." Petra's fingers stiffened around her gun. "Why do you think we came to you first? She trusts you."

"What is your plan here?" Mylan asked. "Break into her apartments? Even if you drag me with you, Leviathan's quarters are not so easy to breach. And besides our dear Ambassador Lunitia here, you are all susceptible to her control once she wakes. I don't care how strong your convictions are, they're no match for her."

"We'll see who's a match for whom."

"Then you're more of a fool than I thought." Mylan pinched the bridge of his nose, shutting his eyes. "You've undone everything. This isn't how you were supposed to act."

"And I suppose you're about to tell us why?" Finn drawled.

"I did you a favor, boy." Mylan turned sharply to Finn, anger finally breaching his wall of control. "I've worked for weeks to pin this insurrection on you, and you've thrown that opportunity away. She would have settled for your life alone. And now, the rest of them will die alongside you."

Finn moved quickly. He grabbed Mylan by the blue silk of his nightclothes, throwing the old man against the wall hard enough to send a holoframe crashing to the floor. Finn leaned close, rage seething in every word. "Remember when I told you to be careful? How about you start doing that?"

"Finn." It was Petra's turn to caution him. Too much noise, and guards would be on them in minutes. If Leviathan awoke and found them within her reach . . . There would be no coming back.

But Finn didn't release Mylan, his knuckles turning white against the silk. "Tell us how to get that blazing stone, or I'll shoot you myself. And it won't be a leg."

He ended the threat by shoving the barrel of his gun into Mylan's ribs. The man grunted, his face going pale.

Finn looked unhinged. Like he very well could kill Mylan in cold blood and not think twice about it. He was one push away from unraveling completely.

"What made you think I would help you?" Mylan croaked.

"Fine," Finn bit out.

Petra had no time to react before Finn shifted his weapon, shoving it into Mylan's shoulder and firing.

Mylan yelped as Finn clamped his mouth shut, shoving him into the wall again.

"What the blazar are you doing?" Petra dug her fingers into Finn's arm.

Finn ignored her, leaning closer to Mylan. "That was a warning, Mylan. The next shot won't be so generous."

Petra wrenched Finn away, shoving him to Linderly. Mylan moaned, pressing a shaking hand into his shoulder. Finn had probably blown out the entire ligament.

"Get out of here," Petra ordered. "I'll deal with him."

Finn's chest heaved, his eyes frantic and wild. He turned on his heel, pushing past Linderly without a word.

Mylan was losing blood quickly; the upper half of his sleeve was stained a deep purple. He grunted, unsteady on his feet.

"What did you expect from us?" Petra asked him. "Did you think we would just let you have Finn? Did you think we wouldn't go down fighting?"

Mylan grunted again. "I thought he at least would do the sensible thing. Apparently I was mistaken about his character."

Petra bit the inside of her cheek. Mylan hadn't been mistaken. If they hadn't interfered, Finn *would* have given himself up. And he still might—if she couldn't find a way to get Mylan to cooperate.

"You have two choices, Mylan. If you help us take that stone, we'll leave you with her. Free to plot another day."

"And if I don't?" he asked through chattering teeth.

"Then you're coming with us." Petra dug her fingers straight into his wound until blood coated her fingers and Mylan screamed, falling to his knees. "And we'll do this the hard way."

He slumped onto the floor, looking up at Petra with calculating eyes. "Even if I do help you—even if you manage to get it out of here—those humans will still die. It's too late to stop it unless she has Finn."

"*You* can stop it, Mylan. Don't pretend you are Leviathan's tool when we both know you're savvier than that. But what you're doing here, it's a violation of the bond between Reange and So'. This isn't the world we fought for."

Something passed over his face, too fleeting for her to name. But it was gone in the next breath.

"Maybe not," he admitted. "But it's our reality now. Your actions in this city are the one thing Leviathan can't control. You and your friends have become something—you *mean* something. And that frightens her."

"But not you?"

Mylan laughed darkly, a strange mix of pain and amusement. "Fear is a luxury someone in my position cannot afford." He sighed wearily, as though resigning himself. "I need your word that no harm will come to her."

"Does my word mean anything to you?"

"I know you, Petra. You have been many things, but never a woman without integrity."

She held his gaze for some moments, until her eyes burned. Petra often wondered if the choices she made were aligned with the person she wanted to be. Her life now was so different from what it had once been, and yet . . . She'd never felt truer to herself. That had to mean something.

Petra nodded. "We just want the stone. Nothing else."

Mylan returned the gesture, dipping his chin to his chest. He opened his mouth to—

"Petra." Linderly was at the door again. "We have to go."

"Give me ten seconds," Petra snapped.

"Now!" Finn barked, crowding the door with Markes. "We're out of time."

Mylan laughed softly, leaning against the wall. "It's too late, then. She won't just take Finn, now." His eyes drifted to Petra before landing on Linderly and then Markes. "You never should have come."

"If our time's up, then yours is, too," Petra snarled, dragging My-lan to his feet. If they had to fight their way out, at least they'd have a bargaining chip.

"Is he coming with us?" Markes asked. "What if he communicates directly with Levia—"

Finn slammed his gun into the back of Mylan's head. He fell limp in Petra's arms, sinking to the floor.

"What the hell, Lunitia!" Petra yelled, trying to hoist the old man up.

"Markes made a good point." Finn grabbed Mylan, hoisting him up and over his shoulder. "Now it won't be an issue."

"And how are you going to scale down the side of a building while carting around unconscious dead weight?" Petra hissed.

"Megan says to stop fighting and move," Linderly interjected.

Petra rounded on her. "This is one of many reasons we left her on the ship."

"She says she heard that."

Petra rolled her eyes, turning to the door. Their plans were falling apart. Maybe Finn had been right: there had been little chance of it ever working in the first place.

But that changed nothing. Petra would still have walked beside Finn straight into the line of fire. She'd finally found a place where she belonged. She'd found people to whom she belonged. And they were more than a mission or a cause or an ideal: they were a family.

Petra would live up to the honor that Mylan saw in her. She would prove to Megan that she had changed—that she was more than the bitterness that once ruled her life.

More than for them, Petra would prove it to herself.

CHAPTER TWENTY-FIVE

Finn shifted Mylan's weight across his back as they entered the brightly lit hallway. He was heavier than he looked. Maybe knocking him out cold had been too rash.

"Clearly we're not leaving the way we came," Petra said sourly.

Finn looked to Linderly. "What about the elevator?"

She shook her head. "We'll have to use the stairs. Plan C is our only option."

"We have a plan C?" Markes asked.

"Did you even listen when we were briefing the routes?"

He shrugged. "If I don't get to blow anything up, plans tend to lose their appeal."

Petra lead them into the stairwell, starting their ascent.

Finn climbed as fast as he was able with Mylan on his back, pushing himself until his breathing labored. If Leviathan woke while they were still in the building, none of them would be leaving.

Plan C wasn't much of a plan. Especially not with dead weight in tow. Even if they made it to the roof, Origin ships would be on them in minutes once they entered airspace. It would take a miracle to get them out of there.

Finn was sweating by the time they reached the top of the stairs. They paused at the entrance to the roof, waiting for Megan's signal. A door clanged open somewhere in the stairwell below.

"Where are they? We don't exactly have time to idle," Finn whispered harshly.

"They're coming as fast as they can," Linderly replied. "Ninety seconds."

"We may not have that long." Petra moved down a few steps, her weapon drawn and aimed. Markes moved into place behind her, mimicking her stance.

Finn shifted Mylan again. The unconscious man stirred, his body beginning to find form over Finn's shoulders.

Finn cursed, weighing options.

Mylan could be faking his unconsciousness, using the excuse to communicate with Leviathan. Finn wasn't certain if Mylan could wake her from sleep, but he *was* certain that he didn't want to find out.

The sound of footsteps echoed up around them. The guards were drawing closer and they still had to deal with the sentry on the roof. Finn wouldn't be able to both carry Mylan and help the others.

Finn dropped Mylan to the ground, situating him up against the wall. Mylan's head lobbed to the side with a low groan.

"What are you doing?" Petra's focus never strayed from her aim down the stairs.

Finn didn't answer her. He pulled his blaster from its holster, pressing the barrel to Mylan's chin. And then he gripped Mylan's bloodied shoulder, shoving his thumb straight into the fresh wound.

Mylan gasped in pain, his eyes widening on a strangled cry.

The footsteps below slowed to a stop. "Who's up there?"

"Damn it, Finn," Petra growled.

"Get up," Finn ordered Mylan, pressing the blaster into his neck. Mylan's eyes widened further, his breathing rapid and shallow. But he rose to his feet. "If you so much as look at one of us wrong, Markes here is going to put a bullet through your brain."

To his credit, Markes swung his weapon around, aiming straight for Mylan.

Finn made his voice as menacing as possible as he added, "And I wouldn't test him. You know how much he likes seeing things explode."

"Twenty seconds." Linderly's hand moved to the door controls.

"Remain where you are!" The voice was closer than ever. "Drop any weapons! Keep your hands raised!"

"The minute they realize it's you, she'll be notified," Mylan said, his voice rasping. "Once she knows you're here, not even I will be able to stop her."

Finn cracked a smile, grabbing Mylan's shirt and pushing him roughly to the front. "Then I guess we'd better get a move on."

"This isn't going to end well," Mylan said over his shoulder. "For any of you."

"We'll see about that."

Linderly gave Finn a quick nod. "They're here."

"Petra?" Finn called her name without looking over his shoulder.

"I'll be right behind you."

Finn leaned in close to Mylan's ear, shoving him against the door. "You better hope the guards out there aren't trigger happy."

Mylan tensed.

Linderly slammed her hand against the door panel and it swooshed open. The wave of brisk night air chilled the sweat-soaked hair at Finn's temples.

Finn pushed Mylan forward and he stumbled out onto the roof. The building's two towers arched up overhead on either side of them, angular metal spires rising into the night. Between them, a narrow walkway extended straight through their center.

There would be nowhere for the ship to land, but they'd known that going in. The unique design made access infinitely more difficult in a society that prioritized air travel. In Finn's experience, underestimation of his recklessness tended to work out in his favor. Even if he hadn't stretched those muscles in a long time.

Only three guards emerged from the shadows, halting immediately upon recognizing Mylan. The woman at the front assessed him quickly, her eyes navigating to the bloody patch on his shoulder as she lifted her weapon. The others followed suit, waiting for direction.

"Mylan?" the woman asked, gripping her weapon.

Petra's shots rang out behind them. The guards flinched, their weapons jerking nervously. But still, they waited for Mylan's order.

"They're here," Linderly said nervously, sticking closely to Markes. Her gaze darted up into the dark, searching the sky.

The walkway lit up blue from blastfire as Petra continued her barrage. She tossed an explosive down the stairs as she backed out and slammed the door shut. A quick shot to the command pad and the door locked itself shut.

Finn shoved his blaster into Mylan's ribs. "Tell them to lower their weapons."

The lead guard shifted her weapon, training it on Markes. Finn's stomach lurched. He gripped Mylan's neck with his free hand, digging his fingers into the clammy skin of his neck.

"If you don't tell them to stand down, we will kill all three of them."

Mylan's eyes flickered between the guards, as though he was weighing lives against the cost of their escape. For a moment, Finn wasn't certain of his choice. Mylan had always seemed reasonable. Likable, even. Finn had only agreed to this plan in the first place out of some hope that his instincts hadn't been wrong. That maybe Mylan had sent Krez away to warn them. A stupid, childish hope.

"Let us pass." Mylan's command was stoic. There was no hint of the pain he'd exhibited earlier. "Drop your weapons. Join the others to wait for reinforcements."

The woman frowned, but her weapon dropped a fraction of an inch. "We can't just—"

"They have nowhere to go up here," Mylan interrupted, sounding every bit her superior. "They cannot take me farther than the edge of the building. There is only one human among them."

They all knew what Mylan didn't voice: once Leviathan was alerted, this would be over in a moment. They dropped their weapons.

"Move." Petra waved her gun at the entrance. "Face the wall. Drop to your knees. If one of you turns, I won't hesitate."

"Traitors," the leader spat. But she complied.

They picked up the weapons and headed for the edge of the roof.

Wind tore at Finn's hair, lashing it against his face. He glanced over the side, down into vibrant lights of the city that had come alive over the past year.

"Was this part of your plan?" Mylan raised his voice against the punishing bursts of wind. The billowing shirt of his night clothes whipped around his body. "Don't tell me you want to scale down this building."

"So you can slow us down with that bum shoulder?" Finn replied. "Doubtful."

"There!" Linderly pointed down.

A ship rose from the line of cruisers, gaining altitude rapidly. The illegal movement would be flagged. They'd have three minutes before Origin forces reached them.

The ship drew close, the hatch of its underbelly already open. Megan stood braced at its mouth, a safety belt harnessed on her hips that was tethered to the inner wall. Her pale hair whipped furiously around her, tangling against her outstretched arms.

Petra didn't hesitate. She backed up a few feet and ran full force toward the ledge. Her legs suspended in the air as she threw herself across the five foot chasm. Megan caught her, pulling Petra securely into the ship.

Mylan paled, the whites of his eyes showing. He took an involuntary step backward, running into Finn's chest. "I can't."

"You're getting on that ship if I have to throw you myself."

Linderly was next. She may have been small, but she knew how to leverage her muscles. Her leap looked almost animalistic in its grace. She didn't stop once she was onboard, running to assist Tai on the bridge.

A blast echoed into the night somewhere behind them. The guards had broken through to the roof.

Markes turned to face them, dropping to a knee and lifting his weapon. "Take Mylan first. I'll hold them off."

Finn shook his head. "You take him—"

"I'm not strong enough to haul his rickety ass onto that ship and we both know it," Markes pointed out. He gave Finn a quick smile.

"I'll be right behind you."

There was no time to argue over it.

Finn's hand tightened on Mylan's arm as he backed them both up. They'd need more of a running start to get the momentum they'd need.

Mylan began to shake, his head turning back and forth in denial. "I can't do this."

"You can either help me or struggle, but I'm not letting go of your arm." Finn leaned close, infusing every bit of desperation as he said darkly, "If you refuse to jump with me, then you'll fall to your death. Honestly, either outcome will work for me."

Mylan shifted beneath Finn's stare, swallowing hard. But he nodded. As far as consent went, that would have to do.

They took off as the guards began their assault. Despite his injury, Mylan was surprisingly quick. They reached the ledge and vaulted together, nothing but open air beneath them for one blissful moment. Mylan's legs caught on the ramp, bringing him down hard.

Finn dropped to his knees, hooking his hands beneath Mylan's arms, hauling him upward with a grunt. Megan took over, dragging Mylan up beside her and shoving him down the hallway.

Finn looked back to the roof. Markes was still holding off the guards.

"We need to go!" Megan yelled over the wind, worried eyes moving from Finn to Petra. "They'll be on us in seconds!"

Petra grabbed a heavier blaster from the wall and knelt to support Markes's defense. It wouldn't be enough.

"Throw me your weapon!" Finn yelled at Megan.

She complied immediately, offering him the one from her back. Finn caught it with one arm, hooking his leg around the hydraulics as he took aim. "Now get to the bridge—send the others back here."

"I'm not leaving you two."

Finn didn't waste any more breath arguing. He took aim and fired at the Reanges on the roof, ignoring the faces that lit up in the night from the glow of each blast.

Markes saw his opening. He rose to his feet and broke into a run for a leap of his own. A shot hit him squarely in the back, his eyes widening in shock as he went down mid-stride.

"Markes!" Megan shrieked.

Markes crumpled and collapsed, his body sliding from the momentum of his sprint. He came to a stop a few feet from the edge.

"Get up!" Petra's scream blew away on the wind.

Markes lifted his head, his eyes meeting Finn's across the expanse. He couldn't stand. He would never make that jump alone.

Finn slung his weapon over his shoulder and crossed the platform to Megan, unbuckling her harness. "You didn't stick to the plan. You're our only hope of getting out if Leviathan wakes up. Get back to the bridge—lock the others out."

Tears filled her eyes as she fumbled to help him. He attached the harness to himself. Megan bit her lip but didn't argue.

Finn didn't wait to see if she obeyed his order.

"Cover me!" he yelled at Petra.

And Finn launched himself back to the roof.

The landing was too close. Finn's boots barely cleared the edge as he rolled with his momentum to his knees, his blaster at his shoulder. He got off a few shots before relying on Petra for support.

Finn pulled Markes to his feet in lurching movements. "Can you run?"

"Just leave me, Finn," Markes wheezed. He curled in on himself, his eyes wet. Hot blood poured out of his wound, coating Finn's hand.

"So you can take all the glory? Nice try, kid." Finn gave him a reassuring grin. He removed the harness from his own hips, attaching it to Markes. Finn gave the straps a solid tug. "If you want to send up a prayer to the moons, now's the time."

Markes choked out a laugh, blood splattering across his lips.

Finn placed a firm hand on Markes's neck. "Now hobble over to that ledge and jump."

"But, Finn—"

"Now!" Finn's voice cracked. "That's an order!"

Finn took a knee, facing the soldiers. They were closer than ever, nearly breathing down his neck, trusting that Markes would obey him for once. And that Megan had taken over the controls of the ship. She was their only chance at getting out of there alive.

Any moment now, the others would be compromised. Leviathan would wake, and they'd be completely screwed.

More guards surged from the stairwell, their assault intensifying. If Finn tried to make the jump again, if he turned his back, he would suffer Markes's fate.

"Get out of here!" Finn yelled over his shoulder, risking a glance and locking eyes with Petra.

She stood at the edge of the hatch. Markes had made it: Tai and Linderly were pulling him deeper into the safety of the ship. Finn gave Petra a quick nod as the ship rose up. He wanted her to know it was all right. This had been his choice.

Her vibrant eyes narrowed on him. She took a step forward.

And then she was out of sight. He could only see the belly of the ship as it lifted into the night sky.

Finn returned his attention to the fight. It was always meant to be this way. He had made the decision already. At least now his death would mean something twofold. In kidnapping Mylan, the others would have a valuable bargaining chip.

Finn would die at last. He hoped that Leviathan would be content without a public exhibition.

Something slammed into the roof beside him in a flash of blue hair and tumbling limbs. Petra rolled across the surface to sprawl at his feet.

"What do you think you're doing?" Finn screamed at her.

"Helping." Petra rose to a knee.

She pulled a gargantuan yellow weapon from her back, resting it atop her shoulder as she took aim. But that was one of Markes's—

The roof shook as she fired, the missile finding its way straight toward the group of soldiers that had them pinned. The explosion was louder than Finn expected, a flash of blue light blinding him as hundreds of electrodarts whirled out in all directions. The group collapsed. Their cries of agony were chilling as they fought against the stimulation of their pain receptors. It was a brutal defense, but effective.

"Moons above," Finn said in awe, lowering his blaster in the wake of Markes's new weapon. "I guess it wasn't such a bad idea after all."

"Let's go." Petra was on her feet, heading for the stairs, its entrance a mass of rubble.

"Please tell me you have a plan that doesn't involve us going back into the building full of people out to kill us."

"I have an idea."

"Why doesn't that make me feel better," Finn muttered, moving past her.

Whatever Petra's plan entailed, it didn't involve a rescue. The others wouldn't be able to come back for them. Megan would have to haul ass out of Milderion like their lives depended on it.

Finn froze.

Petra's gun pressed against the back of his head, cold and heavy.

He turned slowly to face her, the gun running the edge of his temple. Her hand shook as the barrel pressed haphazardly against his skull.

"Petra?" Finn whispered, fear curling unpleasantly in his belly.

Her breath came in pants, quick bursts of air in and out of her nose. Her dark blue brows drew together, wrinkling her forehead. She was fighting it—fighting Leviathan. Her green eyes were wide, brightened by a sheen of moisture. Of tears.

Finn wouldn't raise his weapon against Petra. Leviathan would know that. Worse still, she would use it against him.

It was over.

CHAPTER
TWENTY-SIX

Finn watched the sun rise over the city with nothing but dread in his stomach. He stared blankly as yellow rays crested over the snow-capped mountains, bright fingers of light extending down to caress the curving arches of Milderion's tallest buildings.

He'd been locked in that room for hours with nothing but thoughts of his failure. Sleep was out of the question. The sunrise, while breathtaking, marked the official start of Su'elben: his last day alive.

Petra had gone with the others willingly. Her eyes had been cold and empty by the time Origin reinforcements arrived. He had no idea about the fate of the others. With Leviathan focused on Petra, maybe they had broken free of the city. And if Mylan was telling the truth, it was Finn that Leviathan wanted. Perhaps she would be content with that.

Mylan's kidnapping would benefit their team in more ways than one. Their small resistance had gained a powerful tool against Leviathan by capturing her closest adviser. Finn wouldn't be around to learn Mylan's motives, but he hoped they were honorable. If Mylan's faith in Leviathan's rule was faltering, it could be the opening they needed.

But the price they paid for Mylan was steep. Losing Petra would be a heavy burden for the others to carry.

It wouldn't matter, either way. Once Leviathan delved into Petra's mind, she would know everything. The sanctuary they'd found in Nos Lenti would be obliterated. But the others would know that by now. They would move. They would survive.

The door to his makeshift cell opened as the sun finished its climb into the blue sky. The guards that dragged him out were rough, refusing to answer any of Finn's taunts as they towed him through the halls and shoved him into the elevator. He watched the floors pass as they traveled upward. It wasn't hard to guess where they were taking him.

The assault continued as they forced him over the threshold into Leviathan's apartments. Finn's pride was hurt more than anything else when they drove him to his knees before her. He stayed down.

"Mylan was certain your sense of honor would result in your voluntary surrender." Leviathan's words were hard, each consonant clipped and blunt as stone. She sat ramrod straight in her seat on the couch before Finn, knobby knuckles clenched around the cane she always carried. The necklace they'd come for sat heavily on her chest, a thick chain of silver that featured a round pendant of translucent stone. Resting against her pale gray robes, it nearly glowed. They'd been so close. "I daresay he didn't expect you try some juvenile scheme that was bound to fail."

"Him and me both." Finn sat back on his heels, his aching quads screaming in protest. He eyed the two guards standing near the entry way, wondering if trying to stand would be the worth the risk of a beating.

Leviathan lifted her chin, looking farther down her sharp nose at him. "Of course. This was the others' attempt to save you. It's almost charmingly naive. I expected more from Petra. She had such potential as a child."

Finn's fingers dug into his thighs. "Let her go, Leviathan. It's me you want."

"She belonged to me well before she ever heard of you," Leviathan snapped.

"She belongs to no one."

"Ha!" Leviathan slammed down her cane. "You think she fights with you out of her own volition? It is for Avery whom she fights, make no mistake. And she belonged to Avery as much as she did to me."

"Avery never forced her. Avery never took away her free will."

"Semantics, boy, nothing more. Reanges were created to follow their So's orders and so they shall. Now that we have control over our own world again, we will reshape it to illustrate these convictions. Avery's power held a promise that was too alluring for Petra to resist, whether she was directly controlled or not."

"Petra followed Avery for the same reason we all did."

"Yes, yes. You love Avery and believe in her vision for a world where we can all live together." Leviathan ended with a flourish of her hand. "It's all foolish—a childish fantasy. Never mind that she is one of the last So' of her generation, but she is powerful beyond anything I've seen. And what did she do with all that natural talent? Threw it away. Squandered her chance to truly lead."

"You stole that chance from her!" Finn snarled, coming up on his knees. A hard shove from the guard forced him back down. Finn barely caught himself from falling flat on his face.

Leviathan frowned. "You have led me away from the topic at hand. There is no sense in squabbling over this now."

Finn laughed. "I've got nowhere to be."

"Oh, but you do." Leviathan smiled. "We both have quite the day ahead of us. I'd like to get this part of it over with."

Finn recoiled at her reminder, at the way it sent reality barreling into his gut like a physical blow.

"Now." She lowered her chin, narrowing her eyes. "Tell me where your miscreants have taken Mylan."

"Or you'll kill me? As you just reminded both of us, that's already on your agenda." Finn's mind reeled. Why was she asking about the others? She should see it easily in Petra's mind.

Leviathan slammed her cane down again. "Speak, boy, before I have them shoot you right here!"

"I don't think so." Finn tilted his head, relishing in this small bit of control left to him. "You promised all of Echo a show. You wouldn't ruin the main event."

"An unfortunate reality I'm coming to regret. No matter—Petra will reveal it soon enough." She leaned forward, her nostrils flaring as she added, "But rest assured, when I find those traitors hiding with your human rescues, I will not give them the quick death bestowed upon you today."

Rage surged up Finn's throat, fueled by the blinding fear that had haunted him since dawn. Finn was at her throat before she could react, his fingers wrapping around her thin neck, his fingers tangling with the very necklace they'd come to steal.

He would die today regardless. And by the moons, he would go down fighting.

Whatever physical power Leviathan wielded jerked Finn's body backward, ripping his hands away from her throat and the stone, sending him flying into the wall. His head cracked loudly, the impact reverberating through his spine. He slumped to the ground, stars blooming across his vision.

The guards descended on him with booted kicks and the butts of their weapons. Pain blossomed with no origin and no end. The copper tang of his blood was vibrant in his mouth, nearly blissful in its ability to rob him of the overwhelming terror for his friends.

Somewhere far away, Leviathan was choking loudly, her wet coughs interspersed with a desperate chorus of wheezing. And that was better than nothing.

Finn smiled as darkness took him.

The sound of the crowd woke him.

Finn squinted at the bright light of a midday sun. It streamed through the windows that lined the entire wall, warming him to the point of discomfort. Someone had thrown him into the row of seats that faced the view. More than one of his limbs had fallen asleep. His legs stung as he sat up, the uncomfortable sensation at odds with the pounding of his skull.

A hand settled on his shoulder. Finn jerked away wildly, spinning to his feet.

"Calm down." Petra backed away a step.

Finn sucked in air as he looked her over. Besides the wary frown on her face, she seemed fine. Better than fine. She seemed . . . like herself.

"Petra?" Finn rubbed a hand over his forehead. He winced as he hit a fresh wound, pulling away red stained fingers. Right—the beating. He'd almost forgotten nearly killing Leviathan.

"Did that blow to your head finally wipe your skull clean?"

Finn let out a rush of laughter. "I'm just surprised. You're . . . you."

"And the revelations keep coming."

"The last time we saw each other, you were decidedly *not* you."

The sound of the crowd surged in a sudden cheer, making them both flinch. Petra stiffened. Her eyes shifted to the windows.

Finn finally realized where they were. The rows of seats . . . the wide windows . . . the sounds from the other side of the glass . . . It was the Milderion arena. As his role as ambassador, Finn had been to many events in these very suites overlooking the field beyond. But none where he'd been this invested in the outcome.

A part of Finn had wondered if Leviathan might let him live, after all. Pardoning him could bring her approval and demonstrate mercy. Perhaps that was worth more than what obedience his execution would bring.

But she had no desire for approval when she had control.

Finn stared down at the field. Hundreds of performers danced in unison, their bright banners snapping and twirling in the wind. A traditional Reange orchestra sat on a podium in its center. The crowd roared with approval. Su'elben was a lesser known holiday, centered on the value of sacrifice and loss. Even if it hadn't been honored in popular circles, the rite was of utmost importance to the Origin. And no wonder, given their mission.

In a way, the display moved Finn. He hadn't seen this many

Reanges celebrating anything in unison since his childhood. The half-assed attempts of the humans to honor Reange customs had been laughable.

Finn rested his swollen hands on the window sill, bracing himself against the throbbing pain of his torn palms. These would be the last few moments of his life. He wanted to make them count.

His eyes moved across the thousands of smiling faces that filled the stands. It seemed as though the entire city had shown up to attend. Families. Friends. Liberated Reanges, enjoying their life without any trace of fear. Even if Leviathan controlled this new world, at least in some ways they were still free.

A raised platform of gray steel sat untouched in the front of the celebrations, empty and barren. It stood out in stark relief against the vibrant costumes and flags surrounding it. It could only serve one purpose.

Finn's palms turned clammy. He would not be intimated by its reality—not when he had chosen this path for himself. He was ready.

And directly across from the dais was a section of the stands designated for the Origin Council. Finn recognized many of the faces. Milupe stood out, her pale pink hair now streaked with more gray than she'd ever had before. She had been a vibrant member of the Rebellion Council, both kind and fair. He wondered if there was any part of her left.

Leviathan sat apart from the others, centered and at the front. Of course she'd want the best view. He knew that beneath the high collar of her blue coat, a ring of bruises would remind her of his life for weeks to come.

"The others?" Finn kept his eyes on the celebration. "Did they get out?"

Petra moved to stand beside him. "I don't know," she answered quietly. "When I—woke up, I was here. With you."

Finn turned to her. "You didn't speak to Leviathan?"

"No." She shook her head, watching him closely. "I'm assuming that means you did?"

"Unfortunately. She wasn't exactly hospitable."

She took in a dramatic breath, pressing a hand to her chest. "Leviathan? Not hospitable? I'm shocked."

"Did you just make a joke?" Finn laughed in disbelief at her pathetic attempt. "I really must be about to die if you're taking that much pity on me."

She sobered. "Don't make light of this."

"Why not?" Finn lifted a shoulder and let it drop. But he couldn't meet her eyes. He pivoted back to the window. "It's not like that audience out there is going to find me funny. Might as well use my last good lines on you."

Petra stood in silence with him.

There wasn't much they had left to say to one another. Finn wasn't exactly going to point out that he had been right. He should have just turned himself in. They had failed. There was no point in dragging them both through the pain of that reality.

"Why would she bring me here?" Petra asked so softly, it was almost to herself.

"Who?"

"Leviathan. It doesn't make sense. Why would she let me see you before . . ." She trailed off, her unsaid words loud in both their heads: *Before you die.*

"As far as last requests go, I'm not sure I'd choose to spend my final moments with you—no offense. You and I don't exactly have the best track record for feel good vibes."

"She would be more likely to execute me alongside you than offer a conciliatory visitation."

Finn's shoulders stiffened. He'd never even considered that Leviathan might choose to kill Petra as well. The whole reason Finn wanted to turn himself in was to protect the others.

The whole reason he'd done *any* of this was to keep them safe, to protect them the way Avery would have.

Leviathan wouldn't kill Petra. She couldn't afford to. Not when—

"She can't kill you. Not yet," Finn said confidently. "She still needs you . . . Something she said before, when she was interrogating me for information," Finn explained, growing more excited. "I don't think she can read you, Petra. She can't get into your head. Not fully, at least."

"But . . ." It was Petra's turn to look dazed. "That's impossible. She took control of me, she—"

"I know. But it's true," Finn stopped her, nodding as things started to make more sense. "If she could read your memories, she wouldn't have had me brought to her apartments this morning. She was trying to get the answers from *me*." He searched her face, hope surging. "Whatever you're doing, you need to keep it up."

"I'm not *doing* anything."

"Petra, please." Finn rested his hands on her shoulders, squeezing hard. She had to understand—he had to *make* her understand. "If she gets fully inside your head . . . If she sees where the others—"

"I know!" She broke out of his hold, turning away as her shoulders sagged. Her next words were fragmented, disordered in a way so unlike Petra that it frightened him. "I didn't realize Leviathan hadn't already . . . Then the others are still—then Megan is still . . . ."

"I hope so," Finn said shakily. "For all your sakes."

A gong rang out, loud enough to shake the glass, and they both jumped. The entertainers on the field moved into formation, slowing in front of the stands. Rows and rows stilled, their faces turned up to Leviathan and her council. The crowd grew louder, shaking the very foundations of the arena.

Leviathan stood. She moved to the railing, pressing a small mic pinned to her lapel. "Once again, I want to welcome each and every one of you to the first true Su'elben celebration we've enjoyed since the liberation of Echo!"

More cheers surged as her voice filled the arena, echoing dimly through the glass. She smiled, but the expression was more calculated than genuine. Not that anyone in the stands would notice.

"It truly is an auspicious day of celebration for those bonds we share with one another as a united people. But let us not forget that the purpose of this joyous occasion. Our sacrifices have been great, and our loss profound. Our history is not a stranger to suffering. Let us not forget the lives both taken and destroyed at the hands of unchecked human violence."

She paused and the energy of the crowd shifted, descending into jeers and violent screams.

Finn's stomach churned. He glanced at the door, wondering if there was any point in trying to run. Not that exiting into an arena filled with angry Reanges would be any better. He was a sacrifice awaiting his five minutes in the spotlight, no matter how that materialized.

Leviathan's smile turned into a vitriolic grimace, the echo of her emotion spreading through the stands. "And violent means require violent answers." Her strange eyes cut a line up to the windows where Finn and Petra watched.

Finn faltered, stepping out of her sight. He wouldn't give Leviathan the satisfaction of seeing him falter.

Petra faced him with arms crossed. Her jaw was set, her eyes glassy.

Finn tuned out Leviathan droning on in the back of his awareness. He knew what was coming. Listening to her diatribe would do nothing but make him sick.

Finn ran a shaky hand through his hair. "Listen, Petra—"

"Don't."

He paused. She was shaking. Her face contorted, fighting against stubbornly against the reality that now faced them.

Finn stepped closer. Had she been anyone else, he would have wrapped her in an embrace. The last vestige of friendship and love he'd have in this life. But he didn't—she'd loathe the touch anyway.

"Maybe bringing you here . . . Maybe this is her way of trying to break you," Finn said gently. He waited for her to meet his eyes. "Don't let it, Petra. Whatever happens to me out there, know that this was my choice. I chose this."

She flinched, turning away from him.

"If you hadn't stopped me back on that ship, the result would have been the same. But we gave the others a fighting chance—Mylan will be an asset in the battle ahead." Another gong sounded. A shiver rolled down Finn's spine. He did reach for her then, his fingers pressing into her forearms. "Protect the others as best you can. Don't let her in."

Petra nodded stiffly. "Finn . . . If I've been . . . In the past, if I've—"

"Stop right there, blueberry," he said quickly, giving her arms a reassuring squeeze. "I know you well enough by now to know."

She gave him a rueful smile, grateful that he had saved her from saying the words outright. At least he could give her that.

Heavy footfalls sounded outside the door. A line of soldiers filed past the window, their deep blue uniforms blurring together in his peripheral.

Petra tensed. She moved in front of Finn, bracing her feet, ready to fight. Finn almost smiled.

But as the door opened, her body began to shake, harder than before. Her back straightened. Her hands dropped to her sides. As the shoulders entered, she turned back to him. Her green eyes were blank.

"Petra?" Finn whispered.

But Petra was gone.

Whatever readiness Finn had scrounged together slipped uselessly through his fingers. And he knew. Throwing them together in these last moments hadn't been to break Petra.

It had been to break Finn.

Finn didn't fight Petra as she threw him to the ground, his knees cracking on the hard floor. She tied his hands with a cord behind his back, tightening the bonds until he could no longer feel his swollen fingers.

The crowds erupted louder than ever before as they proceeded down the staircase to the field. Finn's world became a ringing blur of sound and motion until he found himself on the platform at Leviathan's feet. Petra stood beside him. She was motionless, her face empty, the perfect image of a seasoned soldier awaiting her next order.

"May the moons be kinder to your soul than you deserve." Leviathan's blessing reverberated around them, amplified through the mic on her lapel.

She passed a bony hand over Finn's head, the floral scent of holy oils filling his nostrils as she anointed him with the final rite. He tried to rise, desperate to use this last moment to resist, but Petra's hand found his shoulder, shoving him back to the ground roughly. Leviathan gave him a final withering look as she turned away, a priestess dressed in red robes taking her place. His resting prayer was read and his energy purged. He was prepared to meet the afterlife.

The world blurred again and Finn was alone on the dais with Petra. She dragged him to his feet, walking them both to the center of the metal platform. Someone had placed a table there, swathed in a maroon cloth. Atop it, the hilt of a laser sword rested on an ornate mount of carved black stone.

Realization dawned. Petra would be the one to do it. *Petra would be the one to take his life.*

The blood drained from Finn's face as a new fear clawed its way up his ribs. She would never be able to live with this. The memory of it—and he was sure Leviathan would make her remember—would destroy her.

Petra shoved him to his knees again and he lost his balance, nearly tumbling off the front of the platform and down the dry field some ten feet below. By the time he righted himself, Petra had the sword in hand, a sparking yellow blade firing ominously from its burnt metal hilt. She stalked toward him, her body following the unspoken command of Leviathan's will.

Finn met her eyes. But they weren't blank, as before. Tears brimmed over those green depths, spilling out and down her cheeks as she halted over him. Leviathan had devised the ultimate torture for them both: to give Petra her awareness, only to force her to carry out his execution herself with a body beyond her control.

Finn's eyes stung. He wouldn't make this harder for her. Whatever Leviathan hoped to accomplish with this, she would fail.

Petra was strong. Stronger than Finn. Stronger than most. And she still had a chance to protect the others. Finn had to believe that.

He let out a shaking breath, dropping back onto his heels. He leaned his head forward, nearly to the ground. He would make it as easy as possible.

Petra's shadow crossed over him, her black boots entering his line of vision. He stared unseeing at the specks of dried dirt strewn across the platform, his breath no more than sharp whooshes in and out of his nostrils.

The seconds stretched into an infinity that was a torture all its own as he waited for the blow. Would it hurt? How much would he feel? How *long* he would feel? Panic fizzled up his spine, making him dizzy.

"It's all right, Petra," Finn choked out, hoping his declaration sounded less like a sob than he feared. He could be strong. He had to be. So he repeated it. "It's all right."

The gong sounded again. One more peal and Petra would strike.

Finn closed his eyes, letting his mind slip to that place that he'd kept forbidden. He conjured a vision of Avery, her memory rushing into his mind on a wave of grief and pleasure that mingled into something approaching euphoria. For the first time in months, Finn didn't hold himself back—he let his mind turn fully to her.

Her golden eyes, piercing and beautiful and powerful. That smile that softened whenever she looked at him. The freckles that crinkled into new constellations with every laugh. He would end his life bathed in the beauty of her. If memory was all he had left of Avery, then he would revel in it until his last breath.

The final gong rang out, and the entire world faded away.

A thud shook the dais. Something—or someone—landed in front of them.

And then a vicious snarl curled around the newcomer's command. "Don't you fucking touch him."

For a moment, Finn thought he conjured her voice from his dreams. Even the crowd quieted in the wake of her command.

"That's enough, Petra."

Finn's eyes shot open. But he didn't move—he couldn't. He stared at the ground, at that same pattern in the dirt smeared across metal. He'd know her voice anywhere, even when it was low and deadly and filled with rage. But she couldn't be there. It was impossible. Maybe death had come quicker than he thought.

Finn tilted his head upward, and a part of him died anyway.

Avery stood above him, her body outlined by the fierce light of the sun above them, making his eyes water. Her bare hand gripped the laser blade just above Finn's neck where it had been inches away from detaching his head.

It was her. *It was her.*

The arena descended into chaos.

CHAPTER TWENTY-SEVEN

Avery could feel Finn's eyes boring into her, their heat somehow more intense than the winter sun blazing overhead. She allowed herself to glance down at him, trusting that her skill would keep the laser blade hovering millimeters above her fingers instead of slicing straight through them. The blue of his eyes, both familiar and strange to her now, nearly sent her to her knees.

Finn's lips moved, mouthing something silently as those eyes filled with tears.

Her name.

"Hey." Avery's voice caught.

His eyes widened, anticipating. But still, he said nothing.

A grin pulled at Avery's lips. If that made him speechless, what she was about to do next would really knock him on his ass. "I'm sorry about this."

Finn frowned in confusion.

Avery raised a free hand to shove him away on a wave of pure energy. He flew across the dais, tumbling only until he regained his senses. He rolled up into a crouch a safe distance away.

The crowd roared to deafening heights. Thousands of Reanges watched as Avery turned to Petra. Qav was out there somewhere, trying to calm the crowd. He would be able to counter at least some of

Leviathan's influence. But Avery's fight was right in front of her—she had to focus solely on Petra.

Already, Leviathan probed the edges of Avery's mind, searching for an opening. Her assault was strong, but Leviathan was weakened by the sheer scale of the crowd. She couldn't hope to focus her power on an attack while maintaining her grip on the Reanges present. And Leviathan needed them too much to let go of her hold.

Tears streamed down Petra's cheeks, fresh from her near miss as Finn's executioner. Avery pushed the blade up until their hands were raised overhead. Petra's wrist shook.

"Petra." Avery said her name quietly. She reached out to her mind, searching for the familiar vibration of Petra's energy. It was faint but there, encased in a net of granite that could only be Leviathan's doing. Avery tested the net, her power sliding along Leviathan's, looking for an opening.

Petra's free hand jabbed at Avery, catching her in the side. Avery threw her elbow up into Petra's chin, bringing her hand down and knocking the laser knife from Petra's grasp. It sizzled out as the hilt lost skin contact, sliding uselessly across the stage.

Petra was on Avery in the next breath, fighting in earnest. Avery countered each blow, backing away rather than deal damage. They danced across the stage, each movement met with another that was equally skillful. Petra was sweating as Leviathan pushed her body to keep up. She wouldn't last much longer.

Something pulled at her, a tendril of warmth that beckoned to Avery with a familiar promise. She'd felt it before—she'd listened to its call. It *knew* her.

Avery glanced at the stands. Leviathan's gaze was sharp, the neon violet of her eyes shimmering across the yards between them. The old woman leaned heavily on her cane, focusing entirely on Avery and Petra. Good. If her attention was on them, then she'd never be paying attention to the crowds. Or to the rest of the Council. With any luck, Qav would be able to work his magic without detection.

Avery may have leveled up her own abilities over the past year, but it was clear Leviathan was still formidable. They couldn't take her in a direct fight—not yet.

"Look out!" Finn's yelled warning was too late.

Petra's leg swept beneath Avery, knocking her from her feet. She hit the platform hard, the air leaving her chest in a solid whoosh. She'd allowed that strange feeling to distract her—a stupid mistake. Syla would be disappointed. Avery scrambled to her feet, surprised when Petra didn't press her attack. She realized why as Petra launched at her with the laser sword she'd retrieved, slicing straight for Avery with unnatural strength. Avery pivoted, the glowing yellow blade glancing off her upper arm with a burning hiss of pain.

What was Qav waiting for? He knew Avery needed Petra free of Leviathan's grip. She had been clear: she refused to leave either of them.

Petra swiped again in a flurry of strikes, forcing Avery back another three steps. Enough was enough.

Avery stood her ground, dipping her chin as she sent out a wave of energy. Petra lifted off the ground in mid-stride, flailing as she fought for balance in the air.

Avery shifted to face the stands.

"Let her go," Avery called.

Leviathan's stoney power hit her again, testing Avery's boundaries. But Avery did more than keep her out this time. She pushed back.

In a moment, Avery was inside Leviathan's mind. A series of thoughts and memories flashed by, too quickly to track; a young man standing on a cliff's edge in the moonlight; a baby with the same purple eyes as his mother; the crumpled body of a young girl, dead in the middle of summer. The wild emotion that came along with each was overbearing, consuming any hope of control. Avery fumbled, trying to hold on to one—to any—but they slipped out of her grasp, elusive and untouchable.

Avery staggered back a step as Leviathan pushed her out violently. The stone wall fortified, completely immovable. There would be no getting back in.

Leviathan raised a white brow. *Been practicing, have we?*

Her voice in Avery's head was as unnerving as it was familiar. Avery longed to block even this small connection, but keeping Leviathan distracted was paramount.

Avery splayed her hands out at her sides in an unspoken warning. *You have no idea.*

It seems you have also developed a taste for the dramatics, Leviathan continued. *Waiting until the last possible moment to rescue your human. How droll.*

In Petra's mind, Leviathan's heavy net was beginning to crumble. Qav was doing his part, just slower than they'd anticipated. Avery kept her shoulders tight, her muscles ready. If they played this right, Leviathan would assume Petra's freedom had been Avery all along.

They just needed a final distraction.

I learned from the best, Avery replied, holding her focus. *You can feel my strength, Leviathan. Let me walk out of here with my people, and we will leave you be.*

You may have elevated your capabilities, but you lie as poorly as ever, my girl. Leviathan's lips pursed. *No—you will not be leaving.*

Avery smiled. *I thought you might say that.*

Avery raised a hand at Petra, pulling the laser sword from her grip with enough force to send her body spinning. The weapon soared across the arena in a direct line for Leviathan, its deadly blade kept alight by Avery's power.

For a moment, Avery had a wild hope that she would finally end this thing with one sporadic decision. But fate had other plans. A Council member screamed. Someone jumped toward Leviathan, pushing her out of the way. He cried out as the blade sunk into his shoulder, burning through tendon and bone. Piltor, an Elder she recognized from her time assisting the Council the previous year. He'd always been reasonable. Funny, even. Avery had liked him.

Avery paled, but she couldn't afford to worry over the miscalculation. He would live.

The misdirection had served its purpose. Qav had freed Petra from Leviathan's control. Avery let her body drop and Petra crashed into the metal stage, bleary-eyed and dazed.

"Get up!" Avery was at her side in a moment, dragging her to her feet, pulling her toward Finn. They may have thrown Leviathan for a few minutes, but Avery was uncertain how long she'd be disoriented. First and foremost, this was a rescue mission, and nothing said rescue like brevity.

"On your feet!" Avery yelled at Finn.

He stayed on his knees as he watched them approach, his mouth open, his hands shaking.

"Finn! We have to go!" she growled, hooking an arm under his and hauling him to his feet. "Get your ass up, damn it."

Petra took his other side, finally present and aware. She yanked on him hard enough that he stumbled.

"Lunitia," Petra snapped, jabbing his side.

Finn grunted, but the blow seemed to knock some sense into him and he took off running beside them. They sprinted for the edge of the stage, nothing but the open field beyond. At least the performers had scrambled when she appeared—there would be less chance of casualties.

The roaring crowd faltered, letting out gasps and cries of surprise as the ship materialized at the end of the dais, some twenty feet above. The sun caught the sleek silver lines of its body, flashing brightly. Even on Echo, with its advanced capabilities, Cora's tech was a true marvel.

The loading door slid open on the ship's belly, revealing a cavernous docking space. Syla leaned out, her large gun trained on the crowds behind them, ready to fire.

"Are we jumping that?" Finn yelled, his voice cracking over the din of the crowd.

"That's the plan!" Avery replied over her shoulder, grinning.

"We'll never make it!" Petra countered, but her pace didn't slow. She would follow Avery regardless.

"Just trust me!" Avery vaulted off the stage.

There was no time to doubt her, and they followed suit, launching together. Avery lifted their bodies, extending the arc of their momentum with an assist of energy that carried them two . . . three . . . five seconds through the air.

They hit the floor of the ship, rolling to crash into the wall. Avery was caught in a tangle of warm limbs, a wide hand cradling her head from impact. She pushed up on her forearms, looking down at Finn. His hand trailed down to the back of her neck, his long fingers curling into her braid.

She allowed herself to look at him—really look at him. The familiar strong line of his nose, the dimple in his cheek, the hints of gray that shot through his blue eyes, threatening to pull her down into their depths. His fingers tightened against her hair, his long eyelashes fluttering. He breathed her name. Her stomach flipped.

He stared at back at her, his eyes roaming hungrily across her face, taking in every detail. His other arm wrapped around Avery's waist, digging into her hips, pressing her against him like he would never let her go again.

But there were new things about him, too. Revelations that cracked open a deep wound, squeezing Avery's heart until she could hardly breathe. A mottled scar took up most of the side of his face, red and angry, pulling the top of his lip. He bled freely from a fresh gash across his forehead. A deep bruise was forming along the line of his jaw. What had they done to him?

It didn't matter. It was Avery's fault—whatever had happened to Finn was because of her.

How would she ever find the right way to apologize? What would it take to show him how much she regretted? Finn had suffered. Greatly, by the looks of it. *Because of her.*

"Finn, I—"

"Avery." Syla's voice was low—worried.

Avery pulled herself out of Finn's hold, on her feet and at Syla's side as they lifted away from the field. Along the edge of the arena, soldiers had gathered in formation, long-range weapons already mounted on their shoulders.

"Shit," Avery said under her breath. "Leviathan prepared for every eventuality."

"We don't have time to deal with this," Syla said curtly. Her dark eyes moved worriedly over the crowd. To get everyone safely out of the city, they needed to stick to their timeline. A trickle of sweat ran down the side of Syla's cheek. "Should I fire?"

"No," Avery commanded. "We don't harm anyone acting under her control."

It would complicate things, but Avery was adamant. She refused to harm innocents. The face of the Elder she'd maimed only minutes earlier flashed through her mind, declaring her a hypocrite.

If she wouldn't let Syla openly attack the Origin soldiers, then Avery would have to deal with them the old-fashioned way. The wind whipped her braid across her cheek, the hair stinging her cheeks in the cold. She looked over her shoulder where Finn was helping Petra to her feet.

Avery was back on Echo. She had actually made it back to him. To all of them.

Finn and Petra both looked up in unison as though they sensed her stare, their forearms still clasped. A bright smile took over her face, her elation unruly and vibrant and real.

Neither of them would enjoy what she had planned.

"I'll be right back," she said quickly with a reassuring nod.

Finn's brows drew together sharply, his body tensing.

Her smiled widened, and she gave him a wink. "I promise."

She dove out of the ship, barreling through the air toward the ground and guns below.

CHAPTER TWENTY-EIGHT

Avery focused on her descent, ignoring Finn's shout behind her. She tucked her arms into her sides, aiming for the row of gunned soldiers, encasing herself in a shield of power. She slammed directly into the line. For a moment Avery was nothing more than a cloud of dust in the dry soil, fully obscured within the crater from her landing. Soldiers scattered away from the blow, falling to their bellies. A few lay unconscious around the divot of Avery's impact, their massive gray weapons useless in the dirt.

Alarm flared through Syla. She saw Finn through Syla's eyes—saw him run for the opening—saw him try to throw himself out after her. He would have, if Syla hadn't grabbed him by the collar of his shirt, shoving him back into the belly of the ship.

Avery cut off her connection. She glanced up toward the blue sky where the ship gained altitude and speed. Finn's anger would have to wait.

One solid leap and Avery emerged from the dust. The soldiers looked up as her shadow moved over them, their terror battling with the control Leviathan held in an iron grip. Avery would not harm them—any more than necessary. Their free will had been stolen. They would not pay the ultimate price for Leviathan's crimes.

Avery came down on a soldier who struggled to mount their oversized gun back on their shoulder, driving a knee to their chest. Two more lunged for Avery, launching in a swift battle of jabs and punches as they moved across the hard soil. She latched onto an arm, swinging the larger one around and into the other. Their bodies rolled together in a tangle across the field and out of range.

The crowd around them roared, their jeers reverberating through Avery's skull until it was hard to tell them apart from the blood thumping through her veins.

A gun pulsed, charging up. Avery snapped her head to the line of opponents that was left. Three soldiers ran at her as the one remaining gunner took aim behind them. But not at Avery. The weapon was locked on the retreating image of the ship clearing the arena.

She moved without thinking, running straight for the oncoming soldiers, vaulting over them, stepping through the air and dancing on a wave of pure power. The soldier fired.

Avery reached out toward the blastfire as it exited the barrel of the gun, a whorling white mass of destructive energy. But it had form. And Avery realized with sudden clarity: she could harness it.

She hit the ground with hands still raised, her fingers clawed in concentration. The blast stopped in midair. She jerked her arms and its trajectory skewed, sending the writhing ball of heat barreling across the arena and exploding into the base of the stands.

The stadium thundered, the cries of the crowd turning frantic, mingling with screams. Emotions reached Avery. Fear, anxiety—confusion. Leviathan's hold on the crowd had been strong when they had arrived. She had influenced the perception of the event, bending the people to her will. But now that hold was slipping. Leviathan was losing them.

The stands devolved into hysteria as the Reanges began to realize what they were witnessing. They flooded the aisles, barreling over one another for the exit. No one would risk staying in the vicinity if a true battle was at hand. Not even for sport.

Avery crashed into the soldier who'd fired the blast, taking them down with one punch. Avery pulled up the massive gun, aiming it for the remaining three who had regrouped to face her. They halted in their tracks. One clutched her head, another doubled over. There was fear on their faces, something more than just blank obedience.

Avery looked to the stands. Leviathan stood near the edge of the railing, her eyes focused on Avery. A fine sheen of sweat was visible across her ashen forehead, even from the hundred-yard distance. Had Qav been able to break through her defenses?

Someone shouted and Avery turned. A new wave of forces sprouted from the arena entrance. She couldn't wait around to find out if Leviathan's hold was faltering—it was time to go.

Avery crumpled the enormous blaster in her hands, the metal crinkling beneath her power like a useless toy. She flung it to the side as she sprinted for the stands. One glance at the clogged exits told her that avenue was pointless. Even if she could conceal herself in the crowds, it would put the Reanges at risk.

She didn't stop as she reached the high wall of the front seats, jumping up and over into the empty aisle. She bounded up the stairs five at a time, each jump more powerful than the last. At the top of the stadium, the final leap across the railing was no more than a thought. Her fingers gripped the cold metal as she shoved off into freedom and struck the ground, launching into a full sprint.

She used her powers to conceal her movements, cloaking herself from sight of the Reanges around her. Qav had taught her how to manipulate perception, ensuring passersby only saw what she wanted. It was unnerving to think that he possessed such a skill. But it proved useful. Avery moved through the bustling city as a ghost.

It took no time at all to reach the darker interior of Milderion, where the shadows of the high rises welcomed her in the fading light of the afternoon. Only when she was sure she hadn't been followed and that Leviathan's influence was far behind her did she slow to a walk, tucking into an empty alley. At last, she stretched out her power, feeling through the Reanges in proximity.

Took you long enough. Qav's cold presence curled up against her mind. *And you say I'm the one who likes to show off.*

Where are you? Avery ignored his baiting. If he was poking at her, that meant everything had gone well on his end. Her stomach dipped in a sudden rush of anxiety. Maybe she should have waited to rendez-vous with them alongside the others. Megan would be—

"We're right here."

Avery spun at Qav's surprise reply. He had been closer than she realized, able to sneak up behind her. Limiting the use of her power had put her at a disadvantage, especially where he was concerned. Avery didn't like it.

A rush of sweet perfume and golden curls bounced into Avery's arms, latching her in an immovable embrace. "Avie," Megan whispered. Her voice was gravelly. Her hold tightened further and a buckle on her jacket dug into Avery's neck.

Avery's throat dried against the wave of blinding familiarity. How many times had Megan greeted her in the exact same way? A hundred? A thousand? But it had never meant this much—it had never felt so essential, like an integral part of her had finally been restored with one simple hug.

Avery let out a huff, something between a sigh and a sob. It was so . . . normal. Megan's greeting loosened something inside her, pulling tears from Avery's eyes. They slipped down the slope of her cheeks, drying against Megan's pale hair.

Avery found control of her limbs again, wrapping her arms around Megan. They held each other fiercely. Her shoulders racked as she cried, hiding her face in Megan's shoulder. They stood that way for a long moment, lingering in the comfort of one another, rocking in unison as they both wept.

"You're okay," she said wetly, muffled by Megan's collar.

"As far as things go," Megan replied. She pulled back, laughing tearfully as she met Avery's eyes. Her hands slipped into Avery's, holding on to her still. "So are you?"

Avery nodded through her tears. She tried to speak again, but the tears erupted once more. The apology Avery had practiced saying a thousand times floated away in the face of Megan's unyielding devotion. She wasn't angry, although she had every right to be. She picked up their friendship effortlessly. As though nothing had ever happened.

But what Avery had done to Megan . . . How could anyone ever forgive that?

It was more than Avery had prepared herself for. It was more than she deserved.

Qav cleared his throat. "We've got a timeline to keep, ladies. Markes and Grigg are waiting."

"He's right. We'll have time for our sobfest later." Megan laughed, wiping tears from her eyes before pulling a gun over her shoulder. She unlocked the safety and tucked it into her shoulder. "Leviathan has spies everywhere in the city, in places she can't reach. Even with your fancy new skills, we can't afford to linger."

Avery's eyes widened. Megan may have greeted her the same, but she was different. She had changed. The superfluous exterior she had always used as a shield was gone, left behind in her life on Earth. Something fierce had taken its place. It was different but not unknown. A side of Megan that only Avery had seen before, now visible to the world.

But what Avery had done had forced it to the surface.

A flash of a memory appeared: Megan's limp body lying in a pile of rubble. Avery hadn't been able to protect her from anything, least of all herself.

"Avery," Megan snapped, drawing her attention back to the present. "Let's go."

"Get off me!" Finn writhed against the women holding him down, desperate to go after Avery. To help her. To follow her back into that arena.

"Not until you calm down." Syla's edict was raspy and harsh in his ear. She leaned over him, her knee digging into his chest, one arm on his shoulder, pressing him into the cold floor.

Petra—the traitor—held his other arm down.

"You can't—"

"I said get off!" Finn bellowed, catching Petra in the chest with a leg. She crashed into the white-plated wall and sunk to the floor. She stayed that way, staring at him with a look of disgust.

The outer door slid shut, closing them inside. Finn's panic surged. Avery was still out there! They couldn't abandon her again. *He refused to leave her.*

He twisted, dislodging Syla's knee and getting in a solid blow to her face. She lost her balance enough for Finn to get as far as his feet. But the warrior was too good a fighter to let something like surprise get the better of her.

Syla was up faster than light, blocking Finn's path as he charged. She side stepped before he could blink, latching onto his wrist and vaulting him over her shoulder in a complicated move that would have made Grigg jealous. Finn's heart twisted. He leaned into the pain, landing on his back. The air left his body. Stars flickered across his vision. Syla followed him to the floor, wrapping her legs around his neck and pivoting until his arm wrenched into an unnatural angle.

"I said. Calm. Down." Her voice was flat. Level.

"We can't—" He paused to suck in breath, wheezing. "We can't just leave her—"

"She's a big girl, Finn. She can handle herself."

But he could feel the ship on the move, lifting up and away, farther from Avery. Farther from everything he'd spent an entire year wishing would come back to him.

Finn lurched against Syla, his movements frantic. She tightened her grip. Pure agony lanced up his arm, blinding him with pain.

"Don't make me break your arm."

He considered struggling anyway. But the adrenaline was already beginning to ebb, the discomfort in his arm restoring some semblance of reasoning. They were already too far for him to go after Avery straightaway. He didn't even know who else was on the ship. He needed to gather more information, to make a plan.

But Petra was with him. And they were both alive.

Still. This was Syla. She was no more than an extension of the So' she served. It was as good as Qav holding him immobile. The thought of submitting to her . . . .

"Do it, then, and get it over with," Finn spat.

She frowned, her neon pink brows drawing together. He'd shocked her. Good. At least he won something.

"I knew you were thick, but this is another level."

The comment, uttered with such familiar annoyance, stopped his him from struggling. Syla let him twist around enough to see the entrance to the main walkway.

Nova stood with her hands on her hips, frowning with disapproval. "Avery said she'd be back, and she will be. Don't be stupid."

"Good luck with that." Petra pushed to her feet with a muffled grunt, one hand on her ribs.

Finn grimaced, but he relaxed in Syla's grip, and she released him at once. He rolled to his knees as the surprise of Nova's arrival crested over him. Tears blurred his vision. His throat constricted. He couldn't look at her face. He didn't want to see what grief he knew awaited him. If he faced her, then they'd both know.

Grigg was truly gone.

The three of them had once been inseparable. They'd trained together, seen battle together. They'd grown into adults side by side. And Grigg had been a brother to Nova before Finn had ever met them.

And now that Nova was home, she would see her family again. Only without Grigg, who had always been their heart.

He was dead because of Finn. Because of Nick's desperate attempt to reclaim Finn's allegiance. Their family was to blame for all of this. From the very first tests that wiped out the So'Reanges to the death of his closest friend. The darkness threatened to swallow Finn whole, coating his awareness with a blanket of guilt so heavy that it hurt to breathe. Finn slumped over, dropping his head.

Warm hands settled on his shoulders. Nova knelt in front of him. "Look at me, Finn," she said gently. Her presence was soothing, restorative in a way Finn didn't realize how much he'd missed.

But he couldn't look at her. That darkness kept him shackled to floor.

She pulled him into an embrace, wrapping her arms around him. He choked on a sob.

"I promised I'd protect her, didn't I?"

He let out a desperate laugh.

Nova *had* promised Finn that, all those months ago in the wake of battle. When Avery had banished him, threatening to kill them all under Qav's influence.

And Nova had stayed behind, forsaking her home. Her family. Everything she'd ever known. Not only for Avery's sake, but for Finn's as well. Because she understood he'd never be able to live without knowing she was protected in some way. Because Finn never would have left Avery if he'd had any other choice.

And he owed it to Nova to face her.

Finn let out a shuddering breath, leaning back on his heels. Her blue eyes met his, clear and confident. There was no blame there. No grief. Only understanding.

"And Syla is right," Nova said. "Avery can take care of herself."

Petra laughed sourly. "That's what she's always been good at, isn't it?"

"Watch it, Petra," Nova snapped. She stood, hauling Finn to his feet. "You haven't seen the things she's done. What we've been through. You haven't been there."

"And whose fault is that?"

"None of yours," Syla said calmly. "The fault is with Qav alone."

Finn flinched at the name, his fists clenching painfully around his wounds.

"Do not blame Avery for his meddling."

Petra shook her head. "She could have resisted him. We all know her strength."

"The way you resisted Leviathan on that platform?" Finn wouldn't stand by and let Petra disparage Avery's mistakes. Not when they'd all made their own.

Hurt flashed across Petra's face, there and gone in a moment.

"Get your shit together," Finn hissed. "Avery just saved you—she saved us both."

"That doesn't just erase everything she—"

"It has to!" Finn yelled, his own outburst surprising even himself. "Don't you get it? She's back. That means everything is different—*ev-*

erything. Forget about Qav."

"Forget about Qav?" Petra shook her head in disbelief slowly, like she pitied him. "For a solid year now, just the mention of his name has sent you into a full blown rage. And now you want to just delete him? Like he never even existed? Like what Avery did for him never even happened?"

Finn gritted his teeth. "She did nothing *for* him."

Petra crossed her arms over her chest. "You think we can forget about Qav? Don't kid yourself. Ask Nova what she hasn't told you yet."

Finn frowned, the hairs on his neck standing up. No . . . He didn't want to believe it. Avery never would have been that stupid.

"*Avery* didn't free me from Leviathan."

Finn's stomach dropped. The reason for Syla's presence suddenly came into focus with alarming clarity.

It couldn't be true. Even if Avery had been naive enough to trust Qav again, Nova never would. Not after what he had done.

But Nova wouldn't meet Finn's eyes.

Petra laughed again, the sound at once both bitter and broken. She confirmed Finn's worst nightmare with four simple words.

"*Qav is with them.*"

CHAPTER
TWENTY-NINE

Avery trailed behind Megan as she wove them through the city like a trained soldier. She had a knowledge of Milderion, of its streets and alleyways and tunnels, that could only have come from intensive study and use. Her golden hair was bound in a pony tail high on her head, mimicking the style Nova always sported in favor of practicality. Avery had never seen Megan with her hair up, not since they were children.

When they'd come through the Gate, they'd been ready for Leviathan to still have control of Echo. But there had been no Origin guard stationed outside of atmo. Leviathan either didn't realize the Gate was a risk, or she didn't care. Which meant whoever had been sending messages to Earth was keeping their intel to themselves.

Avery had been able to pinpoint Markes, Linderly, and Tai easily. Even limiting her powers, Avery's connection to her friends was immediate, like some sort of intrinsic gravitational pull. Especially in their extreme emotional state, with Markes gravely wounded and their hopes destroyed. Their ship was hidden on the outskirts of the city, tucked beneath the lush greenery of the forest at the edge of the plains.

According to a tearful Linderly, Megan had tricked them after their wild escape from the city where they'd kidnapped Mylan from his own bed. Claiming that she was the only one who could get close to Leviathan, Megan had locked them in the galley—along with Mylan, who was suffering from his own injuries—and left. Presumably, she had some insane idea that she could rescue Petra and Finn. Even if Megan had Syla's skills and training, the odds of that plan finding success were slim to none.

Only desperation could have driven Megan to such a choice. More likely than not, she would have died in the attempt. But the only other option would have been to do nothing. To watch Petra and Finn die. Avery would have done the same regardless of the outcome.

Finn's execution had been plastered all over the city, on every vid screen on every block. They had arrived just in time to scrounge together some kind of plan to get both him and Petra out of danger. But there wasn't enough time to stay as one unit, so they'd split into teams.

Mylan and Markes both needed immediate medical care, and Rem was still unsteady on his feet after his collision with the ceiling. Avery couldn't afford to waste time or energy trying to heal them, so Linderly volunteered to pilot their small ship back to Nos Lenti with the wounded. Rem had been eager to get as far away from the violence as possible.

Qav went alone to infiltrate the arena and work covertly against Leviathan's influence, hoping to map out how deeply her powers had affected the Council. While there, he would find Megan and get her out. Meanwhile, Grigg and Tai would head to the old Federation hangar to disable the Origin fleet before Leviathan could realize she'd need it. And Avery would take center stage. They'd escape from the city and incapacitate Leviathan's most powerful weapons in one fail swoop.

It took a quarter hour to reach the rendezvous point, slipping in and out of alleys and moving swiftly past the few pedestrians that populated the sidewalks. There were no humans anywhere—the city had been revitalized with more Reanges than Avery had ever seen. To some degree, it was wondrous. Avery had a glimpse at the world Echo had once been. Bustling and alive and filled with Reanges who lived their lives without fear.

But it was a false utopia. Although they no longer suffered, the people were still at the mercy of corrupt leadership. Worse than that, Leviathan had taken away free will. She had exploited not only her position on the Council, but the very sanctity of her power as a So'Reange. It was sickening—enough to boil Avery's rage into acid that bubbled up her throat.

Megan finally slowed as they approached the back entrance of a towering office building. The door pushed open before she could touch the handle and Grigg stuck his head out, a wide smile on his face.

Megan let out a squeal, throwing herself at him into a hug as they all tumbled inside. Avery's heart warmed, watching their reunion. Grigg was getting more pleasure from his resurrection bit than he had from any joke he'd uttered in the past decade.

Avery didn't expect the next embrace, when Tai pulled Megan to him. Even the briefest peek into his emotions revealed the bliss of relief that she was unharmed.

Their group had become a tight unit. They seemed as deeply connected as Avery now was to Nova and Grigg. She was glad for it, but Avery felt . . . like an intruder.

The two of them turned together like a well-oiled machine, moving quietly through the halls and down a central stairwell. Avery, Grigg, and Qav followed in silence. At the bottom, tucked beneath the angled stairs, Megan opened a supply door, and Tai dropped to a knee, lifting a hatch in the floor.

"Tell me we're not going down there." Qav scrunched his nose, peering down into the pitch-black hole.

"Best way to get around the city," Tai replied cheerfully, delighting in Qav's discomfort.

Grigg slapped his back. "Maybe you should redo that fancy hair. Wouldn't want it to get dirty in the muck."

"I hope nobody's afraid of the dark." Megan activated a light stick that hung from the strap across her chest.

"I don't think you'll need that." Grigg gestured to the glowing yellow stick. "Qav and Avery have those radioactive irises—we'll just let them lead the way."

"At the very least, we'll just follow the hot air coming out of your mouth," Qav muttered.

"Just get in the hole." Avery shoved Grigg at the hatch. They descended one at a time, with Qav at the rear. Despite his bravado, he didn't seem excited about a drop beneath the surface. Ironic, given where he'd built the Sanctum.

Avery's boots hit the ground with a soft thud. Her eyes adjusted swiftly. They had dropped into a tunnel that opened up around them in a wide curving cylinder. Avery trailed her fingers over the damp walls. She'd been there before.

"The Origin used these tunnels," she said softly.

When she'd first come to Echo, Finn had nearly died when they'd escaped Nick the first time. Mylan had found them in the city, with Fiora and Krez. He had convinced Avery to trust them. Krez had carried Finn himself the entire way to the Origin stronghold deep beneath the city. To Leviathan.

Avery had been so frightened, nearly powerless. She had been forced to trust the Origin when there had been no other option. She had been naive to think everything would be settled once they exposed Klein's crimes to the public. Avery had thought everything would end if they just revealed the truth.

It had only been the beginning.

Shame crept up Avery's spine. Not her own—Tai was watching her. He hadn't been a part of the Origin, but Petra had built her life around it. She had been an orphan recruited to serve Leviathan, the same as Markes and Linderly. Raised to abhor humans, trained to kill them. It was a burden Tai carried for his sister. He had avoided that fate, thanks to her.

"You're right. The Origin did use these once." Megan marched ahead at the front. Tai stayed close by her side, his weapon drawn. The eerie white glow of her device spread out some ten feet ahead of them before shadows devoured it. "But once Leviathan took the city, they were abandoned. They've been an integral part of our recovery missions."

Worry pooled uneasily in Avery's gut. "Is that wise? There's no way Leviathan won't realize you've been down here."

"Relax, Avery," Qav said, somewhat amused. "No one would be able to sneak up on us even if they tried."

"You've never even set foot on this planet," Avery snapped. "Don't pretend like you have any understanding of the way things work around here. Especially when it comes to Leviathan."

Qav stepped back, his silver eyes going wide. But he descended into blissful silence.

"Leviathan can't keep her control trained on everyone in the city at once. She focuses mainly on the Council and other Reanges with influence," Megan explained. "Which works out for us. She doesn't comprehend the scope of the tunnel web—she relied too much on delegation for that. So we developed a system to take advantage of her blind spots."

"But Mylan knew these tunnels. And Krez did, too," Avery pointed out. "I can't believe you wouldn't consider the possibility that—"

"That clearly hasn't been an issue," Megan said firmly.

"Krez isn't with Leviathan anymore anyway," Tai added.

"What?" Avery asked carefully. The familiar pang of guilt she carried over Fiora's death passed through her. Losing Krez to Leviathan had only made it worse. But she hadn't had a nightmare about them in months.

"Krez—as of last week, he's on our side," Tai informed, oblivious to Avery's faltered steps. "He broke free of Leviathan and tracked us all the way up the mountains. Petra was pissed."

Avery halted. "And you believed him? No wonder they were able to capture Petra and Finn. How ignorant do you have to be to—"

"We didn't exactly have many options, Avery." Megan leveled Avery with a glare that even Petra would be proud of. "It's not like you were here to tell us if he was lying. We've done what we can with what we have, and that's been enough. It had to be."

Avery's face flushed so deeply that she was thankful no one could see her clearly. It had been a long time since someone had chastised her so thoroughly. She had almost forgotten . . . Avery wasn't the unequivocal leader here. They had formed a new family without her—and the only one to blame for that was Avery herself.

She needed to back off, at least until they could process everything that had happened. If she didn't listen to their opinions, Avery would be doomed to walk the same path as before. Straight off a cliff and into disaster.

"You're right. I wasn't here." Avery reached for Megan's hand, grateful when she didn't pull away. "I trust your judgment. You're the smartest person I know, Megan. You always have been."

Doubtful. Qav's single word slithered coldly from his head to hers. She shoved him out.

"Let's just keep going." Megan's tone gentled, but she was still angry. "We've got another twenty minutes if we pick up our pace."

They jogged the rest of the way, and even then it took a half hour. Avery was thoroughly lost by the time they finished their zig zagging progress through the interconnecting passages. They stopped at a small ladder that curved up the edge of the wall, marked only by a single splotch of white paint.

"I'll go up first." Avery stopped Megan when she placed her foot on the first rung. "Let me clear the area."

Megan nodded, backing away without argument.

The metal was icy and damp beneath her fingers as she climbed. Her muscles were uncomfortably tight. Once they left the city, she could start to make amends. She just needed space to breathe. She would earn their forgiveness, no matter how long it took.

Avery twisted the handle on the hatch above her, swinging it outward to reveal a cloudless, darkening sky. She scurried up onto the grass and stood, taking in her first lungful of air in hours. She shivered in the cold wind. The tunnels had brought them to the foothills of the mountains, out of danger of the city limits. Avery spread her power out through the open fields, searching for any hint of danger.

The towering mountains rose up against the horizon, their snowy peaks shining dimly in the twilight. The sun had set in their time underground, turning the evening sky an effervescent blue. The three moons rose in a trio of heavy spheres offset by the first winking stars of night. Avery turned to the city, now miles behind her, its striking sleek towers arching into the sky with their own glow. The scent of salt water from the ocean beyond danced along the breeze, teasing tears from the corner of her eyes.

Nova's energy reached Avery just before a gust of air careened over her in the wake of the invisible ship. It materialized just above her, its hatch already open. A figure crouched down as the ship descended.

Finn didn't wait for it to land. He leaped down, catching himself easily in the tall grass and aiming straight for her in a purposeful, long legged stride. Avery's pulse skipped along her veins, crackling with electricity beneath her skin.

And then he was there, his hands on her face, his warm fingers threading into the hair at her temples. His mouth parted, the ghost of a smile teasing its corner. His eyes darted over her face frantically, like he was scared she would disappear.

"You idiot," he breathed.

He caught her laugh with his lips, angling her head to fit against him as their bodies pressed together. It wasn't furious and rushed, like she'd often fantasized, but tender. Soft. As though with that one kiss, Finn would convey the longing that had plagued him as badly as it had Avery. His mouth moved leisurely over hers, tasting her slowly, exploring her again.

Avery met him, one stroke at a time. Somehow she had forgotten—everything about Finn was home. His smell. His touch. The brush of his lips against hers. He made her feel whole, just with the parts of himself that he put into a single caress.

It was the kiss Avery had dreamed of for over a year.

"I guess it makes sense what was taking you so long."

Qav's dry observation penetrated Avery's haze, and she jerked away from Finn. She'd forgotten about the others entirely.

Finn's body had gone rigid against hers, his eyes trained behind her. His dropped his hands. His jaw set.

"Finn, listen—"

Finn moved faster than she'd ever seen him, tackling Qav to the ground with a muffled growl. Avery's brain caught up quickly enough.

Finn was livid. She should have known, she should have prepared him.

Avery took one step toward them before someone grabbed her arm.

"Let him," Petra said fiercely. Her fingers dug into Avery's jacket, hard enough to hurt.

Avery's eyes flickered back to the two men struggling in the dirt. Finn straddled Qav, slamming one fist after another into his face. "He'll kill him."

"I don't see *them* going to his rescue." Petra nodded over her shoulder.

Syla and Ennis stood watching the fight from the belly of the ship. Unconcerned. By all rights, if anyone should do something, it would be them.

"Well, shit." Grigg popped his head up from the hole in the ground. He came out of the hatch faster than anyone of his size should be able to. He grabbed Finn's shoulder, hauling him off Qav with a loud grunt. "Don't be an idiot, Lunitia."

The sound of Grigg's voice did more than his strength ever could. Finn's anger was forgotten as Grigg faced him with large hands on his shoulders. Finn's face was pale, his eyes red.

"Grigg." Finn tripped over his name, the sound pained and ragged. He gripped Grigg's arms, like he was afraid he would disappear, too. Avery clutched her hands to her chest.

But Grigg laughed loudly, his delight in the reveal the most satisfying one yet. He gave Finn a brotherly shake and tilted his head. "Bet you didn't see this one coming."

Finn dragged Grigg to him, crushing his oldest friend in a hard embrace. Joy cascaded over him, clean and fresh and overwhelming. It surged through his limbs, chasing away any exhaustion, nothing compared to the disbelief he'd felt when Nova had gently broken the news to him that Grigg was still alive. Seeing him in person, hearing his laugh . . . A piece of Finn that he'd kept locked away, forbidden and forgotten, was suddenly set free.

"It's good to see you, brother." Grigg's voice was raspy in Finn's ear. He shook Finn again, lifting him from the ground.

Finn pulled back, locking his hands on the sides of Grigg's face, taking in the reality that was now staring him in the face.

Grigg was alive.

In Finn's wildest dreams, he'd hoped to see Avery again, to somehow find a way back to her. But this? Finn smiled, a real laugh bubbling up and out of him. It was the first genuine smile—with no strings of darkness or grief attached—that he'd felt in ages. The happiness was overwhelming, nearly enough to make him forget about the groaning pile of shit on the ground behind him.

Said pile of shit rose to his feet, spitting out blood and brushing off his pants. His silver eyes cut through the dark to pin Finn with a malevolent stare. But he had the decency to keep his mouth shut as he meandered past them to the ship.

Finn tensed, ready for another fight.

Grigg placed a hand on his shoulder. "Unfortunately, we don't have time for that."

"He's right," Avery agreed, approaching alongside Petra. She was smiling, the remnants of tears in her eyes. "We've been lucky this far. Let's not push it."

Finn swallowed his ire, burying it down in his belly. If he had to accept Qav in their crew, then he would find a way to deal with it. At least until the asshole proved himself the traitor he'd always be.

Finn let go of Grigg only to grab Avery's hand. Her fingers threaded immediately into his own, sending a curl of pleasure through him. It felt right. *She* felt right. She always had.

Petra continued past them to help Tai pull Megan out of the hatch. Megan took Petra's hand before glancing nervously to Avery. Finn wondered if Avery would notice, if it would make her uncomfortable. Not the relationship itself but the uneasiness of Megan's gesture. He doubted they'd had time for a heart to heart in their rush from the city.

But Avery ignored them. She gave them space, tugging Finn's hand and leading him to the ship with Grigg and the others.

The bridge was spacious, but their group had grown in size enough that they filled every seat. Syla and Qav were forced to stand as Nova piloted them away from Milderion toward the mountains they called home. In the span of a few hours, something had been healed that Finn once thought broken forever.

The ship itself was a marvel—a special design Cora had cooked up and for some reason let them borrow. Finn still found it difficult to believe that she'd been instrumental in helping them get back to Echo. Nova had done her best to catch him and Petra up to speed on all that had happened during their separation.

Avery explained more of the situation on Earth, and how they'd left it. The impact of the Gate's destruction had touched every part of Earthen society. Klein had blamed it on the Reanges, using the excuse to wage a cultural war against them. Petra was seething by the time Avery described the camps they'd been trying to dismantle. Finn couldn't believe the World Council would approve such a measure. But fear was a terrifying motivator that could drag anyone down to the worst version of themselves. That went for politicians, too.

Grigg was the one to detail Avery's escape from Klein's apartments—and how she'd had to face Nick to do so. Finn froze when he heard his brother's name. Avery had faced him and survived. According to Syla, she'd done so in no small part thanks to Qav. Finn tuned out after that.

He chose instead to focus on Avery speaking beside him. It was easy to let himself be completely mesmerized by her. The warmth of her thigh pressed against his. The familiar lilt of her voice. The way her face moved when she spoke, animated and full of energy. She used her eyebrows to convey points more than her hands, every expression offering insight into the emotion underneath.

She fell so easily into the role of leader, like it was made for her. He could watch her just exist for the rest of his life, and his would be complete.

"... think we need to expect?"

Finn blinked.

Avery was looking at him. Her eyes were incredible, a beautiful, arresting gold that called him into their depths like warm, sweet honey. Had she asked him a question?

Heat crawled up Finn's neck.

Petra scoffed. Grigg barked a laugh.

"What happened to that smart mouth, Lunitia?" Qav asked dryly, his eyes passing over Finn's mottled face. "Or perhaps those burns fried some of your brain cells, too."

Megan was on her feet before Petra could stop her. The crack of her palm hitting Qav's cheek was loud enough to silence them all.

"If you ever say anything like that again, I'll kill you myself," Megan bit out.

The console started to vibrate as Avery shook beside Finn. Her features were rigid, her golden eyes deadly as she stared at Qav. He had the decency to look ashamed as Megan's palm print deepened to a dark pink on his face.

Finn placed a hand on Avery's thigh. As much as he was delighted that Qav's comment had garnered her wrath, he'd like them to make it to Nos Lenti in one piece. All Qav was doing was digging his own grave.

"I'd be happy to go for round two," Finn told him, keeping his tone light. He needed to defuse the situation quickly. They'd be no good to anyone if they all started fighting.

"Round one was a gift," Qav replied.

"Don't embarrass yourself, Qav," Syla turned away from windows, dragging her eyes from the shadowed mountain range that grew ever closer beneath them. "Powers or not, Finn handed you your ass back there. You've got no one to blame but yourself."

Qav rolled his eyes. "Spare me the lectures. I'm not in the mood."

"How far is your camp?" Ennis asked, redirecting the conversation back on course. Finn had forgotten about the scar that ran down the side of her face. Hers was a single slash that traveled from the edge of her eye to her chin, barely more than a soft raise of skin.

Finn's was decidedly . . . more than that. He'd leaned into the burns after they'd healed, relying on them to remind him of every-thing he'd done wrong. He wasn't the face of a movement anymore; he didn't give interviews and go to parties. The scars had given him more than they'd taken away. But now . . .

Finn tucked his chin, angling his ruined side away from Avery. The last thing he needed was her pity.

"The cloaking tech will mask us from scans so we'll be able to fly straight to the village." Petra pulled Megan to her seat again, answering Ennis's question. "No need to hike in on foot."

"Finally some good news," Tai said wearily. "I don't think I could have handled a frigid night hike after the past forty-eight hours."

"You and me both, kid." Finn slumped in his seat. His eyes were already drooping. He'd been surviving on adrenaline and shock for twice that amount of time.

Avery leaned her shoulder into his, wrapping her hands around the one he still had on her leg.

"As far as what we'll find," Finn continued, finally answering her original question. "I'm hoping the others are keeping to the protocol."

"Which is?" Avery asked.

"Stay low. Cut off any form of communication. Wait to hear from the ground team."

Avery frowned, clearly unhappy with that explanation.

"That protocol would have meant allowing your death," Ennis pointed out.

Finn shrugged.

"Finn hasn't exactly had a healthy respect for what that means lately," Megan said pointedly.

He bit the inside of his cheek, wishing she could keep her blazing mouth shut. But she had never been good at that.

Avery stiffened. "What is that supposed to mean?"

"Nothing." Finn tilted his chin. He needed to pilot the conversation away from dangerous airspace. "Besides, Linderly will already be there ahead of us. They'll know we're coming."

"Thank the moons," Nova said, relieved. "I didn't love the idea of shocking my parents out of their wits by showing up unannounced."

"Speak for yourself," Grigg added sullenly. "I was looking forward to their reaction the most."

Megan relaxed enough to smile softly at Avery. "Your grandmother is going to blow a fuse."

"Good." Avery shook her head with a laugh. "It's about time I pay her back with a few surprises of my own."

CHAPTER THIRTY

Nothing could have prepared Avery for the picturesque reality of Nos Lenti—not even the hours Nova and Grigg had spent talking about it over the past year. The buildings were modest and cozy, nestled against the snow lined cliffside that overlooked the majesty of the far-off mountains. The sun had set, but the moons were full, bathing the magnificent peaks in pale light as they stood watch over the village.

They touched down just inside the stone gate that marked the boundary. A bell tolled. The few people out in the square looked up at the ship became visible. They panicked, running for safety. The two guards by the arch had fled behind the cement barricades at the foot of the hill. Linderly appeared, running toward the ship in the snow, yelling at the guards to lower their weapons.

Avery billowed her power out ahead of them, connecting with every Reange in the vicinity. She calmed them, soothing their fear and explaining the situation with a single thought. The confusion was dispelled nearly as soon as it had come.

By the time Nova had opened the access door, Avery was already making her way down the ramp. The others followed closely behind her as she took her first steps into the snow.

A large man stepped out from behind the corner of the closest building, cloaked almost entirely in shadow. He lowered his equally large weapon. Avery knew his stern face, outlined in the cool light of the winter moons. She recognized the intense energy that accompanied his stare.

Krez *had* left Leviathan after all. And he roamed Nos Lenti free-ly—Megan had left that part out.

Krez, Avery spoke for his mind alone.

He flinched, like her presence in his head was as much of a shock as her sudden appearance. He stepped forward, his boots deep in the snow drift. There was a moment of utter disbelief, the few seconds when he doubted the reality in front of him. His eyes filled with tears as he dropped to his knees.

My So'. He bowed his head to her, casting his eyes to the ground.

"Avie?!" Gran's cry bounced across the frozen square.

Avery forgot Krez altogether as Gran came running from some-where down the curving stone lane. She passed through the light of the lanterns in the square, and Avery caught sight of a blaster strapped across her back. Even Gran had become some kind of revolutionary.

Avery sprinted forward to meet her, trying to return the call, em-barrassed when all that emerged was a childlike sob. Gran didn't slow as they met in the empty square, and they crashed into one another when Avery threw herself into her grandmother's arms.

She never thought she'd be able to feel this again, to be held by the woman who had comforted every ailment she'd ever had. She smelled like green tea and lemon, a combination Avery would never have been able to name until that exact moment. It was a comfort un-like anything she'd ever experienced, a reclamation of something that had been lost forever alongside her childhood. Avery held on to Gran for dear life, praying she wouldn't embarrass herself by dissolving into a scared little girl.

Gran was thinner. Her heavy gray coat barely concealed the way her frame had become so sleight underneath. As much as she was the same, so many things were different. Avery gripped Gran tighter, burying her face in the collar of her coat, trying to hold in her sobs.

"It's all right, my little Avie," Gran whispered softly, her own voice unsteady. Her fingers ran a soothing trail down Avery's hair, tracing the braid that was so like her own.

Avery could say nothing. She was barely able to stare down at her fingers where they dug into the wool coat on Gran's back, tucked just beneath her weapon.

"It's all right," Gran said again. And again. She was repeating it over and over. Like the words were a chant, the only thing keeping them both from falling apart.

Someone screeched Nova's name and the intensity of the cry pulled Avery out of her daze.

Nova sprinted past Avery. She was caught in the arms of an older woman with her same build, her same buttery-blond hair, tinged with gray. A man wasn't too far behind, enfolding both women in his wide arms. Nova's parents.

Their happiness crested over Avery, a wave of pure elation brighter and more vibrant than the heart of a star. It blended with her own until Avery could no longer tell which tears of joy were hers and which were theirs. She laughed, tucking her arm around Gran's waist as the others approached.

Grigg sauntered up beside the small family, watching the trio warily, almost nervously. Nova's father lifted his head, heavy tears cascading down his cheeks as he cried out. He dragged Grigg into his arms before the four assimilated into an amoeba of delight.

Finn stood close by, a wondrous smile on his face. He caught Avery staring, and he winked. Avery's heart flipped over itself.

At last, something marvelous had happened. Only days ago, the universe had seemed like such a wretched, bleak abyss. The seeds of hope stirred to life in her heart, hurling her forward straight into its brightest stars.

Avery felt Lissande approach before she stepped into the light beside Gran. "Avery," she said softly, her kind eyes crinkling as they filled with tears. "Welcome home."

And Avery let down her defenses, allowing in every bit of love and relief from the Reanges around her. She opened herself to Lissande, to Nova, to Grigg, and Nova's parents . . . The warmth of their connection passed through every cell in her body, chasing away the chill that seemed to have sunk into her very bones. Avery was no longer alone.

"Look at you." Gran cradled Avery's cheeks, wiping away free flowing tears with cold fingers. "I knew . . . I knew somehow you'd find your way back to us."

"You absolutely did not," Lissande said with a beleaguered laugh.

Gran smiled indulgently. She reached out for Lissande's hand, bringing her in close. She took Avery's in her other. Lissande and Avery completed the circle, until the three of them were linked together.

"I had hope," Gran said. "And that was enough."

Perthos and Naileve, Nova's parents, wasted no time in pulling the entire population of Nos Lenti together for an elaborate reunion celebration. The fact that Avery's return coincided with the week of Su'elben was taken as no small sign that the moons were on their side. What had been intended as a week of somber reflection turned into a raucous party in the span of mere hours.

And with not just one So'Reange defending them, but two . . . The people in Nos Lenti felt some measure of comfort for the first time since before the war with Earth. They had a chance—a real chance at last—to remove Leviathan from her seat of power.

Qav had taken particularly well to his new role as a savior in Nos Lenti. He reveled in the reverence the Reanges bestowed on him, more pronounced than even what he received in his own city. Rem's quick recovery had also put him in an excellent mood—a hydration patch and sleep had brought the uppity coder back to his usual self. Qav would never admit it, but Rem's injuries had weighed on him heavily.

Finn insisted on seeing Markes before letting Gran give him a full medical evaluation. He didn't have to wait long: the boy in question had come barreling out of the lodge not long after they exited the ship. Lissande's treatment had healed his blast wound, but he'd be sore for a few days.

Avery spent the early-evening snuggled beside Megan in Gran's living room, catching up on everything they'd missed over their year apart while Lissande gave both Finn and Petra a full exam. She sent them to their quarters with strict instructions to rest. Neither of them argued the orders. Megan chose to doze on the couch next to Avery.

Krez stood outside the cottage in the cold, refusing to come inside and yet refusing to leave Avery's guard. A quick evaluation of his mind had revealed that Megan had been right: their trust in his word was not misplaced. He had truly broken free of Leviathan's hold, from distance and will alone. The only mystery left to solve was in Mylan's actions.

Lissande had healed Mylan's wounds, using valuable meds to do so, and stabilized his condition. He was under full guard watch until Avery had the energy to deal with him. But the reality of deciding on their next steps could wait, if only a few hours.

Before dinner, Bedria lead a small Su'elben ceremony beneath the open night sky attended by both humans and Reanges alike. They held hands and stared at the three moons, aligned and full above the cliffs, honoring everything they'd sacrificed to bring them to that exact moment. Krez lingered near Avery, his shoulders stiff, his tears silent. It was as much mourning as they'd ever done for Fiora. But once this was over, Avery vowed they would say goodbye to her properly. Together.

Meat was roasted, intricate dishes prepared, and wines uncorked. They cleared out the whole lobby of the lodge to accommodate the entirety of the village, and even then, some spilled out into the square beneath the stars, surrounding the warmth of the large bonfire. A small band played jaunty traditional tunes as partners and friends danced the night away. Perthos pulled out every fine liquor he'd been saving for decades, sending Nova into a state of shock. She didn't refuse a single pour.

Avery sat with her friends at the main table that dominated the great room. The roaring holofire in the enormous hearth chased away any hint of winter chill, even as the front door opened and closed with people mingling between the indoor and outdoor spaces. The lodge was full to the brim, generating enough heat between the revelry and the dancing to make it almost too warm.

Qav had taken up a spot between two beautiful Reanges by the fire. One stroked his battered face, applying some kind of oil salve, while the other sat on his lap brushing out his long silver hair. The looks on their faces were nothing short of overt invitations that Qav gave every indication of accepting. Avery did her best to stay out of their heads—the last thing she wanted was to hear the direction their evening was going.

Avery was glad Qav kept his distance. She was already worried about keeping an eye on Finn, just in case he got any fresh ideas about beating their second best weapon into the ground again. Syla could say what she wanted about Qav's lack of fighting skills, but he had held back. Qav had *let* Finn pummel him. And Avery wasn't exactly sure why.

Avery settled in more comfortably against Finn's side. He had pulled their chairs together as close as possible, his arm resting heavily over her shoulder. And right then, in that moment, Avery actually felt content. Like if they were together, beside their families and the ones they loved, then nothing could touch them. More tears stung her eyes. Her heart clenched so hard that it hurt to breathe.

After dinner, with everyone tipsy on wine and stuffed to the point of bursting, their conversation turned at last to their next steps. Avery was loath to face that reality, but knew it had to be done. Klein would only need a few months to mobilize, and they needed a firm position on Echo before she did.

"We can't just go after the blazing stone again," Finn argued against Petra's suggestion. "Leviathan will be expecting it now. Without the benefit of surprise, we'll never stand a chance. Even with Avery."

"And Qav," Ennis added.

Finn's jaw worked, but he thankfully said nothing.

Petra leaned back in her chair. "Avery should have gone for it in the arena. That was the best shot we had at taking it from her once and for all."

Avery stiffened. But she wouldn't defend herself against Petra. Not when Megan was sitting right beside her. She had no right.

"The priority was getting you and Finn out of there," Nova snapped. "A little gratitude would be nice."

"Petra is right." Avery cleared her throat. Finn's thumb brushed across her shoulder. "I felt the stone when I was there. I felt its pull. It *wanted* me to take it."

"What about him?" Megan nodded at Qav, too far away to be a part of the conversation and too distracted to care.

"Leave him out of it," Finn said quickly.

"You can't afford to leave him out of it," Syla pointed out, studying her glass of wine.

"The last thing we need is that egotistical sociopath getting his hands on a rock that will amplify his power tenfold," Megan said brusquely.

Ennis grinned toward the man in question. "Egotistical, yes. Sociopath is pushing it."

"We never asked you to come here," Petra bit out.

"You're right—Avery did."

Petra's lips thinned, her eyes snapping to Avery's. Anger seethed just beneath the surface that she kept placid by sheer will alone. And she had every right to that emotion. At last, Megan leaned into Petra's shoulder, and she relaxed, looking away.

Avery bit the inside of her cheek. She needed to talk to both of them, to explain what had happened. No—more than that. Avery needed to beg their forgiveness.

"We may not have the necklace," Linderly said reluctantly. "But we didn't come away totally empty-handed."

"Damn straight," Markes added, nodding to the far corner of the room.

Sitting the shadows, Mylan watched them all carefully with a single guard to mind him. It didn't seem fair to keep his guards from the revelry, so they'd decided to situate him within their direct line of sight. The closer he was, the easier he would be to control.

His eyes shifted, sensing Avery's sudden attention. *You can't avoid me forever.*

Avery ignored his thought. She had almost forgotten that he could open the path between them himself. Just like Bedria, he could speak to her directly. And he was immune to the So's influence. It was one of the reasons Avery had trusted Mylan in the first place, because of his gifts. And look how well that went.

"Mylan is more of a risk than a benefit here," Avery said, returning her attention to conversation. "He can't be controlled, and he can't be read."

"If it's information we need, Syla and I will be happy oblige." Ennis's cunning eyes slid to the man in question.

Syla nodded quietly beside her, a serpentine grin spreading across her face.

"We don't do that here," Finn bit out darkly.

He was livid, ready to believe the worst from their comments. But Avery knew them for what they were: a scare tactic meant to put Mylan on edge. Nothing more.

Finn hadn't spent a year with the two women. Avery had trained with them and laughed with them and healed beside them. They were good people. Even Qav, for all his faults, was not evil. He was only . . . misguided.

Avery placed a soft hand on Finn's thigh, relieved when he settled.

"Easy, Ambassador." Syla laughed.

Ennis tilted her chin, threading her fingers beneath it. "Just floating ideas."

If you want information from me, then all you have to do is ask, my So'.

Avery's head snapped toward Mylan at his taunt, startling the others. Finn sat forward, his focus solely on her. Grigg and Nova followed Avery's gaze, half rising from their chairs. Even Qav's eyes moved lazily from his companions to the commotion.

If you have something to say to me, then get it over with. Avery lifted her chin, squaring her shoulders. She was done being played.

You need something—

"You speak to all of us or not at all." Avery raised her voice so that it carried over the music and across the cacophonous room.

The musicians faltered in their tune, a few of the dancers looking warily to Avery and her table. Mylan stood from his chair, eyeing the human beside him who acted as his guard. The hall stilled, the music going silent. Alarm permeated through the revelry, spoiling the peace of the evening.

Mylan gave a short bow, tucking his hand to his chest. "As my So' commands."

"Come closer," Avery said.

Mylan began the walk to their table, the crowd parting ahead of him. A little boy whimpered, scurrying for a place behind his mother's legs as the older man passed.

Avery needed to tread more carefully. The moods shifted so easily among the survivors. They were more delicate than she realized. Avery relaxed, releasing a soothing wave of reassurance through the Reanges, shifting the glum atmosphere in the span of one breath to the next. The fear was soon forgotten as they turned back to the festivities, the music drowning out any hint of disquiet.

Naughty. Qav watched her closely, his fingers brushing against his chin in thought.

Avery was well aware she had broken one of her own rules. She warned him before they entered Echo's atmosphere that the Reanges were off limits. Still . . . to be censured by Qav? A thread of remorse curled its way sourly through Avery's stomach. She wouldn't do it again.

Mylan halted in front of her, close enough for Avery to see how much he had aged since she last saw him. His once-peppered hair was almost entirely white. The wrinkles on his forehead had deepened, the crinkling at the corners of his eyes more prominent than ever. He was tired. And not just from age.

"This better be good," Avery said gruffly.

"You've grown up," Mylan observed with an appreciative smile.

"Necessity will do that."

"Among other things."

Avery paused, considering. Mylan never said anything without purpose. He never did anything without intention. He sent Krez away from Leviathan, starting the chain of events that would bring Finn to his own execution.

"You'd better start talking, Mylan." Avery gestured to Ennis and

Syla, who watched him closely. "Before I let those two try to force the answers out of you."

Syla sucked on her teeth, waggling her eyebrows for effect. Grigg's shoulders started to shake with mirth. Nova elbowed him.

"To assume you have the leisure of time is folly." Mylan cleared his throat. "While you revel here in these mountains drinking and considering your next moves, Leviathan will already be making hers. Speed is essential."

"And I suppose you've come to offer us the perfect solution?" Finn asked casually. "You defected from your supreme So' without so much as a fight."

"Unlikely," Petra sneered.

Markes and Linderly watched Mylan carefully. Even Krez had pushed away from the wall to move closer. Those who had been under Mylan's command in the Origin knew his cunning nature. Although Avery could feel Mylan's sincerity, she could not read his mind. And her friends understood him better than she ever would.

"Without her Elder Council, Leviathan won't be making moves anytime soon." Qav had at last joined the conversation, sauntering over.

"You were able to turn them?" Mylan faced Qav, seeming impressed. He tilted his head. "That changes things."

Avery gritted her teeth. If Qav revealed anything else, she'd silence him herself.

"You want the Essence stone for yourself," Mylan continued. "But with Leviathan's amplification, you'll never be able to take it from her. Not even with the might of two So'. She is more dangerous now than she has ever been. More erratic, more volatile. She's unpredictable."

"What are you saying, Mylan? That you've had enough of her?" Finn asked.

Mylan sighed, some part of his stoicism fading away to reveal the exhaustion he hid underneath. "I'm saying that stone has changed her. Leviathan has always been a hard woman—her life has not been easy. None of ours have been. I know the methods may seem harsh, but any decisions the Origin made have been for the greater future of Echo."

"I've heard this before," Avery challenged. "You gave me a similar speech right after she restricted my power and locked me in a cell."

"Exactly my point. I have always agreed with Leviathan's vision of a free Echo led by and for our people. But the longer she uses that stone, the more limited her vision of what that means becomes. Leviathan has had a taste of absolute power. There is no one who can stand against her—there has been no one who can even try."

"You expect us to believe that?" Petra seethed. "You've stood by Leviathan for months, letting her desecrate the sanctity of her position. You're the one who convinced her to execute Finn—you said so yourself."

"By necessity alone. I never imagined you'd try to come as a unit to take the stone by force. It was a foolish plan."

"That would have worked if you had cooperated."

"Just because I am immune to her control doesn't mean I'm willing to risk my life for the sake of a human."

"Charming," Megan muttered.

"Are you suggesting the stone has induced some kind of dementia?" Lissande asked from her position at the end of the table beside the other Elders, pivoting the conversation. As women of science, Gran's expression was as curious as her partner's.

"Not just her mind," Mylan explained. "She can't go anywhere without the necklace or her body begins to shut down. Some months ago I tried to convince her to let it go, that we didn't need it any longer. That . . . didn't go over well."

Lissande nodded, considering the implications. "The So'Reange power is deeply connected to the physical form. That level of power is flooding her body past its natural ability to harness, like running a basic cruiser on the power of a star."

"I can only imagine the kind of stress that places on the body. The genome itself would be experiencing degradation on a massive scale," Gran observed softly.

Finn's arm stiffened around Avery's shoulders. "Then the stone is too dangerous for Avery to use anyway."

"So we destroy it," Nova suggested.

"You won't be able to get near her again," Mylan warned. "She won't make the same mistake twice."

"Do you actually have anything useful to say?" Petra asked irritably. "We can send you back to her, if you'd like. I wonder how she treats traitors."

Mylan turned to her with a melancholic smile. "You were always her favorite, Petra. Nearly as much vitriol in that heart of yours as Leviathan herself."

Petra went utterly still, her hands balling into fists on the table. Her shame slithered through the air and teased Avery like a living creature, venomous and unruly. Avery felt her throat constrict, unable to keep from feeling Petra's humiliation. Unwilling to let herself ignore it.

"She is *nothing* like her." Megan's quiet response was hard, the edges sharp enough to make even Mylan flinch.

After a moment, Mylan spoke again, finally getting to his point. "The stone did not come to Leviathan by chance. I found it hidden away in the bowels of the capitol building, placed there for safekeeping to prevent the humans from ever getting their hands it."

Avery was drawn back to her time in the cell of dark rock beneath the capitol, where her powers had been extinguished. She'd only been able to free herself from that prison because of some unseen energy that can called to her, leading her to safety through the halls of that place.

It was the same feeling as the warmth from the arena that had called out to Avery from the stands. From Leviathan's neck. If that energy was the Essence, Avery had a feeling it was more powerful than any of them knew.

Maybe Finn was right—meddling with that much energy was definitely dangerous. But Avery would be the only one at risk. And if it meant taking back Echo and having a real chance at keeping Klein away forever, then perhaps it was worth it.

"The stone was never meant as a weapon," Mylan continued. "It was given to the last Elder Council before the war, brought to them by the western sea villages. A child found it by chance on the cliffs of the far coast."

Petra's eyes narrowed at the mention of her home. "What game are you playing, Mylan?"

"Why do you think we were there all those years ago? Do you think we came across you and your bother in that cave by chance? I had read about the piece inside the capitol, but there was no way to access it. Leviathan had grown too weak to lead an army . . . We were looking for more. To strengthen her."

"So your solution is to send us after it, too?" Avery laughed. "You spent years searching for this rock and never found anything. What makes you think we'll have any better luck?"

"You are a So'Reange," he said simply. "Only you can follow the thread in the labyrinth."

"But not Leviathan?"

He shook his head. "She was too feeble then to even make the journey."

"Why should they trust you?" Krez spoke at last, his deep voice booming and steady.

Mylan smiled. "I am an old man. And Leviathan is older still. Maybe once we had a right to determine the way forward for our people . . . but now I'm not so sure. I see the way your Elders here let you lead your own minds, let you make your own decisions. This is how it should be. So'Reanges were never meant to rule; they were meant to connect us to one another, to cultivate understanding in order to maintain a truly just society. With her choices, twisted as they are by the power of that stone, Leviathan has betrayed our way of life." Mylan paused, facing Avery again. "I may not have the strength to stop her myself, but I can point you in the right direction."

It made sense. If Avery and Qav took Leviathan head-on, innocent people would die. If there was any chance to avoid that and keep her friends safe, then she would take it.

"Qav, how long before your influence on her council wears off?" Avery asked, her mind working.

"It shouldn't wear off at all," he replied casually. "The old man is right—Leviathan was weak, barely holding on to that crowd while she fought you. But let's say she discovers my tampering . . . I'd estimate five days. Maybe six, if we're lucky."

"That gives us just under a week."

"You can't actually be thinking about going through with this," Finn protested. "Let's ignore the fact that the man is a bona fide terrorist. He just said using the stone will kill you."

"Not right away," Avery reasoned. "Do you have any better ideas?"

"What if we build our own army?" Megan supplied, hopeful. "The humans aren't susceptible to her influence. And there are plenty of us here who would willingly fight."

"And start another war?" Avery shook her head. "We just stopped one. I won't pit our people against one another again. That cycle will end with us."

Something tugged at Avery, a deep knowing that resonated with her promise from some unreachable place, warm and watchful.

Did you feel that? Qav's question came unbidden. He stood straighter, his eyes unusually bright.

She only nodded, too overwhelmed by the strange presence to do anything more. Finn watched their interaction, his expression severe.

When she brought her eyes to Finn's, Avery swore she could feel his fear. But it was there and gone in a blink.

Avery. Mylan's thought, whispered only to her, brought her attention back to him. *There is something in those caves you need to see—only you.*

Avery raised her chin. "I don't keep secrets from them. Not anymore."

"Then you do your position credit," he acknowledged with a bow of his head. "You will make a better So'Reange than she ever was."

CHAPTER THIRTY-ONE

Qav watched Avery and Finn walk across the square in the snow, holding hands and leaning into each other. They were an enigma to him, in sync in a way he'd only ever known with one other person. But Veena had been a Reange. Avery's ability to love a human, to tether herself to him, was fascinating. She had no guarantee of her love being returned, no assurance of her heart's safety. She was able to open herself wholly without fear.

And not just with Finn—with them all. Qav envied her for it.

Connection had always come easily for Avery. She laid herself bare to her friends, embracing them not as followers but as confidants. She had never been alone the way he had.

But Qav was self-aware enough to realize he was to blame for his own isolation. He had put himself in that position willingly. It had been safe. Predictable. Controlled.

But that security no longer gave him the satisfaction he needed. It didn't help him sleep at night. In fact, his bizarre desire for connection kept him awake into the early hours of the morning. Avery had changed the way he saw the worlds, and no matter how hard he tried, Qav couldn't go back.

He had sworn he would never visit Echo. That had been a dream for his child self, one he left rotting in the past along with the rest of his naive fantasies. He had built a life on Earth, and that had been enough. In many ways, it still was.

But he was now on that planet, against his better judgment. He had left the Sanctum vulnerable. Avery needed him, but even that wouldn't have been enough to sway his decision. He had agreed to the scheme for Syla and Ennis alone. He didn't have siblings, but he assumed they were as close as he'd ever get to sisters. And *they* believed in Avery. They trusted her and supported her, enough to threaten and cajole Qav into lending her his help. They had chosen to follow Avery, and Qav had chosen to follow them.

"I never thought I'd see the day when you'd set foot on Echo's soil."

Qav groaned inwardly.

Bedria's nagging energy hit him like an itchy cloud as she sidled up to him at the window. "Have you finally grown out of your agoraphobia?"

He glanced at her, raising an eyebrow. "I'm not in the mood."

She chuckled. "That's a fine hello. You're clearly still the same where it counts."

"Hmm," Qav grunted. Bedria had been a constant thorn in his side in the Sanctum since her arrival there half a decade ago. He couldn't bend her to his will, and that had meant trouble. But he had grown used to her presence all the same.

"After all this time, you've finally come home," Bedria said softly.

"Home?" Qav breathed, staring through the glass to the moons above. "Is that what this place is?"

"Surely you feel it. The planet pulls at your powers and draws you close. It welcomes us in a way Earth cannot."

Qav laughed skeptically. "How much of that wine have you had?"

Bedria's craft had always seemed like fairy tales to Qav, a scam to peddle her wares in the Sanctum markets. But . . . Qav couldn't deny that he *had* felt something when they passed through the Gate.

"I know you feel it. I can see it in the way you hold yourself. You are more alive here than you've ever been on Earth."

Qav remained quiet, weighing her words against his experience. He *had* felt a resonance. He'd assumed it was from the sheer number of Reanges on the planet, more than he'd ever felt in one place. But could it have been the planet itself? What if Bedria was right?

Qav grimaced. Since when had he started to agree with a mad woman?

But she was right about one thing: he *was* different. At least, he wanted to be.

"I'm proud of you, Qavarion." Bedria placed a wrinkled hand covered in silver rings on his shoulder. Her squirrel watched him from the safety of Bedria's coiled hair, its black eyes almost too knowing. As she left him, she added in mind, *Consider what this place means. Not just for you but for us all.*

He was once so sure that his future was on Earth, with his city safe in the ground. But Echo was different than he'd thought. Strange and wonderful and somehow familiar. The Reanges in the Sanctum relied on Qav, trusting him to keep them safe. How many of them felt the way Bedria did?

If this planet called to them, then they deserved to feel that sense of place. If Qav wanted his people to have true sanctuary, then maybe they should have the right to choose their own path. Soon Earth wouldn't be viable to sustain any sort of life. If he didn't help Avery secure Echo, the Reanges on Earth would be doomed to roam the stars, refugees without a home twice over.

But offering his people that choice would undo everything Qav had spent his life building. It would mean starting over.

"What did she want?"

Qav hadn't realized Syla was beside him until her question broke his thoughts. Even Ennis had approached with her. He was more distracted than he realized.

Just being a general pain in my ass, he answered silently.

It's good to know some things never change. Ennis watched Bedria say her goodbyes. The party was winding down at last, only a few stragglers chatting and laughing by the fireplace.

Rem had left hours ago, eager to avoid the boisterous celebration for the calm quiet of the ship. There were rooms for them in the village, but Cora's vessel was more luxury than anything Nos Lenti could offer. Qav didn't love the idea of sleeping on some cheap, scratchy mattress.

The two Reanges who'd offered him a pleasurable night lingered together, tracking his every move. The woman's pale feline grace countered her friend's dark masculine beauty. They were both tantalized by the idea of sharing a So' between them. He had yet to turn down such a deliciously delivered offer in his life, and he wasn't about to start now.

"So we're in this for the long haul, then?" Ennis asked, drawing his attention back to them.

"You're asking me?" Qav raised a brow, truly surprised. "Since when are you interested in my opinion? You two have been doing as you please for the past year."

Ennis grinned mischievously. It had been a long time since smiles had come easily to them. "And yet here you are. With us."

"And yet here I am."

"Don't romanticize him, En," Syla countered. "He didn't come here for us. He came to prove something to Avery."

"Is that so?" Qav let his gaze settle on Syla, feeling out her emotions. She was hurt but not surprised. She truly believed what she said. Qav wasn't entirely sure if he wanted to correct her.

"Much good it will do you when Finn is ready to rip out your throat." Syla gave him a smarmy smile. "It will be hard to get in her good graces with her partner determined to kill you."

Qav's fingers went to his busted lip, the wound courtesy of the man in question. "That reminds me, thanks so much for your help earlier."

Syla snorted a laugh. "I didn't want to intrude. It looked like you were just getting to know one another again."

"Did it?"

"You had it coming," Ennis said, before adding quietly, "You've had it coming for a long time."

Qav let out a long breath. Despite his goading, he knew exactly why neither of them had intervened. It was the same reason he hadn't fought back. They all knew the truth.

But Syla and Ennis both thought Qav had gone to Echo for Avery. It wasn't a false assumption—he did want her forgiveness. He needed it. Still, that was nothing compared to the way he needed *them*. Qav wouldn't endure the way his soul cracked when they'd abandoned him to join her all those months ago. It had been the second most painful experience of his life. And he was an expert at avoiding pain. At least, he had been once.

It wasn't just Avery whose trust he needed. Syla and Ennis had lost their faith in him too. And he actually *cared*. Fabulous.

But change wasn't just a state of mind; it was a series of actions. If Qav wanted to be different, it was time he started acting that way.

He cleared his throat delicately. "I didn't just come here for Avery."

"What?" Syla chuckled awkwardly as her eyes shifted to Ennis and back.

I didn't just come here for Avery, Qav repeated to them. *I came here for you. For both of you.*

"What does that mean?" Ennis asked slyly, her grin widening. Suddenly she was eight years old again, giddy and stealing candy from his pockets.

Syla shoved his shoulder. "Do you, like, love us or something?"

Qav rolled his eyes as her words slurred. *You're drunk.*

Maybe, Syla admitted, raising her glass to her lips for another drink. But her eyes danced, happiness radiating off her as easily as any of the other Reanges present that evening. It was . . . charming. Syla could be charming?

Ennis watched him, her own eyes clear of any alcohol-induced haze. "That wasn't a no, Qav."

"No," he replied, grabbing Syla's glass and draining it himself. If being honest with them was the only way to repair things, then he'd have to do it completely. "It wasn't a no."

Ennis smiled at Syla, a feeling passing between them that Qav let them keep secret. Some things were not meant for him.

Qav turned back to the window, and they joined him. Together, the three of them watched the snow glistening beneath the light of the three moons.

Finn took Avery to the far end of the village, her hand cold in his from the frigid temperatures of the alpine air. Their boots crunched in the snow, loud over the distant laughter of the hall they left behind. Even the cutting wind, common at the high altitude, seemed to have taken the night off, gifting them a clear, cloudless sky.

But it was still freezing, and Avery wasn't used to it. Finn had wrapped her in one of his extra coats, and she tucked her chin into the collar, breathing in his warm scent. Her toes curled in her boots.

"Almost there." Finn looked over his shoulder at her, his words dissolving into puffs of steam.

They left the last buildings behind them as the main road transitioned into a smaller path, winding around the cliffside. The walkway was no more than ten feet across, its edge dropping into a ravine that dipped between the sheer face of the mountains. Avery peered out over the brim. The drop descended into the shadows that even the moonlight could not reach.

"If you brought me out here to shove me off this cliff, I'm warning you, I won't go easily," she teased.

"Just watch your step," Finn said, pulling her closer.

He slowed when they reached a staircase carved into the side of the cliff, each rise slumping in the center from years of use. But they were clear of snow and dry, obviously well maintained. He led her up let her pass over the threshold ahead of him into the hollowed out cavern.

Avery gasped as the air turned steamy and warm. She laughed. "A hot spring?"

He returned her smile, his eyes devouring every inch of her delight. His hand came up to brush her cheek, his thumb caressing the corner of her mouth.

Avery's breath caught exquisitely in her chest.

She cleared her throat, looking around the cavern. There was a single pool in its center dug out of the rock, large enough to hold ten people at least. Its steaming surface was mostly still except where a metal pipe supplied fresh water from beneath the rock. The bubbling sound of its splashes echoed invitingly around them.

"We have it all to ourselves?" Avery asked.

"There's a curfew for bath use," Finn explained, letting go of her to shrug out of his coat. "It's too dangerous to come out here at night, especially this time of year. But I figured we could break a few rules for you." He draped his coat over a bench in the corner, bending down to unlace his boots.

"I don't have a swimsuit."

"Neither do I."

Avery's cheeks went up in flames.

Finn tucked his socks into his boots. He grabbed the hem of his navy shirt, pulling it up and over his head.

Avery's mouth went dry.

The muscles of his chest stood out in harsh relief beneath the rays of moonlight that teased the edge of the cave. His hands went to the belt threaded through the waistband of pants that hung low on his hips.

"You guys beat us to it!"

Avery whirled away to face Markes, stumbling into the cave. The frigid air felt like ice against Avery's scalding cheeks. Grigg was right behind him, sloppily slinging an arm over Tai's shoulders. Linderly and Nova brought up the rear, giggling. *Nova* was giggling. Megan and Petra were absent.

Grigg stumbled to a halt, his brows waggling as he looked back and forth between them. "Did we . . . interrupt something?"

Avery groaned, covering her face.

"Not yet," Finn muttered sourly.

Avery sunk further into the despair of humiliation.

"Leave them alone, Grigg," Nova chastised. She draped a clumsy arm over Avery's shoulders, making them both stumble. "I'm sure Finn had nothing but chaste plans for our little Avery. Right, Finn?"

Linderly dissolved into a fit of new giggles.

Avery held Nova up, smiling at this new version of her friend. Nova hadn't taken so much as a single sip of alcohol over the past year, even on the nights they'd gone out to relax. Grigg hadn't hesitated to let loose, but Nova . . . She hadn't let go of her control. Not once.

Avery hadn't pushed Nova on it, but maybe that had been a mistake. How much had Nova sacrificed of herself to keep Avery safe?

"Get off her before you tumble down the cliffside," Finn chastised, pulling Nova away from Avery, but even he couldn't hold back a grin.

His eyes found Avery's, and his smile turned molten.

Her stomach flipped over itself, recognizing the promise in his gaze.

Finn pivoted, pointing an accusing finger at Markes, who was already stripping off his pants. "Keep your blazing clothes on until the women get in. Have some manners."

"You're the one who's half-naked," Markes whined.

Finn frowned, rebuttoning his pants.

Grigg and Nova found this riotously funny, their laughter bouncing off the steam coated walls. Linderly, the only one to claim any semblance of empathy for Avery's plight, guided her to the back of the cavern, where the shadows and a screen offered some modicum of privacy.

Finn hauled the boys out into the moonlight, where they faced the mountain ranges until Avery slipped into the spring with Linderly.

The water was perfect, hot just to the brink of scalding, and Avery moaned as she lowered herself to one of the seats situated at its bottom. Finn's bare back stiffened, the line of his spine straightening with corded muscle. His head turned almost imperceptibly to the side. Avery balked, sinking lower into the water.

A flash of long legs had Nova crashing into the pool, sending water flying and Linderly squealing. Markes took that as the all-clear and spun to race Grigg to the back corner to disrobe. Finn took a much slower route, watching Avery with every step. She glanced down to make sure the shadowed water covered everything important.

After the boys joined them—Linderly and Avery had been trusted to cover their eyes—Nova shook a finger at Finn from across the pool. "Respect the bath rules, Finn. Boys on that side; girls over here."

"I know the rules." Finn shook his head at her, running wet hands through his hair. Dark locks fell in spiked curls over his forehead.

Avery's fingers twitched beneath the surface.

"Are you sure?" Grigg asked mockingly. "Because it definitely looked like—"

Finn grabbed Grigg's neck, shoving his face into the water. Markes and Tai laughed, moving out of the zone of impact while they roughhoused. Nova rolled her eyes at Avery as if to commiserate over their combined stupidity.

After a few minutes of this, they calmed enough to settle against the tub's edges, their elbows braced behind them. Avery kept her own arms beneath the water, not confident enough to flaunt anything above the waist. Linderly didn't seem to mind the occasional chest-baring, she was so acclimated to Nos Lenti culture that the partial nudity didn't seem to bother her. Nova didn't care at all. She leaned back with her arms splayed out on the stone, nothing but the long golden hair trailing from her ponytail over one shoulder to cover her.

And they talked—about everything.

What they'd been through over the past year, the political state of Earth and the danger of its Reange camps, the humans' fate on Echo and the So' lineage registrations, how Avery had carved out a true place for herself alongside the three most powerful women on Earth. How Megan and Linderly had developed tech that allowed them scale up their rescue efforts on Echo. How Finn had come up with the idea of a sanctuary in the first place.

They talked about the changes they wanted to make and the world they wanted to build once Leviathan was out of power. They discussed what mediation would look like between the two planets and if they'd have to deal with Klein to make it happen.

And most importantly, they laughed.

Nova teased Grigg for being unable to beat Syla in hand-to-hand combat, and he retaliated by bringing up her awkward fling with Cora Najisuki. Finn had been duly impressed by that revelation, going as far to throw Nova a fist bump that she left hanging. Markes called out Linderly for finally hooking up with Tai, wishing her luck on her prickly future sister-in-law. That ended with Tai challenging Markes to a dare to see who could sit naked on the icy steps longer. Markes lost.

Nova pulled another bottle out of her coat, snatched from what was left of her father's collection. They passed it around, some taking small sips, others longer pulls. They made fun of each other and splashed water in one another's faces. They ran into the snow to freeze their asses off before scurrying back to the hot water to warm back up.

And when they laughed until their bellies were sore and tears gathered in the corners of their eyes, Avery felt a part of herself heal that she'd thought was broken forever.

CHAPTER THIRTY-TWO

Avery and Finn followed the others out, lingering behind as the group sleepily walked toward the village. At some point Grigg began howling, his wail reverberating down the frozen gully below. Somewhere far off in the distance, a nocturnal animal called out its shrieking reply.

"Let's hope he doesn't continue that all the way into town," Finn drawled.

Avery stifled a giggle, and Finn pulled on her hand, stopping them on the path just outside the spring. She could make out the line of his bare chest under his open coat where he'd tossed it on over wet skin. His scars were barely visible, his face cast in shadow from the arcing moons overhead. The snow sparkled in their light, echoing the blanket of stars struggling to compete against their vibrant glow.

Finn studied her, his head tilting, his full lips quirking up at one corner. The dimple she'd ached to see for months deepened.

"What?" Avery asked finally, her soft laugh suddenly breathless.

"It's just . . ." He leaned toward her, his fingers moving up her arms to cradle the sides of her neck. His grip on her was firm, a solid weight that made her feel safe and alive. "I can't believe you're here, standing in front of me. I can't believe you're real."

Avery could hardly stand to see the look in his eyes, the anguish that simmered beneath the surface.

"I should have been there." She covered wrists, her warm fingers curling against his pulse as she leaned up on her toes to place a careful kiss over the raised flesh of his scarred cheek. "I should have been there for this."

His hands tightened, but he didn't release her.

"Finn," she whispered, her eyes filling with tears. "I'm so sorry—"

His mouth crashed down on hers before she could finish the final syllable. And this time there was no aching tenderness, no soft exploration. Finn and Avery came together like two stars colliding, fierce and powerful, an explosion that threatened to dislodge the planets themselves. Finn's mouth opened on hers, and she met him with equal desperation as his hands roamed over her body. His tongue was hot against her own as they devoured one another, relearning every part that they'd thought lost forever.

Avery fingered his damp hair, gripping the roots and angling him to her, taking control. He grunted in approval as his fingers dug into her hips. Her back hit the icy wall behind them, and Avery realized Finn had moved them away from the cliff's edge. He pressed into her, his mouth trailing kisses down the side of her face to her neck. She held on to him for dear life, seeing stars of her own that mingled with the twinkling ones above.

He tasted so good, like sweet wine and mint and something else entirely Finn. She'd nearly forgotten how she'd longed for every single part of him. He bit the side of her neck, and she lost her breath. She couldn't stand it. She would die if he stopped.

His fingers found the zipper on her coat, undoing it slowly enough to make Avery whimper. She pulled at his hair, and he chuckled against her neck. His hands slid inside the warmth of the thick wool, his fingers grazing nothing but skin.

Finn went still as his breath caught against her throat.

"I—I had to use my shirt to dry off," Avery said lamely, her face on fire.

Under Finn's coat, she was just as topless as him.

Finn let out a groan, kissing her neck softly. "Very sensible," he mumbled into her shoulder. His thumb hit the edge of her freshly healed wound, and Avery sucked in a sharp breath. Finn halted. "What's this from?"

"It doesn't matter." Avery tried to kiss him again, but he pulled back.

"Everything that's happened to you matters to me." He covered the large scar with his palm, like he was trying to take away whatever pain she'd felt from the wound that had left it.

"Blastfire," she said simply. When he still wouldn't move, she relented. "The fight with Nick. He shot me, remember?"

Finn's other hand clamped onto her side. "My brother did this to you?"

"Well, he kind of wants me dead, so . . . yeah."

"Don't make jokes."

"I learned from the best." She tilted her head up at him playfully, but it didn't take away the tortured look in his eyes. Finn was more hurt than she realized, healing from more wounds than just the ones on his face. Avery placed a hand against his cheek. "Finn, I'm all right. Nick is gone. For now, at least. And it was Qav who saved me from—"

"I don't want to talk about Qav."

"Okay," she breathed, running her fingers along the hair at his temples and down to his nape. She stared into his blue-gray eyes, falling into their depths. The connection she'd felt to him before was stronger than ever, a living line of warm energy that pulsed between them. Qav had been right—she *could* feel Finn. Avery was certain of it. "Then what do you want to talk about?"

"Call me crazy, sweetheart." His mouth quirked up and he leaned into her, finding the crook of her neck again. His breath tickled her skin. "But I don't want to talk at all."

Avery wholeheartedly agreed. He nibbled the sensitive place beneath her ear and she writhed against him, gripping his hair. Finn's fingers found movement again, tracing soft lines up the curve of her waist that left Avery shaking. Her legs actually wobbled as his hands reached the side of her breasts, and he laughed, his arms wrapping around her back.

"Easy, sweetheart. Wouldn't want you taking us over the edge of this cliff."

"Just kiss me," Avery ordered, dragging his mouth back to hers. And Avery lost herself in Finn as time and reality floated away, distant memories that held no meaning.

"I've missed this," he whispered between caresses, his hands achingly gentle against her. "I've missed you so damn much."

When she felt his hand move to the buttons on her trousers, Avery pulled her mouth away from his, dragging in heavy gulps of icy air that stung her lungs.

"I need you, Finn." Her voice was ragged and raw, strange to her own ears.

"I *always* need you," he whispered.

The cold air piercing Avery's lungs drove some semblance of clarity back into her. They were out in the open, leaning against a wall in the snow. But she'd never make it back to the village. She couldn't wait—she wouldn't. "Will anyone be back here tonight?"

Finn's brows shot up, his thumbs stroking her hips, threatening to drive her insane. "Doubtful."

Avery nodded, her decision made. She grabbed his hand, pulling him back up behind her and into the warm cave. The steam curled around them, silver clouds of heated moonlight that chased away the shadows.

Finn stopped her with a light tug. "Are you sure?"

Avery smiled and let go of his hand. She took a breath, gathering whatever courage the mind-consuming lust had bestowed upon her, and shrugged out of her coat. It dropped to the floor.

Finn inhaled sharply, his eyes widening.

"Give me your coat," Avery said, delighted when he complied. She ran her fingers over his abdomen as she took it from him, his shivers sending a rush of pure adrenaline through her. Avery spread it out alongside hers, turning back to him as she lowered herself down to the ground. She looked up at him through her lashes. "Yes, Finn Lunitia. I'm sure."

Finn closed his eyes, turning away to face the entrance. "I just need—" He inhaled deeply, then exhaled for twice as long. "Give me a second."

She must have been insane from desire, because Avery stood. She threaded her arms around his waist, clasping her hands together until her breasts pressed lusciously against his back, skin to skin. She kissed his spine, moving over cords of muscle and tracing scars that hadn't been there a year before.

He turned swiftly to wrap his arms around her, holding her flush against his body. "You are so beautiful, Avery. You make me ache . . . in ways I never knew possible. I never want to be parted from you again. I don't think I could—" He choked on the thought, screwing his eyes shut. He lowered his face and pressed his forehead to hers. Their breath mingled. "I don't think I could bear it. Not again."

"You won't have to."

But even as Avery promised him, she knew she couldn't make such a guarantee. They knew better than anyone that the future could change in an instant. Fate could look at the plans they had, at the promises they wanted to keep, and laugh.

But they had the now. And that was a moment Avery would live in for eternity.

Finn captured her mouth in another kiss, this one more frenzied and consuming than any that came before it. And when he lowered her to the ground, they endeavored to show each other how long eternity could truly be.

Later, they walked leisurely together back to Finn's room in the lodge, their hands tangled together. Avery clung to Finn's heat and took in the quiet village around her, marveling at how far she had come.

Even if their future was uncertain, Avery had faith in herself and the family she had found among her friends. She was more powerful than ever, and she intended to use that to change both worlds. And if she had to prove herself to the others—to Petra and Megan and anyone else—then she was ready.

The icy wind had picked up at last, swirling dry snow around their feet. Something whispered to Avery on the air, winding up from beyond the hidden corners of the mountains, from beneath the thick drifts of snow. She glanced over her shoulder, sure that someone—or something—was watching them.

And when the wind blew across her face again, it called to her, beckoning with an unspoken promise of its own.

Finn sat up in bed with a gasp. Sweat beaded down his temples. The back of his neck was damp. The soft gray light of morning filtered through his windows, casting the simple furnishings in muted shadows.

Beside him, Avery lay sleeping on her stomach. Her face was turned toward him on the pillow, her back bare. The line of her spine curved exquisitely to disappear beneath the sheets.

A nightmare. It had only been a nightmare.

He forced air in and out of his nostrils in measured counts, guiding his heart rate back down. Avery was there beside him, not in Leviathan's control. She didn't have a laser sword pressed against his throat. She wasn't screaming at him to leave with broken-hearted tears in her eyes.

She was there, and she was fine, and it had only been a stupid dream.

But Finn couldn't find sleep again, no matter how hard he tried. No matter how good Avery smelled and how right it felt to have her by his side again. No matter how soft her skin felt beneath his fingers as he ran them across the warmth of her back.

So he lay there, staring at the ceiling with nothing but that nightmare and his racing thoughts to keep him company.

As flattering as it was to think Avery had found her way back to Echo for Finn, he knew that he wasn't her only reason. Avery cherished everyone in her life. Gran and Megan meant the world to her.

Petra was one of her closest friends. She would have done anything in her power to restore Nova and Grigg to their home.

Even so, Finn still felt like he was weighing her down. She had carved out a place of real influence for herself on Earth. And instead of being able to focus on her new purpose, she'd been forced to come clean up the mess that Finn couldn't handle.

That same melancholy that had plagued him for months crept in, clawing at Finn's chest until her felt like he would rip in two. It had abated for a while, long enough that Finn hoped it would leave him forever. But he couldn't hide from his failures. He saw them, every time he looked in the mirror.

He would just let her down again. The only reason Avery had faltered before was because of his mistakes. He hadn't trusted her enough; he hadn't listened to her, not really. He had pushed her—straight into Qav's control.

If Finn pushed Avery too far this time, there would be no coming back. Leviathan's power with that stone made Qav look like a child playing house. Forget controlling her, Leviathan would strip Avery clean and never look back.

When Avery had burst into Finn's cell on the Port Station and he'd seen what she could do—what she was—Finn hadn't thought of her at all. Only of what she could bring to the Rebellion. At his noblest, he'd acknowledged what her powers would mean for the thousands of Reanges without hope. But the truth was, bringing Avery to Nos Valuta was a way to finally prove to Nick that Finn had value beyond being a poster boy for his brother's political machinations.

But Avery never *truly* had a choice. Finn had forced her into it. Just like he had forced her to come rescue him from his own execution.

She moved differently now. Avery had jumped out of that ship and straight into battle. She floated effortlessly among the others, leading them like she had been born to the role. Even the way she acted around Qav was different, more understanding and less volatile. It was working for her, clearly. Enough to face Leviathan and come out alive. The kind of partnership she could have with Qav would be unlike anything Echo had seen in centuries.

Finn rolled out of bed, shutting off his mind. He crept from the room toward the showers, eager to get started with the long day ahead of them. Even if all Finn was good for was putting the people he loved in danger, he wasn't ready to let Avery go. He wouldn't be able to—not yet.

And if that was cowardly of him, then he'd just have to learn to live with it.

So he set the shower as hot as he could handle, scalding his back and letting it run over the scars that marred his face. The memory of Avery's kiss on his cheek was still fresh in his mind, of her aching apology that he'd been unable to hear. Finn leaned into the water. The stinging pain was a necessary reminder of the mistakes he had made and of the risks he'd taken that lead to nothing more than disaster.

CHAPTER
THIRTY-THREE

"Are you sure you want to go through with this?" Gran pulled the collar of Avery's coat up higher around her neck, brushing snow off her shoulders from the early-morning shower. The flakes had begun falling in fat fluffy puffs, turning all of Nos Lenti into a frosted wonderland.

"You know Leviathan won't stop," Avery replied resolutely. "Now that I'm back, it's only going to get worse. If there's any chance at changing Echo's future, then I have to at least try."

Gran smiled softly. "You've always been brave, Avie. But suddenly I feel like I'm standing in front of a grown woman instead of the little girl I raised. When did that happen?"

"I don't feel brave." Avery's voice was almost a whisper. Her eyes stung. She looked down at her boots that were wet and shiny in the snow.

It was the truth. Avery had never felt brave, not once in her life. She had found strength in the action of making decisions, of moving forward on the path she chose, but little else. Did that count as bravery? Avery doubted it.

Each choice she made determined the fate of millions of people, both the Reanges she served and the humans who lived alongside them. It was a burden that Avery finally understood, and one that she was still struggling to accept. She had hesitated before, doubted herself before, and it had resulted in immense suffering.

Avery swallowed hard, trying to find the courage to admit her thoughts. "I've done horrible things, Gran. I've *caused* them. I'm so far from that little girl that I'm not sure I'll ever find my way back."

"Avie," Gran said gently, lifting Avery's face to hers with a finger under her chin. "I don't want you to find your way back. You think we all haven't done things we regret? Me more than most. We do our best to make the choices that honor us, and when we lose our way, because that is inevitable, we adjust our course. There is nothing braver than that."

Avery nodded shortly, her lip trembling as Gran squeezed her hands.

"You *are* different now but no less precious to me," Gran continued. "You are capable and strong, a woman who has stepped into her power, into her role as leader. Horrible things or not, you're already more than I ever hoped you'd become."

Avery's throat constricted painfully. She had no easy reply. Even Gran seemed at a loss for words as her fingers stroked the backs of Avery's hands, her eyes shining in the cold.

"I wish you'd come with us," Avery said, almost childlike, voicing the thought that had been bothering her for hours. She didn't like the idea of leaving Gran so soon after their reunion. But Avery couldn't linger—not when time was breathing down their necks.

"You know I'm too old for all that," Gran replied. "I'll serve you much better here in the village. And Mylan needs a watchful eye, someone whom Leviathan cannot touch."

Avery nodded again. They'd already discussed Mylan's incarceration. He was to be held away from the other Reanges, kept in strict isolation.

"I'm leaving Krez with you," Avery said softly, her eyes tracking the tall warrior as he helped Syla and Grigg choose weapons from a pile they'd assembled. Markes hovered nearby, moping over the fact that they ignored his new creations.

Gran smiled. "He won't like that."

"He doesn't have to. He wants to earn my forgiveness? This is how he'll do it. I won't leave you unprotected. Especially now, when being back here feels so . . . strange."

"What do you mean?"

Avery looked at Gran, wavering between her desire for reassurance and her fear of sounding like she was losing her mind. "I think . . . I think I can *feel* the Essence. I think it's been trying to reach out to me." She glanced over her shoulder, making sure the others were still distracted. "The way my powers manifest, it's a kind of pull on my mind, like an invisible force that connects me . . . to everything."

Gran nodded, her brows knitting. "Go on."

"But when I'm on Echo . . . that feeling—that connection—becomes more tangible. I don't think I truly noticed it before, but being back here after so much time on Earth, it's impossible to ignore. Like I can reach out and touch it . . . like the air itself can reach out and touch me."

"Have you told anyone else?"

"No. Not yet."

"Not even Finn?"

Avery shook her head. "I didn't want to frighten anyone. Especially after what Mylan said about Leviathan losing her mind. But I couldn't leave without . . . I wanted your opinion."

"So much about the So'Reange power is still unknown. I spent much of my professional life trying to unlock and unravel the mysteries of your genetics, and I barely cracked the surface. It's why Project Lares was unsuccessful."

"Until last year, you mean," Avery pointed out. "Until Nick gained powers."

"That was my fault," Gran said bitterly. "They never would have found the key if I hadn't modded your genetics to mimic a human's. I left too many breadcrumbs. Even so, his powers are a mere shade of your abilities, the physical gifts and nothing more. But Minister Klein wants the other half—she won't rest until she has the ability to control human minds. And once she does, the Federation will be unstoppable." Gran paused, tilting her head. "Unless you become untouchable."

"Then you think I'm right to go after this Essence stone? What if it *is* Leviathan trying to play tricks on me? What if Mylan is still in her pocket?"

"I doubt she would stoop to that level of theatrics," Gran commented. She smiled indulgently. "But I can't answer those questions for you, Avery. Not anymore. You have to answer them yourself."

Lissande called for Gran from the medic building, and she looked over her shoulder to wave. "She'll need help finding supplies for your packs. I love her, but that woman wouldn't be able to find a bottle of antiseptic if bit her in the ass."

Avery laughed, hugging Gran close.

"Trust yourself, Avery. Trust your gifts. You don't need my counsel anymore." Gran kissed Avery's cheek before turning to jog away.

Avery watched her go, yelling at Lissande as she drew closer. It was just like Gran to give advice without actually giving any. She'd never been one to hover, not when it came to learning lessons. But maybe that was exactly why Avery had been able to come so far. Maybe it was why she was still willing to fight.

"That was sweet. Almost made me wish I could tolerate my parents enough to speak to them."

Avery jumped. Qav had sidled up beside her while she was distracted, standing too close for comfort.

"You have parents?" Avery wrinkled her nose. "I thought you crawled out of the sewers fully formed."

"Only one day reunited with your precious Finn and his atrocious sense of humor has already rubbed off on you. Besides, you've pillaged around my head enough to know everything about me." He stepped even closer, his arms going behind his back as he leaned forward to whisper, "You're the one person with whom I have no secrets."

"What do you want, Qav?" Avery bent away from him to grab her pack, shoving a blanket farther down into the black nylon. "Don't they need your help?"

He looked over his shoulder where Syla and Ennis were arguing over how many guns to strap to their gear. Rem watched passively nearby, looking down his nose at them. "I'm not much of a hands-on kind of guy."

Avery snorted. "As if that needed to be said. I don't think I've ever seen you without a fresh manicure every five days."

He curled his hands, hiding his fingers.

She laughed, delighting in his discomfort. Tai looked up from where he'd joined Markes, his eyes narrowing. Petra would be hearing about this.

"Look Avery, I . . ." Qav followed her line of sight and sighed, giving up on trying to speak aloud. *I know it's hard to have me here. Your friends . . . They don't exactly trust me.*

Avery turned to him, genuinely curious. It was the last thing she'd ever expect for Qav to admit. He didn't look away from her, his expression earnest and open. She reached out to his energy, feeling the gratitude he was laying bare for her.

But I trust you. Avery surprised herself when the words came to her. They were true nonetheless. *You wouldn't be here if I didn't.*

His silver eyes brightened as a thrill sparked across their connection. *Even if you don't really mean that yet, even if you're just hoping that you can . . . It means something to me. And I won't let you down, Avery. Not again.*

Qav pressed his energy into hers, letting down every wall he'd ever erected to keep her and everyone else out, the same one she'd had to level an entire building to break through before. And he kept it open to her, his mind as vulnerable as a newborn child.

Avery let her pack drop, her hands going slack from shock.

His raw, biting power curled toward her mind, spreading out with icy fingers as chilly as the snow-covered ground. And Avery met him, unafraid, wholly understanding what Qav was offering, what he was trying to prove. With a single thought, she could break him effortlessly. She could wipe his mind until there was nothing left of him except wisps of cold silver and the faint scent of lavender.

Deep laughter tumbled over Qav's shoulder and Avery's eyes lifted. Finn strolled across the square beside Nova. If Qav was the frigid iciness of winter, then Finn was the melting heat of a sun, warm and vibrant and necessary for life. Avery reached out to him, desperate to feel Finn the way she could Qav, not caring that it was impossible.

But something *was* there at the end of her power—a blast of heat that made her suck in a hissing breath. Finn stumbled, looking up at her sharply. His face had gone pale, his scars standing out in harsh relief. He noted Qav and his face hardened, changing course to stalk straight for them.

Qav grimaced. "I'm beginning to think his frown is permanent. What a waste of a pretty face." But remorse seeped across their open connection, in direct contradiction to his bravado as he retreated. "Good luck with him."

Finn reached her side, crossing his arms over his chest as he glared at Qav leaving. "What did he want?"

"Just wishing us luck," Avery said. It was a decent enough explanation. Their group would be splitting in two—another benefit of having two So'.

Qav would lead a separate expedition back into Milderion, where he would continue his subversion work on the population and keep a close eye on Leviathan's movements. Syla and Ennis would join him, along with Linderly, Markes, and Tai. They'd gather supplies and prepare for Avery and the others to join them in a few days. Rem had chosen to stay behind in Nos Lenti, ill at ease with the idea of close combat.

The others would journey with Avery to the coast to search the Essence stone, if it even existed. Everyone was more at ease to know that Qav would be nowhere near the stone—even Avery. She thought of his show of vulnerability, of how she'd just told him she trusted him, and guilt spread nauseatingly through her belly.

Avery turned to Finn. She let her eyes travel over his features, searching for that feeling of warmth again and finding nothing. But she was certain—*something* had been there.

"Good riddance," Finn said to Qav's back. "I'm sick of looking at his face."

"He said something similar about you," Avery drawled. "Maybe you're more alike than you think."

Finn gave her a surprised look so comical that she burst out laughing, the sound traveling up and over the hills. Finn grinned as he watched her, his expression softening.

His hand went to the back of her neck, pulling her toward him, and Avery rose on her toes, meeting him halfway for an open-mouthed kiss. He nudged her with his lips, brushing his nose against hers as he drew away. They stood there, foreheads touching, their breath mingling in soft puffs in the cold.

"What was that for?" Avery asked quietly, her pulse skittering across her veins.

"For the way you laugh."

She leaned up to press her lips against his again, claiming his mouth more thoroughly. He'd avoided her all morning—he was gone when she finally woke up in his bed. She was relieved that her worries had been nothing more than misplaced insecurity.

This was Finn. This person who radiated enthusiasm for life, who said things out of the blue that made her want to fall in love with him all over again.

"You're in public, you know!" Megan yelled as she sashayed by, but even she was grinning ear to ear. Petra walked beside her, averting her focus straight ahead.

Avery stepped away from Finn. Making out in broad daylight in front of their entire group might not be the best idea. Especially when Petra was barely speaking to Avery.

Megan and Petra had kept to themselves the previous night, disappearing entirely. Megan hadn't spoken about Petra at all, not once in the hours they'd spent catching up together. And no matter how much she longed to, Avery couldn't bring herself to ask Megan about it.

Her memories of what happened in the Sanctum were blurry, but Avery knew she'd been jealous. Not of their romance, but of their attention. They were two of her closest friends and she'd blamed Megan and Petra for loving one another. As though Avery had the right to claim each of them as solely her own.

The memory of Megan's face when Avery had accused her of lying, of sneaking around behind her back . . . It haunted Avery. She had no right to interfere with their relationship. Not then, and certainly not now.

Finn bumped her shoulder. "Don't worry about it. You know Petra. She'll warm up."

Avery bit her lip, her stomach sinking. Even Finn could tell how much it bothered her. "I'm not used to Petra taking your side over mine."

"Just give her time. She's been through a lot."

"So have you. So has everyone. Because of me." Avery let out a beleaguered sigh. Her heart broke a little when he didn't contradict her. "But you and Petra becoming besties? I can't say I saw that one coming."

"What about you and Qav? Looking awfully chummy back there."

"That's not the same thing." But she felt her face grow warm.

"Then explain it to me."

"He is an asset, Finn. Nothing more."

Finn looked away from her, his jaw clenching. "It's not safe, Avery. *He's* not safe. Not for you or any of the others."

Across the square, Qav was arguing with Syla about the weight of his pack. He'd done everything in his power to gain her forgiveness. Even leaving behind the Sanctum.

"He can't hurt me, Finn. He wouldn't," Avery stated. "And I trust him."

Finn's brow flinched, his mouth working, like he wanted to say something more. But he only grabbed her pack and slung it across his shoulder along with his own.

"You know what you're doing," he said curtly. "Let's get going. We're burning daylight."

Avery jerked as though he'd slapped her.

Finn was never short with her, never anything other than optimistic and candid. Did Qav's presence alter so much?

Only last week Avery had felt the same way. She couldn't blame Finn for his hesitancy. It would be good for Finn, and the others, to get some distance from Qav for a while.

But eventually, they'd all have to find a way to trust him. For better or worse, if they couldn't find the Essence, the only way to defeat Leviathan was with Qav by their side.

Petra sat beside Nova, learning the components of Cora's ship over the course of the hour it took them to reach the coast. The journey would have taken at least two in any other cruiser currently on the market. Its speed was nearly as impressive as its cloaking tech. Petra was only surprised that Finn wasn't breathing down her neck to get his own hands on the neural controls.

Petra could have just programmed in their coordinates, but she was eager for some semblance of control on the journey. She hadn't been home since before they'd left for Earth on Avery's publicity tour, nearly two years ago. Even though she'd ached to visit Dru-udi in the past year, Petra was too worried Leviathan would have it monitored. But Petra would never have left Megan unprotected anyway, not in those first few months when they didn't know if she would even live.

Letting Tai go with Qav's team had been a test of Petra's willpower. They'd fought over it. Her brother's place was by her side, especially if they were going to their home town. But Qav needed a guide, and both Markes and Linderly had volunteered. That had sealed Tai's fate—he went where Linderly did. He claimed he would monitor Qav and report back, but if that silver haired asshole decided to mess with Tai's mind, there would be nothing he could do.

Qav may have convinced Avery, but Petra would reserve the right to judge him as she saw fit. Even if Petra hated him, she could acknowledge the value of his skills on their side. She was certain Mylan had sent them on a mission doomed to fail, merely a tactic to waste their time while Leviathan regrouped. And when they were forced to face her without a stone of their own, they would need all the extra help they could get.

Finn, however, wasn't taking Qav's presence on Echo well. Petra doubted he could see past his own rage to acknowledge any semblance of practicality.

He'd stood near the back of the bridge since they took off, silently watching the landscape pass beneath them as they soared through the skies. The euphoria of Avery's arrival had brought him out of whatever personal purgatory he'd sentenced himself to, but even that was beginning to wear off. He was spiraling back into the darkness that had settled over him for months, faster and deeper than ever.

Even Avery could see it, her golden eyes flickering to him more often than not. He kept his distance from her, always finding something to do when she walked his way. It made everyone uncomfortable, especially when they'd spent the past twenty-four hours practically in each other's laps. Nova was already glaring at him. Even Grigg seemed put off by Finn's brusqueness.

If Finn thought his sudden shift in behavior would be enough to push Avery away, he was more of an idiot than she realized. Petra couldn't wait to see it blow up in his face.

The sea came into view at last, a vast, endless blue that continued on to shimmer against the horizon. They touched down in the high grass fields that lined the northern cliffs, acres of green swaying in the morning sun. Petra grabbed her gear and led the others out.

The bright rays of sunlight hit Petra's face, making her squint as the salty scent of cold sea air filled her nostrils. All at once she was five years old again, heading out on her father's boat, allowed to sit at the bow alone for the first time in her life. She closed her eyes, leaning into the longing for the life she should have had, breathing in the air of her youth. Letting it hurt.

Fingers slid into Petra's, holding fast.

Megan stood beside her, a soft smile on her lips. The others passed them without hesitation, heading for the cliffs. Grigg winked suggestively, and Petra fought the heat that rose up her neck.

Avery's eyes lingered on their joined hands for a moment before catching Petra's gaze. There was nothing in her expression except longing and regret. Petra didn't need to read Avery's mind to know they were both thinking of that day, when Avery had been consumed with paranoia, screaming at them of their betrayal.

When Megan had nearly died.

When Avery had nearly killed her.

Petra pulled her hand away from Megan, striding ahead to join the others. She swung her pack to the ground, detaching her harness from its clips and fitting it over her waist. "We need to get a move on. The patrols won't be around these parts for hours, but we don't want to be around here when they do."

Things had been easier when Petra was working for Leviathan and the Origin. In this new life, she felt too much. Things were always too complicated. Sometimes, in her darker hours, Petra wished she had never left.

Those moments in the arena, when Leviathan had been inside Petra's head . . . Losing control of her own body had been horrible. But there was also relief. With Leviathan in her head, Petra hadn't needed to feel . . . anything. And she hadn't been that empty in a very long time.

Her fingers fumbled on the buckles, the metal slipping and clanking against itself.

"You'll break your neck that way." Finn took over, untangling the straps for her.

Petra settled, allowing him to help her. Finn had become a source of comfort in the past year. What a bizarre realization.

Avery watched them with wide, bewildered eyes. She didn't understand—she would never understand—how they'd needed each other when she had cast them out.

Petra fastened her harness as Finn threw the second one at Megan.

"You two go first," Finn said. "We'll descend in pairs to the bottom."

Nova tapped her communicator and the ship disappeared behind them, not even a trace of shimmer on its outline.

"Damn," Finn said in awe, a flicker of his old self coming through. "I don't think I'll ever get used to that."

Petra double-checked Megan's harness and got into position, leaning out over the edge of the cliff. The sea swirled up and around the rocks below, the waves lapping harmlessly in the low tide. It would start rising in another hour.

Megan's breath came in rapid puffs beside Petra as they braced their feet against the ledge.

"Hey," Petra said softly, calling Megan's pale eyes to her. "It'll be fine. Just lean out and trust the—"

"I know what I'm doing." Megan pushed out from the rock to vault backward, dropping on the line faster than Petra had ever seen before. She descended the complicated crags like a seasoned professional.

"Well, shit," Grigg said in admiration.

Finn jerked a thumb toward the drop. "I guess you better go after her, blueberry."

Petra threw up a middle finger at him, wrinkling her nose in disgust. And then she kicked off, swinging after Megan, trying to catch up. Finn's laughter followed her all the way down to the briny rocks below.

CHAPTER THIRTY-FOUR

Finn shoved his hands in his pockets to keep from touching Avery as she jumped down from a boulder, landing gracefully on her feet. Nova caught his eye, one blond brow lifting in question. He turned to survey the ocean, hoping he looked more preoccupied than despondent.

They'd spent the past half hour walking along the shore, following Avery's instincts as far as direction. Finn still wasn't sure what they were supposed to find. Did Mylan expect them to come across Essence stones on the shore, like pebbles waiting to be collected?

"I think there's something here!" Avery called out.

She had move so far ahead of them that she was practically swallowed by one of the large caves, encased by its shadows until Finn could barely see her. His palms turned clammy as his heart stuttered. They didn't know what Mylan had sent them into—it would be stupid to venture so far from one another.

Nova and Grigg wasted no time in picking up their pace to vault over the large rocks as they followed her. Even Megan pushed ahead to join them. Petra lingered back with Finn as he maintained his slower gait.

"How does she know where she's going?" Petra's voice was low, quiet enough that it almost disappeared beneath the sound of the crashing waves. "She's hiding something from us."

Finn frowned, the twist in his gut confirming what he'd been afraid to admit to himself. Avery had been cryptic after their walk back from the spring. Something had spooked her, he could tell. And again that morning, when she'd spoken in hushed tones with Qav in the square.

Finn may not have been by her side for a year, but he could tell when she was uncertain about something. And apparently, so could Petra.

"She'll tell us when she's ready," Finn replied.

He'd made his decision to give her space, and he would abide by it. His interference only made things worse when it came to Avery, spoiling her choices and rotting her self-confidence. He wouldn't be the one to drag her down again.

"I don't like secrets," Petra murmured.

"That's ironic, considering you were on an espionage mission masquerading as a human when we met you."

Petra let out a short huff that sounded suspiciously like a laugh. She stayed close to Finn, only moving away from him to join Megan once they reached the others.

"There's nothing in here," Petra's accusation bounced up around them. "It's just a cut out from the cliffs, like all the rest we've passed."

Avery walked up to the rock face, placing her hands to its surface.

"The tide will start rising soon," Petra said impatiently.

Avery walked along the wall, her fingertips trailing its wet, craggy surface. She bent low, brushing rocks off a notched section, and closed her eyes at last. She crouched there for a minute, unmoving.

She stood with a sigh, wiping her hands on her thighs. "I'm sorry. I really thought there was . . . Maybe we should go back up and wait for the next low tide tonight."

Petra pinned Finn with a knowing look. But he was too busy watching Avery. The way her face fell, dejected over what she thought had been an answer. He swallowed down the urge to tell her to try again. He felt nauseous.

Avery looked up at Finn sharply, a frown scrunching the freckles strewn across her face. What did she—

A rumble started beneath their feet, shaking the ground. They pressed their backs together as loose rocks crashed down from the cliffside. Avery held up both her hands, forming some kind of shield that sent the heavy projectiles bouncing away harmlessly. He'd never seen her do it before—some new trick she'd picked up in her time on Earth. They backed away from the curved wall, watching in awe as the cliff face shifted in on itself.

As soon as it had begun, the stone settled into stillness, revealing a sliver of an entrance just big enough for one person to squeeze through.

"Moons above," Nova whispered reverently, echoing everyone's thoughts.

"I guess that means your instincts were spot-on." Megan grinned at Avery, giving her a playful shove.

"Mylan was right," Avery said, clearly pleased with herself as she ran for the entrance.

They entered single file by necessity. Grigg cursed as he struggled to squeeze his large frame through in front of Finn. Thankfully, the thin corridor was no more than a couple of feet deep before it opened up into a larger cavern. The daylight barely made its way in behind them, illuminating a single line of pale white on the stone ahead.

Avery was already exploring, receding into shadow.

"Avery, wait," Finn called.

She turned back to him, her eyes unusually bright against the blackness. The ground began to rumble again. Finn turned, pushing everyone away from the shifting entrance. It closed behind them, sealing them inside.

"Shit." Grigg's curse bounced around them, fading away into the black.

Petra activated her light stick, illuminating the area in front of her with its yellow glow. The cavern narrowed down to a tunnel that stretched out ahead of them.

"Does this mean we go forward?" Megan asked.

"My communicator's not working," Nova said, tapping the tech on her wrist.

"Maybe we should turn back," Grigg suggested. "Avery can wave her hands over the rock and it will open again, right?"

Avery shifted on her feet, looking to the wall where the entrance had been. For a fraction of a second, she seemed scared.

"Avery?" Megan asked again.

Avery shook her head, turning to the path. "We keep going."

There was no light except for Petra's glow stick. There was no sound. They had been shut inside a tomb. But Avery chose to move forward.

"We should conserve the sticks," Finn said curtly. Their charge wouldn't last forever. "The opening is only wide enough to walk in pairs anyway."

"I'm in front with Avery!" Megan chirped, latching onto Avery's arm. "Finn got you all last night, so now it's my turn."

Finn met Avery's eyes, and they both looked away awkwardly. Moons above, was he blushing again?

"Then I'll take the middle with Nova," Petra said sourly. "The two heathens can bring up the rear."

"Ouch." Finn pressed a hand to his chest. "That one really hurt, Petra."

"I've heard the truth often does."

"Damn," Grigg said appreciatively. "Petra's grown a funny bone since the last time I saw her. Fascinating."

"Don't flatter her," Finn warned. He activated his own light stick, securing it to his shoulder. "Next thing you know, she'll be doing stand-up routines in Milderion."

"I'd pay to see that," Megan said from the front, her voice echoing back to them.

"You'd pay to watch her paint a wall," Finn teased loudly.

Avery watched the interaction, surprise written across her face. She wasn't used to the way they'd fallen into a new dynamic without her.

If only she knew . . . their love for Avery was the entire reason they'd all come together after the Gate fell. The pain they'd gone through from losing Avery had changed them all.

Which was why Finn had to let her go.

He shifted his pack, slapping Grigg on the shoulder. "Looks like it's you and me in the rear."

"At least buy me dinner first."

"Was that an option?" Finn laughed. He twisted to Nova with a wink, knowing his next words would find their target. "And here I thought only Nova fell for my good looks."

Nova froze, frowning curiously at Finn. Her eyes darted to Avery and back before she said disapprovingly, "That mistake was almost a decade ago. And one I don't intent to repeat. Ever."

Her reproach sent shame curling like rotten food in Finn's gut. Avery turned to start down the angling path, but he caught the edge of her face in the soft light. He'd hurt her.

He knew the comment would—it had been his intention. The more space he could put between them, the better.

"Let's keep moving." Avery's voice was stilted.

Megan hurried to catch up with her as they began their descent but not before giving Finn a condemning look of her own.

Finn's hands balled into fists at his sides. Maybe he had gone too far. He wanted to distance himself from Avery, not break her. The darkness sunk its claws in deeper beneath his ribs, crushing his heart.

Finn took a deep breath to steady himself.

If he couldn't be with Avery, then he would at least do his best to protect her. Even from himself.

Qav was sick of the snow. An hour of hiking in the frozen landscape of Echo's high mountains and he was ready to force them all to turn back. The temptation was so visceral that he had to focus on the pain of his toes going numb inside his boots to keep himself from actually doing it.

Avery had asked him to monitor Milderion and gather more information on Leviathan, and that's what Qav would do. It wasn't exactly easy for him to take orders. He wavered between biting his tongue and passively observing so often that it made him physically ill. But the alternative was drastically unappealing to him now.

If he went home—if he even could get through the Gate unassisted—Syla and Ennis wouldn't be with him. Rem would be a sad substitute for their company. And was Sanctum even somewhere he wanted to be without them by his side?

Qav had only ever cared about building walls. He'd even built that giant mansion on a private island away from everyone else in his city. But now the idea of the isolation bothered him. His ego had been blinding him for years, hiding painful memories that he'd never wanted to revisit. And Avery had shoved his face right into them.

Qav couldn't go back to the person he'd been before. As comfortable as that life had been, it was only a facade, a shadow on the wall that distracted him from reality. He'd sheltered himself in a stasis for years.

Unlike Avery, who truly lived her life. She didn't hide herself from the people she loved; she leaned into them. And when he had tried to separate her from them, the backlash had unleashed a power unlike anything Qav had ever seen.

Ennis paused on top of a rock to wait for him, her shaved head covered by a gray woolen cap to keep her scalp warm. "Why are you lingering? We need to make it to the ship before noon."

Qav gritted his teeth. "I didn't sign up for outdoor excursions. I can't feel my blazing feet."

"It's not so far now," Linderly said beside him. The girl was barely out of breath. Qav told himself she'd had longer to adjust to the altitude.

Syla appeared from behind the boulder, her breath puffing with the extra exertion she undoubtedly unleashed in running back to them. "Aw—is the poor little So' feeling tired?"

"You are lucky I'm too cold to send an avalanche down on top of you."

"Come on, the children are doing a better job than you." Syla gestured ahead where Tai and Markes waited patiently, their thumbs hooked into their packs. At least Linderly had the decency to go at Qav's pace.

"Syla, I really don't need your censure right now while I'm trying to climb a mountain."

"Technically you're descending it." She raised a pink eyebrow, delighted when he sent snow flying at her with a flick of his wrist. "If you would actually train more with us, then—"

"And I certainly don't need another lecture on how I don't join you enough in the gym." Qav adjusted the straps on his pack, hastening to pass them.

Maybe you'd actually be able to take on Avery if you put a little effort into your physical form. Syla's chastising thoughts hit him from behind.

The surest way to annoy her would be not to reply. Qav bit the inside of his cheek to keep from speaking, pushing forward through the fresh snow.

It aggravated him even more that she was probably right. Avery never missed a day in the gym. The breadth of her physical powers put even his mental skills to shame. Qav nearly gagged: he was going to have to start sweating on a regular basis. It would ruin his hair care routine.

Another thirty minutes of hiking in silence and they finally reached the designated coordinates. The ship was so ancient, he was surprised it would be able to get off the ground. The fresh snow from the morning shower had covered its outdated angular lines in a thick layer of white.

"Your chariot awaits, my liege," Syla teased as Markes opened the access door.

Qav rolled his eyes, lingering outside to catch his breath as the others disappeared ahead of him. Something in the air brushed against him, a soft, familiar pull at his chest. Like it was testing his ability to discern it.

He spun, his eyes scanning the icy landscape, looking for the threat. The cold rocks and snow-covered bushes sat still as the wind howled over the peaks in the far distance.

The pull tested him again, drawing his eyes upward. Qav's breath halted.

On the highest outcropping of the cliffside, a small white fox stood nearly invisible in the snow. Qav's mouth fell open. It was a tsek.

On Earth, the Reanges called him by the same name. Of course, Qav knew the legends, but he hadn't thought they actually existed. Not really.

Its tail flicked. The wind picked up and pulled at Qav's hair, silver strands brushing across his face along with the icy air.

The pull grabbed him again, a deeper presence than he'd ever felt before that curled up and settled warmly against his heart. Qav saw a vision of Finn, staring at him in the snow with tears in his eyes. And he could *feel* Finn. Despair, weighted and stinging, billowed out from him like poison.

It wasn't strong, nothing like what Qav could do with his skills, merely a shadow of the merge's true depth. But it was enough. And more bizarre still: Qav wanted to help. Or maybe whatever had shown him the vision wanted it. Somehow he doubted the distinction mattered.

But Qav knew one thing for certain at last: he was on the right path.

Following Avery, leaving Earth and coming to Echo, fighting for the freedom and peace of both Reanges and humans . . . This was where he was meant to be. This was his home—these people were his home. And choosing to stay by their side was no choice at all.

This planet *was* different; it was alive. Whatever that energy was that kept playing with them, they needed to explore it more. Somehow, he knew it was the answer. He needed to speak with Avery.

Qav closed his eyes, reaching out across the planet, careful to avoid the capitol and any chance that Leviathan would detect him. He'd kept a soft connection to Avery, light enough that she'd barely feel it, keen to keep at least one eye on her despite the distance.

But she was gone—her energy was gone.

Qav pressed as hard as he dared, expanding farther, searching for the familiar electric sting of her power. But she wasn't there.

If something had gone wrong, Qav would know. Even if he

couldn't find her, the warmth in his chest assured him that she was all right. Protected. Watched.

There were strange things about Echo that affected his abilities in ways Qav didn't yet understand. But this deep knowing . . . It came to him as naturally as breathing.

When Qav opened his eyes, the tsek was gone, nothing but snow billowing on the cliffside where it had been. He wondered if it had even been there at all.

CHAPTER THIRTY-FIVE

For miles, the tunnel remained straight, a steady descent along the narrow path into the bowels of the rock until its weight overhead began to press down on them. Finn was grateful he had spent so much of his youth in the Rebellion base of Nos Valuta, but even that stronghold built into the center of a mountain had never felt so oppressive.

The tunnel itself was rudimentary, a jaggedly carved arch over an uneven damp floor. The air was stale and thick, almost difficult to breathe. The dark stone surrounding them swallowed both sound and light.

Even after stopping to rest and eat a meager lunch of leftovers from their celebratory feast the night before, they were all uneasy. But no one suggested turning around, no matter how uncomfortable the lack of light made them. Avery was trusting her instincts. If she felt the call of the Essence, then they had to be on the right path.

But the descent was getting to even her. The deeper they went, the tighter her shoulders became, the less sure her gait. Finn couldn't find a reason for the change in her demeanor when she was the only one among them with a connection to the outside world. She was the only one who could be certain that their journey forward would be worth the effort. The rest of them were just operating on blind faith—in her.

Megan did her best to keep things cheerful, the only one willing to keep conversation going. She went off on long tangents about her and Avery's childhood. When they were fifteen, they'd snuck out to raves on the ground level every weeknight for an entire month. Even Gran had never found that one out. When they were ten, Avery had developed an obsession with Megan's older brother, Denny, over the holiday break—a detail that Avery remembered very differently. It got so bad that Megan stopped inviting her over until he went back to university. Avery retaliated by sharing how Megan had failed every single physical fitness test she'd ever had in school. Petra found this particularly amusing and validating. Megan pertly pointed out that Avery was right there beside her at the bottom of the rankings.

And when those stories started to wane, Megan moved on to things that had happened on Echo over the past year, catching Avery up on everything she'd missed. Like Linderly convincing her to get tattoos together—a falling star on her lower back that she would show Avery later. Or Markes nearly blowing himself up testing outdated explosives they found on a raid. How Tai had spent an entire month exploring the upper altitudes in his free time to find a rare flower Linderly had seen on an old data sheet.

But her stories left out the things that would make Avery sad. Like how Finn spent more time alone than ever before, disappearing for entire days. And until last week, Megan had barely spoken two words to Petra in the past three months. Or how it had taken Megan weeks to relearn how to walk once she woke from her coma. Or that Megan had even *been* in a coma.

Only Finn and Petra knew the omissions. Only they felt the awkward weight of their absence.

There was some excitement when the tunnel at last opened up into an atrium. Its circular space was large enough that they could all fit inside with ample room to breathe. That enthusiasm quickly dwindled when they realized there were three new openings ahead of them, three potential paths forward.

"Well?" Petra asked Avery, her hands planted on her hips. "What now?"

Avery bit her lip, her eyes darting between the three options. Her hands trembled at her sides before she brought them together behind her back. At last, she let out a long, steady breath before turning back to the group. Her face was cast in the eerie yellow light, her eyes bright and gold and shimmering.

Finn's fingers twitched, yearning to touch her, to hold her, to tell her everything would be all right. Even when he could never make such a promise. It was her actions alone that would lead them out of this. It was her choice, her belief in Mylan, that had brought them there in the first place.

When she spoke, her voice was small. "I—I don't know."

"What do you mean, you don't know?" Petra bit out savagely.

"Petra." Nova said her name like a warning.

Megan stepped in front of Avery. "We're all tired, okay? Just give her a moment."

"I don't know," Avery repeated. She sank to her haunches, huddling before them with her hands on her head. She screwed her eyes shut. "I don't know because I can't feel anything. I think that I . . . I think that this rock may be the obsidian stone. The one they used in the cells beneath the capitol."

No one so much as breathed.

Petra cursed, turning to the tunnel behind them.

Finn felt the blood drain from his face. He stared at the streaks of yellow light casting shadows along the ceiling, trying to keep himself from punching the nearest wall of solid rock.

Nova let out a steadying sigh of her own. "You mean the stone that nullifies your powers?"

Avery nodded once, struggling to hold it together. "That would be the one."

"So Mylan really did send us to our deaths." Grigg let out a disbelieving laugh. "I didn't think he had it in him."

"Can't we go back up the way we came?" Megan asked hopefully. "Surely Avery can activate the passage again. There has to be a way to open it from the inside."

Avery finally stood, her voice shaking as she admitted, "I won't be able to. Once that entrance closed, I couldn't feel . . . anything. I think we've been walking through a passage made entirely of the black stone since the moment we stepped foot in this place."

"And you lied to us about it this whole time," Petra sneered, whirling to press in on Avery until she backed away. "Why am I not surprised?"

Finn grabbed Petra's arm, his instincts kicking in. "Easy, Petra. Back off."

She ripped out of his grasp, curling her lip at him. But she stalked off to the other side of the atrium, pacing the wall.

Finn stepped close to Avery, keeping his hands to himself, waiting until she lifted her eyes to meet his. The meek demeanor was unlike her. Her uncertainty would cost them. She had sent Qav into the city alone, millions of Reanges ready for his manipulations, a fate even worse than Leviathan. If they never escaped the tunnels, Qav would use that opportunity to carve out his own rule even greater than what he'd determined in the Sanctum. The humans would be doomed—Nos Lenti and everything they'd worked for would be lost.

They never should have listened to Mylan. He must have been working for Leviathan from the start. Whatever machinations he had in play, Mylan had won.

But sitting there, crying in uncertainty and fear, was not the Avery Finn knew. She was strong and bold and fierce. Whatever was holding her back was only making things worse for all of them. He would force sense back into her.

"I don't care that you lied." Finn turned his voice to ice. "I don't care that you hid things from us. But you trusted Mylan, against our advice. You brought us all here, Avery. You are the leader—*now lead.*"

"Hey," Grigg said angrily, shoving Finn away from her. "You don't get to say that shit to her."

Finn kept his eyes on Avery, ignoring the way Grigg's loyalty to her hit him with a strange combination of betrayal and pride. She still had protection, even if it didn't come from Finn. At least she would have that when he was gone.

Avery stared at Finn wide-eyed. A single tear escaped down her cheek, trailing wetly over her freckles.

Finn's chest wrenched painfully. She didn't understand—and Finn didn't want her to. He had to make her listen to herself. Even if her powers were blocked, she could still get them out of there. He had to believe that.

And a part of Finn *was* angry. A part of him had wanted to say those words to her, if for no other reason than to show her how worthless he was now. All he had left of himself were the putrid remnants of who he'd once been, ready to throw his own fear in her face with cold comments and censure. There was no place for something so foul in her life.

"Three corridors, three pairs," Grigg said, trying to defuse the tension. "Let's just split up."

Nova shook her head. "We should stay together. Who knows where they lead, and with Avery's power out of commission, we'll only be more vulnerable separated."

Finn said nothing. Even if he agreed with Nova, he wouldn't voice it.

Avery was frozen in place, her eyes vacant.

"Come on, then. Let's just choose one." Megan grabbed Avery's shoulders, pushing her around to face the tunnels. She looped her arm in Avery's, gesturing to the farthest tunnel on the right. "This one smells the best. That's as good a start as any."

And so they pressed on into the dark.

CHAPTER THIRTY-SIX

They wandered for two days.

The tunnel they chose was much like the first: cold, rough walls curving overhead a narrow pathway. But it no longer followed a straight path, instead winding ominously and spiraling them deeper, disorienting them until they couldn't tell what direction they'd started from.

Avery's spirits plummeted further than their descent into the deep stone.

Finn's words cycled through her head on repeat. But she was no leader—not like this. Cut off from her gifts, she was no more useful to the others than a faux figurehead.

More than just losing her direction, Avery had lost her ability to connect with the others. She couldn't judge their moods or feel their emotions. Avery was more of a burden than when Leviathan had curbed her powers the previous year. At least then she had maintained her physical abilities, able to provide some kind of contribution to their team.

Avery had forgotten what it felt like . . . to be weak. She was hardly able to cling to her sanity, much less any kind of plan. Only Megan's optimism helped her stay the course.

It would be folly to turn back now. Their time was running out—it may have run out already. Qav's estimate on Leviathan's recuperation was just that: a guess. If they didn't find a way out of the ground soon, then she would make her move. She would attack Nos Lenti, and everyone in the village would die. Even Gran.

Qav alone wouldn't be able to stop Leviathan—*if* he chose to fight back. Avery hoped he would at least try. He had given her his promise.

On the morning of the second day, the walls began to smooth out. They encountered another atrium that split into two more paths. Avery couldn't bring herself to randomly choose one again, knowing it might lead to their doom. Spirits were low.

Megan suggested they pause and take a break for lunch—a few measly bites of shared protein bars. They'd begun rationing food.

Avery leaned her head against the rock as they chewed in silence, counting her breaths to distract her from her own anxiety. She'd done it again: she'd hidden things from her friends, and it had led them there. Even Finn saw the truth; he had as good as said it. Avery was worth nothing without her powers, nothing without—

"Call me crazy," Nova said slowly, interrupting the quiet around a mouthful of food, "but I think it's a maze."

"What?" Avery asked tentatively.

"Why?" Petra demanded. Her mood had turned absolutely rancid, her every action and response barely civil.

"Something Mylan said." Nova tilted her head. She passed the bar to Finn, her long legs stretched out along the path, crossed at the ankles. "*The thread in the labyrinth.*"

"Shit," Finn whispered, his hand stalling on its way to his mouth. He sat up, looking at the openings before them, two yawning arches of shadow. "I think you're right."

"*Only Avery can follow it.*" Megan sat forward, dropping her own half-eaten bar.

"Hey," Grigg whined, grabbing it from the dirt. "The rest of that was mine."

Megan clutched Avery's leg excitedly. "Mylan didn't send us into a trap, Avery. *It's a test.*"

Avery's pulse skipped, hope glimmering faintly to life.

"The entrance, the multiple paths," Megan continued, "even the rock blocking your powers. It's all designed for you."

Nova nodded. "Mylan must have known she would find this place. He didn't send us here to find some stone on a beach."

"Look, Avie." Megan took Avery's hands. Her fingers were frozen, colder than even Avery's. "This entrance to the maze could only be opened by a So'. Which must mean—"

"It can only be solved by one," Avery finished softly. She rose to her feet, staring at the two archways before them. She closed her eyes, opening herself fully as she approached. And she felt . . . nothing. Avery fisted her hands at her sides.

"It's fine, Avery," Megan said softly. "We're right; I'm certain of it. If it's a puzzle, then it *can* be solved. We just have to find the right formula."

Avery gave her a weak nod, her eyes flickering to Finn. She could barely see him in the light of the single glowing stick—they only had two left. But he said nothing. He did nothing.

Her chest caved in on itself, squeezing the air from her lungs. She wouldn't let herself cry again. She'd done enough of that while the others slept.

Finn was putting distance between them, in all the ways that mattered. Avery knew coming back to him would be difficult, that her mistakes had been enormous. Perhaps Finn, like Petra, had finally decided to make her pay for them.

After the night they spent together with nothing between them except the light of the moons, Avery thought that Finn *had* forgiven her. He had worshiped her, body and soul. They had worshiped each other. But now . . . Avery felt more alone than she had when the length of the universe had separated them.

In the end, they decided to choose the path with the more even floor. They encountered three more diversions, choosing their progress in the same way. It was a paltry method, but it gave Avery some semblance of control.

By that evening, the walls started to become wet. They continued on until water was trickling down the sides of the tunnel in thin rivulets, pooling in divots on the floor. Water was good. It meant a pathway to the ocean, to freedom. So they changed their method, following whichever paths and directions were wettest.

Avery was the first to hear it. A deep, thunderous whooshing, muffled by layers of rock and distance. But since the others said nothing, Avery said nothing, worried she was finally going mad. She'd be certain this time before voicing anything.

Megan looped her arm in Avery's, jostling loose her sudden stiffness. "Don't let them get to you," Megan whispered. "If you found your way out of that rock in the capitol, you'll find your way out now."

Avery smiled, leaning in closer as they walked together. How could Megan still believe in her? She was the one person who had suffered the most from Avery's mistakes.

Avery glanced behind them, thankful that Petra and Nova had spread out. Grigg chatted amiably with Finn, doing his best to lift spirits. The ambient noise of their conversation gave Avery and Megan the illusion of privacy.

"I don't deserve you, Megan," Avery admitted quietly, her throat going dry.

"Of course you do." Megan said sweetly. "We deserve each other. We always have."

"No, I . . . I haven't apologized for what happened," Avery croaked, her vision blurring. Familiar memories surfaced, nightmarish and frightening, of the way Megan had looked in Petra's arms, so pale and lifeless—

"You don't need to."

"No, I do. I need to say this. If I—"

"Please. Don't." Megan grew serious, glancing behind her. She sighed softly, like she had been dreading the conversation too. "What happened wasn't your fault, Avery. It wasn't you—it could never have been you. I know that, okay? Qav took advantage of you when you were vulnerable. He manipulated you and tricked you and messed with your mind. There's no one to blame for what happened except him."

"But if I had been stronger, if I had just realized what was happening, I could have fought it. It was still me who—" Avery choked, struggling to finish. "Who hurt you."

Megan grabbed Avery's hand, interlacing their fingers as they walked and squeezing tightly. "If you want to forgive someone, then forgive yourself. You owe me nothing."

Avery couldn't stop the tears, angling her head away from Megan to stare at the blackness. She had spent so long torturing herself, blaming herself for what had happened. Her shoulders shook. Tears ran down to the corners of her mouth, warm and salty.

"You think I can't tell when you're crying?" Megan asked playfully, swinging their joined hands back and forth like children. "With the echoes in this tunnel, I'm pretty sure everyone can hear you sniffling."

"Fabulous." Avery laughed tearfully, wiping her nose on her sleeve. But Avery still hadn't told her. The whooshing in her head grew louder as she pulled them to a stop. "I need to say this, Megan. And not just to you—to all of you."

Petra crossed her arms over her chest, meeting Avery's gaze and holding it.

But Avery would not be intimidated. She owed it to them—she owed it to herself.

"I made so many mistakes last year, and I just . . . I want you all to know that I learned from them. What happened then won't happen again. Ever."

Avery's tears came more swiftly, spilling onto her cheeks, making her face hot. Something inside of her released, a dam that held back a year's worth of grief and regret. The whooshing turned to a roar, louder than before, drowning out her thoughts.

"We know, Avery," Nova reassured her.

"No. We don't *know*," Petra spat, her voice unnaturally loud. "She can't make a promise like that. Not now. Not when we're most likely going to die here on her orders."

Avery flinched, her hand retreating from Megan's.

But she realized at last that the whooshing wasn't in her head at all. It was below them, Avery was certain. She could feel it, the power of the water running beneath their feet, a raging river under the stone. And it called to her, tugging at her chest as clearly as the wind in the mountains of Nos Lenti.

But Petra continued, like a ship thrown off course. "And she brought Qav here. *Here.* To our home—to a planet full of fresh Reanges just waiting to be caught in his web. From where I stand, Avery's making the same mistakes as always. And this time, we'll pay with our lives."

"Petra," Finn chided, his voice hard. "Enough."

"No—it's not enough," Petra countered, her voice rising.

And Avery could finally feel her.

Anger surged out from Petra and slammed into Avery's chest like a force of gravity.

"If Qav gets his hands on Leviathan's stone, then what? At least we stand some kind of chance against an old woman. But if *his* powers are amplified? It will be over."

Avery knew Qav was a risk. He had done terrible things, and a part of her would never be able to forgive him for that. But he had changed—he was changing. At some point, that had to be enough.

"He wouldn't dare," Nova said in the quiet. "You didn't see what Avery did to Qav. How she broke him."

"I didn't need to," Petra bit out through clenched teeth. "I watched as she used her powers against Megan. As she tried to *kill her.* Or did we conveniently forget that?"

"No," Avery whispered. "I didn't forget." She refused to look away, refused to shield herself from Petra's pain, white-hot and scalding, searing Avery from the inside out. Had Petra been living like that? The burning agony was proof of what Avery had done to her. Every ounce of censure and condemnation from her was deserved.

Megan stepped between them.

Avery saw nothing but her back, blond curls hanging low across the shoulders of her blue jacket. She was shielding her from Petra. From the truth.

Shame ate through Avery's stomach even as she stepped forward to gently push Megan aside. "I haven't forgotten, Petra," Avery repeated. "It's haunted me. It still haunts me."

Nova was frowning, her hands balled at her sides. "Petra, I don't think you understand. It took Avery weeks to even—"

"Megan was in a coma for months!" Petra screamed, her voice booming around them, a painful echo in their ears. "I don't give a fuck if Avery *felt bad*. She deserved to feel like the scum of the universe. We didn't know if Megan would *live*. And don't get me started on what her choices did to Finn, how they broke him."

"I said enough," Finn growled, jerking Petra's arm and sending her stumbling behind to join Grigg. "Shut your mouth before I shut it for you."

The walls rumbled ominously, pebbles scattering down from the ceiling. Grigg looked up warily, his hand going to the wall.

Avery couldn't breathe. Megan had been in a coma? For . . . *months*? Her heart split open along the fractures that had just begun to heal, the guilt suddenly as fresh and painful as the day she'd broken free of Qav.

Megan was stiff, her eyes trained on the ground.

"Is that true?" Avery asked shakily.

Megan sniffed, looking up at Avery with a quick shrug and a smile. "What's a little coma between friends?"

"Don't." Avery held up a hand.

Megan couldn't fix this. Megan couldn't even *forgive* this.

"You know Petra," Megan said, her bravado fading fast as her voice wavered. "She's exaggerating. Ultimate drama queen."

But Avery had heard enough. She closed her eyes, diving straight into Petra's mind.

Avery wasn't sure how she'd regained her powers, but they were back and suddenly at her fingertips. Once in Petra's thoughts, Avery didn't have to look far. Petra's memories were right at the surface, bubbling over into Avery's hands.

Megan's lifeless body lying on a couch in the city, every inch of her exposed skin bruised and mottled. Her nose was broken, her hair matted with blood.

Later, in a bed somewhere, wires attached to Megan's temples. Gran hovered over her, checking her pulse, monitoring signals on a med tablet.

Petra speaking with Gran about the odds, fear and uncertainty clouding her familiar eyes. Petra's utter despair, her fear, wholly consuming and unbearable.

There were so many . . . Weeks and weeks of memories, each one more vibrant than the last, guarded and protected and exact. Like Petra didn't want to forget them.

Avery pulled away with a cry, falling her to her knees on the hard, wet floor. The water called to her, the whoosh surging through her head from somewhere far below. It was warm. Alive. Avery welcomed it, letting its energy fill her, willing it to take away the despair that clung to her, refusing to let go.

And it did.

Avery sucked in a gasp as her power rushed back with more force than she'd ever felt. It collided with her emotions, exploding outward in a wave of energy that she was helpless to stop, carrying her anger and grief along with it.

The tunnel boomed as the walls began to shake, great chunks of the ceiling breaking away to crash into the floor around them.

"Cover your heads!" Nova yelled, huddling against the wall.

Avery breathed rhythmically, in and out, reeling the power back into herself. The opening was caving in around them because of her. She had lost control. But she could fix it—this time she could *do* something.

Avery tossed Megan toward the others where Petra caught her. She held up a hand, forming a barrier that protected her friends in a bubble of safety as the passage fell apart. Something slammed into Avery's shoulder, and she stumbled back. She'd forgotten to shield herself.

But the cave-in had already begun to settle. Piles of stone littered the tunnel, the air filled with dust, illuminated only by the single light stick. They began to cough, but no one seemed hurt. Megan was fine. Finn stood, dusting off his clothes.

Avery let out a shaking breath.

Grigg limped into the tunnel behind them. Avery would have to check his leg. "Well, I guess we're not going back that way. It's blocked."

"What the blazar was that?" Finn stalked to Avery, his eyes wide and angry, nearly black in the dim light. When he saw her shoulder, he frowned. "You're hurt."

Her jacket was torn open, the white shirt beneath stained red with blood. Avery didn't even feel it. A wealth of power flowed through her veins, making her dizzy. She lifted her arm, pulling at the fabric. "It's nothing. Just a—"

The world shifted as the floor gave way beneath her. Avery's stomach dipped when she fell backward, her arms flailing as she dropped into an abyss.

And Finn jumped after her.

CHAPTER
THIRTY-SEVEN

Finn latched onto Avery as they plummeted together, wrapping her in his arms and pulling her close into his body. They twirled head-first through shadow. In seconds they slammed into solid rock, barely buffered by some instinct Avery had to soften the blow.

She yelped in pain, and Finn released her as they rolled across wet stone, terrified he would do more harm than good. He heard a splash against the roar of moving water near his face.

"Avery?" Finn called out.

There was no reply.

Finn pushed up on his knees, fumbling for his light stick. It flickered to life, casting a pathetic yellow glow across the ledge they'd landed on. The ceiling arched overhead in a yawning cavern at least a hundred feet high. And beside him, a raging river flowed past, its white caps crashing violently against the rocks.

Finn whirled. "Avery!" he called out again, but his voice was swallowed up by the water.

She was gone.

He was on his feet in an instant, scanning the churning water, desperate for some glimpse of her. Finn's heart beat so loudly, he was sure it would burst through his chest. He tossed his pack to the ground, gripping the light stick in a shaking hand. He wouldn't lose her. Not there. Not like this.

Finn took in deep breaths, expanding his lungs to hold as much oxygen as they would allow. His eyes scanned the black river. Waiting for something—anything.

A flash of gold sparked in the corner of his vision. He didn't hesitate, aiming his dive straight for her.

The icy water hit him hard, its piercing sting threatening to force out any breath he had prepared. He swam through complete darkness, nothing but the light clutched in his hand to guide him and the hope that Avery was somewhere ahead. His lungs burned, his limbs lost all feeling, and he swam on, fighting against the current.

Something pulled him forward, nothing more than the barest hint of a thought—a feeling telling him not to give up. Not yet. Just a little farther.

And as he reached his breaking point, his lungs near bursting, Finn pushed even harder. When at last black spots crossed his sight, his hand brushed against something soft.

He gripped the collar of Avery's jacket, jerking her against him as he kicked up, praying to the moons it wouldn't be too late for them both.

Finn broke the surface, gulping in air and coughing painfully as he oriented himself. He hooked an arm around Avery's core, using whatever strength he had left to pull their weight against the current and toward the shore. By some miracle he was able to throw her up to safety, crawling up behind her.

She wasn't moving. Her face was pale as death, cast in yellow from the stick he'd managed to keep holding on to.

"Come on, Avery." Finn pushed back wet hair that stuck to her cheeks. She was cold. "Damn it, Avery!" he cried, slapping her face.

She remained still.

Finn swallowed hard through tears as reality caught up with him. Idiot! He was wasting time.

Finn rolled her, ripping her sodden pack from her shoulders and slinging it away. He positioned her flat on her back, tipping up her chin. And Finn receded somewhere far into the back of his mind as he started chest compressions.

CHAPTER
THIRTY-EIGHT

Avery opened her eyes to the star-soaked vastness of space, stretching out around her in every direction, never ending. Her feet dangled beneath her, both arms extended outward. She was weightless. Painless. At peace, floating among the stars.

"Avery!"

The call was only just audible, like it had been screamed from very far away. She spun in the air, looking for the source. The sound faded away into the nothingness, easily forgotten.

There was nothing to worry about there. She was safe. Free.

"Come on, Avery!"

Something pressed against her chest. She frowned. The sensation was distinctly unpleasant.

Was there something she had forgotten?

"Avery."

She twisted around again and found herself standing on a cliff's edge, overlooking the mountains of Echo. The skyline of Milderion glimmered in the distance, its sleek buildings flashing in the late evening sun. The sky was cast in marvelous shades of orange and pink, melting together in glory as it faded into night.

And Avery was not alone.

"Fiora?" Avery gasped, her heart wrenching.

"Hey, kid." Her once trainer and guide stepped out of the shadows. The pink light hit her red curls, turning them so vibrant that they glowed.

She was resplendent. Like Fiora was lit from the inside out. She was more alive than she'd ever been.

Avery blinked away tears. She lurched forward, reaching out blindly.

Fiora stepped back. "Not yet. You still haven't decided."

"What?" Avery frowned, confusion tumbling her thoughts. There was something she needed to remember. Something she wasn't understanding.

"Where are we?" Avery looked around again. They were perched on a small ledge, and behind them a hatch in the floor lead into the mountain.

She recognized it. Finn had brought her there once, not long after they'd first met, after she'd first come to Echo. He showed her that special place so she could breathe when she thought she might suffocate. So she could feel a modicum of freedom from the weight of her newfound responsibilities. It was the first time she'd ever seen Finn as something more than he'd been to her.

"Come on!"

Something pressed on her chest again as she looked around for the source of the words that faded into the warm wind. "Finn," Avery whispered, recognizing his voice at last. He sounded frightened. He needed her. "Where is Finn?"

Fiora smiled, her features soft, her eyes understanding. She looked out to the horizon, watching the moons that were thin crescents above the city.

"Where is Finn?" Avery repeated, uncertainty clawing her brain.

But she was beginning to understand. She could feel the warmth that emanated from Fiora, so familiar and so strange. Avery had felt its pull before—had listened to it.

"You're not Fiora."

She glanced back at Avery, those eyes shifting and glinting against the fading sun, a glimpse into the unsettling familiarity of infinity.

How had Avery not noticed? How had she missed it?

"I am," Fiora said softly. "And I am not."

Avery swallowed but said nothing. She waited.

"It is difficult to explain. For some understanding, mere speech is insufficient. And it would make no difference to you, Avery. You already know what I am."

"You are . . ." Avery's voice dropped to a whisper. "The Essence?"

Fiora nodded, a smile teasing her lips. "You have always been a quick study—you have learned to harness your gifts faster than most would have in your place. Faster than most souls we have welcomed since your people found us. And you've only grown stronger. It is not easy to feel us—not easy to reach us so far beneath the rock."

The rock.

Avery took in her surroundings. She wasn't supposed to be there. She was supposed to be in the dark and deep. She had fallen.

"Where are we?"

"Again you ask questions, the answers to which you already know."

Avery let out a slow, shuddering breath, a fearful tear slipping from her eye. "Is this . . . I'm dead?"

"Not quite. Not yet, at least," Fiora confirmed. "If you had truly passed, you would already be a part of us. We would have no reason to come to you like this, with Fiora as our vessel, to give you solace. But you are still tethered."

The pressure built on Avery's chest, sharp and aching.

"Finn," Avery whispered. She could feel him—he was with her. Waiting for her.

"But the choice is yours to make," Fiora continued. "You can return to him. To your friends. To the pain and the division and the loss. Or you can join us now and watch as it unfolds. You can wait for them in peace."

The yearning for that tranquility was nearly overwhelming. The utter rightness of that place . . . It was serenity beyond safety.

Two figures of light materialized behind Fiora, their faces obscured. Avery's eyes refused to focus on them no matter how hard she tried. And yet she knew who they were, would know them anywhere.

Her parents.

Avery gasped, crying in earnest as tears ran down her cheeks. She'd never allowed herself to dwell on thoughts of them. Gran had always been enough. But there was a part of her that wondered, that hoped . . .

She let the tears fall, too scared to look away. Too scared that the feeling of belonging would slip through her fingers. Too frightened of the truth she already knew: Avery wasn't ready.

"My friends . . . They need me," Avery choked out. "They still need me."

Fiora tilted her chin like Avery had said something she found amusing. Like she had expected that exact answer.

And then Fiora was beside her, leaning in close to whisper in Avery's ear, "Then you need to go deeper."

Pain seared through Avery's chest as she curled on her side, coughing up water through her burning throat. Her eyes watered, her body convulsing as she struggled to suck in oxygen.

The next thing she knew, she was nestled in Finn's lap, his warm arms wrapped around her as he rocked them back and forth, whispering her name. His hands shook as they rubbed her arms, his breath unsteady.

"Finn," she croaked, leaning back to see him.

He was barely holding on, his eyes wild. His cheeks were splotchy and red, like he'd been crying.

"Finn," she repeated, her hands coming up to hold his neck. His skin was still damp but warming much faster than hers. "It's all right. I'm okay."

He didn't respond. His breath came in rapid, short bursts. His long eyelashes fluttered.

"I'm okay," Avery whispered, wrapping herself around him, holding him close. She tucked her head into his neck, breathing in the familiar smell of his skin as his stubble tickled her lips. His wet hair was cold against her cheek. "I'm okay."

CHAPTER THIRTY-NINE

They sat there long enough that Avery began to shiver in her wet clothes. Finn's breath slowed to normal, and his shaking eased as they curled into one another on the ground. Avery started to lean away, but his fingers dug into her hips. His silent protest made her pause.

"I'm cold," she said awkwardly. "We need to change into something dry or hypothermia is going to become a real issue."

"Right. Sorry." Finn nodded, letting her go. His throat was hoarse, like he'd been screaming.

Avery picked up the light stick beside them, finding her pack against the wall. It was soaked, but at least it was waterproof. Her change of clothes inside was gloriously dry, but there was no helping her sodden boots. She shed her wet garments, throwing them to the ground with a slap at her feet, heedless of privacy. The gash in her arm stung, reminding her of the stone that had collided with her back in the tunnel. At least it had stopped bleeding.

Finn's clothing rustled behind her, and Avery snuck a peek in his direction. In what little light they had, she could only see the hint of his outline moving in shadow.

Her mind was reeling. Avery had just communed with the Essence in some strange place between life and death. Or had it just been a peculiar dream, her body's attempt to make sense of her time without a pulse.

No . . . It had been real. Avery had felt it—she had *felt* Fiora. She had felt her parents, or whatever was left of them, on the other side.

Even now, Avery could feel that warmth, pulsing and vibrant and linked to her heart. And when it pulled again, it was a living thing, guiding her forward, stronger than ever.

"Do you think they're still up there?" Finn stood near the roaring water with this head tilted back. "That drop had to have been at least a hundred feet."

Avery finally remembered what had happened, how she had fallen through the floor and plummeted through the air. And Finn, like an overemotional idiot, had thrown himself after her.

Anger flooded her veins in a hot rush as she realized how close they had both come to dying. The floor rumbled under their feet as she rounded on him and shoved his chest.

"Why did you jump after me?" she yelled as he stumbled backward.

"I was trying to help!"

"How? By dying with me?"

He shoved a hand through his hair. "I don't know. I wasn't exactly thinking, Avery."

"No shit. If you hadn't distracted me, I would have been able to handle that drop fine! You saw me land in the arena—I can practically fly."

"How was I supposed to know that? Literally ten minutes before that cave-in, you couldn't access your powers at all."

"So your solution was to fall to your death beside me? Yeah, that makes a lot of sense."

Finn let out a frustrated sigh, walking away. "Avery, I can't do this right now. We need to find the others."

"I *want* to do this right now," Avery protested, stepping into his path. "*Talk to me.* What is wrong with you?"

"What's wrong with me?" Finn laughed, shaking his head in disbelief. "I just watched you die, Avery. Give me a fucking break."

"I'm just confused," Avery said slowly, her tone suddenly delicate. Her hands itched to touch his chest, but she held them glued at her sides. "You've done nothing but push me away since we entered this place. I thought you . . . I thought maybe you decided I wasn't . . . I wasn't what you wanted. Anymore." She dropped her eyes, cringing at how lamely she'd finished the thought.

Finn stepped closer to her, his heat filling the space between them until she lifted her gaze to his. "I will *always* want you, Avery Vey. I can't *stop* wanting you."

Tears burned her eyes, spilling out and down her cheeks. She was desperate to reach him. "Then what is wrong? Tell me. *Please.* Help me understand, Finn. I—I love you."

He stepped back, his walls going back up as he retreated from her. His head shook; his brows drew together in pain.

"I love you, Finn," she repeated, determined.

"Stop," he said. The word ripped her heart in half. "I can't. Don't you see how hard I'm trying to—" He drew a steadying breath. "I just can't, Avery."

"No, I don't see," Avery said, frustration sharpening her words like knives. "So you're going to have to explain it to me. I can't exactly read *your* mind, can I? Just tell me what you're trying to say."

Finn stood in silence, refusing to speak for so long that she thought he wouldn't reply. And then he did speak and she wished he hadn't.

"We can't be together, Avery. It wouldn't work. It doesn't work."

"What?" Avery felt like she'd been slapped. The blood drained from her face. Her fingers felt numb.

"It's over, Avery."

But he wouldn't look at her. His brows drew low over his eyes, his jaw absolute granite. This was why he'd been pulling away, why he'd been so hard on her.

Avery turned away from him, her mind filtering through a thousand paths. She wondered if she would beg. It wasn't entirely out of the realm of possibility.

Finn blamed her for what had happened, that much was clear. He and Petra both did. And they were right. Avery had disappointed them, betraying their trust on such a grand scale that she didn't know if it could ever be repaired.

But she had to try. She would never forgive *herself* if she walked away now.

"Listen," she began, turning back to him as she pressed a hand to her chest. "I know I messed up, but I'm sorry. I'm so sorry, Finn. I know you think bringing Qav to Echo was a mistake. I know you haven't forgiven me for what I did—"

"That's not it," he snapped, suddenly furious. "Can we just drop it? I'm done with this conversation."

Avery's jaw set, her teeth clenching so painfully that she thought they might crack. The walls around them trembled, her emotions fluctuating so wildly that she could barely control herself. He couldn't actually be serious. Only a few days ago he had *shown* her how much he loved her. She had felt it. And despite his words, she could *still* feel it.

Avery shook her head. "No."

Finn let out a breathy laugh. "Of course you'd try to tell me I can't break up with you. Avery, you—you can't love me."

"Why not?"

"Because it doesn't make any sense." He tried to move around her.

She blocked his path again, forcing him to meet her eyes. "*Why not?*"

"Because I'm *nothing*, Avery!" Finn exploded, his voice ricocheting around them, laced with shame and anguish. And when his revelation faded to silence, he repeated weakly, "I'm nothing."

Finn's breath came in shallow pants. He couldn't keep talking—he had to stop himself.

Avery already carried the weight of an entire planet on her shoulders. He couldn't burden her with his own shit that was so oppressive he struggled to breathe under its pressure. It was too self-serving, too greedy.

But then, Finn *was* selfish, especially when it came to Avery.

And once he had yelled out the truth, his strength abandoned him, releasing everything in one fell swoop. He was helpless to stop himself. He wasn't only selfish but weak as well.

She stepped closer to him and grabbed his hands. "Finn, you're more than—"

"No!" It was Finn's turn to stop her. "All I do is hold you back, Avery. The only reason Qav was able to get into your head is because of *me*," he said desperately, pulling away. "And I'm no better than him. All I've done is try to control you in my own way. I won't do it again. I swore it. I won't watch you question yourself again because of me."

She stood still before him, her eyes wide and bright, like she was scared one wrong move would send him over the edge. Her wet hair was still plastered to her head, a reminder of her brush with death that knocked the breath out of Finn all over again. The only thing worse than pushing her away would be losing her forever.

Avery's features hardened, and he thought for one blissful, agonizing second that she would leave him.

She stepped closer.

"Listen to me," she said quietly in a voice as determined as her expression. "Qav was able to get inside of my head because I had my own holes there. My own weaknesses. Not because of you." She gripped his arms, her fingers clinging to him over his sweater. "You've only ever made me stronger, Finn. You've believed more in me than anyone else. You always have."

Finn's breath was heavy in the silence that fell between them now. He struggled to control it, to keep tears from falling. He didn't want to talk anymore. He wanted to walk into the black and never look back. His eyes drifted to the water, savage and promising.

Avery opened her mouth to speak, her throat working painfully, like she was trying to decide the best way to say what came next. "What Petra said back there, about Megan and—and about you . . . What did she mean by saying I broke you?"

Finn jerked away from her violently. He shook his head. He couldn't do this.

"Damn it, Finn, don't walk away from me!" she growled.

And he froze.

Because Finn was no longer in control of his body—Avery was.

CHAPTER FORTY

Avery gasped as she fell headfirst into Finn's mind.

She was so desperate to connect with him, to understand him, that she'd reached out blindly with her powers. It was instinct and habit, a result of living alongside Reanges for the past year.

But something shifted, clicking into place. And Avery had stepped straight into his head and ordered him to a halt.

Finn's energy was bright and soothing, the soft heat of the sun on a warm day that eased up against her, a balm created for only Avery's soul to know. It was undiluted and effortless . . . So quintessentially Finn. She would know him from that sensation alone if they were nothing more than wisps of energy floating in the infinite expanse of time and space.

It took mere moments for memories to pour past her, surging around her like a sped-up holovid. Avery couldn't get her bearings to control them, couldn't wrap her head around what was actually happening enough to slow them down. Flashes of Finn's childhood surrounded her.

Eating dinner at a long glass table with his parents. Nick sat beside him, only a teenager, smiling and winking at Finn with food in his mouth.

Chasing Nick through a field of tall grass until they tumbled together down a hill, shrieking and giggling up at the blue sky.

Holding back tears at his father's funeral, somber and quiet and full of despair. Watching his mother waste away as depression and alcohol stole her away next. Standing in silence as both brothers watched their mother's body be incinerated into ash at the funeral home. Nick placing a hand on Finn's shoulder, squeezing gently.

And then Avery saw herself, pinned beneath Finn in his cell on the Station, her eyes wide and frightened and an ordinary shade of pale brown. Her freckles stood out harshly against her face. But Finn had thought her beautiful, even then.

And the memories surged, flying by in a series of moments too fast to stop.

Avery laughing. Avery's blurred face leaning over him. Avery sitting on a throne in the Origin, her pale green dress accentuating every curve. Avery leaning against the mountainside as she stared up at him, loneliness in her eyes. Avery giggling, her nose scrunching perfectly to form his favorite series of constellations.

Her existence redefined what beauty meant, his entire understanding of the word shifting on its axis to embody the singularities of one particular woman.

And Avery knew—more completely and assuredly than she ever had before.

Finn loved her.

He was desperate to be near her, desperate to be anything she needed. Leaving her on Earth had been the most difficult decision of his life. When the Gate had collapsed and separated them forever, it had driven a hole so deeply through his heart that it was still a gaping wound.

Finn blamed himself for it. For Qav. For Nick. He blamed himself *for everything*.

Avery saw another memory—Finn staring at the mirror, fingering the raised flesh that covered a quarter of his face. He loathed it. He clung to it. It was a constant reminder of everything he had lost, and how he had failed. Finn was glad for the physical pain that came with the scars, forcing him to suffer as he deserved.

Finn hated himself and what he had become.

He'd lost his father and failed his mother. He'd let Nick down so badly that Finn would never get him back. And he'd pressured Avery so intensely that she'd broken beside him.

He was nothing. He was no good to anyone. He wanted to sink into the ground and disappear forever.

And then another memory.

Finn with Petra, screaming at each other on a ship bound for the capitol. Leviathan's call for Finn's execution had finally given him a way out, a chance to leave the others behind and make his life mean something in the process. He was ready. He would finally let the anguished darkness take him to a place he'd never have to feel again.

Agony tore through Avery, launching her out of Finn and back into herself. She had nearly lost him. More than just separated by the Gates, Finn had almost made the one choice he would never be able to come back from. He'd almost done the one thing that would have truly destroyed her.

How could you? She whispered in his mind. Tears flowed steadily down her cheeks, her own terror mingling with his, spooling rapidly into something overwhelming for them both.

Finn jerked away from her, breathing hard as he realized what was happening, as he gained control of his own body again. His eyes were wide. Shocked.

Avery stepped closer. He stiffened.

"How could you, Finn?" she asked aloud, sounding more accusatory than she'd intended. But she couldn't contain her own horror.

She had nearly lost him—to himself.

If he had made that choice, if he had given into it, then there would have been nothing she could have done to bring him back.

His full lips quivered, his chin angling away from her as he countered brokenly, "How could I not?"

Avery grimaced, a painful groan emerging from her as she endured everything inside of him, every riotous miserable feeling. Anger, desperation, hopelessness, despair.

But she didn't shirk away. Avery opened herself to it, pulling the emotion into herself, making space for the suffocating darkness to spread out and away from him. She may not have been able to stop his emotions, not yet, but she could give him space. She could show him that he could let go of the torment, if he'd only try.

Finn gasped, his gulp of air offering pure relief. He sagged, dipping to the ground on his knees before her. Avery followed him, catching his weight as she pulled more into herself. Misery rolled through her, its intensity lessening as it found space between them both.

Avery had been there before, felt the same emotions before. Trying to fight it would only make them worse.

She wrapped herself around Finn, cradling his head to her chest as he threaded his arms around her waist. He shook, his fingers clutching her shirt as a cry seeped out of his lips.

"I'm so sorry, Finn," she whispered. *I'm so sorry you were alone*, she said in his mind, soothing him with the warm assurance that he was safe. That he was loved.

His arms tightened around her waist.

As the wave began to ease, Finn's body loosened, slackening against her. Avery leaned back to rest fully on her knees before him, holding his pale face. She leaned forward, kissing his cheeks, his eyes, his forehead, his nose. She stroked his mottled skin, wiping away silent tears that still escaped the corners of his eyes.

"I was miserable too," she whispered. She inched closer to him, making sure to hold his gaze. "Without you, I was miserable."

Finn smiled derisively. "But you're you, Avery."

"What does that mean?"

He sighed. "It means that you are valuable to everyone. You can change the tides of history with a single wave of your hand."

"So that's what this is about? My powers?"

"No!" he cried, pulling her hands to his, their fingers entangling. "I love your strength. Almost as much as I love your laugh."

She smiled. "You can change the world too, Finn."

He chuckled.

"It's true," Avery said sternly. "Look at what you've done here, what you were able to build with the others, the lives you've saved. You bring people together, Finn. They would never have been able to get this far without you guiding them." She took in a deep breath, filling her lungs to steady herself. "The only thing that kept me going this past year was the knowledge that you were still alive somewhere in the universe."

He grinned, his dimple a deep shadow in the dim yellow light. He reached out to brush loose hair behind her ear. "And how would you know that I was alive, sweetheart?"

She caught his hand against her cheek. "I just knew."

He leaned into her, brushing his lips against hers in a feathery kiss that was only a soft caress of skin. And when he sat back to lean against the wall, she crawled into his lap like a child, suddenly so exhausted that her eyelids grew heavy.

Neither of them spoke of what had just happened, of what they'd shared. Perhaps it was too raw, too vulnerable to analyze. They'd bared a part of themselves they'd never thought possible, dispelling emotions so powerful they had once threatened to separate them forever.

And for that moment, as Avery fell asleep against Finn's warm chest, huddled together in the dark, it was enough to just feel.

CHAPTER FORTY-ONE

Finn watched over Avery as she slept. He didn't dare move her, even when his leg lost all feeling from her weight in his lap. He kept still, playing with the end of her braid, her hair soft and damp in his fingers.

A smile pulled at his lips. For the first time since crash landing on Echo all those months ago, he felt . . . like himself. For the first time in a very long time. It was like taking in a lungful of clean air when he'd spent an entire year gasping for one suffocating breath after another.

And it was because of Avery.

Finn pressed a kiss to her head, rubbing his lips across her hair. She had reached inside of him and pried the black claws out of his ribs, absorbing the worst parts into herself.

In retrospect, Finn should have been angry with her. Stepping into his mind, delving into the deepest parts that even he kept hidden from himself, was a violation of his privacy. Not to mention, taking on that darkness was too much a risk. It could have swallowed her whole, too.

But Finn couldn't muster up any reaction other than elation and gratitude.

She hadn't wiped it entirely. The melancholy that had plagued Finn so wholly wasn't gone, but it was . . . receding. Like a muscle cramp that had been unbearable in one moment and no more than a sore, lingering ache the next.

Healing him was one thing, but a So'Reange merging with a human . . . It shouldn't have been possible. Everything they knew about the powers of the So' suggested it was unfeasible. As far as Finn knew, it had never been done before, not in hundreds of years of shared history.

But Avery wasn't just a So'Reange—she was a beautiful marvel, always pushing the limits, always breaking right through them.

Finn relaxed into her, drifting in and out of sleep as he shifted their bodies closer together. They would find the others once they'd had time to rest . . .

"Taking a nap? Really?" Grigg's accusation startled them both awake.

Avery jumped out of Finn's lap and to her feet. He had to dig his fingers into his thighs to keep from pulling her back to him.

"Took you long enough," Finn replied, rolling his neck. He bent his knees, shaking out his legs to wake them up.

"We thought you were dead." Megan dragged Avery into a fierce hug, coating her in the dust that lingered on their clothes from the cave-in. Their faces were filthy in the dim light. "We've been searching for hours."

"I told you they'd be fine," Petra said, but Finn knew her well enough to recognize the signs of her relief.

Grigg helped Finn to his feet before looking upward. "That's one hell of a fall."

"I guess this means you got your powers back," Petra observed tightly.

Avery nodded. "At least some of it, anyway."

"Can you reach the others outside?" Nova asked.

"I still can't get through the rock," Avery revealed. "Whatever power I have, it's limited to the boundaries of these caves."

"The fall wasn't so bad," Finn added before nodding to the river. "It's the water you've got to watch out for."

Avery's eyes caught Finn's before flying away awkwardly to the others. Nova raised one blond brow in question.

Avery cleared her throat. "How did you find us?"

"That cave-in opened another passage," Nova explained, her eyes tracking Avery's discomfort.

Megan looked up, taking in the vast expanse above them. "We tried to rappel down the hole, but our cables weren't long enough to see anything below."

Nova moved to the edge of the river. "No wonder you never responded to our calls. You can't hear anything over the sound of this water."

"The only other option was to see where the pathway led," Megan concluded. "Straight to you two, apparently."

"And to another dead end." Petra had stalked past them, investigating the area. She waved her light stick in the air, its yellow glow moving over the wall of solid rock that extended up into the shadows. "Looks like that blazing path ends here."

"What about the river?" Grigg asked. "Shouldn't it lead out to the ocean?"

Petra turned. "Have you suddenly developed the ability to breathe underwater? That current is too strong. Jumping in there would be suicidal."

Avery and Finn looked at one another with wide eyes. She barked out laughter just as he snorted. The irony of Petra's comment sent them into a fit of misplaced humor, devolving into ludicrous, exhausted giggles.

The others stared, watching the two of them like curiosities in a gen mod experiment gone wrong.

"Are you two done?" Megan asked, clearly puzzled.

"Nearly," Avery got out between hysterical hiccups. But one look from Finn sent them back into hilarity.

Megan rolled her eyes. "Then the grown-ups will talk while you two continue your spiral."

"If one part of the maze was hidden behind a wall, maybe there's another," Nova mused.

"Even if that's true, how do you propose we find it?" Petra asked. "We can't exactly go around blasting holes in a fragile tunnel system encased in heavy stone."

Avery blew out clarifying breath as their laughter finally receded.

"I think I can help with that."

Avery meandered past them to the wall Petra had just investigated. Her hands pressed up against the rock, her fingers moving delicately across its surface.

"Is she doing the thing again?" Grigg whispered.

Megan shushed him. "Let her concentrate."

"We need to go deeper," Avery murmured cryptically. And as though the words unlocked an answer, she leaned down to press her palm against a rock that jutted out of the wall, slightly perfectly round to be natural. She twisted it and her palm began to glow, its bright white light illuminating the wall, chasing way all shadow.

The sounds of shifting rock rumbled underfoot. Finn pulled Avery up to stand beside him as the others backed away from the edge. A large boulder set near the water began to shake before beginning a slow drop into the river. The rapids fell away, forming two walls on either side of a set of metal stairs that descended beneath the surface.

Avery held up Finn's light stick, striding ahead toward the opening, unwilling to wait for the others. She paused at the top of the stairs, her face settling into determination. Like she was listening to something.

"Avery," Finn warned, reaching out for her. "That's probably not a great idea to—"

Avery disappeared down the staircase and into the water below.

"And there she goes," Finn said on a beleaguered sigh. But he jumped to catch up with her, the others close behind. "Sure, we'll follow you down the mystery staircase into the river that almost killed us."

"What?" Megan asked frantically.

"We didn't die, though, did we?" Avery asked over her shoulder.

"That's up for debate," Finn deadpanned.

His palms turned clammy just remembering how pale her face had been, how still and lifeless. He'd spent too many harrowing minutes slamming her chest, breathing air into her lungs, praying to the moons and every god he'd ever heard of to bring her back to him.

And at least one of them had listened.

CHAPTER FORTY-TWO

"**W**ho almost died?"

Avery winced at Megan's shrill question. "Would you two stop talking? I'm trying to focus."

"I think we all deserve some answers to what—ow!" Megan dropped into silence, glaring daggers at Petra beside her.

Avery smiled. *Thank you,* she said silently to Petra.

Petra's only reply was begrudging acknowledgment. Even if the gesture had been small, it meant something. Petra wasn't freezing her out completely, like she had before. Avery would take what she could get.

Avery held the light stick over her head as she continued down the metal stairs, following the warm pull of the Essence. Avery trusted it implicitly, letting it guide her without fear. It had told her to go deeper, and she would follow that counsel. There was something it needed her to know—something it wanted her to find.

The roaring water soon faded until nothing filled the silence except their boots clanging on the grates beneath their feet. The staircase was no more than five feet across. They could see nothing beyond it except more yawning darkness, but the air felt wide and open, like the metal structure was suspended in some enormous chamber.

Grigg began to lag behind, the dull ache of his pain finally reaching Avery beyond her focus. His ankle was in agony, throbbing and sore against the snug confines of his boot.

"Why didn't you say anything?" Avery chastised when they knelt on the stairs to assess the injury.

He shrugged. "Didn't seem that important."

"Idiot," Nova muttered, more frustrated that she'd missed how badly he was hurting.

Petra was already digging through her pack for supplies to stabilize the joint.

"We won't need that," Avery said quietly.

She leaned over Grigg's leg, placing her hands on his ankle, over his boot. Power flowed up and through her, spreading like warm rays of sun down her arms and out of her hands. That familiar, pale light glowed beneath her skin, pouring out of her fingers and into Grigg. It was easier than ever before, like her body remembered how to heal before Avery herself did.

"Damn," Finn murmured in awe.

Grigg laughed, standing and twisting his foot back and forth.

"You can just . . . do that now?" Petra asked.

"This is nothing." Grigg bounced on his toes. "You should have seen her in the wastelands when she pulled a kid's guts back into his body."

Nova rolled her eyes. "Don't exaggerate."

"Still," Megan marveled. "That's going to come in handy."

Avery stood, ignoring the dizziness that plagued her. She was more drained than she realized. Finn frowned, watching her closely as she continued on ahead.

At last, the stairs leveled out onto a platform with a single walkway extending forward.

Avery paused. They'd been following the stairs for at least an hour. Even if she *knew* this was the right path, she needed to make sure the others wanted to keep going—if they wanted to turn back, she would find a way.

Avery looked at them gathered behind her, their faces illuminated in the pale yellow light.

"We're with you, Avery." Nova read Avery's question on her face, before she could even ask it.

"Right behind you, sweetheart," Finn added with a wink.

Avery flushed, whirling back around. Since when had it become difficult to look him in the eyes?

They hadn't told the others . . . what had happened between them. Avery still wasn't sure what had happened herself. Somehow she'd been able to form a merge with Finn. But the ability seemed to have faded. When Avery had woken and tried again, she'd felt nothing beyond the warm tether that ran between them.

As Avery started forward on the walkway, she let her power flow into the light stick she held. Its glow expanded, illuminating out much farther than it had been designed.

"Moons above," Petra gaped in wonder.

Their walkway was not the only one around them. Hundreds of identical metal paths crisscrossed above and below, a spiraling web that extended as far as the light could reveal in both directions.

"What is this place?" Megan's question echoed eerily around them, left unanswered in their stunned silence.

The pull was even stronger, the presence of the Essence more intense and alive than ever before, drawing Avery closer. Her power surged and the light stick followed suit, flickering like an overloaded circuit.

"There's something ahead." Nova moved closer to Avery's side, peering past them.

A large column, at least forty feet in diameter, extended vertically in both directions without end. Concentric walkways wrapped around the column, one on top of the other every twenty or so feet. Their own path ended on one of the enveloping circles and they followed the curve of the cylinder, passing other similar entrances from unknown directions. The same pattern repeated on every level.

Avery slowed as they made their way around the structure, her hand grazing the cold, curving metal. Her fingers tingled, electricity buzzing at the end of her nails. The Essence was there—somewhere close. Its presence was alive in everything, from the grates beneath their feet to the molecules in the air. Her power bubbled up to the surface, a humming promise that lingered beneath her skin, waiting to be set free.

They rounded the column and finally met an opening in its center, revealing the hollow interior. The entire structure was an enormous metal plated tube. Their walkway met a single path that bisected its center.

"Are we sure this is a good idea?" Megan peered over the edge, down into the emptiness below.

"Who knows how long that fall is." Finn shuddered.

"You can stay here if the big bad shadows are too scary," Avery teased over her shoulder. She was confident that there was nothing to fear. The Essence would have warned her.

Inside the tube, the air was more oppressive, stifled and thick and undisturbed for far too long. At the end of the solitary path, at the direct center, a console lay waiting on a grated landing. The tech was obviously Reange: smooth, curving lines of metal where style met function and intuition. The touch pads were old, tactile sensors set into the metal that spread out before a large black screen. Everything was covered in a layer of dust.

"Strange," Nova murmured, on edge. She ran her index finger along the ends of the metal, leaving a streak of shining silver in its wake. "No one has been here in a very long time."

"Not even Mylan?" Petra's query was valid.

Megan turned to her. "How could he? The tunnels were designed for a So'Reange."

If Mylan hadn't been there himself, how had he known to send Avery? What had he expected her to find? What had he wanted her to see?

Grigg leaned over the railing. "This structure is massive. Do you think it's some kind of transport?"

"It's a mine." Megan's revelation pulled all eyes to her. She looked upward, taking in the curved panels and the support arms that held them together. "We studied the process for mineral extraction on the outer planets my first semester at university."

"Are you sure?" Avery asked.

"The setup is slightly different, but . . . I'm pretty certain. What else would they be doing down here?"

"Then why the secrecy?" Nova wondered. "Seems like a lot of trouble to go through, hiding something of this scale."

"Mylan said they found the Essence stone on the beaches aboveground." Petra's comment lingered, heavy with implication.

"Of course," Avery whispered. *Of course.*

The Reanges before them had been desperate to find more of that stone. If it amplified So' powers, then it must have been coveted more than any other mineral on Echo. Enough to mine down into the depths of the planet itself to obtain. Maybe Mylan knew that—maybe he had wanted her to find not just one stone but more than Leviathan could ever hope to counter.

Avery moved to the console, blowing off the dust on its central touch pad. It felt familiar somehow. Like she'd been there before, or a part of her had. She lifted her palm above it, following her instincts.

Finn grabbed her wrist, inches above the metal.

"I'm okay," Avery reassured him, her reply echoing in her memory to the moments they'd shared by the river. "I can't explain it, but I think I know this place. Or maybe it knows me."

"That's reassuring," he grumbled. But he released her hand, hovering close beside Nova.

Avery pressed her hand down on the top of the cool sensory plate. A soft blue light glowed to life beneath her palm.

The main screen booted to life, the rest of the controls coming online and backlit in a soft white. Beneath their feet, blue lights flickered on, activating every few feet behind them and spreading to every path they'd seen on their way in, both above and below. Inside the tube, rings of blue light spread out in either direction, one running the line of each level. It repeated in both directions, too far to see.

Grigg whistled low, following its progress below. "I wonder how far it goes."

The console beeped as the screen in front of Avery opened an access window. It was asking for log-in credentials.

"It's in English," Megan said in shock, shoving Finn out of the way to move beside Avery.

"Is that a surprise?"

"Humans didn't invade Echo until the Gates had finished construction. That was only a couple hundred years ago."

"This dust build up is at least twice that age," Petra surmised.

Megan took over the control pad, working her magic on the screen in front of them. "And I don't recognize this operating system. It's almost like advanced Earth tech. But we've never had capabilities like this."

"What about the early human settlers that colonized Echo?" Finn asked.

Megan shook her head. "Impossible. There were barely a thousand of them, and they assimilated fully into the existing Reange culture. Evidence of human influence didn't become obvious until the Gate had been built."

"Construction of a mine this large would take hundreds of years in itself," Nova added.

Avery tilted her head skeptically. "So your theory is that we're sitting in some ancient marvel of Reange ingenuity that happens to have human programming?"

"Only one way to find out." Megan's fingers flew across the touch pads.

In moments, the log-in screen had disappeared, revealing lines of blue code. She typed in commands faster than Avery could follow, the system responding to her inquiries and generating new prompts.

Megan let out a satisfied laugh. "That was easier than it should have been—they must not have been concerned about security. There's nothing on here except a few schematics of the structure. Not even an operations program."

"So it's not able to run?" Avery asked.

"Do you want it to?"

"We came here to find more of the Essence stone. If that's what they were digging for, then maybe we can use it ourselves."

"The piece Leviathan uses is small enough to sit on the end of a necklace," Megan pointed out. "Do you realize the sheer amount they must have been pulling out of here with an operation this big?"

What kind of powers would be unleashed with so much raw Essence at Avery's fingertips? She was afraid she already knew. This place vibrated through her very bones, making her blood sing.

"We have to try," Petra declared decisively. She looked at Avery. "We came this far. If there's a chance that we can get our hands on enough to stop her, then we have to take it."

Avery turned to the console, intending to look at files herself. But as soon as her hand touched the pad, the screen glitched, going black again. The blue lights around them stuttered, bringing them in and out of the darkness.

"As if this place couldn't get creepier," Finn said slowly, glancing behind them.

Grigg drew out his blaster.

The screen came back to life as the lights steadied. But instead of the access screen, a vid opened on its own. An older man with cropped gray hair was centered in its frame, his stark white uniform standing out against brown skin. It began to play automatically.

"*Greetings. This is Commander Felix Rosenbaum of the exploratory vessel Soter. The year is 2253 by last origin measure, according to our date of departure from Earth.*"

"That's impossible," Finn whispered.

Avery's mind was reeling. Humans hadn't discovered Echo until a thousand years past that. Was this some kind of trick?

"*If you're watching this, you are one of the Altered. Like me.*" The commander paused to look behind him, but Avery could make out nothing but blurred shadows over his shoulder. "*We are . . . no longer human.*"

"What?" Megan breathed, her voice shaking.

"*When our operation first left Earth, we never imagined finding such a verdant planet for expansion, even in our wildest aspirations. The worm hole that threw us so miserably off course during the first fifty years of travel led us to this galaxy—nearly straight to this planet itself, like we were meant to find it. And maybe we were.*"

"Beyond its ideal biome for human life, the mineral we found lining the shores was a near-perfect fuel source. Once refined, Luxetite produced unheard of levels of energy that propelled our technology forward exponentially over the course of one generation. It was nothing short of a miracle. We quickly developed this mine to harvest it from the planet's core.

"But the continued exposure to Luxetite also had . . . adverse effects. The mineral harbored a unique radioactivity, unstable for human proximity. It has changed us—irrevocably manipulated our genetic structures until we were no longer human. Those who remain so call us Altered. Nearly eighty-five percent of our colony is now a new species. And our children . . ." He rubbed a hand over his face. *"One hundred percent affectation. The next generation of our colony—the future of humanity in the stars—will no longer be able to call themselves human."*

CHAPTER FORTY-THREE

Petra's breath stopped as she watched the screen in horror. She couldn't tear her eyes away. Her brain filtered through the information assaulting them, struggling to make sense of the words.

The man—Commander Rosenbaum—continued.

"Effective immediately, I'm shutting down all mining operations planet-wide. I cannot in good conscience continue to delve into this resource at the cost of our health. Who knows what it will do to us the longer we expose ourselves." He glanced behind him once more before leaning in close to the cam and lowering his voice. *"And I've begun to hear things. To feel things. This rock . . ."* He picked up a piece of white stone on the desk beside him, so pure that it nearly glowed in his hand. *"It's almost as if . . . as if I can hear it trying to communicate with me. Or maybe the radiation has truly driven me mad."*

His feed cut out as another window popped up. Another recording. This time it was a woman, her tan face framed by pale blond hair cropped to her chin. She wore a white uniform similar to the commander's.

"Lenora Rosenbaum, acting president of the Letor Colony. Today I record a similar missive to my predecessor and grandfather. Nearly a hundred years after he closed these mines, the colony voted to reopen operations, eager to study the mineral, hoping to learn more about the burgeoning abilities of our new species. The stone our ancestors once used so callously

for fuel has given us a gift beyond their wildest imaginations—along with an understanding of its true nature. Luxetite is sentient. Not the kind of alien life our ancestors had anticipated encountering in their travels, but alive all the same. It wants to connect with us, to merge with us. And we have harvested it for our personal gain, killing it mercilessly. We've dug so deeply, destroyed it so thoroughly, that no more can be extracted from this mine beyond a few thin veins too small to countenance. Even so, there are those within Letor command who wish to dig deeper still, unable to feel the energy that flows through this planet. Their greed for advancement drives them, but they cannot feel its pull. They do not know. And this desire to harvest Luxetite ruthlessly, we cannot allow.

"A few of the Altered, like myself, have developed gifts that will enable us to wipe this place from memory. To wipe the Luxetite itself from memory, along with our history. We have left humanity behind, and thus we must continue forward, fearlessly, into a new reality of peace and understanding. The Luxetite has shown us this path, and we will defend it at any cost.

"If you have found this recording, I beg you to maintain the sanctity of this choice. Walk away. Keep this secret for the Altered who have come before you. It is the only way to protect our peace and prosperity for the future. The only way to protect the Luxetite. Humanity is our past. This . . . is our future."

The vid stopped, frozen on the young commander's pleading face.

Petra gulped in air, staring blindly at the screen that glitched back to a still image of the mine schematics. The metal walkway beneath their feet began to shake, vibrating perilously as Avery struggled to control herself.

"Easy," Finn murmured. He stepped closer to Avery, his focus on her. "Breathe, sweetheart."

Whatever had happened between them had ironed out the issues he'd been struggling with for the past few days. Petra felt the familiar twinge of jealousy writhing in her chest. For whom or for what, she didn't know. She worried her collar bone, staring up at the rings of blue that disappeared into the mine above.

"So we're . . . human?" Grigg was the first to speak, his tone sub-

dued. Apparently he actually was capable of taking some things seriously.

"This can't be real," Megan said, her voice shrill. She stared at Avery. "Can this be real?"

Finn took Avery's hand. He gave her a nod so imperceptible that Petra would have missed it entirely if she hadn't been so attuned to him lately. Watching over him had become a strange sort of habit.

Avery turned to them. "Now might be a good time to reveal something. In light of what we just saw."

"More secrets?" Petra couldn't stop the question from bubbling out of her, cold and unwelcome.

Petra chewed the inside of her cheek, disappointed with her own reaction. She'd sworn to herself that she'd make an effort. The few hours they'd been unable to find Avery and Finn had been torture. And watching Megan nearly unable to bear it had been even worse.

Petra truly wanted to understand Avery. To forgive her. She should have known it wouldn't be that easy. Petra had never been able to let go of the past without effort. She'd always found it simpler to let the rage take her away from it all.

I'm trying, Petra, Avery said to her in mind. Her golden eyes were wide and glistening, compassion seeping down their bond, softening them both.

Petra fought against herself, the two halves of her unable to reconcile. She didn't want to ignore Avery's plea. And yet the tension that built in her throat only seemed to harden her obstinacy.

Avery drew a small breath. "After Finn and I fell down to the river cavern, I was able to merge with him."

"What?" Nova gripped the railing.

Petra shut her eyes against sudden tears, willing herself to process what Avery was saying. She had been able to connect with Finn, a human. But Reanges had once *been* human. It was contradictory to everything Petra had ever known—everything she'd ever clung to in order to survive.

She pulled in stale air through her nostrils, trying to fight the light-headedness that sent black spots dotting across her vision.

"And you're just dropping this on us now?" Megan shrieked. "That's not something you should be keeping to yourselves."

"It just happened," Finn explained. He ran a nervous hand through his hair. "We haven't even discussed it with one another. You found us before we had the chance to even figure out what it meant. What it means."

"Can you merge with me?" Megan didn't hesitate to throw her question at Avery.

Another pang of jealously struck Petra, her lip curling with disgust. And what was worse, again Petra couldn't decipher its origin. There was a part of her that didn't even want to try.

All Petra clung to was the certainty that she could not let go of her anger. Only last year, Avery had banished Megan and Finn for being human. And now she was claiming she could connect with them? It was too much.

"I don't know," Avery admitted. "I haven't been able to do it again since that first time."

"We were a little too preoccupied to run tests, Megan," Finn added wryly.

Megan scrunched her nose. "Gross. I don't need a play-by-play of your sex life."

Avery blanched. She shoved Finn. "That's not what happened—"

"That's not unusual, though," Nova said, already analyzing the possibilities. "New facets of your power have always come in waves similar to this one. You discover them, and then you hone them. Like your healing."

Grigg nodded. "You just need time to train. Imagine the weapon it will make, being able to control them, too."

"It's not a weapon," Avery said defensively. "These powers were never meant for that. If the Essence has shown me anything—if this vid capsule has shown us anything—it's that we're not meant to harm others with it."

"Then what about liberating the humans in captivity under Leviathan's laws?" Megan suggested, growing more animated. "We could finally organize effectively. We could free them all."

Petra listened in silence as they delved into the possibilities.

And all the while, Petra's rage simmered, searing through her veins like lava, destructive and unstoppable. She pushed it down, desperate to ignore the sensation. Petra was so tired of being angry, of hating everything and everyone around her, of *feeling* so intensely and so often.

None of them understood Leviathan. But Petra did.

She knew how desperately the old So' would cling to her own convictions, to the very end. It had been the only way for Leviathan to survive, and she wouldn't abandon her hatred now. Even with the revelations about the nature of humans and Reanges, it would change nothing. It solved nothing.

Petra had listened to their conjecture long enough.

"It doesn't matter," Petra hissed, but the others kept talking, her words lost beneath their conjectures. So she shouted, "It doesn't matter!"

Silence. They stared at her like she'd lost her mind. And maybe she had.

"Didn't you hear those commanders? Any hope we had of defeating Leviathan is gone!" Petra was yelling, unable to keep the agony out of her voice. "The stone is *gone*! Used up! Nothing we're talking about here is actually going to change anything. It's not going to stop Leviathan. Nothing will stop her except a power greater than hers. It. Doesn't. Matter."

Avery started for Petra, but Finn grabbed her, holding her back. For once, she listened to him.

"It doesn't matter?" Megan tilted her head, tears rushing suddenly into her pale blue eyes. Her voice shook. "How can you say that? To me, of all people?"

Petra's heart twisted, tangling around so many emotions that they threatened to strangle her from the inside. She didn't want to hurt Megan anymore. She was tired of hurting people.

But she refused to lie, to herself or anyone else.

"Because it's the truth," Petra clipped.

"It's not!" Megan screamed. Her words bounced around the cylinder, repeating over and over. "I'm so sick of you pushing everyone and everything away!" She shoved Petra with more force than her slight frame should've been able to allow.

Petra stumbled backward and crashed into Grigg's enormous wall of a chest. He grabbed her shoulders to keep her from tumbling off the edge of the platform.

She jerked away from him, heat flushing her face as she steadied herself. That reaction had been unexpected. Megan was hungry for a fight.

They had been dancing around this exact conversation since Avery had blown back into their orbit. Even on the night they'd spent together, when everyone else had ventured off to the hot baths, there had been little talking.

Petra dipped her chin. "Do we have to do this here? In front of everyone?"

"Yes." Megan's eyes were glistening and full of fury.

Petra cackled. "Fine. Then I'd say that claiming *I* push people away is a load of shit. You know damn well I've been trying to do the exact opposite of that for twelve months. *You've* been the one keeping us at arm's length. Not me."

Megan's demeanor softened. "You know why I did that. I told you why."

"I know. But Avery is fine." Petra waved a wild hand in Avery's direction. "She's standing right there."

"And you've been making her pay for what happened every second since coming back, when you know it's all I wanted," Megan accused. "All you've ever cared about it how different we are from one another. Humans versus Reanges. And we finally have proof that can change all that. Not just for you and me but for the people we're trying to save. For the future we're trying to create, for both our worlds. This information will change *everything*. The fact that you have the audacity to stand there can claim otherwise is infuriating!"

"Infuriating?" Petra questioned. The vitriol Mylan had claimed she possessed rose with a vengeance, spewing out of her as she lost control. "What's infuriating is that despite everything we've been through, despite everything we've sacrificed and lost, it's still not enough. There is no guarantee that we are going to get through this. The only hope we had to overpower Leviathan was that stupid rock, and it's *gone!*"

Petra turned away from them, rage pouring through her so violently that her skin turned to ice. She sucked in a breath, then let it out in a slow stream between her lips. Then she crumpled, her shoulders sagging, her lip trembling as she struggled not to cry.

"I'm tired," Petra confessed. There was barely any strength left to maintain her defenses. "I'm tired of feeling so angry all the time. But when I think about the alternative . . . anger is all I have."

"That's not true," Megan said immediately. And she sounded so sure of herself. So incredibly sure.

"Isn't it?" Petra asked. "It's easier to fight than to hope. And I've been fighting since I was a child—since the Federation murdered my parents. But when I met Avery, when I saw not only what she was but *who* she was—" Petra choked, eyes darting to Avery. If this was going to be a confession for Megan, it might as well be for Avery, too. "*You* made me hope again. I thought that maybe . . . maybe it wasn't all a stupid dream. Maybe we could actually find peace for our people."

A tear slid down Avery's cheek. If she had spoken, Petra knew she wouldn't have been able to continue.

"And when you—when Qav used you to banish us—it proved that the dream was an illusion after all. It was like I had lost myself all over again."

"That's not fair," Finn said harshly.

Avery touched his arm. "Let her speak."

"I know it's not. You think I don't know that? I hate myself for it. But I nearly lost Megan, too." Petra stepped toward Megan and spoke directly to her. "You're right. About a lot of things. I've survived by pushing people away. But I don't want to do it anymore. I don't want to push *you* away."

Megan's breath shallowed as she stared up at Petra. "You were right—I don't think we should do this here." She backed away.

Petra grabbed her arm, pulling them closer together. "No—we are absolutely finishing this here and now."

Two weeks ago, she would have given anything for this kind of chance to talk. If it had to happen there, in front of everyone, then so be it.

"What I'm trying to say is that I'm scared, Megan. Hope has never gone well for me. But if my options are to cling to my fear of losing you or cling to my hope that you'll love me back . . . then I choose the latter."

Avery sucked in a breath. Finn was grinning. Grigg and Nova graciously showed no reaction.

"What?" Megan squeaked.

"I love you, Megan. I've loved you for a long time. I just had to get out of my own way to admit it to myself." Petra took Megan's hands in hers, their dirt-covered fingers wrapping around one another. "And yes, the fact that Reanges are descended from human explorers who landed here thousands of years ago will change things for both worlds. But it changes nothing for me. Not when it comes to you."

"Oh," Megan breathed, her mouth forming a perfect bow. Her blond eyelashes fluttered, her eyes dropping to Petra's lips.

And even if they were standing feet away from four other people, Petra leaned in and claimed Megan's mouth in a kiss, gentler and softer than she ever had before. They pulled apart, lingering close enough that Petra's next promise brushed their lips together again. "Maybe I can find the strength to hope things can change too. If you'll let me stand beside you."

Megan smiled, her eyes soft and fierce. And she kissed Petra, running her fingers through her hair, fitting their mouths perfectly together. Petra grabbed Megan's hips to hold them both steady, her fingers digging into her jacket.

When at last Megan pulled away, she took Petra's hand. "Next time, maybe lead with that."

Petra barked out a surprised laugh.

Something bright crested through her heart, sparkling up through her body and filling her eyes with tears. It felt . . . wonderful. To fully let go. To say aloud what she'd been carrying trapped in a cage for months. It bubbled up through her body, starting a rumbling laugh deep in her chest as a smile cracked across her face.

Petra let the laughter take her, tripping up and out of her mouth until the peeling sound of her euphoria filled the cylinder around them.

And the others watched her with wide eyes and faint smiles of their own, absorbing the bewildering evidence of Petra's happiness along with the realization that everything they'd ever known was about to change.

Avery watched as Petra laughed. That bitterness that had come to define Petra was gone, only exhilaration and delight left in its wake, so overflowing and vibrant that it left her breathless.

Finn squeezed Avery's hand in his, and she looked up at him. He was smiling. She couldn't feel him, like before, but she knew his emotions mirrored her own. They were both grateful, indebted to fate for giving them a second chance. Not just for themselves, but for their entire family. And this time, they wouldn't waste it.

"Is she all right?" Grigg watched Petra cautiously, like she might punch him if he made a wrong move.

"Don't be an ass," Nova chastised.

"Me? An ass?" Grigg pouted comically. "You wound me."

"Highly doubtful," Petra drawled. She still held Megan's hand, their bodies pressed together. "But if it bothers you that much, I'll keep the laughing to a minimum."

Finn released a theatrical breath. "Thank the moons for that. I don't think my brain could process the ongoing confusion."

Petra made a face at Finn, sticking her tongue out playfully. Avery watched with fascination. Petra actually loved Finn—Avery could feel it radiating from her, like the gentle warmth of a holofire. It left Avery speechless.

"But I stand by what I said," Petra clarified, carefully steering the conversation away from her emotional outburst. "Without the stone, we don't have much going for us against Leviathan."

"And I stand by what *I* said," Megan countered. "Once Avery can influence humans, it will be enough."

"If Qav figures this out, then we're screwed," Finn added darkly.

"It's a valid point, Avery." Petra cut off Avery's objection before she could speak. "None of us trust Qav. He's a liability."

Megan was quiet, as good as an agreement as anything else. She sided with Petra and Finn.

But Avery couldn't forget how Qav had stood before her in the snow of Nos Lenti, baring himself to her, opening his mind until he was completely vulnerable. Doing so would not have been easy for him. It had been Qav's way of proving his loyalty, of showing that she could unequivocally trust him. And surprisingly enough, Avery realized she *did*.

"If Qav was still the same person he was last year, I would agree. But he's not," Avery said delicately.

Finn stilled beside her. Avery squeezed his hand again, refusing to let him go but determined to make her point.

"Grigg and Nova and I never would have made it back here without his help. He left everything back on Earth to follow us—to help repair what he destroyed."

Petra frowned skeptically.

"But you're right, Petra," Avery continued. "We don't have a stone of our own. Even if the information we found here will change both worlds, it won't help us go up against Leviathan. To do that, I will need Qav's help."

"Okay," Petra said simply. But she wasn't looking at Avery. She was watching Finn. "So we hone your new power, like Megan suggested. If there's one thing Leviathan won't expect, it's a coordinated attack from the humans themselves."

"There's nothing down here for us regardless. We need to find a way out," Nova reasoned. They had been gone too long, cut off from the world above. Anxiety snaked around Nova's every move, her worries going to her home and her family that they'd left undefended. "Leviathan won't be bound by her council for long—Qav said as much."

Grigg sighed heavily. "If she makes a move on Nos Lenti, they won't stand a chance."

"Qav wouldn't let that happen," Avery replied. And suddenly she knew it was the truth. He would defend her family; she was certain of it.

Megan was already at the console. "There was a ventilation system on the schematics. The entrance may have been sealed, but air gets down here somehow."

"Great," Grigg drawled. "I've always been a big fan of cramped spaces."

Megan pulled out a drive from her jacket pocket. "I don't care what those vids said about keeping this place a secret; I'm taking the data with us."

"Wait a second," Finn protested. "If we leak that vid, it's not going to magically end the conflict between our planets. It could cause more unrest than ever before."

Nova tilted her head. "And you say you're not a politician—you sound just like Alex Peña."

Petra placed a hand over Megan's to stop her from connecting the drive. She looked up at Avery. "What do you want to do?"

Avery's heart swelled. Petra was making the choice to trust Avery again.

Thank you. Avery infused every bit of gratitude she could into the bond between them until Petra cheeks flushed. But she didn't look away.

"You all are my family," Avery said quietly. "Closer than family. I value your opinions more than anyone else on both worlds. Whatever we decide here and now, we will all honor. We can walk out of here and never speak of that vid again . . . Or we can use it to try and make a difference."

They were quiet for a few moments as the weight of the choice settled over their entire party. Their eyes drifted over each other, waiting for someone to reply.

But it was Petra who spoke first, a tentative smile cresting over her face as she clasped Megan's hand. "Then I say we choose hope."

CHAPTER FORTY-FOUR

There was no way to reach the ventilation shaft except an arduous climb up the stairs. Avery was thankful they at least had a pathway to traverse from one level to the next and didn't have to rely on her powers. She would not have been able to muster enough strength to make a difference.

The climb itself was exhausting in its own right. The narrow staircase ran along the edge of the stone, forcing them to walk in single file. The farther up they went, the more the Essence dissipated. It lingered, pulsing in the air around Avery, but never so vibrant as in the heart of the mine.

After two hours of climbing, Avery's quads were burning. Sweat had gathered beneath her shirt, making her sticky and hot. The sounds of their breathing were heavy over the trickling of the water that ran down the wall beside them.

Megan hounded Avery to explore her new power, and she had no choice but to obey the commands. Avery *did* need to figure out how it worked, and the sooner, the better. But she had little success.

But Megan was determined. "What were you doing when it happened the last time?"

"I don't know," Avery snapped. She wiped sweat from her upper lip, trying to concentrate. "We were arguing, and then . . . I just fell into his head."

"And it's gone now? Completely?"

Finn halted midstep. "Give her a break, Megan. Maybe she just needs to rest."

"We don't have time to rest. This is important."

"Trying to force it won't help anyone," Finn said sourly. "Especially if you kill her in the process."

"She's just trying to help," Petra practically snarled.

They slowed to a stop, and Avery took the opportunity to catch her breath as they argued. Avery hadn't felt so exhausted from physical activity since her time in the Origin, when she'd been new to the concept of training at all.

Maybe nearly drowning had taken more of her strength than she realized. She was only beginning to realize how weak she felt the farther she moved from the mine below.

Avery angled against the wall, leaning her head onto the cool rock. Her fingers trailed over the stone, until her skin touched the cold stream of water that flowed down its jagged surface.

Power pulsed through her, calling to whatever was left of her reserves, setting her on fire. Her eyes flew open, her back straightening.

Finn's energy hit her in a rushing wave of heat. She would never get used to the way he felt, so visceral and alive and completely hers.

In the next breath, Megan's mind barreled forward, like she had been trying to project herself at Avery, all force and excitement. Thoughts came at her faster than lightning, so quickly that most passed her by. The few she did catch were all about Petra and her delectable—

"Ew!" Avery screeched, pulling away from their energy, ripping her hand out of the water.

"What?" Finn whirled behind her, his weapon drawn, ready for an attack. Grigg and Nova were in the same position at the top of their line.

Avery leveled outraged eyes at Megan. "You are seriously disgusting."

Megan's eyes lit up. "You did it, didn't you?" She grabbed Avery's hands, bouncing up and down on her toes. "I knew it would work—I knew it!"

"Then why didn't you censor your thoughts?" Avery made a gagging noise. "You make Grigg's mind look chaste."

Grigg chuckled impishly, holstering his blaster to his hip.

Finn took Avery's elbow, his hold soft and supportive. "Don't push it, Avery. We can figure this out when you're less exhausted."

"It didn't feel like it drained me at all," Avery said, frowning. "But you're right. I probably would have fallen flat on my face if I hadn't—" Something clicked into place, realization dawning. "I touched the water."

Avery pressed her hand into the cool stream without hesitation. Power flooded through her, the warm pull of the Essence as vibrant as when she'd fallen into the river itself. It revitalized her, filling her very cells with renewed, limitless energy.

"The Essence," Avery whispered.

"What?" Petra stared at the water like it would bubble out from the wall and take them all with it.

"I can feel the Essence—it's everywhere," Avery withdrew her hand, staring up into the shadows around them.

She could almost taste its presence in the air, like the salt from the ocean on a sea breeze. How had she missed it before? That subtle warmth, its constant pull. It had been speaking to her since the moment they came through the Gate. No—before that. Its call had echoed through the stars.

"They said the stone was radioactive." Megan shifted away from the wall. "Do you think everything down here has been affected by it?"

Avery turned to the water, pressing both her hands on the stone beneath its easy flow.

Awareness surged through her, lighting every molecule in her body, connecting her to a power so ancient that it defied understanding. But she had felt the Essence before, had stood in its presence in its own dimension. This feeling, no matter how incredible, was merely a fragment of its true infinity, a stale trail left behind from the days when Luxetite had been harvested from those very mines.

But a trail was all Avery needed.

She sent her mind out along the water, and it flowed down the stone wall to the bottom of the mine and farther, deep into the planet below, where the pale, translucent veins of Luxetite rested undisturbed. And when her consciousness met that stone, a pure, undiluted cradle of true Essence, Avery's mind exploded in a thousand directions at once.

She gasped, her fingers digging into the rock, bits crumbling wetly away beneath her strength. She didn't move away—she couldn't.

Avery traveled through the veins that spread throughout Echo, following them through the planet's core and out the other side. There was so much Luxetite that had remained untapped, even if their ancestors had taken everything from the surface. It ran in wide, unending rivers beneath their feet, below the oceans, inside the mountains . . . even under Milderion itself.

And it could feel everything. It could *see* everything. It waited patiently and quietly, unmoving for millennia as eons passed overhead. Avery could barely understand—could barely perceive—how to go about harnessing such a power, if it was even possible. All she could do was feel . . .

There was so much pain, so much immense despair. Avery recoiled, desperate for relief that never came. Reanges and humans alike were suffering, their torment and terror consuming her from the inside out. They were dying—*they were all dying*—and Avery could do nothing to stop it. She could only exist and observe as the world above burned.

Avery couldn't focus to find the source of their torture, to figure out what was happening. But she could feel every last ounce of their anguish—and it was unbearable.

Silver eyes flashed in her mind—Qav!

He was desperate and hurt, his cold presence grasping at her as though he'd thought her dead. Something was horribly wrong. Avery pushed toward him, trying to reach him despite her liminal existence in that place, trying to ask him what was wrong.

But she couldn't speak. She could feel the cool thread of his power, only a whisper of its usual intensity, as it slipped away from her.

Avery had no control there. She could not use the Essence from afar, even if she held a trace of its force in water flowing over her hands. She could merely travel through it, a passive observer at the same mercy of the Essence's limitations without a host.

Violet eyes slashed toward her, angry and accusing. Leviathan had felt Avery there, no matter how insignificant Avery's existence was among the vast infinity of the planet itself. The old So' jerked Avery forward, dragging her violently into Leviathan's mind.

They were in the central hospital, though its lights were dim and the central hallway that looked out over the city was strangely empty. Warning sirens wailed. The building shook, debris falling to the floor as bits of ceiling broke off around them. And outside the gargantuan arching windows of the upper lobby, the night sky pulsed with an artificial orange glow.

This is your fault, girl. Leviathan's accusation rang through Avery's head like a searing toll, making her dizzy.

What was her fault? What was happening? Avery tried to scream her questions, but nothing emerged. She was stuck. Powerless and aware in the midst of a nightmare.

Avery could only watch as Leviathan hobbled on her cane down the hallway, straight to a group that knelt on the ground. Two guards stood over them, blasters at the ready for any sudden moves. Avery's heart stopped.

Krez was there, along with a few others she recognized from Nos Lenti. Two Reanges. Three humans. And at the end of the line, her arm around one of the human girls . . . Gran. Her gray eyes were defiant, her broad shoulders rolled back. A gash on her forehead bled profusely, its dark trail staining her silver braid red.

It had to have been an illusion. Gran wouldn't be in Milderion—they had left them only days ago, safe in the shelter of the mountains.

You brought this down on all of us. And you have brought what comes next down on yourself, Leviathan hissed.

She lifted her hand to Krez.

He stood, his eyes blank, his features going slack. He pulled the blaster from the holster still strapped to his thigh. He raised it. And shot himself in the head.

Blood sprayed, staining the wall with dark splotches as Krez's lifeless body fell to the ground. And Avery watched in horror—*felt* in horror—as his light faded away forever. He was gone.

Avery screamed, as much as she was able in that strange in-between place.

Leviathan flinched. She lashed out at Avery, striking her hard enough to knock Avery backward, straight into her body on the stairs.

Avery was still screaming, the sound startling them all as she jerked away from the water. She hit the railing behind her, the force of her momentum breaking the old metal away, and she plunged over with nothing to stop her from plummeting to her death below.

Petra jumped, grabbing Avery's pack and swinging her back up onto the stairs. They fell in a heap against Megan as Avery sobbed uncontrollably.

"What's wrong with her?" Megan ran her hands over Avery, trying to find some kind of wound. "What happened?"

"Finn," Petra called anxiously, moving away so he could get to her.

Finn sat on the stairs behind Avery and pulled her to him, curling his body around hers as her screams dissolved into cries.

She couldn't stop herself. She had gone too far—she had felt too much. No one person should ever have to feel what she had felt, to understand the truth in that way . . .

Avery had seen Krez lying dead at Leviathan's feet. He had been taken from her, the same way Fiora had. Even with all that raw energy, she had been helpless to stop it.

And Gran was still there.

"Breathe, sweetheart," Finn whispered in her ear, his voice low and steady and sure. "I've got you."

She could do nothing for them. All that power and she could do *nothing*.

All Avery could do was breathe.

CHAPTER FORTY-FIVE

"What do you mean, they have Gran?" Megan asked in disbelief.

"Who were the others from Nos Lenti?" Nova's fear struck Avery, sending bile up her throat.

"I don't know." Avery clutched the fabric of her pants, desperate for something to hold on to.

Nova was never scared. It rattled her, making Avery's skin crawl.

"What about Tai?" Petra's question shook.

"No," Avery replied at once. "He wasn't with them. Just Gran and . . . the others. I could only see what was shown to me. That place . . . I had no control there."

"But you have your powers back." Petra nodded sharply. "Reach out now—feel for them now."

Avery shook her head miserably. "I can't penetrate the rock."

"Then you have to go back." Nova took a step down, closer to Avery, who was still huddled in Finn's arms. Her blue eyes were wide, bright in the light of the stick on Petra's pack, her face cast in harsh shadows. "We need answers. You have to go back into the Essence."

"She can't, Nova." Grigg placed a hand on her shoulder. "It's too dangerous."

Finn nodded against Avery's head. "If Leviathan knocked her out of there, she'll be waiting for Avery to show her face again. Who knows what she can actually do to her."

Nova let out a shuddering breath and turned to lean over the railing, staring out into the nothingness. Her knuckles turned white on the metal.

"Leviathan would never attack the city itself," Petra reasoned. "If there was a bombing, it wasn't under her command."

Finn pulled Avery closer to him. "No offense, Petra, but Leviathan isn't exactly known for making understandable choices as of late. Maybe she finally lost it."

"That doesn't explain why the others would be in the city," Nova said over her shoulder. "Or why they left the protection of Nos Lenti."

Avery started shivering. In the back of her mind, she feared she already knew. That hospital had shaken beneath the weight of some kind of blastfire. Only heavy artillery would cause that kind of damage.

"Klein."

Avery looked up at Grigg as he voiced her thought aloud.

None of them had wanted to admit the possibility. But it was the most logical answer, even if it was the most feared. They thought they'd have more time, that they could deal with Leviathan first. What a stupid, naive assumption.

"Klein couldn't have moved that quickly," Nova said. "She'd need to mobilize half the Federation forces to attack a city the size of Milderion. The World Council would never approve that in just a few days. Alex wouldn't let it happen."

"But it *could* happen," Grigg argued. "After we got Avery out of the city that night, Klein as good as disappeared. Even Cora couldn't track her."

"You're suggesting Klein revealed that she built a second, privately funded Gate for her personal use?" Nova shook her head. "She'd lose any support she gained over the past year. The public would turn on her."

"Tensions have been high. The people are more frightened than ever—Klein saw to that," Avery reminded them. "Earth always has a much higher tolerance for Klein and her machinations than we ever expect."

Nova's breath quickened as she stared at Avery, her jaw working in silence. Avery could feel her reining herself in, pulling the wild pieces back together into some semblance order.

Finn hugged Avery closer. "We won't know anything until Avery can connect with the others."

"Then we have to get aboveground." Nova's voice had leveled, returning to its usual calm control.

Avery thought of climbing out of the mine, of how long it would take them. They'd estimated at least another full day.

Krez filled Avery's mind. His blank look as he rose to his feet. Grabbing his blaster. The sound of the shot—

Avery choked back a sob.

She forced herself to think of Gran, to see only her face. She had looked tired kneeling on the ground beside the others. But not broken. It would take more than fear to do that.

"Leviathan has Gran," Avery said, hating how pitiful she sounded. Hating the way she felt so powerless, even now.

"I know," Finn replied, running a thumb over Avery's hand on her thigh.

"She'll be okay, Avery." Megan scooted closer to her on the stairs until they were flush against one another.

"Leviathan won't kill her," Petra said succinctly. "She only used Krez to frighten you. Your grandmother is too valuable for that."

Despite Petra's terse comments, Avery could feel the grief Petra kept on a short leash. Losing Krez meant more to her than she let on.

Leviathan hadn't considered Krez worth more than a quick death at his own hand. Avery's stomach rolled, nausea bubbling up her throat again.

Fiora had given her life for Avery. And now . . . her husband's life had been stolen from him while following the same path.

Avery had only said a few words to him that night of the Su'elben celebration. She thought they would find a way to mourn Fiora together once this was all over. He had died as a pawn in Leviathan's fervor to break Avery. The same way Fiora had died as a pawn in Klein's.

"We're going to get her back, Avery." Megan brought Avery out of her spiral. "Leviathan needs Gran to draw you out. That means she needs her alive."

Avery nodded, dazed and struggling to shake off the overwhelm. But seeing the city under attack, knowing Gran was in Leviathan's control, watching Krez die . . . Witnessing that horror was only a small part of it.

Avery finally understood the vast awareness of the Essence and its place on Echo. She had felt the yawning infinite reality of who she was outside of the limitations of her physical form. More frightening still, something in her yearned to become a part of that awareness. To return to it.

"Now get up." Petra loomed over Avery, her face contorted.

And there, mingling with the grief, was regret. Petra had left things unsaid with Krez, too.

"Now is not the time to let Leviathan get into your head. I don't care what she did to you in there." Petra extended her hand to Avery.

And then, louder than her words, Petra pushed every bit of obstinacy and determination she could muster straight at Avery. It hit her in the chest, filling Avery with a strength she wouldn't have been able to muster alone.

Petra spoke again, her words soft yet bound with steel. "Get up and stand beside us."

Avery rose unsteadily to her feet.

She had to keep moving. She'd handled Gran being in the enemies' hands once. She could handle it again.

With her friends by her side, Avery began to climb.

CHAPTER FORTY-SIX

They ascended for hours, until the darkness and the repetition made Finn dizzy with disorientation. He forced Avery to drink the last of their water. The past few days had taken a toll on her that was visible to anyone who looked at her. Her face was pale, her skin no more than a translucent base for the smattering of discolored freckles.

Finn kept a close step behind her.

There was no way he could fully understand what falling into the Essence had been like, but he could see how it had drained her. They all could. And only Finn knew she'd drowned a few hours earlier. Even as a So'Reange, her body had its limits.

Nothing good awaited them on the surface. At best, Avery would have a few measly hours to gather herself. More likely, she'd have to act immediately, regardless of her exhaustion. The thought alone was enough to turn Finn's stomach.

If Klein really was attacking the city, Nick would undoubtedly be with her. Finn wasn't ready to face his brother again. But maybe Qav had taken care of Nick once and for all when they'd fallen in Alexandria. Finn would actually thank that smug asshole if he had.

When at last they reached it, the ventilation shaft wasn't as easily accessible as they'd hoped. The small metal flap was set high on the adjacent wall, at least ten feet from the edge of the railing.

Avery didn't fight Finn when he forbade her from using her power to open it. That should have been validation enough that she felt like shit. Instead, Grigg hauled it off with brute force via a deftly thrown grappling hook. Petra threw the second cable, a red lined beacon leading them to their escape.

Shimmying across in groups of two, their harnesses the only thing keeping them from falling into the abyss. They left their packs behind, and any semblance of open air, crawling on their bellies over rough-hewn stone through the tiny opening. A tense silence descended. If it hadn't felt like a tomb before, it certainly did now.

"My claustrophobia is thrilled with this turn of events," Grigg grumbled sullenly from the back of their line.

"Save the complaints for when we're out of here," Finn muttered back.

"If we ever *get* out of—" Grigg grunted.

Avery laughed wearily. "Thanks, Nova."

Finn smiled. Avery knew their actions without even having to look. She had become a part of them.

Another half hour of crawling and Finn was ready to lie down and die right there in the rock. His hands were raw and blistered. His kneecaps felt like nubs of bone clanking against the stone beneath him.

Finn startled when Megan yelped. His knees jostled, sending shooting pain up his spine.

"I can see the sky!" she exclaimed. "The vent finally turns up-ward—according to the specs I downloaded, it's maybe another hun-dred feet."

"Great," Grigg remarked. "Straight up through a jagged rock tun-nel barely the width of my shoulders."

They all ignored him.

Petra helped Megan transition their gear to belays and anchors, and they began clawing their way up the final stretch to freedom.

Halfway up, Avery tensed. She stopped in front of Finn, her body outlined against the distant rays of light trickling in from the opening above. Her fingers gripped the edges of the obsidian rock, their tips pale even in the shadows.

"Avery?" Finn wrapped his hands around her thighs, assuring himself that she was secure. That she was safe.

"What's wrong?" Nova was already close on Finn, crowding in from below.

"Nothing," Avery replied, already in motion. She pulled herself up and continued to climb.

Finn wouldn't press her. Not when they were all at their limits.

When they finally emerged from the opening, Finn fell to the ground beside Avery, both of them gasping for breath on their backs in the evening twilight. They stared up at the dimming sky with relief so tangible that Finn swore he could feel it himself. And maybe he could. Maybe Avery's power was connecting them all.

The breeze was cool on Finn's face, drying his sweat to salty crystals. The air was crisp, the wind quiet. He couldn't hear the ocean. They must have traveled farther inland than they'd realized.

Finn rolled his head toward Avery. Her cheeks were pale and streaked with dirt against the lavender smudge of the sky behind her. His fingers tangled with hers. "You okay?"

She turned to him, her stunning gold eyes meeting his. "Qav is unconscious. I can't reach him."

Finn cursed.

"What about the others?" Petra was already rolling to her knees.

"With him. They're in your safe house in the city, but beyond that . . . I don't want to risk using too much of my power in case Leviathan is watching. But the city—" She cleared her throat, taking a small breath. "Klein *did* follow us. And she brought an entire army."

Nova was on her feet, already calling Cora's ship to their location with the communicator still on her wrist.

"Does that mean we're in a full-scale war again?" Megan let Petra pull her to her feet.

"I thought we'd have more time," Avery said softly, almost to herself.

Nova looked at her severely. "We all did, Avery. Don't take this burden on yourself alone."

"She's right," Grigg agreed. "We made the choice to come through the Gate together."

"You heard them." Finn stood and reached out a hand to her.

"Get used to the company, sweetheart."

Avery's laugh dissipated into exhaustion as she shook her head. But she took his hand, and she stood, accepting the companionship and help of her friends. Finn fell even more in love with her in that moment than he ever had before.

Nova was the only one with excess energy, her long legs pacing as they waited for the ship's arrival. Beyond Avery's limited use of power, they were truly in the dark.

Sending comms to the city could alert their enemies to their location and attempting to contact Nos Lenti was out of the question. Its secrecy was paramount, especially now. They no longer had Leviathan alone to contend with, but Klein and the Federation army in its entirety.

Petra wiped at Megan's face. Her cheeks were covered in splotches of dirt, her blond hair stained with streaks of black. Grigg ran a rough hand through his hair, sending soot flying everywhere. After days without a shave, he was almost sporting a full beard. Avery and Finn were by far the cleanest, but that was only a result of their unexpected swim in the river. Given the option, Finn would have rather remained filthy.

They were quiet as the ship arrived, appearing out of nothing, not even a hint of a shimmer in the air before it materialized. Finn would never get used to the tech, no matter how many times he witnessed it.

They were still silent as they piled into the bridge. Nova took her place at the controls as the ship pulled up and away from the ground. Finn was too tired even to offer to pilot.

Nova looked over her shoulder as Grigg settled into the comm seat beside her. "You all should go shower. Get some food and rest. We're going to need it."

Avery was ready to protest. "But I—"

"Just take the offer," Petra interrupted. She softened her tone as she added, "We're all exhausted. You more than the rest of us."

Avery's fatigue won out in the end, thanks in no small part to her desire to appease Petra. If Finn had to guess, Petra knew exactly what she was doing in demanding it from Avery.

"Finn?" Nova called, stopping him as the others made their way for the cabins. Her voice shook, her hands slipping on the control pad. Coming to the surface made everything so much more real. "Make sure she sleeps. If we have a battle ahead of us, she'll need all the strength she can muster. We all will."

Finn's heart stuttered.

Putting Avery in more danger was not something he was eager to run toward, but they had no choice. Even if Finn wanted to tie her to the nearest boulder to keep her from harm, she would overpower him. She would never leave the innocents of the city without the aid of her gifts. And Finn would never ask her to do so—he'd learned that lesson once before.

His musings were beside the point. To stand up against a force like the Federation, they *needed* Avery.

And no matter how much Finn wanted to deny it, there was no avoiding the secondary truth: they would need Qav, too.

Finn couldn't sleep beyond the fifteen minutes he was able to claim. He woke fitfully next to Avery and left her to rest. Her face was clean from her quick shower, but she still bore the strain of the past few days, evident in the dark circles had formed under her eyes. Finn would give anything to not force her straight into more conflict.

It seemed most of the others had gathered in the bridge by the time Finn arrived, silent as he entered, their bodies rigid. Petra sat at the controls. Nova was nowhere in sight. They must have swapped shifts to take advantage of whatever rest they could.

Miles ahead, beyond the expansive windows of the ship, Finn could just make out the arching skyline of the city in shadowed relief against the fading orange glow of the sun.

Except it wasn't the sun—it was fire. Finn's blood ran cold in his veins.

Milderion was burning.

CHAPTER FORTY-SEVEN

They touched down farther from the city than Finn would have liked. Massive Federation warships hovered above Milderion, dominating the skyline. Their presence was a looming promise that blotted out the stars, their curving hulls gleaming in the light of the moons.

Avery had to be woken from her sleep, so deep that Finn feared for a moment she wouldn't wake at all. When she joined them at last, she walked out of the ship like some kind of avenging warrior, clad in an outfit of all black that clung to her body like a second skin. A structured layer covered her torso, immovable across her chest. Individual pieces of the same material wrapped around her forearms and over her shoulders.

Avery had donned armor—a gift from Cora Najisuki.

She gave the sky and its looming warships no more than a cursory glance as they made their way down into the tunnels below the surface.

After their journey into the depths of the mines, no one in their party was too thrilled to be entering darkness again. But it was the only way to move in and out of the city undetected. And it would take at least an hour of travel to reach the safe house, an unassuming apartment they used as a base during their raids.

Finn, at least, was comforted by the familiar route. He and Petra had run the same paths so many times that it had become second nature, a pattern he followed to ease his anxious mind. Finn could almost convince himself that what lay ahead was no more than a group of humans awaiting their opportunity for freedom.

When they rose up onto the streets from a grate in a side alley, nothing could have prepared them for the eeriness of the city under siege. The bombing had stopped, and Milderion sat quiet in its destructive wake. The air was still, not even a breeze to clear out the acrid smell of fire and smoke.

No cruisers passed by overhead; no pedestrians walked the streets. The energy had shifted, like the city was waiting within a stasis of its own fear.

They paused on the main road where great chunks of concrete lodged into the street, blocking their way. The rubble was covered by a blanket of broken glass. Above them, a deep gouge had been torn out of the side of the apartment complex's upper half. Clouds of orange-tinged smoke billowed out and up into the air as it continued to burn. Somewhere far away a siren wailed.

"Why did they stop attacking?" Megan whispered with dread as they maneuvered around the rubble.

A troop of soldiers rounded the corner a block away, and Petra clamped a hand over Megan's mouth, tucking her into the tall chunk of concrete behind them. They huddled together as the Feds passed, listening to the organized sounds of their boots marching away.

Avery's entire body shook beside Finn. He took her hand, willing her to stay put. It would serve no purpose to confront them—not when they had no idea what they were up against or what had happened.

Finn breathed a sigh of relief when at last the street was empty and Avery had kept herself in check. They pressed on. No one spoke, too overwhelmed by the devastation to do anything other than move forward. The Federation had disabled the power grid, leaving each block in near total darkness except for the bright light of the moons overhead. It cast strange shadows around them, pale ghosts that followed their every move.

By the time they reached the apartment, they'd passed enough empty buildings to realize this area of the city had evacuated. Finn was surprised there'd been no bodies on the ground, but he knew without a doubt the ruins piled around them hid the deathly consequences of the Federation's initial assault. Finn had seen enough war to know those strikes had taken lives.

They piled into the small elevator with barely enough room to fit them all, grateful for the internal generators that kept the lift functional. Finn pressed against Avery, but she was rigid, staring into nothingness as they ascended. Her wrath seeped into the atmosphere around them, making the air particles themselves vibrate, charging with potential the way a sky turned heavy and metallic before a bolt of lightning.

Markes was ready and waiting for them, standing just outside a door at the end of the dimly lit hallway. He widened it as they approached, his pale face regaining color as his eyes drifted over them, counting heads.

"Thank the moons," he said breathlessly as they filtered past him.

Finn placed a hand on Markes's shoulder, gripping it firmly as the others passed inside. "All safe?"

Markes nodded.

"I got it." Finn gestured to the door, nudging Markes back into the apartment. Finn needed to secure the barrier himself. He latched the five bolts they'd added and threw the bar down into its slot. It wouldn't stop Leviathan—or a group of Feds—but the scant security could offer them time to make a quick exit.

"We've been trying to reach you for days." Linderly hugged Megan close, her voice muffled against her coat.

Petra pulled Tai to her, touching their foreheads together. For once, the kid didn't fight his sister on the public display.

"Where have you been?" Syla watched them with her arms over her chest, her back to the single window in the living room. "Qav lost contact with you almost as soon as you left Nos Lenti."

Avery knelt down beside the couch where Ennis sat with her legs tucked beneath her and Qav's head in her lap. His eyes were squeezed shut in pain, his long hair plastered to the side of his temples with sweat. A nasty gash ran down the length of his forehead, red and angry where the jagged flesh still oozed blood.

"What happened?" Avery pressed the back of her hand against Qav's cheek.

Finn ignored the twinge of jealousy that curled in his gut. He almost felt sorry for Qav—he looked like he'd been dragged through the nearest meteor field.

"It was during the first wave of attacks—two days ago," Ennis explained calmly. "Civilians were still in the streets when a building collapsed."

"Qav got in the way." Syla bit out roughly. "Blazing idiot."

"He didn't just get in the way," Markes clarified in awe. "It was insane."

"He held the whole structure up," Linderly said softly. "Long enough for us to evacuate and get the innocents out of there."

Syla turned away stiffly. "At what cost? He's no use to anyone like that. And if the head wound isn't enough, his arm is broken straight through."

Grigg made his way to Syla's side, staring out at the city beside her.

Finn's brows raised. *Qav* had saved people? At risk to himself? It was difficult to believe.

"Why hasn't Leviathan done anything to protect the city?" Petra asked. "How did Klein even get into atmo?"

"She *couldn't* do anything," Tai replied solemnly. "The Origin fleet has been offline since Grigg and I scrambled their execution protocols. Linderly's coding worked too well—they haven't been able to undo it."

Grigg ran a hand over his face. "That was supposed to be a good thing."

"Yeah, well, it wasn't," Syla said bitterly. "The city was undefended. The Feds just waltzed right in."

"We haven't been able to get through the city to undo their work," Ennis added. "Not that it would matter now."

"What about Dr. Vey?" Finn asked. "Avery saw her and others from Nos Lenti here in the city."

Linderly nodded. "She knew the hospital would need more hands. They came through yesterday before heading on."

"And you let her leave?"

"Krez was with her," Markes replied, frowning at Finn. "Along with half a dozen others. As far as we can tell, they've been leaving the hospitals alone."

"Well, Leviathan hasn't."

"But you're back," Linderly said tentatively. "That shouldn't matter, right? Avery can take her on with the stone and—"

"It was a dead end," Avery said miserably. There was no point in expanding further.

Linderly dropped into one of the chairs, her eyes drifting to the dirty floor. "Then it's over."

Avery let out a slow breath, leaning closely over Qav's body, her face contorting as she worked through her options. Her hand drifted to his arm, and she spread her fingers out. She paused for only a moment, reaching some final decision, before her eyes slid closed.

"No." Finn gripped Avery's shoulder, stopping her. "You barely have enough energy to keep your eyes open—you can't afford to waste any more on healing him."

"I can't afford *not* to," Avery countered. She didn't look up at Finn. She didn't pull away from him, either. She waited.

In the quiet of that room, Finn had to face what everyone else had already realized. Regardless of how Finn felt about Qav, he was nearly as powerful as Avery. If there was a chance to have him back in fighting shape, they needed to take the risk.

Finn dropped her arm, stepping back.

Avery placed her other hand on Qav's forehead, her chin dipping to her chest as her eyes closed once more.

The air shifted, coming alive. The hairs on Finn's neck prickled.

And Avery's skin began to glow.

A soft, pulsing radiation illuminated her from within, growing more vibrant as it reached her hands. Sweat trickled down the sides of her face, her nose scrunching up in concentration. Avery pressed down on Qav's body with one hand, clutching his black sleeve. Her other hand dug into the silvery hair at his temple. A line of blood trailed down her lip from her nose.

It was too much for her. At this rate, she wouldn't be able to handle the demands on her body.

Finn stepped forward—but then a hand gripped his arm.

Nova. Her eyes were pleading, her hold on him firm. It was enough to curb his instincts.

Qav lurched up to sitting, sucking in air. His wound was gone, now only a faint pink line that ran the length of his scalp. His silver eyes were bright, piercing through the shadows of the apartment.

Avery slumped forward against Qav's lap. She was unconscious.

Finn fell to his knees, pulling her into him, brushing hair off her clammy forehead. Her skin was too pale, her lips nearly blue under the blood that coated one side of her mouth.

Qav ran a shaking hand over his freshly healed wound. He twisted his wrist, testing out the viability of his once broken arm. He glanced at the newcomers before zeroing in on Avery, his attention fixed on her face slumped against Finn's chest.

"What did she do?" Qav's question was slow. Deadly.

Finn looked up at him, at the brows that drew down over his striking eyes.

Qav was angry. Furious, even. As livid as Finn would have been with Avery had their roles been reversed.

And the realization that he cared—that Qav cared about Avery enough to put her well-being above his own—was no small thing.

CHAPTER
FORTY-EIGHT

"Why are they just sitting up there . . . watching us?"

Avery twisted her head on Finn's lap. Megan stood by the window, watching the warships that hovered in the stillness.

Finn lightly stroked Avery's hair, his fingers tingling her scalp. The movement eased her aching skull. She'd been out for nearly an hour after healing Qav. Healing him had cost her.

The meager med patch from the first aid box had done little to restore her strength. What Avery really needed was more rest, a luxury none of them could afford.

"Classic Federation war tactics." Finn's voice was a comforting rumble against her cheek. "The first wave is always long-range attacks, meant to the frighten the population more than anything else. They don't want to damage the infrastructure any more than necessary."

"And the second wave?" Megan asked warily.

"Ground fighting," Petra answered for him. "They'll let the city shake in the dark until fear overpowers any ideas of resistance. And then they'll take it with sheers numbers on foot."

"Okay," Qav said tactfully. He swirled a hot mug of tea between his hands at the scant dining table. Some of them had tried to eat, with little success. "Then that gives us some time."

"To do what?" Syla scoffed. "There's no way we can assimilate a force large enough to take on that many humans."

"She's right," Markes said. "Each of those ships up there probably has three thousand soldiers per vessel."

"Then Qav and I will unify the city." Avery pushed herself up to lean into Finn's warmth, tucking her bare feet under her legs. "We did it in the Sanctum. We can do it here."

Qav shook his head. "You're strong, Avery. If I'm being honest, stronger than I thought was possible—for either of us. But even you've never used your power on that big of a scale."

"She held your city well enough," Petra countered, bristling.

Qav laughed. "That was a population of ten thousand. Milderion has at least a million Reanges. Even with both of us at full capacity, there's no way we'll be able to harness that many minds."

"We don't need all of them," Avery reasoned. "Just enough to hold off the Federation."

"Oh, my mistake. Three hundred thousand is totally doable," Qav said sarcastically. "Have you always been this delusional, or did healing me finally push you over the edge?"

"Hold off the Federation for what?" Finn's question was gentle as his fingers laced together with Avery's. "Klein isn't going anywhere, Avery. Are you prepared to kill all those humans? We're not going to get out of this without bloodshed."

Avery sighed, slumping deeper against Finn. She *couldn't* just kill them—but would the humans stop? Gran's face flashed in her mind, bloodstained and tired. Her heart squeezed beneath the cold fingers of panic. If they could just hold off Klein's forces, it would buy them time to get to Gran.

Maybe Avery wasn't thinking clearly. The need to find Gran—to save her first—was almost too great of a temptation to bear. Avery's power wasn't meant for that, and Gran would never want it. Now, more than ever, Avery understood.

But she was done killing.

"I'm so sick of it," Avery muttered, tears pricking her eyes. "All this pain and loss is pointless. We keep killing one another, and for what? It's not right that the lives of so many are decided by the will of a few." Avery looked at Qav. "Even us."

Qav dropped his gaze to his steaming mug.

"The point of our power is to bring peace and understanding. We are here to facilitate empathy, not force others to our will. I won't be used as a weapon any longer." Her voice shook, her throat constricting as the floor rattled underfoot. "Not even for my own gain."

Finn leaned over to press a lingering kiss to Avery's temple. Her breathing settled. The shaking floor stilled.

"Leviathan never understood that," Petra commented. She shared one of the larger chairs with Megan, their limbs tangled together. "She always saw the So' first and foremost as the most powerful weapon we had."

Avery looked out the window to the burning city beyond. "And look at where it has brought us."

"We can still go after the stone," Tai said delicately. His green eyes shifted uncertainly as so many heads turned to him. He cleared his throat. "I mean . . . if more power is what we need, isn't that the best option?"

Markes nodded fiercely. "That was our plan from the beginning—why change it?"

"If Leviathan still has the stone, why hasn't she used it to fight back against the Federation?" Megan asked.

"Half her council abandoned her," Ennis explained. "They tried to broker peace with Klein on that first day."

"And?" Finn asked.

"It didn't work."

"The Federation killed them all," Tai added fervently. "Blew up their cruiser before it could even reach their command."

Finn cursed.

Avery's chest tightened. She could see the image of it in Tai's memory, the white banner they'd tied across the front of the vessel, the fiery rubble falling from the sky.

Klein had ignored the plea for negotiations. More than that, she'd defied basic rules of war in broad daylight. It was tantamount to treason against the World Council. When it came to light, she would be prosecuted immediately. Why would she so foolishly compromise her position?

"After that, Leviathan mainly kept to herself in the capitol building, hiding behind what soldiers she can control, letting them take the city," Qav said. "But she's weak. Even more so than the day we arrived."

"Mylan said her power was waning," Avery mused. "Maybe pulling me into her mind took a toll."

Syla rubbed a thoughtful hand over her chin. "If she's too weak to use the stone, then maybe she's too weak to keep it."

"It won't matter what she is as long as we can take it from her," Nova said pointedly. "Forget three hundred thousand Reanges; we'd have the entire city of Milderion at your fingertips."

Linderly shifted, her eyes bright. "Leviathan would be the least of our worries."

Avery raised an eyebrow at Qav. It would be a huge gamble to put their friends in the way of Leviathan's reach. If things went south, they would have to bear the burden of that choice.

What do you want to do? Qav asked silently.

Finn stood to pace the room. "With the merge connecting those kinds of numbers, we could subdue the Federation easily. Potentially without any bloodshed. Do we have weapons?"

"The armory is still stocked from the Federation occupation two years ago," Grigg supplied. "Tai and I came across the cache when we disabled the ships. The Origin left it largely untouched."

"Enough?"

"To equip a couple hundred thousand at least."

Finn turned to Avery. A small grin tugged his scarred lips. "It could work."

"Okay," Avery said, hope making her breathless. It emerged like effervescent fog from every person in the room, rising up and around them until even Qav was heady with the sensation. "We'll need weapons in the hands of every able bodied Reange in the city."

"That will take time," Nova said.

"Because we have so much of that," Petra grumbled.

"What's life without a little challenge?" Finn shrugged playfully.

Avery turned to him, all business. "When will the attacks begin again?"

"First light. Maybe before."

Qav leaned back in his chair. "That's a few hours at best."

"It will have to be enough." Avery's eyes drifted over the people who surrounded her, the friends she'd made that had somehow become more precious to her than any family ever could. "Qav, Syla, and Finn will come with me to face Leviathan. The rest of you we'll need moving through the streets as fast as you can. We need to get the ships operational, the city back online, and weapons into the hands of as many people as we can manage before day break."

"What?" Grigg rose halfway to his feet. "No way, Avery. We're not leaving you."

"She doesn't have time to argue with you," Finn said curtly, ignoring Grigg's frown. "She needs you on the ground. We have a few hours to make this plan happen—breaking up is the only way to do it."

"But we . . ." Grigg's eyes flickered to Nova. "Who will protect her?"

Nova shoved him with a half-hearted laugh. "She has a room full of people to do that."

"As if *she* needs protection," Qav murmured.

"When we go up against Leviathan, I don't want any of you near that battle," Avery explained. "She can control Reanges—that makes everyone in this room a liability. I'll need Qav close once I have the stone, and Syla's combat skills make her invaluable for the journey getting there."

Grigg crossed his arms, looking sullenly at Syla.

"But when we get there . . ." Avery knew none of them would like the truth she was about to deliver. "I'm going to face Leviathan alone."

Megan squeaked when Petra flinched.

"Like hell you are," Finn fumed.

"It's not like I haven't thought about this. Our priority is getting that stone off her neck. I can't focus on that if you all are in danger."

Megan sat forward. "Then Finn and I are your best defense. She can't hijack humans, Avery."

"We don't know that for sure," Avery countered. They hadn't gone into detail what they'd fond in the mines, but it weighed on her mind. "Leviathan already has Gran, and I won't put anyone else at risk. I lost all three of you once. I don't think I can handle that again—I won't."

"You don't get to decide that for us, sweetheart," Finn said quietly.

Avery looked up at him. His eyes were locked on her, dark and unmoving. He would not yield, not this time. Avery didn't have to feel his emotions to know that—if she even could open that part of her powers again. She was too exhausted to even attempt it.

"We need to rest," Finn said firmly. "*You* need more rest."

"Finn's right." Qav stood, moving to Avery's side and placing a heavy hand on her shoulder. "Without sleep, our biggest liability will be you."

Qav's eyes met Finn's over her head, and he quickly withdrew his hand from Avery.

As long as they agreed to divide their efforts, Avery would agree on her need for sleep. But as she and Finn entered one of the three bedrooms, Avery lingered in the hallway, waiting for Petra. Finn and Megan shared a look before disappearing into their respective rooms.

Only Avery and Petra remained in the hall. She had always been comfortable in the silence.

But then, to Avery's surprise, Petra spoke first. "Your grandmother will hold her own, Avery."

It was Avery's turn to stay speechless. She was mortified by the moisture welling in her eyes.

Petra cleared her throat. "She's strong, like you. She won't break easily."

Avery nodded curtly, and Petra turned to her door.

"Wait," Avery said before she lost her nerve. "I just wanted to say that I—I'm sorry. For everything. I don't think I've said that to your face. And I owe you the apology."

Petra's jaw clenched. "You don't have to—"

"Yes. I do."

Petra had watched over everything that was dear to Avery. She had kept them all safe.

Avery took another shaking breath and released it.

"You have done so much for the people I love, Petra. You protected them—all of them—when I couldn't be there myself. When I hurt them. And that is a debt I will never be able to repay. I should have said as much the moment we arrived."

Petra's green eyes regarded Avery mischievously. "You were a little preoccupied with Finn's tongue down your throat."

Avery snorted out a shocked laugh. "I suppose I deserved that."

"Understatement." But beneath the single word, there was still pain. Still the stinging twinge of betrayal.

"I know I hurt you," Avery said softly. "I don't think I realized how badly until . . . But if you give me the chance, I will never let you down again."

Petra's grin softened into a bittersweet smile. "No one can promise that, Avery. Not even you." She took Avery's hand. "But thanks for at least pretending."

They'd finally reached some level of understanding, no matter how tenuous. It was a start.

The fresh silence that blanketed them was comfortable, a familiar remnant of the friendship that had once come so swiftly and easily to them.

As Petra entered her room to join Megan, Avery caught the door before it shut, watching as they leaned into one another.

"For the record . . ." Avery stated clearly. They both turned to look at her. "I'm glad that you found each other."

CHAPTER FORTY-NINE

Avery adjusted the sleek black chest plate of her armor, checking the placement of the gun on her hip for the tenth time. They were heading out into an active war zone, ill-equipped to deal with the threat that loomed above them in the skies and uncertain of what they'd find once they reached Leviathan.

Leviathan blamed Avery for Klein's attack; that much was clear from her actions in the Essence. She wanted to see Avery suffer—it was the whole reason she'd taken Gran hostage instead of just killing her outright, some desperate bid to bring Avery straight to her. But rage was a complex emotion, able to be both an element of fuel and of weakness. Avery hoped that baiting Leviathan would be enough to make her falter.

"It's just under nine miles to the capitol building," Finn said over his shoulder. He stared out the small window of the building's rear exit, scanning the streets for activity. "I'd feel safer in the tunnels."

"So would I." Petra knelt in front of Megan, checking the weapons she'd chosen for her. Two guns across Megan's back, a blaster on the thigh, and a knife in her boot—just in case. "But traveling aboveground is the fastest route."

Ennis looked over Avery's outfit, raising an appreciative brow. "Is that Cora's work?"

Avery nodded, smoothing a hand down the innovative fabric. It hadn't come with a manual, but she suspected it would protect her from gunshots, at least.

"You look good," Syla observed. She was never one to compliment style but definitely the first to admire function.

"Let's hope it does more than look good," Qav drawled. He leaned forward beside Finn, running his own analysis of the ground level outside. "It's been quiet for a while."

Avery could almost feel Finn's mind working as his eyes narrowed, taking in information, sorting through scenarios. He'd become a steady leader in his time on Echo, more than he'd ever been before. Watching the way he moved, the way the others followed him, even Petra . . . Avery was proud to claim a small part of the man he'd become.

It was just after midnight when they exited the sanctuary of their building and entered Milderion's empty streets. Avery wasn't certain the measly hour of rest they claimed was worth it. Although she'd plummeted into sleep on the ship, it had evaded her there. Even with Finn's heavy, warm arms anchoring her to reality.

It was completely dark. What moonlight had trickled between the skyscrapers before was now obscured by heavy cloud cover. The soft hum of the warships above filled the air with a haunting vibration that set Avery's teeth on edge.

It took them a quarter hour to reach the first major intersection. They paused in the shadows of the high-rise on the corner, kneeling together in the stillness.

"This is it," Nova whispered tightly. "We part ways here."

Avery nodded, her eyes moving over her friends. Markes grinned at her, his vibrant hair pale in the shadows. Linderly crouched beside her brother, with Tai on her other side. Avery wouldn't worry about the three of them—they were well trained and could handle themselves in a fight. They knew how to survive. But Megan . . .

She stared at Avery now with kind of secretive determination. Her hair was pulled back in a severe updo, her elegant fingers clutching her blaster. For nearly a year, Avery had been tormented by the possibility that Megan was dead. If anything happened to her, Avery didn't know if she could handle such loss again.

But Nova and Grigg would be with her, as they had sworn they would, to keep her safe. And Megan had Petra by her side. That would have to be enough.

Syla and Qav were already hauling away the massive drain plate from its seat in the adjacent alleyway. Qav tossed the metal onto the concrete and it clanged heavily, the sound ricocheting too loudly.

A raindrop hit Avery's cheek. It trailed coldly down past her chin. A few more landed on her scalp, teasing a coming storm.

"Great." Markes looked up to the sky. He held out a curious hand, catching the falling droplets. "Just what we need."

"Stay belowground just to cross the main roads. They'll only be monitoring the more trafficked areas," Finn reminded them, concealing his stress behind measured orders. He cupped a solid hand on Grigg's shoulder, squeezing. "Be smart. We'll see you on the other side of this."

Grigg gave Finn an exaggerated salute. "On your command, sir."

"Don't be an asshole."

"That's my line," Nova said, throwing Finn a salute of her own. She took off before he could shove her, disappearing down into the tunnels below.

Grigg laughed, winking at Avery as he followed. Markes was close on his heels, with Tai and Linderly just behind. Ennis brought up the rear with Megan and Petra, huddling around the opening as they waited for the others to descend.

They barely had any warning, no more than a soft mechanical buzzing on the tail of an unnatural breeze.

The drone appeared from the shadows in a white blur too fast to follow. Blastfire rained down on them, littering the ground with its assault, sending chunks of concrete flying between flashes of bright blue.

Finn slammed Avery to the ground just as a smoking hole eviscerated the wall behind her. Someone cried out in pain, the sound high and unfamiliar.

A shot tore through Ennis's shoulder, sending a shocking blast of agony straight through Avery.

"Ennis!" Qav screamed, fear freezing him.

But Ennis lay there, writhing in the street, while Petra and Megan struggled to pull her to her feet.

Avery was already up. She swept a hand toward Ennis, sending her crumpled form to the safety of the hole, where Grigg caught her.

The drone swiveled to Avery, setting its sights on a new target.

"No!" But Finn's cry came too late.

Megan screamed.

Avery took the blast straight to her chest. The force sent her flying backward, throwing her into the concrete wall with enough force to shake its foundation. She saw stars, gasping for breath as she slid to the ground.

Finn stumbled to her side, running his hands over her to check her wound. He hissed, recoiling.

"I'm fine," Avery managed, scrambling to her knees. She forced air into her lungs. The armor had done its job; its fine layer of tech fabric had shielded her from the blastfire. It sizzled as errant drops of rain pelted her, the surface too hot to touch.

Petra and Megan hesitated by the tunnel entrance, immobile from Avery's brush with death. The drone shot toward them and fired at their feet, collapsing the tunnel. Petra and Megan dove out of the way just before it pivoted again. It was following them, drawn to their movement.

"Hey!" Qav stalked out into the street. He kept Syla pinned to the wall with a flick of his wrist.

The drone spun, the small white sphere visible now that it had stopped to hover over them. The blinking red light on its sensor pointed straight at Qav.

He swung his hands in front of him, his white hair lifting around his face as he channeled his power. But he ignored the drone. Petra and Megan rose from the ground, tumbling together haphazardly across the concrete and out of danger.

The drone fired at Qav.

Avery rolled to her feet, deflecting the blast. It careened into the nearest building, sending exploding concrete raining down around them. She clawed her hand, grabbing the drone and crushing it beneath the force of her will. The globe crumpled, crashing the ground with a heavy metallic clank. It rolled harmlessly into the main road.

Finn and Syla were already rounding the others close to the building wall, their eyes scanning the air. No one dared to even breathe.

And then they heard it: the same quiet buzzing that had heralded the first drone. Not one, but an entire fleet.

"We have to move," Finn said fiercely, his gun pointed up at the sky.

Megan's eyes were frantic. "But Ennis—"

"She'll be fine." Syla shared a pointed look with Qav.

Avery knew it as well, though it didn't make leaving their friends any easier. If that drone had seen them descend into the tunnels, then the Federation could send more after them. Avery reached out to Grigg and Nova, the bond between them still vibrant at such a short distance.

Don't turn back. The meager warning was all Avery could afford of her energy. As much as she longed to keep a full merge, her exhaustion made it a wasteful endeavor. Avery needed every ounce of strength for the fight that lay ahead.

Nova's reassuring voice filled her head. *We'll do our part, Avery. You do yours. Just keep going.*

"We need to get off the roads." Petra grabbed Megan's arm and shoved her ahead of the pack as they broke into a run.

They rounded the corner and came face-to-face with another white orb. Avery stepped ahead, dragging it to the ground, where it exploded at their feet, disabled before it could fire a single shot.

Behind them, the buzzing shifted, growing louder. There was no way to destroy one drone without alerting them all. Finn grabbed her hand and dragged Avery toward the others, who'd begun running again.

They followed Petra blindly as she wove through the streets, taking alleys and side streets with the expertise of someone who had spent the past year memorizing every detail of the city. Petra didn't slow until they reached a parking facility filled with abandoned cruisers, filing them into the stairwell. Its heavy door slammed shut with resounding finality, blocking them from the cold of the open-air structure.

Avery leaned against the wall, gripping her hands on her knees. Sweat coated her back, despite the cold. Megan dry-heaved in the corner. Finn panted, his blaster still out as he hovered near the door.

They waited in worried anticipation for the buzzing to grow closer. But there was nothing, only their echoing gasps of breath bouncing up the hard stairs as they fought to slow their hearts.

"This place was made with the mountain stone," Petra said, the only one of them that wasn't winded. "They won't be able to scan us."

Finn laughed, dropping his weapon to his side with relief.

"Inspired," Syla said appreciatively, leaning her head against the wall.

Finn slid to the ground and rested his elbows on his knees. "Not bad, Petra."

Qav was on Finn in the next second, dragging him up to his feet. "You didn't say there'd be drones."

"Qav!" Avery snapped, shoving him off Finn.

"He nearly got us killed!" Qav yelled, pointing an accusing finger at Finn. "Ennis is only alive from sheer luck!"

"You think I'd have risked any of us traveling top side if I knew there were blazing drones out there?" Finn snarled.

Avery stood between them, flaring her energy out to slam both of them against the wall on either side of the stairwell. "That's enough!"

Qav ripped away from Avery's power, pacing up the stairs, getting as much distance from Finn as he could manage. His fear for Ennis had driven him over the edge, making him lose his grip on that tight control.

"The feeling is mutual, pal," Finn muttered up at the stairs. He caught Avery glaring at him and raised a bemused eyebrow. He found Qav's outburst entertaining—of course he did.

"The others will be fine," Avery said resolutely. Any other option was unbearable to consider. "They know the city as well as any of us. They know the mission, and they'll continue on it. We have to continue on ours."

"Avery's right," Megan agreed, finally able to stand. "This is a setback, nothing more. At least we're together."

Avery eyed her, recognizing the determination in her expression. "You're not coming with us, Megan. That part of the plan remains unchanged."

"We don't exactly have a choice anymore. What are you going to do, lock me in this stairwell?"

"If that's what it takes."

"You may be able to force the others to do your bidding, but you can't with me—not yet." Megan crossed her arms over her chest. "And until then, I'll do what I want, when I want."

Qav's eyes sharpened. He didn't miss the double meaning in Megan's words. They hadn't told him or any of the others what they'd found in those mines. It would only distract them—especially Qav. But now she wondered if that had been the right choice.

Frustration curdled through Avery, making her lightheaded. The walls around them began to vibrate, and the metal door shook on its hinges.

"Easy." Finn took her hand, his thumb stroking over her skin. "Maybe you need to listen to her. They don't have a chance at catching up with the others. You don't want them out there on the streets alone."

Avery closed her eyes, pulling the energy back. She focused on the chilly air, bright and stinging in her lungs. She listened to the slow patter of the rain that was just beginning to fall, reaching them even through the thick walls.

She turned to Petra. "And you? Are you on board with this?"

Petra shrugged. She gave in to a small smile. "Megan can handle herself."

Megan smiled too, stepping closer to Petra. Fabulous—Avery would get no support there.

"Besides," Petra added, "I'd like to see you ruin Leviathan once and for all."

Avery gritted her teeth. But she had promised to listen to them, to never stand in the way of their own choices, of their own will. And that included Megan.

"Fine," Avery said at last. "But you stick to Petra's side like glue."

"What do you know, that's my preferred position anyway."

Finn made a gagging noise.

Avery ignored them. "Remember—once we're in that building, none of you come out unless absolutely necessary. This is a fight for me first, Qav if needed, and the rest of you as a last resort."

"You gave into her? Just like that?" Syla laughed, bewildered. She turned to hiss up at Qav, "See, this is the kind of communication we need."

He rolled his eyes. "I'll make a note to bring it up with Rem when we get home. Weekly meetings where you all can boss me around and I graciously refuse to use my own powers to prevent it."

Syla gave him a feline grin. "Perfect."

Finn eyed Qav. "If you're done sulking up there, we need to make a new plan. We've still got seven miles to cover and a hoard of drones out there trying to hunt us down."

"So no pressure," Petra added.

Petra's attempt to lighten the mood delighted Avery in its novelty. Finn really had rubbed off on her. Megan's eyes crinkled with amusement as she shared a knowing look with Avery. It was enough to melt away terror of not knowing what would happen in the hours ahead.

Standing there in that cold stairwell with incredible odds against them, Avery was struck with a strange thought: maybe being together *would* be enough.

CHAPTER FIFTY

The rain turned into a steady, freezing downpour.

Avery walked alone down the throughway that lead to the capitol building, her hair soaked straight through from the frigid deluge. But thanks to her armor, the rest of Avery stayed blissfully warm and dry. The fabric didn't just deflect blastfire—it was waterproof as well, conserving every ounce of valuable body heat. If she'd known that, Avery would have donned it before exploring the coast.

A sharp breeze sliced through the buildings, sending raindrops stinging the sides of her face. Avery held her head high and kept her pace steady, focusing on the tall white columns ahead. The anti-human banners she'd seen last year still hung there, tattered fabric that snapped loudly beneath the thrumming sound of the rain.

The smell of wet smoke carried on the wind, agitating her nostrils. Despite the rain, many of the buildings were still burning. The sky above glowed orange while the vibrant neon lights that Milderion was known for were completely absent.

There was no reason for Avery to hide anymore. She opened herself and her power to the building before her, stalking toward it with one sole purpose: to force Leviathan into action. If the stone was driving her mad, all the better. Destroying Avery was her obsession. There was no way Leviathan could resist the temptation of Avery simply waltzing up to the front door. The power-hungry So' would welcome her inside with glee, hoping to devour her whole.

A loud explosion rocked the ground beneath her, reverberating throughout the entire city. Avery glanced toward the sky, searching for the source of the attack. Finn had been so sure the Federation would hold off its assault until morning—had they miscalculated?

Markes. Avery could feel him somehow. Even if she wasn't connected to the merge with her friends, she knew he was in pain. Something had happened—something bad.

Focus, Avery. Qav's missive reached her, urging her forward. He was deliberately going against their plan by opening their connection—Leviathan would hear him, would feel him.

Avery cut off the bond, shutting out whatever was happening to the others along with Qav. She had to trust that they would be all right, that they knew what they were doing as much as she did.

As she passed the last block, she could sense both him and Syla lingering in the shadows to the south. And on the north, Petra. Megan and Finn would be with her, even if Avery couldn't feel their presence. No matter how hard she tried, Avery couldn't bring back the human connection she'd unveiled. She felt its lack bitterly, especially with an entire army of humans overhead.

But it would do no good to Avery if she didn't have the strength to wield it. Even the adrenaline pumping through her veins wasn't enough to keep Avery from feeling the weight of her exhaustion.

Avery looked up at the warships. They would be monitoring the main roads. Klein would see Avery enter the capitol building. With any luck, it would keep their eyes off the movement of the others across the city. The Federation wouldn't know they had a real fight on their hands until it was too late.

She climbed the steps of the capitol, finally escaping the rain. Four guards stood watch by the grand doors, unaware of her approach until she was already stalking out of the shadows. They jumped, raising their weapons just as she stepped into the light.

But then their guns dropped, clanging uselessly at their feet. And in their eyes, their resolve was broken. Avery could feel their fear, sharp and potent, blending strangely with something like . . . hope.

They recognized her. They were *aware.*

Those guards were in full control of their own minds, not just toys for Leviathan to command. Avery hadn't expected that.

"You're here," the man in the center gasped, tears filling his pale green eyes. He fell to his knees.

Another knelt beside him, placing her hand on his shoulder. "I told you she would come," she said quietly. She looked up at Avery, hope lighting her face. "I knew you would come."

The final two stepped aside as she approached, bowing their heads. They had been left untouched by Leviathan, completely unaffected. What kind of trick was this?

Avery couldn't warn the others. She could feel Leviathan's hard presence lingering at the edge of her awareness. If Avery reached out to Qav then, Leviathan would see him for sure. Avery needed him to sneak into the building undetected—she was counting on it for their plan to succeed. As long as she kept Leviathan's eyes on her, the misdirection would work. It had to.

The enormous hall of the capitol entrance was quiet and empty, long shadows stretching across the white tile against the dim generator lighting. Each step of Avery's boots clunked loudly, their soles squeaking on the slick floor.

Gran was there. Even with Avery's new powers barely formed, her connection to Gran was immediate. Avery knew Gran's energy as well as her own, even if it was a faint glimmer in the recesses of her mind.

I expected you to come sooner. Leviathan's voice, seething and restless, filled Avery's thoughts.

The barest hint of movement shifted in the shadows. Soldiers were stationed along the walls, silent and still in their uniforms. Avery hadn't felt them at all—their presence had been shielded. Their eyes were blank. They stood in perfect formation, puppets waiting for their strings to be pulled.

Avery shuddered with rage, her hands balling into fists.

How many of those Reanges felt like the ones outside? How many wanted no part of Leviathan's schemes? They were no more than innocents—they had no choice in this, no free will. They were as helpless as Avery had once been beneath Qav's influence. But worse than that, they had no awareness. Leviathan had taken that from them, along with the hope of saving their world.

Her anger burned, kindling into a fury that scorched her belly, sharp and stinging until she saw white. And Avery welcomed it, letting the wrath flow through her, letting it stoke the embers of her power that had burned low from weariness.

Avery strode past the Reanges toward the towering entrance of the Council room. She threw out a hand and the heavy doors burst open, pounding thunderously against the walls. Avery stalked across the threshold.

Leviathan barely moved in her chair, a great monstrosity of cold white marble that elevated her above the other Council members. What was left of her Elders sat along the table that ran the length of the chamber.

It was no chair—it was a throne.

Instead of reinforcing Leviathan's dominance, the gargantuan seat had the opposite effect, overwhelming her slight form. Leviathan was thinner than Avery remembered, no more than a collection of bones held together by thin, pale skin. Her white robes did little to conceal how frail she had become.

In the arena, only days ago, Leviathan had seemed younger. Or, at the very least, invigorated. The Essence had seen to that.

But now . . . it was as if she had aged decades.

And her eyes—they glowed so brightly as to make them unsettling, magenta orbs set in the deepened sockets of her skull. Perhaps Mylan had been right. The power of the Essence was enough to waste the body away—even a So'.

"Typical of you to barge in here like a heathen," Leviathan croaked, her voice ragged and spent.

"You know I never like to disappoint," Avery said casually. She glanced down at the folds of Leviathan's robes, searching for her target, unable to feel its call. Avery truly was weaker than she realized . . . She would need Qav before this was over.

"Humor—how base." Leviathan shifted in her throne, as though it made her uncomfortable to stay still for too long. "I suppose that human of yours continues to influence you poorly."

"I heard that human of mine has been making your life difficult."

Leviathan glared. "No more difficult than a fly finding its way into my food."

"That showcase you were in the middle of in the arena suggests otherwise." Avery smiled, tilting her head and channeling Qav's nonchalant indifference alongside Finn's nagging humor.

Avery tucked hair behind her ear, letting her eyes dart over the Council members. There were only six left. Half of them were shaking, staring down at the table in abject terror. The other half sported the same blank stares as the guards in the hall.

A woman with pink hair looked up at Avery—Milupe. She had once been a leading voice at that very table. She had been someone Avery trusted, ushering them down a path toward freedom, alongside Earth. And she was fully aware, staring at Avery with a ferocity that revealed an enormous truth: Leviathan held less power than she portrayed.

Another explosion boomed, rocking the building. Bits of stone tumbled down the walls, crashing harmlessly to the floor.

The lights flickered, lurching back to life as the power came back online. The enormous glass chandelier overhead glowed brightly, casting them all in its pale orange glare. Leviathan squinted.

Avery's pulse ricocheted wildly. Linderly and Tai must have been successful on their mission. That meant they were still moving—the others would be at the armory. Their plan was falling into place.

"We expected you much earlier. Silly, emotional thing that you are, I thought my incentives would be enough to bring you running," Leviathan crowed on, her thin fingers clinging to the cane that leaned against her legs. "Don't say Krez took his life for nothing."

Wrath coiled in Avery's gut, spiking painfully through her veins. Her power surged, desperate for an outlet, but Avery held fast. Electric tendrils sparked along her fingertips, tingling her nails. Avery would stick to the plan, no matter how badly she wanted to slam Leviathan's face into the end of that cane.

Qav and the others would be there soon.

Avery ran a casual finger across the table as she walked around it.

"I love what you've done with the place. It needed a little renovation after the state I left it in."

"Yes, you have a penchant for destruction in your little outbursts. Even with your friends on Earth."

Avery looked up sharply. There was no way Leviathan could know about what Avery did to Qav—of how she destroyed his home.

"Let's not be coy, Avery." It was Leviathan's turn to smile. "Did you think I wouldn't know? Did you think I would destroy that Gate without a way to keep tabs on the human activity? They are far too cunning a species to ignore entirely."

Avery froze, trying to piece together what Leviathan was saying. "Then you knew? You knew Klein would bring the Federation here and still you sat and did nothing? You let those Council members die—"

"They went against my orders!" Leviathan shouted, her neon eyes wild. "I warned them—I tried to maintain my hold, but I couldn't stop them. Your crafty little tsek did his work well."

Avery blanched. Leviathan knew about Qav—maybe she had known all along.

"I didn't stop Klein because I couldn't," Leviathan revealed bitterly. "Without Mylan, my flow of information from the other side ceased to exist. This is your fault, Avery Vey, in more ways than one. You and those friends of yours have brought about our doom."

Mylan had been the connection to Earth. The messages the engineer had intercepted . . . They had been his all along. He had sent Krez away just when Avery had made her journey back through the second Gate. *Mylan had known she was coming back.*

Which meant he also knew Klein would have been ready to follow them. Had he sent Avery into those mines to give the planet to the Federation?

No—Avery couldn't believe that. Mylan had been sincere with her. Whatever plans he laid, they were always in service to Echo. And Leviathan was no longer fit to counter the might of the Federation— he had hidden Avery's return from her. Mylan had sent her into the mines with the hope she would find what she needed to take on an entire army.

But Avery had failed even him.

"I can see your mind working, girl. You've always struggled to grasp the bigger picture," Leviathan goaded. "Another sign I should have taken that you were not fit to rule. You never were."

"The So'Reanges are not meant to rule," Avery bit out.

Leviathan waved a thin hand. "A minor technicality. Reanges have struggled against our oppressors without success for far too long. It is time for a different approach: they need to be governed."

"Controlled, you mean," Avery clarified. "You never wanted to lead the Reanges. All you've ever wanted was obedience. Even from me."

"Oh, especially from you." Leviathan's lips twisted, her eyes turning monstrous. "And you were my greatest disappointment. You refused to give up your pets, no matter how hard I tried to shake them from your grasp. And just when I thought I had finally rid our planet of your nuisance forever . . . You barreled straight back with your usual flair, ready to destroy everything that was never yours to begin with!"

She slammed her cane down, the force cracking the floor in a fractured line down the center of the room. The walls shuddered, from Leviathan's ire or another Federation bomb, Avery couldn't tell.

Someone whimpered. Behind the throne, a group of hostages sat on the floor. Their hands were tied in front of them, their heads low as they huddled together. Two Reange soldiers stood over them, their guns trained on only one human.

Gran.

One of her eyes was nearly swollen shut. The gash on her head had dried, leaving a dark trail of crust down the side of her face. She wore a pained expression, her gray eyes trying to convey something to Avery without words. She looked . . . vulnerable. In a way Avery hadn't seen since she'd rescued them both from torture under Klein's orders on the Port Station two years ago.

It was Gran's vulnerability alone—not Leviathan's ranting or shows of power—that finally rattled Avery. Sweat beaded on the back of her neck, her limbs going cold.

"Ah, I see you've noticed my little menagerie." Leviathan looked over her shoulder. "After the first wave of attacks, my soldiers found a few human fugitives loitering around our wounded. Unsurprisingly, your grandmother was with them. And dear Krez, of course. But then, you already knew that."

One of the humans whimpered again. Gran shushed her, pressing her bound hands against the girl's shoulder.

"Let them go," Avery demanded gravely. Power ran beneath her skin like lightning, her hands shaking with the leashed energy. She took another step closer to Leviathan. The floor beneath their feet rattled. The chandelier flickered.

"Stop that!" Leviathan snapped. She slammed her cane into the tile once more, her own energy clashing against Avery, trying to worm inside. But the attempt was hardly an attack. Leviathan was weak.

Avery batted Leviathan away, rearing back as she studied the older So' anew. Her eyes dropped to Leviathan's neck, searching for the stone she had once worn so proudly over her chest.

Leviathan frowned, reaching out a bony finger toward the hostages.

Avery reacted on instinct, throwing out her hand to send a solid barrier around Gran.

One of the soldiers lifted his gun and took aim.

The young girl beside Gran didn't see the shot coming. Gran cried out as blood sprayed across her face, her mouth falling open in a silent scream of horror. The girl's body slumped lifelessly into Gran's lap.

Avery froze—she had miscalculated horribly. Gran hadn't been Leviathan's target.

That girl had been one of the humans from Nos Lenti, a part of the first group Finn and the others had saved. She had been brave enough to follow them into the city, willing to risk her life to help. Just a few nights earlier, Avery had watched her dance for hours, laughing along with the others.

Leviathan lifted her hand again.

"Stop!" Avery yelled, bringing the burning desire to unleash her power under control. The hall returned to stillness.

In the group of hostages, a man cried, doing his best to stifle his sobs. Gran lowered the girl's body to the floor.

Avery turned to Leviathan. "What exactly do you want from me?"

Leviathan stood, hobbling down the riser of her throne, until she stood just a few feet away. Face-to-face at last.

"I want you to be free of your childish attachment to these . . . lesser beings. I want you to be free of the emotions that hold you back."

Ready? Qav's query was the barest of a whisper in the back of Avery's mind, the mere shade of a thought.

Avery kept her eyes on Leviathan's. She wouldn't glance at the empty place on Leviathan's chest. She wouldn't consider what that meant. She wouldn't worry about why Leviathan's attack had been so weak or why she looked like walking death.

"Lesser beings?" Avery repeated in disbelief. "Is that what you think? That our powers somehow make us superior to them?"

"I know it. Your pathetic obsession with the humans needs to end. Look at what it has cost us—look outside these doors! Our city has been ravaged when we should have been free! Humans have ruined us. They have taken and taken and taken, until there is nothing left! They're no more than beasts, deserving of whatever comes to them. I'm only sorry I let the Council talk me out of the mass execution when I had the chance."

"Can't you hear yourself? You're no better than Klein!" Avery yelled. "After a hundred years of conflict, true peace was finally—"

"I don't want peace!" Leviathan's voice cracked. "I want our people to be *free*. I want them to be *safe*. I want them to be—"

"Completely under your control," Avery finished. "Look at what you've done to them! Just look at the people in this room. Is this the way of the So'Reange? To frighten your own council into submission and make the rest catatonic? You can't honestly think that's the future of Echo."

"I won't justify my choices to a child." Leviathan grabbed Avery, her fingers like spikes in Avery's arm as she snarled, "This is only way to ensure the continuation of our species. It is the only way to restore Echo to its glory."

Avery let Leviathan keep her hand there. She was fully distracted, her eyes only on Avery.

"Mylan was right," Avery taunted. "That stone truly has driven you mad."

Leviathan recoiled, the realization that Mylan had turned against her hitting somewhere soft. But she gathered herself in the next breath, dipping her chin with resolve.

"You think I've gone insane?" Leviathan cackled. "Child, the only one mad here is you."

"Finally, something we can agree on." Finn appeared from nowhere—not even Avery had noticed his stealthy approach—grabbing Leviathan's arms and wrenching her away from Avery. "Now!"

Qav wrapped his fingers around Leviathan's skull, forcing her to meet his eyes. He only needed to subdue her long enough for Finn to remove the necklace. She clawed at them, writhing against them both as they brought her to the floor.

Avery plunged headfirst into the guards, ordering them to drop their blasters. The clanging of a dozen weapons hitting the tile told her Leviathan had already released them.

"Avery . . ." Qav's voice was questioning as Leviathan slid to the floor beneath him. She had gone limp, slackening under his power. Qav looked up at Avery, his silver eyes wide. Worried. But he already knew.

"Where is it?" Finn boomed, his fingers running panicked over Leviathan's billowing ivory robes. "Avery? Where is it?"

Avery dropped to her knees, pillaging Leviathan's robes herself.

Behind them, Petra and Syla urged Council members to their feet. Megan ran to Gran and cut her bonds, gathering blasters as she went, supplying them with weapons of their own.

Avery fumbled through fabric, reaching out desperately for the familiar pull that had been so vibrant. They had to find it quickly. Once Qav lost his control over Leviathan, she would be unstoppable—

They heard the deafening blast of the bomb just before its explosion rocked the building. The ceiling of the hall gave way, collapsing onto them.

The Federation had decided to resume their attack after all.

CHAPTER FIFTY-ONE

Finn launched himself at Avery, taking them both to the ground and shielding her from the falling debris. She was too distracted, or too tired, to throw up a barrier.

Qav grunted when a hunk of concrete hit his shoulder, flinging him away from Leviathan and onto his back. The old woman fell, disoriented and immobile.

"Finn!" Petra shouted, pointing up.

A huge piece of the roof swung precariously, only attached by a few wires sparking furiously in the rain. It dropped in the next breath. Finn tucked Avery into him, rolling them both across the floor in a jarring clamor of limbs.

The heavy stone crushed Leviathan with a colossal, resounding thud.

"No!" Avery screamed, coming to her knees.

She clawed her hands out, ripping the piece away from Leviathan, sending it flying into the wall. Leviathan's body was still, her white robes stained bloody and drenched from the rain.

Megan yelped behind them. She and Dr. Vey struggled against the other humans who had risen to their feet in a frenzied rush with their weapons, taking aim at the retreating Council members—at Petra and Syla leading them.

"Petra!" Finn warned.

She looked over her shoulder, her green eyes widening in horror. The humans fired.

Milupe fell, along with two others, their bodies lifeless on the ground. Syla took a shot to the shoulder, raising her weapon to fire back.

"No!" Qav was on his feet again. He twisted his hand out to Syla, halting her movements, preventing her from shooting.

She looked at him in shock, pink hair falling across her forehead. But when the humans fired again, the blasts bounced away harmlessly beneath the shield Avery had placed in front of her.

Finn stared at Qav in confusion. Had he just saved *humans*? From Syla?

But the humans didn't stop—they pressed forward without mercy, out of Megan and Dr. Vey's reach, intent on finishing what they started. As though they had lost their minds.

Avery lurched to her feet to stop them.

"Wait!" Finn grabbed her arm. He jerked his chin to the ship descending through the massive hole above.

Avery pivoted back to the Council members and swiped both hands through the air. The enormous table flipped on its side, swiveling across the tile in a riotous screech, providing the perfect barrier from the humans' attack. Syla and Petra gathered the survivors and crouched behind, safe.

The humans kept their advance, pushing forward with a dogged determination Finn had never seen. He knew three of them—he had rescued all three on the same run from Milderion months ago. They would never unleash that kind of violence without cause. And besides that, they didn't have the skills. They'd barely finished training to just defend the village.

"It's Nick," Avery said raggedly beside him. Her breath came in pants as the cruiser slowly dropped toward them. Her strength was already meeting its limits.

Finn's pulse skyrocketed, blood rushing loudly in his ears. "What?"

"The humans," Avery said quickly. "They're not themselves. They're not in control."

"You think Nick is doing this? *Can* he do this?"

Avery shook her head, her eyes flickering to Leviathan. To Gran.

"He couldn't control minds before—something must have changed."

"That hybrid bastard just doesn't give up, does he?" Qav wiped blood from the corner of his mouth as he limped to their side. "Take down the ship, Avery."

"What? I—I can't."

"You've done it before. In the desert on Earth."

"She wasn't running on zero sleep," Finn argued. "And if she brings it down in here, the explosion will kill us all."

"I don't have to bring it down," Avery reasoned cryptically, lifting her hands. Her fingers stiffened as she braced her feet, focusing all her power on her target. And incredibly, the hulking black vessel halted in the air. Her arms started to shake, her face contorting with effort.

The ship began to lift away, moving back the way it came.

The human survivors behind them dropped their weapons. They straightened, staring at one another in confusion. Syla and Petra leaped the barrier, subduing them in case of another attack.

But the ship had reversed course again, dropping swiftly despite Avery's efforts.

She let out a frustrated yowl, taking two stilted steps forward. A slow trickle of blood seeped out of her nose, running down the edge of her lip.

Finn's chest tightened with panic. Avery would never last—she needed that stone or they'd all be dead. He looked to the ship, trying to see through the black windows of its bridge. He knew Nick would be there—waiting for him.

If Nick had one constant, it was his desire to have Finn by his side. Even in the Sanctum, when he'd invaded Qav's home and killed hundreds with his Federation forces in tow, it had only ever been for Finn.

Which meant Finn was the best distraction they could ask for.

"It's me he wants!" Finn said frantically. "I can draw him away from here. Give you time to find the stone."

"No, Finn—"

"It's the only option we've got right now, sweetheart!" He backed away from her, already moving on his plan. "Just keep him busy!"

Finn found a route up the carnage of the building, climbing the debris until he reached the top. The stone was freezing beneath his fingers, wet from the icy rain that soaked him to the bone and set his teeth chattering.

Finn crawled onto the roof, standing just above the vessel as he pulled around the blaster he'd strapped to his back. He looked down its sights, ready to fire—

"That's your plan? Shoot at him? You might as well throw a rock."

Finn jumped out of his skin, swinging his weapon toward the intruder.

Qav pulled himself up onto the roof with a grunt. He was out of breath, his white hair wet and stringing.

"You followed me?" Finn snarled. The last thing he needed was some out-of-shape asshole he didn't trust slowing him down.

"Somebody has to help you," Qav said, his silver eyes darkening. "Or did you plan on taking down an entire cruiser with your little gun?"

"Fine. Just stay out of my way." Finn faced his target and fired.

At that moment, an awareness ran straight through him that made him shiver. He was certain that he'd felt Nick turn to look at him from behind the opaque glass. And then the cruiser rose away from Avery, back up through the roof. It pivoted, facing Finn and Qav as they began to back away.

"Okay," Qav said warily. "What's your big plan now?"

Finn shrugged, turning to run. "This is where I usually wing it!"

He took off across the roof at a full sprint, his boots struggling to grip the slick roof in the rain. Surprisingly, Qav kept pace with him. The ship was close on their tail, its engines roaring over the heavily pelting downpour.

When they jumped in tandem over the edge of the building, down toward the street thirty-some feet below, Finn trusted that Qav would buffer them safely to the ground.

Which he did. Mostly.

CHAPTER FIFTY-TWO

Avery watched with her heart in her throat as the ship cleared the roof and pulled away into the storm. She had to let them go.

Protect him, she begged Qav.

Avery saw through his eyes as they careened off the roof, tumbling down across the ground in a rough landing that Qav scarcely cushioned.

Who's going to protect me? Qav asked her bitterly as he rolled to his feet and took off after Finn.

Avery released a shaking breath, letting the connection fade. Then she ran to Leviathan's side, dropping to her knees. There was so much blood. It pooled around her torso, mingling with the water that had gathered in puddles beneath them. The entire bottom half of her body was crushed, nothing but a mangled mess of flesh beneath her robes.

But Leviathan was still alive. Barely.

Syla approached Avery from behind, drawing closer. Petra climbed over debris to join Megan and Gran by the far wall, out of danger.

"Stay away from her," Avery warned Syla, uncertain how much power Leviathan still had. Or what she was capable of.

Syla stilled, watching from a good distance away. Her laser knives were drawn at her sides, their electric white blades crackling against her thighs. She would not leave Avery undefended.

Leviathan's eyes were wide as she fought to haul in air. Avery ran a hand over her shuddering chest. It had all but caved in. Leviathan was dying.

"I need that stone, Leviathan," Avery said darkly. "You want to end this? You want Echo to be restored to what it once was? This is how we will do it."

Those glowing eyes wavered, but the power of speech was beyond Leviathan. Her mouth gaped as she tried to answer.

I need that stone. And you're not going to die until you give it to me.

Avery pressed her palm into Leviathan's wound, calling on whatever was left of her strength. It rose to her bidding, winding out and around Leviathan's body before seeping inside. Avery concentrated that feeling, focusing her healing only on Leviathan's lungs. Her ribs expanded. Her lungs sealed their punctures and filled with air.

Leviathan gasped, choking on her blood, crying out in pain.

Avery had only healed half of her.

"The stone," Leviathan said desperate gasps, "is the least of your worries now. I saw those humans—Klein finally did it." She sobbed. "They will be just like us."

"They always were. More than you ever let on."

Leviathan's eyes rolled back, a wave of pain taking her before she grasped for Avery's hands. "What did Mylan tell you?" she screeched. "What did he tell you?"

I think you know.

And Avery pulled Leviathan into her memories, forcing her to face everything she had seen in those mines. To feel everything she had felt while immobile and minuscule within the vast existence of the true Essence, every terrible and overwhelming second. She would not let Leviathan hide from the truth of the Reanges and how they came to be. She would not let her lie to herself any longer.

Leviathan cried out pitifully, feebly pulling away from Avery. She fell into another fit of wet coughing before revealing a horrible truth of her own.

"There is no stone anymore, girl. I destroyed it myself."

"What?" Avery breathed, dread sinking like lead in her stomach.

But Avery had known. She'd been lying to herself, too. Hoping her own instincts had been wrong.

Avery had known from the moment she'd been able to bat away Leviathan's first attack.

That stone had been their only hope at defeating the Federation, at saving the thousands of innocents that would die on Klein's orders to invade. Without it, Avery would have nothing to amplify her power.

Whatever she and Qav could pull together, it wouldn't be enough. Not against an army that large. Half the city would die in the attempt if they even tried.

"How could you?" Avery's voice shook as she rocked back on her knees. And then she screamed it. "How could you?!"

"I wasn't going to die before seeing my world set to rights." Leviathan dropped her head, her eyes focusing on something beyond Avery, their neon depths dimming, filling with tears. "It's too late now. It's too late. She will take Echo from us once and for all. And our people will cease to exist. I failed." Tears ran down her hollowed cheeks, her voice diminishing into a faint whisper. "I failed."

"You didn't trust me, Leviathan. You refused to let go of your power, even when your time was over," Avery said fiercely. She leaned in close until she was certain Leviathan could see her. "Well it's my turn, now. And I don't intend to waste it."

Avery's tears fell onto Leviathan's cheeks, both mingling together. But Avery hadn't finished.

I will watch you die here and now. And I will never think of you again except to warn myself of what not to become.

Leviathan laughed, choking on her own blood. Behind thin lips, her teeth were stained red. *Good girl.*

Avery took her hand. Leviathan's thin fingers were pure ice. She stared up into the falling rain, her eyes dimming until they were nothing more than a dull purple in the stillness of death.

And at the end, Leviathan had the final word at last.

CHAPTER
FIFTY-THREE

Qav ran with Finn through rain so heavy they could only see a few feet ahead. He steadied their strides, urging them on with unnatural speed through the city. But he was freezing, his muscles already spasming in the cold, wet weather.

"We have to get Nick out of there!" Qav yelled through the rain, aware of the black cruiser bearing down on their heels. "We'll never outrun him while he's inside that ship!"

Finn took a corner, sliding across the pavement as they changed course. Qav barely had time to follow his lead. The ship fell behind, its momentum struggling to pivot so easily.

Finn didn't slow. He pushed into a sprint, trying to put more distance between them. "Can you take it down?"

"Not the whole thing. But I can get you a clear—"

As if Nick could hear them planning, the massive vessel behind shot a round of blastfire at their feet.

They dove away from one another, tumbling roughly across the slick street. Qav's arm screamed in pain as he landed, his earlier break still tender. Avery had not been able to heal him completely.

Qav hesitated, fear paralyzing him in a daze. His attention was pulled between this fight and the one he'd just left. Would Avery be able to handle herself against Leviathan alone? What if he had left her to face her death? The old woman had been weak, almost comically so, but perhaps it had been a ruse.

And on the other side of the city, Ennis was fighting for her own life. Nova had patched up her wound enough that she could stand with the others—but they had drawn enough attention to be facing a battle or their own.

At least she was still alive. They were all still alive.

Finn struggled to his feet with a pained yowl, dealing with some injury of his own.

Qav cut off his connection to the others—his commitment was here. Helping Finn would free Avery to focus on her own fight. Whether he liked it or not, Qav was bound by his promise to keep this one stupid human alive.

The ship surged forward, coming at them faster than ever before.

Qav turned and sprinted straight for the ship, pushing off the street in a leap that launched him into the sky. He landed with a thud on the cold curves of the vessel, slipping wildly across its surface. Qav plunged a hand into the metal, his skin ripping with the force it took to break through the blast plates. But he held fast, even as the sheets of rain pelted his face, a thousand stinging needles made worse by their sheer velocity.

Finn turned to run, but he was slower than before. And Nick was no longer content with their game of pursuit.

Qav clawed his way toward the front of the ship, his fingers digging painfully into the metal with each haul of his body until at last he was just above the windows that wrapped around its nose.

"Now, Finn!" Qav screamed, praying he had heard him over the rain and the engines and the war raging on in the city beyond.

Finn would only have one chance to take his shot. Qav's own life hung in the balance of his success. He would have felt better with Ennis's impeccable aim behind the blaster, but Finn would have to be enough.

Qav vaulted his legs over, bringing his boots down onto the windshield with a heavy boost of energy. It cracked, still not enough.

Qav let out a primal scream and gathered power into his fists, energy crackling down his arms with flashes of white lightning. He slammed his bloodied hands into the windows.

They shattered completely.

Qav could only hold on to the broken glass as the ship careened toward Finn who faced them fully, motionless in the torrential downpour. His legs were braced, his blaster up on his shoulder, aiming for the bridge and his brother within.

But Finn's arms fell slack, his weapon dropping to the ground. His hands shook at his sides, his face contorting as he fought against some internal assault.

No—*no!*

Qav knew that look. He'd been the cause of it himself a thousand times.

At last, Finn lost himself, his eyes going completely blank.

But the ship was still headed straight for him—it would run him down.

Qav angled himself toward the bridge. Nick was similarly horrified, his brows drawn low and panicked as he leaned over the controls Qav had obliterated with his strike. He'd taken out the pilot, too, their body quickly soaking in a useless heap at Nick's feet.

Stupid. Qav should have been more precise. Even Nick wouldn't be able to slow the blazing ship down in time to save his own brother.

For the first time in his life, Qav acted without thinking.

He pushed off, vaulting himself toward Finn. They collided and Qav held fast, cushioning them with the shield of energy he'd seen Avery use a thousand times, just as the ship careened into them both, crushing them between tons of reinforced metal and the immovable concrete below.

Qav drifted in and out of awareness, agony dragging him blissfully into the loving arms of unconsciousness. When Finn stirred beside him, leaning over Qav to curse at his injuries, he at least had the satisfaction of knowing Finn would forever be in his debt.

None of that mattered anyway. Qav was only glad that he hadn't failed her.

A shadow moved behind Finn, rising from the fiery rubble engulfing them.

Qav's eyes widened—the only warning he could give.

But it was too late. Nick wrapped his hands around Finn's throat, dragging him to his feet.

"Did you think I wouldn't come for you, brother?" Nick sneered. Blood coated his teeth, trickling easily down his chin, over his rain-soaked skin.

"Was counting on it," Finn choked out. He clawed at Nick's hands, struggling to find his feet.

"You may have distracted me for a moment. But we'll return to your precious Avery soon enough," Nick promised ominously. His focus shifted to Qav, his image blurring.

Qav tried to lift his hand, pain searing his fingers and up his elbow. He had to do something. To try.

Nick chuckled, spitting blood onto the floor. He dropped Finn to his knees, slapping his face hard to enough to send Finn tumbling through burning debris.

But Finn didn't stay down. He rolled to his feet, ready to fight. His cheek was already turning black from the blow, swelling in the span of seconds. He charged at Nick with a raw cry, nothing but a shard of glass in his hand as a weapon.

Nick tilted his head and Finn halted entirely, as though hitting against an invisible blast door. His motions stilled. The glass dropped from his hand. His eyes turned blank once more.

Qav couldn't save him from this.

At last, Nick smiled. "It's about time you started listening to me."

"Avery," Syla warned.

Avery turned away from Leviathan's body as another ship approached from the open sky. This one was smaller than the last, painted the deep blue of the Federation. And on its door, the stamp of the Minister. It touched down on the rubble, settling into the Council room with a heavy lurch.

"Get behind me," Avery said, getting to her feet.

"Not a chance." Syla sheathed her blades for the huge blaster over her shoulder.

"Syla—"

"Qav told me not to leave you. And I won't."

The door to the cruiser slid open. It was too late to get them out. But as long as Nick didn't return, Avery could handle Klein. In fact, she would revel in mopping the floor with her.

"Avery," Klein crooned, like they were meeting at some official function instead of in the rubble of the city she'd decimated. She carried a rain deflector, the droplets cascading perfectly around her in an arc that kept each perfect blond wave of her hair from getting wet. "I've been looking for you everywhere. You seemed to have fallen entirely off the edge of this planet."

Avery said nothing.

Klein descended the small ramp in obnoxious white heels. They clicked loudly as she reached the ruined tile where she paused beside the fallen Elders. Milupe's pink hair spread out inches from her feet.

"Imagine my surprise," Klein continued, "when our scouts caught sight of *the* Avery Vey marching straight into the capitol all by herself. In the rain, no less. From one politician to another, make sure you have vid bots on you next time. Such a waste of truly superb footage."

Avery let her power crackle at her fingertips, sizzling against the water.

Klein glanced down at Avery's hands, seemingly amused.

"I'm no politician," Avery refuted.

"Oh, I think you are. You want to *change the worlds*. People follow you for that very conviction. And you've fooled them into imagining it possible."

"And you're a fool to come here so unprepared. Do you think I'm just going to let you walk away? After what you've done? These people are *innocent!* Why would you attack completely unprovoked?"

"Unprovoked?" Klein said in disbelief. She tilted her head, laughing strangely. "You and your planet destroyed the Gate—you killed thousands of people on Earth in the aftermath. This is a reasonable and justified reaction to that aggression."

"*You* were the one who tried to destroy the Gate, first. You wanted Earth at war with itself so you could slip away to take Echo for yourself and the precious few who can afford to pay their way in. And once Cora releases proof of your schemes to the world, everyone will finally see you for what you are."

Avery reached out to Qav. Leviathan was gone—there was no reason they shouldn't have merged already. She needed to know where Nick was, to prepare herself in case he came back. With the power to control minds, he could use the humans as collateral to get in her way.

But Qav was unreachable.

His cool energy was close, closer than she'd expected, but he was unconscious. She would be unable to connect with him in that state at all.

"Aw," Klein cooed. "Are we still operating under the assumption that humans will choose the higher path? Haven't you learned by now that we're all just mercenary little creatures out to survive? And trust me, humans want to survive—they want it more than anything else. Let me tell you something, Avery Vey." She stepped a few feet closer, tip toeing around the bodies beneath her. "I am excellent at survival."

"I've had enough of this bitch." Syla's blaster came up to her shoulder, and she took aim.

Klein raised her hand and jerked.

Syla went flying. She careened into the wall with a sickening thunk. She fell to the ground in a lifeless heap of limbs.

Avery didn't think. She bolted for Klein, leaping across heaps of rubble in one great arc to attack the woman who now had powers of her own.

CHAPTER FIFTY-FOUR

Klein's head snapped sideways as Avery connected her fist to that perfect jaw. Klein stumbled backward, tripping over a body and onto her knees into a pool of blood. But she was weaker than Nick. Klein wouldn't be able to go toe-to-toe with Avery—that was good.

Avery paused only long enough to feel for Syla. She was alive, but only just. Avery didn't have time to heal her and hold off Klein simultaneously. She doubted she'd even have enough strength to do both.

Pain rocked through Avery, doubling her over. But not her own—someone was injured badly. Nova or Grigg, she couldn't tell. They needed help, somewhere on the other side of the city. And Avery had none to spare.

She needed Qav. She needed the stone. But neither of those were an option.

Avery only had herself.

We can take her. It's not over yet. Petra's conviction hit Avery like a wave, blind determination fueling her. She had her gun trained on Klein, stalking forward, ready to shoot.

No! Avery pleaded. *I need you to get Megan and Gran out of here. Get them far away, Petra.*

Petra stopped, meeting Avery's eyes with uncertainty.

It wasn't going to end well, Avery knew that much. Klein had powers of her own, along with the might of an entire army behind her. Leviathan had obliterated their chances when she obliterated the stone.

But I can't just—

That's an order, Petra. Avery put the finality of the So' into the command.

Petra wouldn't have been able to argue, even if she tried. Whether she agreed or not, she would get Megan and Gran out or die trying.

Klein pushed unsteadily to her feet. The knees of her cream pants were stained red. It seeped up the ends of her jacket, like they'd been dipped in a vat of crimson dye. The rain protection glitched in and out, her hair going flat.

"Let's go, then," Avery taunted. She took two running steps and leaped, ready to deal another blow.

Something hit her midair, slamming into her side and flinging her across the room. Avery crashed into the table, the marble fissuring.

"It's about time," Klein chastised, her tone harsh and violent. "Why did you let him distract you?"

Avery pushed up to her feet, marveling again at the armor that had absorbed most of the impact. Still, she was out of breath and panting from the exertion. She barely had anything left to give.

Nick sauntered into the room, bending under the huge slab doors that hung haphazardly on their hinges. And behind him, Finn followed.

Finn held something in one arm, dragging a heap along the floor in his wake. A boot—pristine and custom and all too familiar. Qav's inanimate body was no more than a smear of white hair on the wet floor as Finn hauled him by his leg.

The world tilted on its axis.

"Finn?" Avery called out nervously. But she knew he wouldn't answer. His movements too perfect. Too methodical. Finn was gone.

He threw Qav's foot down, slinging his body haphazardly across the tile and into the rain.

"Poor Avery." Klein slicked her hair back. "No lover to save you. No allies to aid you. And by the look of your exhausted face, not much energy left to fight."

Avery let out a shaking breath, weighing her options. There was nothing she could do except stand her ground. She would not run.

Movement caught her eye—Qav's fingers had twitched. He was regaining consciousness but not fast enough. If she could get him back up and by her side, maybe they still had some kid of chance to get out of there alive.

She threw her power out to connect with every Reange she could reach. From the Council members cowering behind the fallen table to the soldiers Leviathan had left vacant in the halls.

Avery's mind surged across the city, calling to everyone who could hear her. Grigg and Tai were close, only a few blocks away, already heading for the capitol. Avery knew they would come to her summons, she knew they would all come.

The Council members rose, picking up errant weapons from the floor. Soldiers filed in, their blasters up and ready to shoot. The four who had let Avery pass the front steps appeared, their eyes bright and fierce, ready for battle.

Every Reange within a five block radius would be there soon, flooding the building with weapons and rage. Nick and Klein may have had powers over humans, but they couldn't touch the Reanges.

Now! Avery ordered.

The Reanges attacked, rushing headfirst into the fight against the two powerful humans. Avery coated them with energy, giving their bodies some protection as they fought in her stead. Avery closed her eyes, risking the vulnerability to concentrate.

She set her power to Qav, searching his physical form for injuries. His arm was fractured again. His brain swelled from some blow to the head. She'd never healed anyone from a distance before, and his wounds were complex enough to give her pause. But she had to try.

Avery opened herself to her power, letting it flow through her and across the room. Her skin began to glow, the raindrops falling around her catching the pale light as it arched out of her palm and through the dark straight into Qav. His face shimmered as her power spread throughout his skull.

Klein slammed into Avery, carrying them both into the wall. Avery's head cracked against the marble, stars shooting over her vision as she struggled to remain conscious.

"That's a neat trick," Klein hissed, her eyes feral as she shoved her forearm into Avery's neck.

The perfect Minister was gone, replaced by this crazed monster.

"Too bad it won't be enough." Klein tilted her head and brought every human in the room under her control.

They picked up the blasters that they'd dropped to the ground, and began to shoot.

Avery cried out. Her shields had fallen from the Reanges as she'd struggled to heal Qav—the shots found their targets. They dropped, one after the other from the attacks they never saw coming. Avery had been determined not to kill, sure that the Reanges could best the humans with sheer numbers alone. She'd foolishly forced them to focus solely on Nick and Klein.

Avery hadn't accounted for Klein's cruelty, for her utter disregard for life, Reange or otherwise.

Avery shoved Klein away with a scream. The woman went sliding, her heels digging into the floor as she steadied herself.

Avery's anger surged until electricity crackled across her skin, lifting her bodily from the floor. She hovered three feet above Klein, debris lifting and swirling around her like a storm of chaos in which Avery was the eye.

She would kill Klein. At last, she would end it.

Klein laughed, sizing Avery up. As though she was delighted to see the power that would one day be hers.

"I'm full of neat tricks, too!" Klein yelled over the storm that surrounded Avery. "Want to see another one?" She raised an elegant hand behind her, away from Avery entirely.

A shot rang out, louder than it should have been in the midst of all that noise.

"No!" Petra screamed, her voice strained and tearful. Her horror traveled up their bond and slammed Avery in the heart, squeezing out all the air in her chest.

Avery looked to the corner where Gran sprawled on the floor, a deep blast hole carved out of her chest.

Megan held a gun in both hands, still steaming in the wet air from the heat of the shot.

No.

No. No!

They weren't supposed to be there at all—they were supposed to be gone, safe and far away from all this.

Megan had shot Gran.

Blood pooled beneath her, too fast—entirely too fast. It surged in heavy spurts, in time with whatever was left of Gran's heart. Avery knew enough about healing to understand what it meant.

Avery lost her hold on the Reanges left in the room. She collapsed to the ground with the debris that had been storming around her.

Petra struggled with Megan, trying to wrestle the blaster from her hand, the same one she'd laughingly chosen for Megan only hours ago. The same one Petra had strapped to Megan's thigh herself.

But she was too gentle with Megan who threw Petra off with a feral scream. She whipped around, aiming the weapon straight for Avery.

The blast rang out for a second time.

But the shot was not for Avery.

It was for Finn.

CHAPTER FIFTY-FIVE

Avery screamed, whatever was left of her breaking in half as she whirled. She sent out a shield too late.

The shot hit its aim true, in perfect alignment with Finn's heart. Megan's months of training had finally paid off. A shot like that was tantamount to instantaneous death.

And it would have been. But Nick pushed his brother out of the way.

"Nick!" Klein screeched his name, her disbelief at war with her control.

Avery gaped as despair crested over her. There would be no more reinforcements coming to aid them. Somewhere in the midst of their fight, Klein had ordered the army overhead to resume its attack. Ships were landing all over the city, sending soldiers on foot out into the streets, into the homes. Not even weapons could save them now—the Federation troops were killing on sight.

And Avery was powerless to unite her people, she was powerless to stop their deaths. She couldn't get herself together. She had lost.

Nick fell to his knees, coughing up blood as he slumped into a puddle. Finn stood motionless behind him, a husk of his former self. Klein had taken over his control.

"Why?" Klein ground out, watching Nick crumple.

"I told you not to touch him," Nick wheezed, blood trickling down the side of his mouth. He pressed a hand to his abdomen, his eyes closing with a grimace. "We agreed."

And Finn wasn't there to see his brother die.

Avery tore herself away while Klein was distracted, stumbling over bits of charred rock and exposed wires. She slid to her knees beside Gran in the grime and blood.

A few feet away, Petra resumed her fight with Megan. The gun waved perilously between them, locked between both their hands.

Gran looked up at Avery, her eyes glassy and half closed. The wound in her chest was too big, a gaping hole that ran straight through. Avery tried to put pieces of her back together, her hands turning hot and wet with Gran's blood.

Avery sobbed, realizing she had nothing left. She could do nothing. And it was too late. Even if Avery had power she could use on Gran, the wound had been a killing blow.

Gran grasped Avery's hands clumsily, stopping her from trying.

"Save your strength," Gran slurred. A tear fell from her eye, rolling down and back into her gray braid. "How brave you are, Avie," Gran marveled, her voice going softer than Avery had ever heard it, her chest spasming as she fought against death. And at last, she shut her eyes, her last breath a single sentence. "How brave . . . you will be."

And then she was gone.

Avery stared blankly at Gran's body. Silent tears spilled from eyes she couldn't close, falling onto their still joined hands. Gran's fingers were already cold.

Gran was gone. Gran was *gone*.

Avery was hollow. Whatever light she clung to faded away with Gran's final breaths. A piece of her had been wrenched away, a more violent and jarring separation than she had ever thought possible. It hurt to breathe. Existing in the space of that moment was agony, tearing Avery's soul apart from the inside.

This had all started with Gran.

Avery had only left Earth in the first place to save her, to rescue her from Klein and the Federation.

And she had—*she had saved her.*

Why had Avery fought so hard for peace, why had she hoped so desperately for a world where humans and Reanges could live in harmony if this was the result?

Avery sucked in air through lungs that refuse to cooperate. Her chest was a vise, contracting her organs until she feared they would burst. She leaned over Gran, clinging to her, squeezing her eyes tightly against a silent scream.

Nearby Megan still attacked Petra who avoided every swing, doing her best not to harm the woman she loved.

But Avery felt nothing—there was nothing left inside her. No power. No feeling.

She looked over her shoulder to Klein who stood watching Avery shatter in the easing storm. She crossed her arms over her chest. And she smiled.

"Why?" Avery sobbed. "Why would you do this? She meant nothing to you—*nothing!*"

Klein lifted her chin, looking down at Avery through long beautiful lashes. "But she meant the world to you. And beyond securing this planet for our future, I will enjoy watching you break at last."

Petra yelped, a wet, gurgling sound that made Avery's gut wrench.

Megan had remembered the knife hidden in her boot and driven it straight into Petra's neck.

CHAPTER FIFTY-SIX

A very collapsed in on herself, like a dying star forming a black hole. It sucked in everything she was or would be, a whorling pit of destruction that promised to swallow her whole.

Blood spurted out around the knife in Petra's neck, covering Megan's face. She held it in place as Petra choked, her hands clinging to Megan's wrists.

Klein's heels clicked behind them as she walked away, heading for her cruiser. She crooked a finger at Finn. He meandered lifelessly behind her into the vessel, a new pawn for her personal use.

"I suppose one brother is as good as the next," she crooned. "Especially when they both look so much like their father."

Megan slipped the knife away and Petra fell to her knees, her fingers fumbling to her neck, her eyes wide. She stared at Avery as blood spurt through her fingers, drenching her arms in seconds.

Megan stood above them, staring at nothing. The knife hung by her side, dripping blood.

Avery couldn't breathe—she couldn't breathe. Klein had taken everything except Avery's life. And that, she feared, would be the worst punishment of all.

The knife clanged to the ground.

Megan's scream filled the room, a haunting cry that raked its fingernails across every surface. She fell to her knees, her thin fingers going to Petra's neck, trying to stanch the bleeding.

It wouldn't work. It was too late.

Megan finally saw Avery, her pale blue eyes wide and clear beneath a face painted red. She crawled over to Avery, glancing down once at Gran before grabbing Avery's shoulders.

"Avery!" Megan begged her name.

It reached Avery through a tunnel, somewhere far away. Avery could barely hear anything over the sound of her heartbeat slowing. Her vision blacked. Maybe she would die there anyway.

"Avery!" Megan shook her violently. "Damn it, Avery, snap out of it!" Megan screamed.

Megan hauled her arm out and slapped Avery with a force that whipped Avery's head back. She saw stars. The pain in her face traveled down her jaw and into her teeth, shocking her back into the present.

Avery looked down at Gran again, cold and lifeless. She looked at Petra, choking on her blood. And Megan, desperate and waiting on her knees before her.

Qav lay on the ground behind them, barely stirring. And Finn . . . Avery looked up at the silver cruiser pulling away with the only man she'd ever loved inside.

They needed her—her friends needed her. A warm pull called to her, sure and familiar.

She wasn't done yet.

Avery screamed, her soul wrenching out and away from her chest as she gathered whatever power she had left. Energy pulsed outward, knocking Megan and Petra onto their backs.

Avery could feel them all—the entire city of Milderion. It wasn't enough to connect them, not nearly enough to establish a merge that would give them a fighting change. Avery had no light left. But she could draw from theirs if they were willing to give it.

And they did.

Avery welcomed the energy pulsing from every living thing in the city, drawing on the radiance fostered in the people's desire for peace. It drove straight and true, like a pulsing ray of sunlight straight into her heart. Their offering was undiluted and clarified, concentrated power in its purest form.

It burst from Avery in an endless well, surging out from the tips of her fingers as she rose to her feet. It was more power than she'd ever felt alone—more than she'd ever thought possible. Through their gifts, Avery connected them all, bringing every Reange in Milderion into the merge along with her.

Avery healed Qav in the next breath, a single thought and he was on his feet beside her. Petra's neck sealed in an instant. And Syla, still clinging to life, sat up in a daze.

Avery walked to the center of the room, her feet gliding, never making contact with the floor.

Qav met her in the middle, his eyes drifting over the carnage. To Nick, to Gran . . . to the dozens of others littering the ground around them.

Qav.

His silver eyes lifted to hers, wary.

I need you to bring the city together.

He frowned, shaking his head, understanding what the request meant.

You need to join the others, to get weapons to anyone who can fight. The ones who can't will need your merge to guide them.

Qav stared up at the dark sky, at the ships descending on the city. The streets were already flooded with thousands of soldiers. *It won't make a difference. Not against numbers like that.*

We have to try, Qav. Syla approached, tossing a blaster to him. He caught it with one hand. *This is our home. And Ennis is still out there.*

"I don't need you to beat them," Avery said to him, her voice strained from her tears. "I just need time."

Avery knew what she had to do. It had been staring her in the face since she delved into the Essence deep beneath the surface. She held out her hand, catching droplets of water in her palm.

The Essence *wanted* to help them—it yearned for peace nearly as much as Avery herself. But its energy was bound to that infinite place between dimensions. It couldn't act—not without a host.

She needed to go deeper.

"What will you do?" Qav asked.

"She took Finn." Avery looked up. The rain had eased to little more than a drizzle. "I'm going to take him back."

CHAPTER FIFTY-SEVEN

In a single jump, Avery bounded upward and landed on the roof. Cold wind stung her cheeks as she sprinted beneath the open sky, keeping the cruiser in her line of sight. The rain had stopped, leaving the surface slick beneath her boots.

Above her, a dozen smaller ships zipped through the sky, beginning an assault on the great Federation warships that had begun their descent to the ground. Flashes of vibrant blue lit up the darkness as they fired at their targets. Her friends had done their part—the Origin fleet was back online. The Reanges would need that victory, no matter how small.

Avery reached the building's edge, vaulting off the roof and reaching out a hand toward Klein's retreating silver vessel. It jerked to a halt in midair, immobile beneath the weight of Avery's power.

When Avery struck the ground, the pavement cracked beneath one knee. She pulled on her hold, dragging the entire ship down with her. It crashed twenty feet ahead, gouging out the road beneath as it slid to a stop in the side of an office building.

The door blew off the cruiser as Klein stepped out, dragging Finn behind her. Her feet were bare on the wet street.

"I didn't say you could walk away!" Avery yelled. Power cracked from her hands, lashing out to the wet ground. "Give. Him. Back."

Klein laughed, a wild guffaw that bounced around the chilly air. She pushed Finn to the side and he stumbled, still unseeing.

"And what will you do if I don't?" Klein challenged. "I've taken this planet, Avery. The Reanges barely had the skills to fight us off the first time. The only thing peace ever brought the Natives of this planet was weakness. You cannot survive on peace."

"There are over a million Reanges in this city. That's more than twice your army."

"And what about now?" Klein yelled, swinging a wide arm across the burning city around them. The sky was tinged with red. "Maybe a day ago. But now my army has captured half of them. And the humans within my control have all but slaughtered the rest. What are you going to do? Bring them back from the dead?"

Avery felt the warm pull of the Essence beneath her, felt its gentle caress against her cheek as the breeze rustled her hair over her face.

"That's the idea."

Avery dropped to the ground, shoving her hands into the concrete, digging her fingers down into the mud and rocks drenched from the rain.

She didn't need a stone to summon the Essence. Luxetite ran in great veins through the core of the planet, resting dormant beneath even the city. All Avery needed was a conduit to reach it—a way to go deeper.

All she needed was water.

She sent her consciousness through her fingers and into the water pooling beneath the streets, down into the tunnels and sewers and farther still. Avery followed the pull, letting its warmth call to her, letting go of her physical form just as she had in the mines.

She hit a vein and power flooded through her, sucking her in. And when at last she was in the seat of the Essence itself, deep within the heart of Echo, Avery let go completely.

Avery had no intention of using the Luxetite to amplify her power—*she would let it use her.*

That's what Avery had always been: a vessel for this sentient being to find form in their reality. Her power was a mere shade of its true ability. And once she gave herself over to it, there would be no limits.

Avery had reached straight into the well of power, a molten core of radioactive sentience that longed for her to let it take control. It surged outward into Avery like a supernova crashing into mortal form.

A wave passed up and through Avery, light pouring out of her and knocking Klein and Finn off their feet. It surged through the city, taking down both soldiers and Reanges, knocking out the power in its wake. And farther, across the entire planet, the ground shuddered.

Avery leaned into it, following the wave as her consciousness expanded to encompass the whole world. She touched each Reange who was harmed, each innocent life that lay dying, restoring their health with a shift of her eyes. She imbued them with hope, with light, with the knowledge that they could save themselves, that help was on its way.

Qav's awe brushed up against her, his utter and complete reverence. Avery touched his cold presence, bestowing more power to him than a single stone could, her magnificence surging in and around every part of his being.

She transferred the merge to him, connecting Qav with the millions of Reanges across the Echo. He would harness what Avery had tamed, an entire army of Reanges, ready and waiting to defend themselves on his command. They would take back their city. They would reclaim their world.

Avery's eyes finally opened as she rose to her feet, her boots lifting from the ground. Bits of concrete fell away from her hands, now glowing with the promise of endless power. Her eyes pulsed, their golden light brighter than they'd ever been.

Klein stumbled back in fear.

Avery floated over to her, trailing electricity in her wake. It snapped at the ground, melting the road. Klein clung to the side of the cruiser, pressing her back into the silver metal.

"What are you?" Klein whispered, quaking with terror.

"Your reckoning."

And Avery dove into her head.

CHAPTER FIFTY-EIGHT

Wind howled in the pitch black. Avery stood composed, watching as Klein tried to orient herself. She was lost in the shadows, stumbling with outstretched limbs.

The place inside Klein's mind was horrible—nothing like the calm fields in Qav's head. There was nothing there but fear and confusion. Nothing but uncertainty and darkness. How had Klein survived in the midst of such misery?

Klein cried out as she hit a chair, small enough for a child, that banged against her shins. She clung to it, sitting down and digging her fingers into the seat. She still wore her bloody pantsuit, ripped and ragged from her fight. Her hair was in disarray, her eyes frightened.

At last, she noticed Avery watching from the distance. Her brows drew low as her gaze shifted to the winds around her.

Avery walked closer.

"What is this?" Klein asked, her voice weak. Childlike. "Where are we?"

"Your mind," Avery said. "You may have stolen the key to unlocking these powers, but you have no concept of how to harness them. And you never will."

Panic crested over Klein's face, her face going pale. She tried to stand but could not. She wriggled in her seat, desperate to move, to run.

"What are you doing to me?" Klein screeched.

"You have only as much control here as I allow," Avery explained.

"Let me out!" Klein yelled, turning violent. "Let me out right this instant! You are only a child! An idiotic girl who doesn't know what she's doing, who doesn't understand the power she wields! You do not deserve it—don't you see? You cannot keep me in here!"

Avery tilted her head, halting Klein's tantrum with a thought. Even within Klein's mind—a human—the Essence was uncontested.

Avery filtered through Klein's memories, dragging her along.

Her youth on a farm on the edges of the central wastelands. Her father teaching her how to grow a plant from a seed. And later, beating her bloody with his belt. A visceral, hateful recollection of him spitting angrily when she left, telling her she'd never amount to anything in the city. She'd proven him wrong by willpower alone. He'd never spoken to her again.

Her father's funeral, sparse and bleak, with only four people in attendance. She'd expected that. She'd gone to his house—her home— only once more, to take his precious collection of whiskey for herself. She drank the first glass while staring in the mirror, watching his ugly, hateful eyes staring back at her. The glass broke in her hand, blood and liquor swirling together down the drain.

"Stop!" Klein cried, tears streaming down her face. "Please!" she sobbed. "Please, stop!"

Avery brought them back to the chair in the middle of the bleak storm. She stood over Klein as she wept. Waiting.

"I—I don't want to see that," Klein stammered. "There is a reason I never look there. Who I was, what he made me . . . That only distracts me from my purpose. Don't you see? He expected me to fail. I can't fail—I won't. Humanity will not fade away into irrelevance and insignificance. I won't let it. I WON'T LET IT!"

Avery frowned. She realized at last . . . perhaps Klein was truly beyond hope.

"There is nothing left to prove, Rebecca," Avery said softly. "Even after all that, you won't see reason?"

"There is no reason," Klein said bitterly, spitting at Avery's feet. "There is only survival."

Avery looked away, sorrow coursing through her like gravity itself, some combination of her own reaction to Klein and the Essence itself.

She was beyond saving.

"If I let you go, you will only hurt more people." Avery knelt before Klein until they were at eye level. She placed a hand over Klein's own, clutched against her knee. It was cold, clammy from fear. "I am not like you. I find no pleasure from what I must do next."

Klein laughed, tears streaming down her cheeks, her eyes full of wild despair. "Then you're more like me than you realize."

Avery tried not to flinch as she wiped Klein's mind completely.

CHAPTER FIFTY-NINE

Klein sat on her knees before Avery, alive but gone. Her eyes were blank, her face slack. Little more than a living corpse.

Sadness wrenched through Avery. In some ways, it was crueler than simply killing her. But Klein wouldn't be stopped—even after facing the proof of her own fears. The worlds were finally rid of her misery, rampaging its way through everything and everyone in its attempt to destroy itself. A person with that much anger, that much fear, should never have held a position of power at all.

But Avery had learned an irrevocable truth. Power alone wasn't enough to corrupt both the heart and mind: only fear could claim such a feat.

Finn stood motionless, left vacant by whatever hold Klein had on him.

Avery stepped toward him and stumbled, gasping in pain. It felt like her bones were shattering into a thousand pieces, barely holding her form together. Her body was already failing.

She grabbed Finn's arms as she fell against him. With a thought, Avery reached into his mind, warm and bright so wholly Finn. She searched for the ties that bound him, cutting them in one swift slice.

He gasped, his eyes lighting with awareness as he took in his surroundings, the warm color returning to his face. He caught Avery as she collapsed into his chest.

Her breath had devolved into lurching gulps. Her head was aching.

"Avery?" Finn was panicked, his fear pouring over her in waves as he held her. "What is it, sweetheart? What's wrong?"

She closed her eyes, gathering her strength to stand again. In the back of her mind, she could feel the Reanges still fighting. Whatever humans Klein had in her direct control hadn't stopped their assault. Much like Finn, they were stuck in whatever state Klein had left them.

And Avery could feel them now, she could feel the humans as easily as any of the Reanges. Qav was there, leading the city in its own resistance. Her friends had been able to gather the weapons and get them into the hands that needed them. They were fighting back—and they were doing it without killing anyone.

Qav had honored Avery's request. His merge with the city came with an ultimate edict: no more death. Tears poured down her cheeks.

"Qav," Avery breathed, gripping Finn's arms, grimacing when pain lanced behind her eyes. "Qav has the city. He'll be a good So', Finn. I promise you—I promise you, he will be."

Finn wasn't listening. His hands traveled over her body, searching for wounds he'd never find. They slid to the ground on their knees and he cupped her face, his warm fingers cradling her head. He was crying. "What's wrong with your eyes?"

Avery could barely hold on. She dragged her hands up, cupping Finn's wrists as she stared at him. The glowing orbs of her own eyes reflected back to her in the depths of his. Everything Finn was poured out and into her, filling her soul with a warmth and light so beautiful that it took her breath away.

She sighed. Finn's presence alone soothed the crushing pain. His radiance would make the end bearable.

"I know what I have to do, Finn," she whispered, tears spilling down her cheeks. He had made her last moments worth living. "Please forgive me."

"What does that mean?" Finn asked harshly, shaking his head. He gripped her hands.

Avery let the Essence take her.

Every inch of her skin began to glow, burning from within, where the Essence had expanded without end. Avery's body lifted to standing and higher, rising from the ground and into the air.

"No," Finn said desperately, trying to cling to her fingers. "No—Avery, stop!"

But she couldn't—it was too late for that.

Their fingers broke apart. She let him go.

And let everything else in.

Avery became the planet itself, her awareness expanding until she no longer existed. Anything that drew breath, anything that had a soul . . . Its life force flowed in and through her, searing her body from the inside out. Every Reange and every human ran through her, as though there was no difference between them at all, as though there never had been. And there never was.

Avery could feel her friends—she *was* her friends.

Megan lay sobbing in Petra's arms, watching Avery rise in the sky from the roof of the capitol.

Syla and Ennis ran through the streets beside Qav. He faltered, feeling her somehow, turning to look behind, where he'd left them.

Grigg and Nova stood with Markes, passing weapons to Reanges in the streets. Linderly and Tai were in the hangar, keeping the Origin fleet online.

And far across the planet, in the mountains, Lissande stood outside in the night, staring up at the early-morning sky, waiting for the sun to rise.

Avery brought the humans into the merge alongside the Reanges, the soldiers and the commanders and the generals surveying from their warships overhead. Avery expanded her reach across the entire planet until everything and everyone was connected, until millions of minds across both species shared one consciousness, one understanding.

Her veins turned molten, blazing a fissured path beneath her skin and up her neck. She screamed, going blind as her vision turned white.

Avery commanded them to stop, to put down their weapons.

And all at once, they did.

The fighting ceased under her orders, true wonder cresting through the hearts of every single human and Reange she touched.

Avery gifted them with her memories, showed them the vision of those mines beneath the surface. She showed them the vast, infinite power of the Essence. She opened their minds to the possibility of a world where there was no difference between Reanges and humans, where there was only peace and genuine understanding. Where they didn't put their faith in a single leader, but in each other. That had always been ultimate power of the Essence: the only one that had ever really mattered.

The searing lava reached her mind, melting it away. Avery was losing herself. But she needed to hold on for one final task, one last gift.

She begged the Essence for power, letting it take her whole form. Energy blasted out from her chest, crashing over the city as the Essence answered her.

And it healed them all—the humans alongside the Reanges. There was no difference between either. Those with wounds were sealed, those near death were brought back to life. Only the ones who had been lost entirely remained so.

And Avery watched passively as the last moments of her life heralded the infancy of peace.

Both sides laid down their weapons. Those on the street stopped to look up as Avery's body rose higher over the buildings. She was no more than a bright, searing light, cresting through the shadowed blocks of the city as the sky above began to lighten with the precursors of dawn.

Avery's sight returned as she looked up at the sky overhead, taking in the beauty of the three pale moons in the early light of day. The pain was gone. The warm pull tugged at her soul, familiar and welcome and ready. Fiora took one hand, Gran took the other, and Avery was not alone.

She had been given such a wondrous gift. If it had led to this, then she was thankful.

When at last her vision went dark, her body fell from the sky.

CHAPTER SIXTY

Finn watched helplessly as Avery floated away from him until she hovered above all of Milderion. Her glowing skin pulsed, flaring so brightly that he had to shield his eyes, bathing the city in light. And when he turned back, her luminescence had gone out entirely, plunging them back into the blue shadows of dawn.

Her body fell, suddenly weighted and dropping like lead. Finn ran, with no hope of catching her. The fall would crush her.

She slammed into the concrete like a cruiser at full speed, the crash ricocheting through Finn's bones, stopping his heart. He reached the crater her body had formed, her lifeless frame spread out at its center. No one could have survived that—not even Avery.

Finn scrambled to her side. She wasn't moving. Her face was pallid, a sickly sort of gray that was somehow worse than the pale cold of when she'd nearly drowned.

And her eyes . . . The shimmering beauty of her power had gone out. Extinguished. They were a dull golden brown, as they had been when Finn had first met her. When she'd thought she was nothing more than a human. When he'd fallen in love with her, even before he knew what she would become.

"You idiot!" Finn shook her arms, crying. He slapped her face, and still she didn't move. Her empty eyes stared up at him, unseeing. Finn choked on a sob, feeling hopelessly for a pulse he knew he'd never find. "You stupid woman!" he screamed, rage making him follow the curse with a strangling, desperate cry.

She had made this choice without him. She had chosen to give herself over to a power that she knew would use her dry—just as it had done to Leviathan before her.

Finn wouldn't let her go. She couldn't just leave. He wouldn't let her.

He ripped the outer shell of her armor off, throwing the priceless garment behind him. Finn started chest compressions for the second time in as many days. He kept going until sweat poured from his brow, until he could barely feel his muscles working at all.

"Finn!" Nova called his name, sprinting for them with Grigg close behind. They skidded to their knees beside him, shoving him out of the way. Grigg took over the compressions while Nova blew air into her lungs.

Finn rocked on his heels, dry tears making him sob. He gripped his hair, pulling at their sweating roots until it hurt enough to make him feel something other than terror.

He couldn't lose her—not again. Not now, when he'd just gotten her back. Not like this. Not ever.

Qav appeared, sprinting from the opposite direction. "Where is she?" he yelled, panicking. "I can't feel her—I can't—" He stopped when he reached their group, horror dawning as he scrambled down to them.

With each of Grigg's compressions, Avery's body shook violently against the hard concrete beneath her.

Syla and Ennis finally caught up, slowing to a walk as they approached the crater, toeing its edge. Ennis's eyes were wide and filled with marveling tears. "She used her whole body as a conduit. That power . . . It was infinite. No one body could have held it."

Syla's face twisted. She turned away.

Finn surged to his feet, advancing on Qav, desperate for some kind of action. He yanked Qav up by his bloodied shirt. "Save her!" Finn spat. He shoved Qav down to his knees beside Nova.

✳

Finn slapped Qav across the face, the crack bouncing across the drying pavement. Pain crested in a sharp burn over Qav's cheek, bringing him back to himself. He looked up at Finn, focusing on the agonized defiance in his blue eyes.

"You are a So'Reange," Finn said fiercely. "Whatever Avery can do, you can too. She said you wouldn't let me down. She promised, Qav."

"I—I don't know how," Qav stammered. He'd only ever seen Avery heal people before. The concept of it was beyond him. "She's more than—"

"Then figure it out!" Finn snapped. His whole body was shaking. "Avery would try—you have to at least try."

Grief crested over him, desolate and overwhelming, as Megan limped over with Petra. They both wept, their eyes locked on Avery's body.

Another cry heralded Linderly's arrival with Tai, both supporting Markes between them. They fell to the ground at the edge of the crater, leaning into one another as Linderly sobbed.

Please, Petra begged, her single word more aching and torturous in Qav's head than it could ever be aloud.

Syla placed a heavy hand on his shoulder. "You can do this."

Qav swallowed with a nod.

Grigg moved aside reluctantly, making room as Qav leaned over Avery, pressing shaking hands to her chest. But her body was completely still. Her eyes were empty, a plain sort of brown that showed nothing of her former glory. They were empty—so empty. Just like Veena's had been at the end.

His palms began to sweat, panic making bile rise in his throat. He couldn't do this. They all thought he could, but it was hopeless for him to even—

She wouldn't want you to suffer like this. Ennis could see his pain, could feel his anguish. Only she shared this part of him. She had been there with him when her sister had died. In some ways, she felt Veena's loss more than Qav himself.

You have to let go, Qav, Ennis said softly. *The key is in the release.*

Just let go—we'll catch you.

Qav drew in a steadying breath.

He had been beside Avery when she healed Syla in the desert, he had offered her his power then. He had *felt* the way she'd healed. It had been so warm and open, a beacon of light in the absolute dark. A breeze drifted over his cheek, blowing hair across his face along with a deep pull.

The Essence.

It was still there, watching them. Observing. Qav could feel its intention, could understand it at last. It *wanted* to save Avery.

And he was no longer afraid.

Qav leaned into himself, opening the well deep within his soul and letting the light out. It poured from him, reaching out to Avery. She was still there, her sparking vibrance lingering around them in every part of the city she had touched, in every human and Reange she had healed. And he called to it, pulling the pieces of her light back into her body.

He dove down into her physical form, sending energy through every vein, through every cell. Qav restored what had been drained, infusing every atom of Avery with the same warmth and light she had once showed him.

As Qav opened to himself, so he opened to the others. Their feeling flowed in and around and through him freely, without boundaries or motive. This was the core of Avery's incredible power, this remarkable vulnerability, this willingness to open her heart to her friends. It was their love that gave her access to a seat of power so deep, it had called out to the Essence itself.

Qav was nothing if not a quick learner.

He opened himself to those emotions, letting their love flow through him and into her. And slowly, her body began to rebuild itself from the inside. Qav wrapped energy around her heart, squeezing it sharply with powerful zap.

Her body spasmed beneath his hands. Once. Twice.

They waited as the sun crested over the mountains, bathing the city in rays of muted orange, the entire sky alight with shades of tangerine and purple.

Avery's chest lifted.

Her eyes flickered, coming to life with an effervescent glow.

Finn's arms went around her as Avery sat up, gasping for air and coughing. Finn was sobbing, his hands roving over her hair, her back, her arms. He anchored himself to her as his shoulders shook. And Avery clung to him, sinking her face into the side of his neck, like he was the only thing keeping her from floating away again.

When Avery looked up over Finn's shoulder, she stared only at Qav. Gratitude radiated down the bond that she opened between them, a vibrant sun casting its warmth straight onto his soul.

I knew you wouldn't let me down.

Qav laughed through his tears. *I'm glad one of us did.*

Avery nodded to Syla and Ennis. *They knew you wouldn't either.*

He turned to his friends.

Syla threw her arms around him, her stature swallowing him whole. Ennis wrapped a hug of her own around both their waists. Qav stood still and uncertain in the middle.

"Damn it, Qav, just hug us back already," Syla mumbled, tightening her hold.

Qav released his breath, letting their emotions reach him, their relief and pride mingling brightly with the gratitude in his heart.

For the first time in his life, standing somewhat awkwardly in the arms of the two people who had always been by his side, Qav understood what friendship truly meant.

CHAPTER SIXTY-ONE

By the time they reached the ruins of the capitol building, relief efforts were well underway along the road leading up to the crumbled steps. Federation medic shuttles lined the road, their gray metal glimmering and wet from the earlier rain. Dozens of soldiers ushered survivors, both human and Reange alike, into their hulls for first aid, supplies, and essentials.

The hospital had been completely destroyed in the attack. Even though Avery had been able to heal a great many people, there were still minor injuries that needed tending.

Megan's ankle was broken, and Avery didn't enough strength left to try and heal her. It seemed too much to ask Qav to try to cross the species barrier. They didn't even know if he would be able to. Perhaps the ability to affect both human and Reange was unique to Avery alone.

Finn left Avery only long enough to see Klein—or what was left of her—taken into custody. Even then, he'd only done so because Grigg and Nova swore they wouldn't leave her side.

The memory of Avery's blank stare, of her body limp and lifeless in his arms, was still too fresh. The reality of losing her was still close enough to make Finn nauseous.

Word spread quickly of Avery's location and soon the area was swarming with residents of the city, clamoring for a glimpse of the So' who had saved them. In a matter of hours, Avery had gone from young leader to newly minted saint, the story of her resurrection passed around in reverent whispers by Reanges and humans alike.

By the time the group of leaders found them—an amalgamation of what was left of the Elder Council alongside several of the Federation officers—Avery excused herself to seek the quiet of one of the empty shuttles. She was overwhelmed and overtired.

Avery herself asked that Finn act as representative in her stead. One look at her pleading, tired eyes, and he couldn't say no. Not even to satisfy his own need to be close to her.

Someone needed to explain what had happened. The next steps moving forward between the planets would be delicate and complex. Half the Federation officers barely remembered how they got to Echo, let alone receiving any kind of direct order from the World Council. Whatever state Klein had left Earth in, it wouldn't be easy to unravel.

Finn stepped into his role as ambassador, possibly for the first time in his life. He would live up to the Lunitia name, if not for his father, then for Nick. The revelations about their family had broken his brother, but Finn would choose a different path. He would not let the mistakes of the past stain the potential of the future.

Whatever their father had been, after everything he had done, he *had* changed. In the end, he found the will to alter his course. He raised his children to believe in the power of peace and the right of all Reanges to determine their own fate.

That was the father Finn knew . . . the one he would remember.

After an hour of discussions, Finn excused himself from the informal peace council. They agreed to keep things locally on Echo for the next week, until the city had time to process and reach some level of stability. They were all eager to listen, leaving ego and artifice at the door. Thanks to Avery's influence there was a strong desire from all present, even the Federation officers, to serve the innocents in as quick and efficient a manner as possible.

The city needed time to breathe. To grieve. To process what had happened and how to move forward.

Avery would need those things, too, in her own way.

The sun was high in the sky by the time Finn exited the small shuttle that had served as their interim Council room. He caught sight of Qav leaning against the cruiser closest to the capitol building, his focus trained on the fractured columns.

Finn halted in front of Qav, drawing those cold eyes to him. The sound of laughter teased up and over them from inside the cruiser. Grigg and Nova, along with . . . Syla and Ennis. It struck Finn as strange that he'd learned to tell them from their laughs, too.

"She's not in there, is she?" Finn nodded to the vessel.

"No," Qav replied. His eyes stayed on the capitol.

"How long?"

"Ten minutes. Maybe fifteen."

Finn nodded, as close to thanks as Qav would get from him.

From the merriment in the shuttle, none of the others knew Avery was gone. So much for Grigg and Nova keeping her safe. Qav had been watching over her, instead.

Finn climbed the stairs alone, passing beneath fractured columns that once held up the entire front of the building. The great hall was eerily silent as he maneuvered over broken stone. The city was too busy gathering survivors from residential areas to worry about the ruins there. Or the bodies within.

Finn squatted beneath the massive double doors that now hung uselessly at the entrance to the Council room. The sun was making its way across the late morning sky. Its pale orange light casting streaks of muted shadows through the jagged remnants of the roof. Most of the space was still shrouded in darkness, still drenched from the downpour of the night.

Avery knelt over her grandmother's body, her shoulders hunched and shaking. She leaned over to smooth Dr. Vey's silver braid across her shoulder, her touch light and reverent. She brought a knife up to cut off the bottom third of hair, rescuing the end that was left in a new clasp.

When Avery rose to her feet, the bit of braid remained clutched in her fingers at her side.

Finn started toward her, keeping his eyes on Avery as he passed what was left of Nick's body beneath the rubble, refusing to look down. Unable to.

"Wait." Avery's back was still to him, her hand still clinging to all she had left of her grandmother.

Finn froze.

Avery pocketed the lock of hair, shoving it deep into the black coat that was too big for her. And from somewhere within the same coat, she pulled a great sheathe of white cloth, draping it over Gran's body.

Her strides were long and sure as she met Finn where he'd stopped at her command. Her face was splotchy and swollen, her golden eyes bright with the sheen of fresh tears. But she didn't hesitate as she approached. In fact, she marched right past him.

She lifted an enormous slab of stone, hauling it up and tossing it away. She knelt beside what she had revealed—Nick.

"What are you doing?" Finn grabbed her arm, trying to pull her up. He still couldn't look at his brother. "You shouldn't be using your powers yet."

Avery tilted her head. "I know my own limits, Finn."

"Your condition two fucking hours ago would suggest otherwise."

Avery didn't take the bait. She looked down at Nick. Finn made the mistake of following her gaze.

His brother's body was lifeless and still, his eyes open and staring into nothingness at the pale sky above. Finn's heart lurched in his chest as Avery knelt.

Finn's memory of what had happened under Klein's control was fuzzy, like a dream he was struggling to piece together. Nick had thrown himself in front of Finn—he had died *for Finn.*

Even if it was the truth, Finn was struggling to believe it. After everything they'd been through . . . after everything Nick had done . . . did it even matter?

Finn dropped to his knees beside Avery, fixating on the gaping blast hole in Nick's chest, identical to Dr. Vey's.

At least he hadn't suffered. Not for long.

Avery's fingers linked through Finn's. She squeezed his hand. "He chose you in the end."

"It was too late," Finn replied hoarsely.

"No," Avery said immediately. She was frowning over fresh tears.

Behind them, voices rose in the outer hall. The others had finally realized Avery was missing.

"It wasn't too late," Avery said. She removed her hand from Finn's to lean over Nick's body. She brushed a lock of hair off his pale forehead. "He found the will to change his path. For you."

Finn startled at her words, so similar to his own thoughts about his father.

Nick had done horrible things, and a part of Finn would never be able to forgive him for that. But in the end, Nick had held on to whatever bit of himself had loved Finn. There had been goodness in him still, despite everything. And Nick had chosen to honor it.

The others filtered in as they finished covering Nick's body with another white cloth. Avery had brought along a bag of the shrouds, intending to honor those who had fallen with some semblance of dignity in their death. She had planned to do so alone, but in the end, she didn't have to.

Their friends joined them in silence, gathering bodies and lining them together in the soft rays of sunlight that reached the wet shadows at last. Even Leviathan—or what was left of her. They worked quickly and quietly, the only sound coming from Megan's soft sobs that she tried unsuccessfully to conceal.

When they were done, Avery was the first to leave. They left as they had arrived, in the solemn quiet, following Avery out of the shadowed remnants of the past and into the sun dappled light of the future.

CHAPTER
SIXTY-TWO

Avery lingered for a week in Milderion before it became clear she would be expected to return to Earth with the Federation representatives. She longed to tell them she would be staying on Echo, but she couldn't deny the reality that they needed her influence.

Qav had offered to go in her stead, but his face was unknown on Earth, he had made sure of that. But he vowed that would change, that he would step into his role as a representative for the Reange refugees who called Earth home. He would step up for the citizens who had found solace in his city beneath the surface.

After the battle in Milderion, Mylan disappeared completely. He'd simply walked off into the snowy mountains and never returned. Avery could have pursued him, but she simply didn't care. If he wanted to see Echo at peace, if that was truly his intention all along, then he had succeeded. Perhaps that had been enough for him.

Lissande took Gran's death hard. That first visit to Nos Lenti had been agonizing. The funeral rites lasted four days. On the final morning, they hiked to the uppermost peak to release the ashes. Lissande and Avery cried in each other's arms as they watched the last remaining pieces of Gran drift away on the breeze. Petra had accepted the honor for Krez, doing her best to remain stoic even as her knuckles turned white in Megan's hand.

And after two weeks, Avery reluctantly left Echo.

This time, at least, she wasn't alone. Finn accompanied her, never leaving her side. He took a majority of the burden of diplomacy off her shoulders. Megan and Petra were in their party, along with Qav, Syla, Ennis, and Rem.

But Avery asked the others to stay behind. There was no one she trusted more than Nova to act in her stead for the days she would be away from Echo's fledgling government. No one more capable to keep everyone in line.

Their interviews with the World Council of Earth lasted two weeks. Klein had indeed left Earth in turmoil. She had acted without approval from the World Council, mobilizing the Federation forces on her own volition with the misuse of her powers.

In the ensuing chaos, Alex and Cora had agreed to release the footage of Klein's plan to destroy the Gate and privatize access to Echo. The knowledge of Earth's impending demise caused more unrest than ever, as they'd warned Avery, but it sealed Klein's fate enough to unseat her from popularity. No one probed into her newly catatonic state. No one cared.

Alex was well on her way to being sworn in as interim Minister by the time Avery and the others arrived. Honestly, it made things easier in the end.

Qav came out of the shadows as a Reange leader in his own right. He was shockingly open about representing Reange interests within the earth government. Once he accepted the fact that he could no longer hide in the Sanctum, Qav became an ideal politician. He'd even let Finn drag him to an interview with Mixtie, the celebrity gossipmonger who could make or break anyone with a single vid on his stream. Qav's soundbites leaped into virality. Earth had found its new obsession.

In fact, he adjusted so beautifully to the role that Avery was surprised he'd never considered infiltrating human government before. When she asked him as much, he said he'd always preferred to just pay people off. There was less red tape.

But Avery felt raw. Her connection to the Essence was more vibrant and alive than it had ever been, like learning her gifts anew. The proximity to humans made things even more difficult. While she could control herself around Reanges, blocking human emotions and thoughts was a new kind of struggle.

On their last night on Earth, Cora threw them all a lavish party on the top level of her hotel in Alexandria, both a celebration and a farewell. Avery had no plans to return.

"I wish you'd stay longer," Megan said quietly.

They stood together in elegant gowns, looking out over the skyline of the city. A few years ago, Avery would never have believed she'd even see the upper levels, let alone be welcomed into them with open arms.

Avery smiled, linking their arms. Megan had chosen to stay on Earth for a while longer. She wanted to spend time with her family, to see her old friends. To heal.

Megan would carry the weight of what happened, of what she'd done under Klein's control, for the rest of her life.

Avery leaned her head against Megan's shoulder. "You know I can't."

"I know," Megan replied sadly. "Can't blame a girl for trying."

Petra cleared her throat. "You'll have me. Isn't that enough?"

Megan pouted, pulling away from Avery to throw her arms around Petra in a grand gesture. "Of course it is, darling. You're always enough."

Petra rolled her eyes but caught Megan against her anyway. They looked good together, Megan in her pale pink gown and Petra in her green suit. And more than that, they made each other happy.

"What about me?" Qav turned to the three women, leaning his arms against the railing behind him. "I'll be here, too."

Megan waved a hand. "Yes, but you're too busy with your whole 'dashingly handsome public figure' thing."

"And—I don't like you," Petra added.

Qav grinned, the expression easy and genuine. It made him look youthful, turning his sharp elegance into something softer, more real.

"Get in line, Petra. I didn't like him first." Finn arrived with a tray of pink drinks in elegant glasses. He looked every bit the suave diplomat in his sleek suit of blue. "Besides, the 'dashingly handsome celebrity' persona is *my* thing."

"We'll see." Qav took one of the drinks and sipped mischievously. "Nobody can resist the white hair."

Finn narrowed his eyes, shoving Qav hard enough to send pink liquid splashing over his ivory suit.

And they all laughed. Even Qav.

CHAPTER
SIXTY-THREE

Three weeks later

"All of Echo at your disposal, and you wanted to come here?" Finn asked, laughing as Avery pulled him out of the small hatch and up onto the ledge beneath the open sky.

"I just wanted to see it again," Avery said with a smile.

She turned to the view, toeing the sheer drop down the side of the mountain. The small platform was no more than a cliffside lookout, carved at the edge of Nos Valuta, the Rebellion stronghold that had held off the Federation for decades. It was the same place Finn had brought her during those first few weeks on Echo, when the weight of expectation became too much to bear.

The Essence had brought her there, too, when Avery had nearly drowned. But after Avery's true death, when she'd burned herself out in the wake of infinite power, she'd seen nothing. She could only feel, like losing every sense except awareness itself.

The wind picked up, colder than it had been in her memories. But the weather was just beginning to turn toward spring. Avery pulled her heavy coat more closely around her.

Finn grabbed her wrist. "Easy. That's far enough, sweetheart."

Avery grinned over her shoulder. "Since when are you scared of heights, Lunitia?"

"Where you're concerned, I'm scared of everything."

"If you fall, I promise I'll catch you."

Finn pulled her into him, wrapping his arms around her waist. "How about we just stay away from the edge regardless?"

Avery rose on her toes, brushing a soft kiss over his lips. "Fair enough."

She turned in his arms, looking out over the mountain peaks that trailed down in a staggering line toward Milderion. The city was just coming alive in the gentle rays of the setting sun. The arching buildings reached up into the purpling twilight sky, their lights twinkling as steadily as any star above.

The Essence had shown Avery this spot for a reason. Fiora had stood there, speaking to her of what came next. And her parents, whoever they had been. Avery hoped that maybe . . . she would feel Gran there, too.

Avery shoved her hand in her pocket, her fingers wrapping around the gray braid that she carried with her everywhere. She couldn't bring herself to put it away. Not yet.

Gran wanted a future where Avery would be safe. Even if she wasn't there to see it, Avery had claimed that reality for herself. The future was no longer some unforeseen possibility stretching out ahead of her—it was in every moment, each one more precious and present than the last. And Avery was ready to live in them.

She leaned against Finn's broad chest, letting her gaze travel out over the white snow that coated the mountains, stained a glacial blue in the late-evening light. In the middle of summer, only the peaks themselves would keep their snowy blanket. The mountain sunsets would lose this piercing beauty of the winter, when the fading rays of sunlight stained the snow vibrant shades of pink and orange.

A gentle warm tug pulled at her chest, catching Avery's breath. The wind picked up again, teasing her braid.

She and Finn were still struggling with their grief. On some days,

Avery could feel Gran there, guiding her toward her fears, toward living a life full of joy and peace. But the surest way to honor Gran's life would be to survive in a world without her. It was an act of bravery she strove for with each new sunrise.

And Avery had Finn to anchor her when the waves swallowed her whole. They anchored each other. Leaning into their loss was its own kind of aching gift, a final tether to the love they never wanted to forget. And through that grief, they never would.

Gran wasn't truly gone. Nick either. If Avery had learned anything, it was that nothing ever ceased to exist, it merely transformed.

Avery had only ever wanted to live her life for herself. And now, after all this time, she was free to do so. Free to make whatever choice she wanted.

They had lost so much in the conflict between the two worlds. Those in power had let fear control their actions, angling them toward hostility and anger, until it nearly destroyed everything and everyone around them.

Avery wouldn't let that happen again—to anyone.

There would still be friction. Avery was not so naive to think she had solved everything from her sacrifice, but the planets were at peace. The leaders in power were just and sensible, and they had So' to help them see all sides.

Avery was at the height of her power. If anyone tried to strip peace away from her people again, human or Reange, she would be able to stop them. She would be ready.

She had floundered between her identities for so long, trying to straddle the line between her upbringing as a human and her new life as a So'Reange. And in the end, it didn't matter. Avery was *both*—she always had been.

"So we're here," Finn whispered in her ear, his voice deep and soft. He pressed a tender kiss to the side of her face. "What's your plan now?"

Avery leaned her head back on his shoulder, closing her eyes. She didn't have a plan. She didn't need one, which was its own kind of freedom.

The wind softened to a breeze, strangely warm against Avery's cheeks. It swirled around her braid again, lifting it off her shoulder.

Avery didn't have an answer to Finn's question.

But she had hope. And that was enough.

ACKNOWLEDGMENTS

There were times along the journey of completing this trilogy that I didn't think I would make it. Writing is not for the weak—it will push you to the edges of your creative endurance and then demand you go further. It takes a great deal of energy and finesse to fan the flames of passion and dedication to finish the art that you begin, as well as an immense influx of support without which I would not be writing this final page.

I owe so much to my partner in love and life, my insanely (literally) supportive husband, Leonel. You have never once wavered in your belief that I can accomplish great things, even when I'm certain I never will. I know it wasn't easy to see me struggle through this phase, but I'm so grateful you never gave up on me, and you do so much every day to make me understand that you never will. I love you to the moons and back.

To my editor, Marinda Valenti, who has been with me on all three of the books in this trilogy. Working with you is an immense privilege and gift. Thank you for utilizing your incredible skill and knowledge to polish my work into something greater than it could ever realize on its own.

My awe and devotion go to Allie Preswick, who created the breathtaking art for all three covers. You have taken my imagination and given her life. I get more compliments on the beauty of your work than anything else, and all I can do is agree whole-heartedly.

As always, I owe so much to my family and friends. To my mom, who is my biggest source of support and is always in my corner. And to my dad, who actually reads romantic sci-fi books about young adults for me. To my early readers and feedback givers, Alice and Ashley, you both are the ultimate hype-women and I wouldn't be here without you.

And to my writing group, which I found only this year. I never understood the power of camaraderie in producing work until I actually tried it. Turns out, I need you. I have a sneaking suspicion that this is the beginning of career-long friendships!

And finally, to the readers. If you've come this far, then you are a true member of Avery and Finn's family—as much as I will ever be. You joined me for this adventure alongside a girl as she finds her way into womanhood and steps into the seat of her power. I hope Avery will continue to inspire you to fight for the things you believe in, even after you close this book. I know she will for me.

J ESSICA LYNN MEDINA has spent the better part of her life sacrificing sleep to devour good stories in one form or another. When she's not writing or reading, she is watching the newest k-drama or digesting extrapolated theories from her latest fandom. Jessica lives in Seattle, Washington with her husband and one quirky hound mix.

READ A FREE BONUS SCENE ONLINE

www.JessicaLynnMedina.com

@medinajlynn